# Billy President

*Tell the world about Billy Pigeon.*
*David H E Smith*

David H. E. Smith

Strategic Book Publishing and Rights Co.

Copyright 2012
All rights reserved — David H. E. Smith

No part of this book may be reproduced or transmitted in any form or by any means, graphic, electronic, or mechanical, including photocopying, recording, taping, or by any information storage retrieval system, without the permission, in writing, from the publisher.

Strategic Book Publishing and Rights Co.
12620 FM 1960, Suite A4-507
Houston, TX 77065
www.sbpra.com

ISBN: 978-1-61897-736-6

Typography and page composition by J. K. Eckert & Company

*For Kurt Vonnegut, God rest your soul.
May students the world over read your
books forever…*

*Why not go out on a limb?*
*Isn't that where the fruit is?*

—Frank Skully

# Contents

Preface .................................................... vii

Chapter 1—Hi, My Name Is Billy Pigeon .................... 1

Chapter 2—Surprise, Surprise ............................. 7

Chapter 3—Work and Think ................................ 12

Chapter 4—Time to Get a Move On ......................... 15

Chapter 5—One Big Vicious Circle ........................ 20

Chapter 6—Hi, My Name Is Julie .......................... 22

Chapter 7—I Need a Tylenol .............................. 31

Chapter 8—Bring Your Savings Book ....................... 33

Chapter 9—5,000 Dormitories ............................. 39

Chapter 10—Mr. President, I'm Speechless! ............... 47

Chapter 11—Barack, Barack, Get Out Here, Quick .......... 64

Chapter 12—On the Road Again ............................ 67

Chapter 13—Pigeon Poop .................................. 92

Chapter 14—The Midnight Train ........................... 100

Chapter 15—Save A Spot For Me ........................... 110

Chapter 16—Chicago, My Kind of Town ..................... 112

Chapter 17—Don't Do It in Dallas ........................ 118

Chapter 18—Let the Games Begin .......................... 129

Chapter 19—I'm with the FBI ............................. 136

Chapter 20—Piss on the Alamo ............................ 154

Chapter 21—Religious Meeting in Progress ................ 162

Chapter 22—I Have a Plan ................................ 173

Chapter 23—Hanky-Panky ............................................. 184

Chapter 24—World War III ........................................... 204

Chapter 25—Kiss My Ass ............................................. 212

Chapter 26—A One-Legged Pigeon ..................................... 216

Chapter 27—Saddle Up, Boys ......................................... 223

Chapter 28—A Change of Plans ....................................... 232

Chapter 29—What's for Supper? ...................................... 241

Chapter 30—Rules of Engagement ..................................... 251

Chapter 31—The Hungry Wolf ......................................... 255

Chapter 32—The Men in Black ........................................ 268

Chapter 33—Deep Throat ............................................. 278

Chapter 34—The Used Car Dealership ................................. 285

Chapter 35—Wrong Horses ............................................ 293

Chapter 36—Jingle Bells ............................................ 301

Chapter 37—Put the File Away ....................................... 309

Chapter 38—The 1800 Boxes .......................................... 314

Chapter 39—Let the Work Begin ...................................... 339

Chapter 40—A Letter for the President .............................. 346

Chapter 41—Another Bare Ass ........................................ 354

# Preface

History has a long list of people who have been bold, innovative and have led countries through incredible changes to their political systems and through difficult wars; people who have changed the world with their technical advances, their brilliant minds, their ability to be different; to go into a closed room to collect their thoughts, to stay in that room for a long, long time, to come out and change the status quo, to shock the world, to think out of the box!

I would like to tell you a story about one of those unique individuals who come along once in a lifetime, who has such a profound influence on humanity, who changes the way we think. Ladies and gentlemen, boys and girls, I give you Billy Pigeon!

# 1

## Hi, My Name Is Billy Pigeon

Billy Pigeon, seventeen years old, is the main character of my little story. He is soon to enter his final year of high school at Bellevue High in Bellevue, Washington. Billy lives in the same neighborhood with the likes of Bill Gates of Microsoft fame, Boeing executives, and Seattle Seahawks football players: a well-to-do neighborhood, to say the least.

Billy's father, Walter Pigeon, worked for WAMU, Washington Mutual, a really big bank, servicing clients all over the Pacific Northwest. Walter was a branch manager for WAMU; he had an excellent salary, benefits, medical and dental, and a 401K pension fund. He really took good care of his wife, Sally, Billy and his sister, Sarah. Their mother, Sally, was a former cheerleader at Bellevue High in her younger days.

Walter Pigeon also took really good care of his clients. He was told by WAMU higher-ups in 2008 to prime the pump with mortgages and to give every customer who could sign on the dotted line a house mortgage. The packaging of house mortgages into mortgage-backed securities was the flavor of the month on Wall Street.

When the housing market sprang a leak and popped big-time, and when it was determined by federal officials in Washington, D. C. that WAMU was undercapitalized, that it did not meet the stress test, and that it had lent way more money than it should have, Walter Pigeon knew his bank in Seattle was in deep doo-doo—that's silly talk for deep shit!

Within months, Washington Mutual was shut down, its assets sold to JP Morgan Chase of Wall Street fame for a paltry 1.9 billion dollars, its branch offices all over the Pacific Northwest closed for now, its depositors all covered by the Federal Deposit Insurance Fund, with thousands of WAMU employees losing their jobs; need I say more?

Walter Pigeon was one of those people, he was forty-six years old, he was out of work for the first time in his life, just like another 8–10% of the American workforce, depending on which month it was. Walter had not seen this coming, he was in total shock.

After he cleared out his Seattle office and walked his boxes of office stuff to the trunk of his brand new Chevy Impala car, Walter Pigeon fired up his made in America vehicle and took a drive to a nearby bar, the bar frequented on a regular basis by other WAMU employees. The bar was overflowing with people that fine Seattle afternoon.

Ex-WAMU employees hugged each other, they cried, they consoled, they discussed their futures. Their futures were muddled; their futures looked bleak, bleak, bleak!

"How could so many smart people be so stupid?" asked Sarah Parker, a teller at WAMU for the past ten years.

"Greed," said Jim Smith, another WAMU teller.

"When is enough ever enough?" asked Jane Morgan, a loans manager at WAMU for the past five years.

"We should have seen it coming; we were writing mortgages for people with borderline credit, with no job guarantees, with little or no assets to back up their credit except for the house itself," said Tracy Jenkins, another WAMU loan officer.

"We were just doing what we were told," said Jane Morgan.

"And we were doing what we were told!" snapped Walter Pigeon. "If it came from the top, it was out of our control."

"And now what do we do?" asked Sarah Parker. "I have a mortgage of my own to pay, a car loan, kids in college."

"We're all in the same boat," said Walter Pigeon.

Over another glass of Jack Daniel's on ice, Walter told his assistant manager Peter Graves that he had no idea what he was going to do, where he would find a job, or how he was going to support his family. He had enough cold, hard cash squirreled away for six or seven more months, but that was it. The stock market was tanking, his 401K pension fund was sinking in value like the Titanic, his house mortgage payment, his car payment, his overdraft payment, his three credit card payments, his cable bill, his electrical bill, his Rotary Club dues, his wife Sally's car payment, his golf club fees, his property taxes, his house insurance, his boat insurance, his boat moorage fees, Sarah's tennis lessons bill were all due at the end of the month. Walter Pigeon ordered another Jack Daniel's on ice; this time he made it a double!

When Walter finally pulled into the driveway of his home in suburban Bellevue, he dragged his sorry ass into the living room to see Sally and Sarah and Billy. The silence in their suburban Bellevue home was deafening. Sally and Sarah began to cry a river. Billy Pigeon paced the living room, his seventeen-year-old mind going here, there, and everywhere, really fast! Billy gave his father a big old hug, told his father that they were a strong family, that this was just one of those bumps in the road of life, and that everything would work out, you just wait and see. Billy excused himself, told Walter and Sally and Sarah that he was going upstairs to study for a math exam and to work on his valedictorian address to his graduating class, even though he had another year to go in high school!

Billy Pigeon stretched his arms above his head, grabbed a baseball he caught with his own glove at a Mariners' game, tossed the baseball into the air, caught it once more, and then closed his bedroom door. He lay on his single bed, his room bare compared to those of most kids his age: a desk, a chair, a plastic replica of the space shuttle Columbia hanging from the ceiling, otherwise empty walls.

He thought of high school graduation, his plans to attend U-Dub for his bachelor's degree in political science, then to Harvard for his law degree, then a job in government, then the Senate, and then the Oval Office; heady stuff for most seventeen year olds, but not for Billy Pigeon!

Billy loved politics; he was a political junkie. He watched *Morning Joe* on MSNBC with his morning coffee, he was fascinated with Wolf Blitzer and the "best political team on television," he listened to *CBS Evening News* with Katie Couric, he watched *The McLaughlin Group* on PBS, loved it when the left and the right screamed bloody blue murder at each other, and when old John said "Bye-Bye." He was intrigued by the left-wing bias of *The Ed Show*, and captivated by the right-wing slant of Bill O'Reilly.

Billy Pigeon was also interested in the goings on in New York City, on Wall Street in particular, and was a student of American capitalism. He watched Larry Kudlow on *The Kudlow Report* and Jim Cramer from *Mad Money* fame, with their boisterous support of large American corporations, and listened to Larry repeat over and over again that capitalism was the best path to prosperity: the American corporate giants like Exxon Mobile and Chevron with their highly paid lobbyists in Washington, D. C., wearing their fancy three-piece suits and carrying their BlackBerries 24/7, the greedy men and women on Wall Street, their total focus in life to make money, to live the American Dream, at whatever cost.

Billy was even more intrigued by the current economic crisis caused by the packaging of mortgage-backed securities by the really big banks on Wall Street, the sudden collapse of Lehman Brothers and Bear Stearns, the tanking of the stock market to Dow 6000, the writing on the wall for America, and a buying opportunity for the richest Americans in the Hamptons, with piles and piles of money to burn.

But capitalism, according to Adam Smith in an economics textbook Billy had read from cover to cover, meant success and failure, not being bailed out by the federal government in Washington, D. C. Billy Pigeon, even at the tender age of seventeen, did not like the coined phrase "too big to fail."

He watched in amazement as the Federal Government in Washington, D. C. bailed out the really big banks, bailed out AIG, bailed out General Motors and Chrysler, with the government purchasing a lot of toxic mortgage-backed securities and company stock. President Obama then spent hundreds of billions of dollars on a gigantic stimulus program, with all the money earmarked for infrastructure projects like repairing roads and building new bridges to rebuild America and give unemployed Americans temporary jobs until the economy recovered. But only a third of the stimulus money actually went to job creation. The rest went to keep on union workers who supported the Democrats and pork-barrel projects to keep politicians in both parties elected, the way Washington works, with the United States federal debt now up to thirteen trillion and counting. The actual unemployment rate is not between 8–10 percent but closer to 15 percent if you took into account all the American workers who had given up looking for a job, with American manufacturing jobs being shipped overseas at an alarming rate because of cheaper wage costs. America is in an economic mess!

"How could so many smart people be so stupid?" asked Billy Pigeon to himself. Billy was no relation whatsoever to Sarah Parker, the ex-teller from Washington Mutual. Billy Pigeon's presidential mind was already in sync with the masses! Billy Pigeon continued to rant, in his own mind of course!

"Their stupidity, their greed, their *me, me, me* attitude, their desire to spend, spend, spend, all of it costing my father his job and millions of other Americans their jobs, too, was about to cause big-time stress in the homes of all kinds of Americans, jeopardizing their American Dream for many generations to come, including mine—end of story!"

Like I said earlier, this was heady stuff for a young man still another year and some from high school graduation. But to anyone who really knew Billy Pigeon, who knew what really made him tick, this kind of rant was nothing new. From Day One in junior high, with all the trials and tribulations of elementary school behind him, he had been a thinker, a dreamer, an idealist; he was always contemplating solutions to difficult problems.

There was no doubt in anyone's mind that his speech to his graduating class at Bellevue High would be a success, would be different, would be talked about by people from all over Seattle, all over the state, all over the country, and all over the world with today's social media.

Billy's command of the English language was exceptional, especially for his age. His appetite for new information was unheard of and he was a walking encyclopedia of knowledge. His wit and charm were endearing to everyone. He was a risk-taker. He loved to explore the capabilities of his mind in a conversation. He loved to go out on a limb, even risking failure and ridicule. He spoke his mind on issues at school, defending democracy and the American way. His discussions in social studies class were the highlight of his day, his fellow students and teacher feeling the same way.

Bottom line: Billy Pigeon was unique, exceptional, one of a kind, a rare bird, a young man destined for greatness, not one who sat in the corner and twiddled his thumbs waiting for the bell to go. Billy stood up in class and scolded George Bush for American involvement in the Iraq war, doubting the existence of weapons of mass destruction from Day One. The war was not justification to bleed American blood on foreign soil. He accused the American government of being in bed with big oil and told anyone who would listen that Americans should have a balanced approach to energy, that we should reduce our dependence on foreign oil, that we had enough natural gas under America to run its vehicles for centuries to come, to run its kitchens, to provide all sorts of energy for an energy starved nation, and that we should focus our attention on other alternate energy sources like wind and solar. He chastised Washington for its inaction on climate control, for wasting money on frivolous government programs, for racking up trillions and trillions of dollars in federal government debt, and for not putting away its credit card. The debt would soon cripple America, lead to zero growth in the economy, economic stagnation rivaling Japan's, and reduce America's stature as a world power, big time!

Even worse, Billy Pigeon was becoming a fatalist, absolutely convinced that Washington politicians did not have the political will or appetite because of political agendas and doctrines to take the bull by the horns, to take the tough measures necessary to turn spending into savings, to have the discipline to actually eliminate deficits and pay down debt, to actually change the culture in Washington. Don't feel bad, Billy; you're not alone in your thoughts!

But Billy's day in the spotlight would come soon, with the seeds of Billy's World germinating as we speak, that glorious night in Bellevue at Bellevue High, just over a year away, when Billy Pigeon would give his famous speech that changed America forever, a speech which was captured on hundreds of cell-phones in the audience and then sent all across social media on You Tube and Facebook and Twitter, with Billy Pigeon's plea to the next generation of young Americans getting hundreds of thousands of hits in the first hour alone.

Billy Pigeon was soon to become a teenage sensation, bigger than Donny Osmond, bigger than David Cassidy, bigger than Justin Bieber—a teenage sensation with much more to offer to the world than silly little love songs!

But all that comes later. Billy Pigeon is only in Grade 11; he has another year of high school to go. He has more early mornings with Joe Scarborough and Mika, he has to Google many more facts about American corporations, pass a few more high-school exams, watch his parents, Walter and Sally, struggle to survive, really get a feel for what America was turning into, a vast wasteland of debt, credit cards, and empty wallets.

By that time, Billy Pigeon would be ready to put the finishing touches on his famous speech, with his seventeen-year-old mind spinning around with ideas, ideas he would soon share with the world, but not yet!

# 2
## Surprise, Surprise

The summer of 2009 was awful for Billy Pigeon. It was worse than awful; it was the absolute pits. He loved his father, Walter, and it broke his heart to see him so distraught. Walter Pigeon was down in the dumps, big time. He moped around the house till dinner each day in his pajamas, reading the Help Wanted ads in the *Seattle Times*, wanting desperately to find a decent paying job. Banks in Seattle and the surrounding areas were maintaining the status quo. With all the economic uncertainty, they were not about to open new branches, or hire any new managers.

"It's not the end of the world, Dad," said Billy.

"Like *hell* it's not! There's just no work out there to be had," said a frustrated Walter Pigeon.

"Maybe you could look for something besides banking," said Billy.

"Like what, cooking fries at McDonald's?" said Walter.

There was silence in the room as Walter went back to his laptop and continued to pump out resumes to prospective employers. Billy Pigeon grabbed his tired old baseball cap, his torn and tattered knapsack, and his battered mountain bike and headed out to his part-time job at a local car wash, knowing that his conversation with his father had come to an abrupt end.

Billy's sister, Sarah, was upstairs in her bedroom with her door closed to the outside world. She was contemplating doing her bills for the month after she finished painting her toenails. Sarah had a grand total of $51.37 in her savings account; payday was in another six days at her part-time job in a small, trendy clothing store for women at a nearby shopping mall.

Like most girls her age in America, her rather large closet was overflowing with clothes, shoes—a lot of shoes—blouses, sweaters, jackets, and purses.

Her bathroom was filled with hair-blowers, curling irons, hair stuff, body stuff, combs, brushes and makeup—lots of makeup—all brought to Sarah's room in Bellevue from factories in far away places like China, Singapore, Japan, and India, places Sarah never even thought about.

Sarah also had a Visa card in her wallet in her purse. The limit on her Visa card was $10,000; the balance on her card today was $9,903.64. Her cell phone bill due two weeks ago was $217.36. Like most girls and boys in America now, Sarah loved to chitchat on her cell phone, making gigantic corporations like Verizon, AT&T, Sprint, and Apple filthy rich.

Sarah's Visa Card company was looking for a payment on her bill—actually two of them. Billy's sister, Sarah, was in deep doo-doo! Sarah was thankful her father, Walter, was chipping in for her tennis lessons, but she could no longer count on him when times were tough, the way he usually bailed her out in the good old days. She could ask Billy, but she knew what he was going to say. He would say the following:

"Stop spending, pay down your debt, start saving!"

And while we're on the topic of Billy, her dear, sweet brother, Sarah knew he had money, lots of money. His savings account was flush with hard-earned cash he had saved forever, and now was even saving more from his car wash job, a job he had been busting his butt at since the age of twelve.

Sarah had walked into Billy's bedroom two short weeks ago. She knew exactly where he placed his savings book and knew exactly how much money Billy had accumulated. As of that day, he had $8,714.75 tucked away in the bank! She also knew he had more money than that, that there was a lot more money invested in the bank in some sort of investment certificates earning him 2 percent or 3 percent interest per year. She also knew he had one credit card, an American Express card, with a zero balance. She knew for a fact that whenever Billy purchased an item on his card, which wasn't very often, he always paid it off before his next bill arrived, always keeping his interest charges to a minimum.

He had no cell phone, rode everywhere on his mountain bike, and hardly ever went to a store to go shopping. Billy owned a grand total of three shirts, two pairs of pants, a pair of sneakers, a pair of dark brown leather moccasins, a pair of work boots, a leather jacket, a raincoat, six pairs of socks, four pairs of underwear, a dark brown leather belt and a baseball cap. That was it! Nothing more, nothing less. When one of his three shirts wore out, he threw it away. He replaced it with a used one from a thrift store, always using his American Express card to maintain his perfect credit rating. He bought his underwear and socks at the mall.

Sarah would also love to know this fact about Billy, but we'll keep her guessing. Besides the $8,714.75 in Billy's saving account, he also had another

$35,000 squirreled away at the same bank, the money placed in seven safe, secure, Certificates of Deposit paying Billy 2–3 percent interest per year, each $5,000 CD rolling over at maturity, with the interest compounding and reinvested automatically by the bank. One of the CDs was actually making 4 percent!

Billy Pigeon had been saving money since the age of four. He always had a part-time job doing something. He rode around the neighborhood on his mountain bike with his bag of newspapers over his shoulder, tossing newspapers on the lawns of Bellevue, and then riding to school. After school, he collected beer bottles, pop and water bottles, and Coke and Pepsi cans on his way home, taking the bottles and cans to the bottle depot for a cash refund every two weeks in a big old cardboard box, getting a ride to the bottle depot with his father, Walter.

Billy also had an old Kodak instamatic camera, a camera he carried everywhere with him on his bicycle. Billy took all kinds of neat pictures of people, animals, and landscapes of Seattle. He took the pictures to the local newspapers and they paid him cash for his pictures. There were pictures of seagulls at the Pike Place Market on the Seattle waterfront, homeless people camping out in back alleys, dogs and cats dressed up in silly outfits, and vendors selling popcorn and hotdogs at University of Washington Huskies football games.

You do the math. At the tender age of seventeen, Billy Pigeon had almost $44,000 tucked away in the bank in cash and CDs. He worked every morning and after school and on the weekends. He had no debt: zero, zilch, nada, not a penny! He purchased everything he needed on his one American Express card. He had more money than most American families.

Sarah had no reason not to believe her brother, Billy, when he told her in her bedroom one evening that he would sit in the Oval Office one day, be our president, change the culture of America, not just politically and economically, but also morally, and do something about that sex, drugs, rock and roll culture so prevalent in today's youth. He was going to figure out a way to do it without shoving religion down their throats as his only course of action. Our image was ridiculed by people in other countries of the world who saw America as a lazy, underachieving, overweight, immoral society going down the tube. Billy was also planning a new political party for America, but we'll get to that later. Billy wanted to put even more on his plate. He wanted to turn America around economically, have us be an America of savers, not big spenders: spenders on stuff that has to go out on the lawn at a garage sale three years later, stuff that has to be put away in mini-storage, with the mini-storage business booming in America, or else stuff hoarded by Americans for no good reason at all, stuff we do not need, but buy on credit cards on impulse at the mall on a Saturday or Sunday morning, Billy Pigeon wanted Americans to have cash, cold hard cash, so a family could actually go on a two-week vacation every summer, go to Disneyland, go camping, pay cash for their trips, not put everything on a credit card, put all their new furniture on a lay-away plan, or put everything they purchase on credit. Billy wanted Americans to have a rainy day account, too, never *ever* having to worry about all the bills coming in. The American family would be much more stable if American citizens didn't have to worry about money all the time. If Americans saw the stock market go up, down, up, down, if interest rates started to climb, if you had cash in your blue jeans, it's no big deal!

Not only did Billy want American citizens to have a healthy balance sheet, he also wanted the Federal government in Washington to have a healthy balance sheet. He was formulating a plan, a big plan for America, and if he got real lucky, he would change America politically, economically, and morally. He would kill three birds with one stone; wouldn't that be something!

To doubt her brother, Billy, was foolhardy. If Billy said he was going to do something, he meant business. And he always backed it up with results. Like when he began high school, Billy hated English classes. He found Shakespeare difficult to read, difficult to understand, and wondered why it was in the curriculum and what it had to do with today's world. Billy got a *D* on his first essay. He had a choice now: 2B or not 2B. He vowed it would never happen again, that he was going to get an A on his next essay. He signed on with the drama club. He acted in Macbeth. His acting was inspirational. He lived and breathed Shakespeare, the way it was meant to be! And the little bugger did exactly what he said he was going to do: he got an *A*. His teacher, Mrs. Ryan, was thoroughly impressed. So were all the other students in his English class.

Billy Pigeon had lots of friends at high school. You'd think a young man who was up at 5:00 a.m. watching the last hour of *Morning Joe,* then was off on his mountain bike to deliver papers, then off to school, then off to the car wash, then hitting the books till ten at night, then spending an hour, sometimes two, sometimes three, focusing on the details of Billy's World would have little time for friends.

On the contrary, Billy had more friends at school than you could shake a stick at. He also found time for the track team and was a real team player. A natural leader, he represented Bellevue High at state championships and even won some races. His specialty was long distance, the longer the distance the better. You talk to anyone at Bellevue High and they will all tell you that Billy Pigeon was headed for greatness; it was written all over him. His teachers could sense it, too. He was the real McCoy. They admired his work ethic and his dedication to task, especially the real difficult problems, the problems needing lots of thought before any solution was obvious. They also admired his ability to command a crowd, to get their participation.

Bottom line: Billy Pigeon was a rare gem. He was special, yet he had that air of mystery surrounding him. He was full of surprises. Students and teachers alike had no idea that he had almost $44,000 squirreled away in the bank, that he would soon be president, that he might even have to be president of a revolutionary government standing up to Washington, that there would be a really good chance that Billy and a whole bunch of other young Americans like him might be surrounded and cut off by real American soldiers, that his life might be in grave danger! How's that for a possibility? Oh, there's one other thing. Billy really liked to fly fish!

Sarah had a brilliant idea. See, Billy, you aren't the only smart Pigeon in the house. She didn't need her brother Billy's money at all. She would pay her Visa bill with her MasterCard! Sarah had $500 to go on that card. She would zip over to her bank, do a cash withdrawal on her MasterCard at the ATM machine, and then zip back over to the other bank with the cash to put against her Visa bill. There you go, problem solved, the American way!

# 3

## Work and Think

Billy Pigeon arrived at the car wash. He looked forward to the mundane work after school when his mind was not focused on Socrates or mathematical formulas or the history of the Roman Empire, but focused rather on Billy's World: his plan to put 20 million young Americans to work all at once. Billy's ideas were still incoherent, still going here, there and everywhere, in no particular order.

He imagined the young factory workers in training, under the watchful eyes of the Generals, with all the dormitories, the trains, the trucks, the buses, and the underground tunnels and the one-thousand room hotels for parents, corporate executives, factory staff, prospective clients, suppliers, and sales people; the bank accounts of all the workers growing in leaps and bounds; an America where four hundred of the richest Americans no longer had more money that 60 percent of the population, where American corporations placed their orders to the gigantic administration building, where they were e-mailed to smaller admin buildings responsible for each of the manufacturing hubs, where single Americans over the age of sixteen and up to the age of twenty-five without a job now had a job, with good, hot, healthy food to eat, three shirts and two pairs of pants to wear, their savings accounts overflowing with cash; the set-up for the food distribution center and the five thousand dining halls was Billy Pigeon's reason for Tylenol. His head was on fire with more thoughts going here, there, and everywhere again. The dots were hard to connect: the overland pipelines to the largest natural gas reserves in the United States, American corporations no longer having to go overseas for cheaper labor, the cheaper labor in the United States happier than a pig in shit with their minimum wage paycheck, the cheaper labor in the U. S. of A. much happier than the really cheap labor in China and other Asian countries, the cheaper labor in the U. S. of A. proud as punch of their made in America products, with their chests stuck out, their backs straight as a whip, their bras inside their blouses; a disciplined, well-oiled working machine, with a roof over their heads, a bed to lay on, friends to talk to, freedom to go to the gym, to the pool, to the post office, to any store they wanted in Billy's World. They could lie on their beds and admire their growing savings accounts, the five thousand banks to deposit their paychecks in, their check deposited automatically—no that's not like getting a real check and walking to the teller and feeling the strength of money. We'll go with personal deposits, with 20 million young Americans saving way, way more than they were spending. Obama was in big trouble in 2012; whoever was running against him as the Republican candidate for president was in deep doo-doo, too. Billy Pigeon had one minor problem: you have to be thirty-five to be president!

I told you Billy Pigeon liked the difficult problems the most—the challenge of coming up with a solution.

"Piece of cake!" thought Billy. "We'll figure it out!"

Billy had much more to do before the primaries and the Presidential Debate in 2012. He knew President Obama could bullshit his way out of a paper bag and had the gift of gab, but Billy would hit him hard, unexpectedly, and blow his socks off. The element of surprise was crucial. He had to keep Billy's World under wraps, at all costs!

His plan for America needed a great name, like President Roosevelt's New Deal in 1933 during the Great Depression. Try as he might, Billy really liked Billy's World; he kept coming back to those two words time after time. Piss on it, until he heard something better, Billy's World would be his name, and he should have a diagram on a big screen like Steve Jobs at Apple does every time he announces a new Apple product, which looks so cool, a portable microphone like Garth Brooks wrapped around his face, and a pointer—that's a really good idea—with Billy Pigeon standing up on the stage by himself. Maybe he could get the top General to come up on the stage, too, introduce him to the crowd, maybe have the General tell the worldwide audience that this was a nice change of pace, that running Billy's World was awesome, that he was tired of dead bodies in Vietnam and Iraq and Afghanistan, that he was tired of signing letters to parents of dead Americans killed in battle, that the boots had the shittiest jobs of all, that the boots all wanted to come home to work for President Pigeon, that the president's plan should definitely be given a big thumbs-up, that's for sure!

"What's your problem, Billy?" asked Willy Reid, the owner of the car wash. "You look like you're in deep thought, like you have the weight of the world on your shoulders."

"I do," said Billy. "I'm worried sick about my father."

"Don't worry, he's a strong man. He'll figure something out. If he doesn't, you can always hire him to count all that money I know you're squirreling away!" said Willy Reid.

"Now there's an idea!" said Billy Pigeon. "A real good idea; I'll work it into my speech for next year."

"What speech?" asked Willy Reid.

"My speech to my graduating class at the end of Grade 12, my speech telling the world I'm running for President of the United States in 2012!" said Billy.

Willy Reid was silent; he grinned and spoke. "You're fucking nuts, Billy. You must be smoking that wacky tobacky again! Now get your ass back to work. That's enough bullshit for one day!" said Willy Reid.

# 4

# Time to Get a Move On

Sally Pigeon was stressing out big time! Billy's mother had lived a charmed life; she never had a real job since the day she married Walter. She had developed a daily routine that would be the envy of most housewives in America: up early to say goodbye to Billy as he headed out to do his newspaper deliveries, a coffee, her exercises, a shower, do her hair and makeup, count her calories for the day, eat a high roughage breakfast, watch Regis and Kelly, do a little housekeeping—enough to keep the birds from chirping, meet her girlfriend Mary for lunch, do some shopping, watch Oprah and Ellen in the late afternoon, prepare a healthy dinner for Walter, watch *Entertainment Tonite*, read her novel of choice, and then fall asleep next to Walter. That's about it for the day!

With Walter at home 24/7, her daily routine was in shambles; her life of Riley was in jeopardy. Money was tight; their cash was being burnt at an alarming rate. Poor Sally! Stress had never been an element in Sally's life. The thought of having to find a job to help support her family was appalling. A better solution would be to help Walter find a job, the way it should be.

Sally's enthusiasm would soon turn to despair. There were no jobs in Walter's future, try as they may. The thought of having to ask Billy for some of his money was also appalling. Billy would certainly need all his money to help get him through college at U-Dub, every last cent of it. The thought of having to sell their beautiful Bellevue home and rent an apartment was even more appalling than asking Billy for money. The thought of having to sell her cute little Volkswagen Beetle to get some cash to pay the mounting mountain of bills on her kitchen table wasn't a pleasant thought either. Sarah Pigeon needed her own wheels for her sanity. The little German car meant everything; it was her freedom. Poor Sally! Poor Sarah! Poor Walter!

As for Billy Pigeon, the writing was on the wall with his car wash job. The car wash business was in slow-down mode. Because so many Americans were cutting back on discretionary items like washing their cars at the car wash when they could easily do it themselves in their own driveway for free, it meant that Willy Reid, Billy's boss, had fewer cars to wash, and therefore less money to pay his bills and his staff. Something had to give, and that something was Billy Pigeon.

"No worries," said Billy, "it's not your fault, and it's certainly not the end of the world. I'll find work somewhere."

Across the street from the car wash was a busy McDonald's restaurant. Billy watched a CNN story on TV one night which said that by the year 2020, 60 percent of Americans would be obese, a polite way of saying "fat, overweight, corpulent, gross, stout, fleshy, heavy, portly, paunchy, well-upholstered, well-padded, broad in the beam, bulky, bloated, flabby, porky, blubbery and podgy," according to the Oxford Compact Thesaurus, one of the few books in Billy's empty bedroom.

"There you go," thought Billy Pigeon, "those 60 percent of Americans would certainly have to consume a lot of French fries and Big Macs to do that. My full-time job this summer and part-time work through Grade 12 would be secure. Next summer wouldn't matter; he'd be on the road anyway, on his way to his new digs in Washington, D. C.

Billy Pigeon took his final $315.64 goodbye-and-thank-you-very-much-and-good-luck-in-the-future check from Willy Reid at the car wash, stuffed it in his plaid shirt pocket and headed across the street to McDonald's to make inquiries.

"We have an opening for kitchen clean-up; the pay is minimum wage," said George Bell, the manager.

"That's fine with me," said Billy Pigeon. "It's not how much you make, sir; it's how much you save that really matters!"

"That's a refreshing attitude," said George Bell.

"It's true," said Billy. "Trust me; I know what I'm talking about!"

"I'm sure you do," said George Bell.

"So when can I start work?" asked Billy.

"Right now," said George Bell, "the kitchen's a mess!"

"I'm all over it, sir!" said Billy with a smile.

So there you have it: Billy Pigeon's brief moment in time as an unemployed American, a short ten minutes and thirty-four seconds! Go figure. He was on his way home from McDonald's, his first shift going all the way till 9:00 p.m. The clean-up after the dinner hour rush crowd was overwhelming, with fry and burger grease splattered here, there, and everywhere, the tiled kitchen floor slippery as can be!

Billy pulled his mountain bike into a small shopping mall, the mall with Billy's bank. The bank had an ATM room, but was now closed for the day. Billy took out his check for $315.64 and put it in an envelope provided for deposits. He put his paycheck into his account. New balance—$9,030.39.

The automatic banking machine then asked Billy if he would like another transaction. Billy pressed the *yes* button. Billy told the machine to withdraw $20 from his savings account. The machine granted his wish and spit out a fresh, new American $20 bill. Billy smiled. His spending money for the next two weeks was safe and secure in his otherwise empty wallet.

New balance—$9,010.39

About three blocks from home, Billy stopped at a small coffee shop and was given a free coffee by his high school buddy Tim Jones. Billy sat at the window table and read the *Seattle Times*. He focused on the headline in the business section: "Where Are The Jobs?"

Billy Pigeon, at the tender age of 17, a full two years before he would become President of the United States in 2012, knew that there were no new good-paying jobs in America's future and knew that there would be doom and gloom for what was left of America's middle class and poor.

Unions across the country were asking way too much from their employers so their union members could buy all that stuff that ended up on lawns in garage sales and stuffed in mini-storage units, and hoarded in bedrooms, attics, and basements. The wages and benefits and medical and dental and pension plans were killing corporate America, and then on top of all that, employers were being taxed to the max by a Federal government in Washington that had its financial house in disarray. The Federal government should only spend $9 out of every $10 it took in from tax revenue. The other $1 should be going to deficit reduction, then debt reduction when the yearly deficits were gone, and then they should find another creative way to put a big chunk of money on the U. S. Federal debt, like taking a billion dollars of gold out of Fort Knox and putting it in a big old treasure chest, taking the big old treasure chest to the White House for public display, telling the world that we are about to have another gold rush, just like the Klondike days, with the big old treasure chest taken and buried somewhere in America. Two billion people from all over the world would pay one thousand dollars each to sign up for the treasure hunt to search all over America for the treasure, with the airplanes, buses, and trains full of excited treasure seekers, with the hotels, restaurants, and bars of America full, too. The tourism business would be on fire, with the president giving out ten clues to where the treasure was buried, the first clue being, "Go west, young man!" There would be one new clue each week, a one trillion, 999 billion dollar profit in two and a half months—not bad, eh. Plus all the other tourism money spent all over America, by people going west and looking for the big old treasure chest, or like maybe turning some of their older Navy submarines into money-making submarines, taking people for a three-day ride into the depths of the ocean, putting some big old windows at the front of the submarine, with some comfortable theater seats and popcorn, some big old floodlights, letting them see big old jellyfish, big old sharks, big old humpback whales, and big old Russian submarines. People all over the world would pay $5,000 a pop for an adventure like that, but Washington politicians would never think like that or be creative like Billy Pigeon. Washington politicians were only thinking about filling their own pockets with Washington money, how to spend taxpayers dollars and keep their political supporters happy until the next election—end of story!

The American government was spending money like drunken sailors, taxing American people and American corporations like crazy, forcing American corporations to downsize in America and ship their manufacturing business elsewhere. The situation was getting worse with each passing day.

The American government was also heading toward 14 trillion dollars in debt, with no debt relief in site. There were no out of the box solutions, with American consumers also up to their ying-yang in debt. The outlook for Billy Pigeon's generation was not a pleasant one, with red ink and more red ink running all over Washington, all over the state capitals, all over the towns and cities of America—all over everybody.

Billy Pigeon knew, and every other American with any kind of head on his or her shoulder knew, that America was on the downhill slide and headed for bankruptcy, that politicians would never change, and that everyone in Washington was protecting their piece of the American Pie, no matter what the consequences.

A lean, mean political machine and a healthy, vibrant economy with people and businesses in the black were essential to the survival of the middle class and the poor in America. Billy Pigeon was totally focused and committed to transforming his nation from a nation of spenders to a nation of savers, to change America, politically, economically, and morally—a notion easier said than done.

Billy Pigeon would make *Birdman of 24 Sussex* required reading for all American politicians. They could start by implementing Canadian Prime Minister John Evans's plan to eliminate WFDS in government: Waste, Fat, Duplication, and Stupidity. That would certainly be a good beginning, with Billy Pigeon busting his butt and burning the midnight oil putting together all the sketches and diagrams to his plan for America: his Billy's World. The initial drawing of the twenty-mile long runway and the four gigantic airports was easily done on his first sheet of 8 ½ by 14 inch copier paper he borrowed from Walter's study, but now he was up to fifty sheets, all held together with Scotch tape, the gigantic construction project probably needing another fifty sheets before he was done, before he could roll it all up into one big roll, hold it together with five or six big old elastic bands, take it to the architects and engineers for analysis, and actually move Billy's World to the design stage and get ready to build.

Billy's World would blow the socks off Washington, with the rest of the world probably wanting Billy Pigeon to design smaller versions of Billy's World on the other continents, too, maybe a franchising opportunity down the road; you never know!

Bottom Line: Billy's World would reduce unemployment in America to zero, put America back on top of the heap, unleash American ingenuity and technology like never before, bring all the change necessary in America and take Billy Pigeon all the way to the Oval Office in 2012!

"I can wait. America can wait a little longer, the world can wait a little longer, but there is no way on God's green Earth that we can all wait till I'm 35! America needs me *now*," thought Billy Pigeon, "and I will not disappoint!"

# 5
## One Big Vicious Circle

On his bike rides from his job at McDonald's to his home in Bellevue, Billy Pigeon was constantly reminded of America's debt issue, Billy's observant eyes saw stuff that other people would never see or bother to take notice of; they would never see the big picture, never see the forest for the trees.

Billy personally knew hundreds of horror stories of families in Seattle who were up to their wazoo in personal debt. Those people now had *For Sale* signs tacked on their motor homes, boats, cars, and 4 by 4 trucks: their prized possessions parked here, there, and everywhere on lawns and empty parking lots all over Seattle. There were more *For Sale* signs up this year than ever before, with people desperate to generate cash any way they could think of.

When he delivered his papers in the morning, Billy saw the mailboxes around Bellevue overflowing with new credit card and personal lines of credit offers. Big banks and other smaller financial institutions were still telling stressed-out Americans on a daily basis that they have been given priority status, that they were specially selected to apply, that with this fantastic line of credit, they could combine their regular credit card and store credit card balances into one neat, single monthly payment so they wouldn't be preoccupied with keeping track of multiple due dates and that the offer was only available for a short time. Billy Pigeon was totally amazed to still see the ladies of Seattle in the teller lines and the grocery store lineups, still opening their wallets with 10–15 credit cards of all colors and pretty designs, all neatly organized in individual slots, all ready to go shopping, to fulfill Americans' insatiable appetite for new exercise bikes, a new hot tub, a new TV, a new barbecue, a new boat, a second, third and fourth vehicle, a second winter home in Arizona or Florida, a condo in Mexico, a cabin on a mountain lake, a weekend in Vegas, a new perm, a facelift—all bought on credit, rarely with cash the way it should be—with consumer debt in America now at 95 percent of the country's Gross Domestic Product. Millions and millions of Americans now had little or no savings, no 401K pension plans, no health insurance, no nothing, just living from job to job, paycheck to paycheck, with consumers pissing away their hard-earned money on stuff that decreased in value over time. With the government essentially broke and relying on businesses to bail them out, and businesses relying on consumers to bail them out, and consumers relying on government to bail them out, it was one big vicious circle getting no one anywhere, really fast! What a mess, what a mess, what a mess, what a recipe for disaster, with America at a crossroads, with options for the government running out, big time!

Thank God that America had Billy Pigeon, that Billy Pigeon was already ahead of the rest of the pack, that he had already studied the writings of Adam Smith, John Kenneth Galbraith, Maynard Keyes, and Milton Friedman, had already written essays on capitalism and socialism, on democracy and communism, had already participated in lively discussions in and out of school about Enron, Bear Stearns, Goldman Sachs, and AIG and was probably ahead of any honor student in political science at any university in the land. Thank God Billy Pigeon was already preparing his high school graduation speech, planning his motor home trip around America, and getting ready to run as an Independent against President Obama in 2012, with a new political party formed in Billy Pigeon's mind as we speak. America was also ready and waiting, desperately needing their knight in shining armor to come waltzing into Washington on a big old white horse and kick some sense into the Washington Establishment, with Billy chomping at the bit, the days not going fast enough, his nights spent on his knees with his gigantic sheet of paper, his quilt of many colors getting longer and longer, wider and wider, and his vivid imagination stretching further than it had ever stretched before!

# 6

# Hi, My Name Is Julie

Now that you know all the political and economic stuff about America, and the really big mess we are in, and now that you know all that you really need to know about Billy Pigeon, except for a few more small details, it's time to get this story into high gear, to set the wheels in motion, to satisfy your curiosity, to see exactly what Billy is up to, what he's really going to do, to watch him change America, to watch him think out of the box, big time!

The remainder of the summer of 2009 was a blur to Billy, his mind focused totally now on becoming president, on building Billy's World, and on fixing America forever. Walter and Sally were still in the dumps, sister Sarah was nothing but a pain in the behind, still complaining once or twice a week to anyone who would listen about the bills she had to pay—her Visa, her MasterCard, her cell phone—and how much she was stressed-out. Give her credit, though; she never once came to Billy looking for a loan.

Obese people, especially young Americans, continued to pile into McDonald's and stuff themselves with French fries and Big Macs and drown their sorrows with gigantic cardboard containers of pop, their cholesterol and blood sugar levels starting to screw up their normal bodily functions, a big problem for future American presidents trying to cut back on the costs of Medicare and Medicaid. It was one of those summers; Billy Pigeon could hardly wait for Grade 12 to begin.

One bright spot for Billy was the big spike up in his savings book balance. His savings account was now another $2,461.73 higher than before and his balance was now at $11,472.12 and counting. Billy had a better balanced cash account than the United States of America! Go figure.

Another bright spot was a really pretty, dark haired, young lady by the name of Julie Sanders. Billy had first run into Julie at that world-famous fish market on the Seattle waterfront. Billy was there, minding his own business, taking pictures of people early on a Sunday morning before he headed off to work at McDonald's. The place was a beehive of activity. Even with all the people, Billy Pigeon stood out like a sore thumb!

Julie's first reaction: "Now there's someone different!"

If Julie only knew! But that's my job, to tell you all about Billy Pigeon, to zero in on what made him such a unique individual, a one of a kind, a rare breed, a special talent, only a hop, skip and a jump, and a heartbeat away from the Oval Office.

Billy Pigeon was standing still, totally focused on the two young workers tossing salmon to each other behind a busy counter. Billy had one hand on his beat-up old mountain bike, the other hand held his old Kodak instamatic camera. He was wearing his worn-out baseball cap, tattered and torn along the edges, his work boots, his plaid shirt, his faded corduroy pants, his battered leather jacket full of scratches, all looking like they had been purchased at a Salvation Army Thrift Store, which they were, but Julie Sanders doesn't need to know that—not yet.

Julie was intrigued as Billy took his camera, rested his mountain bike against the wooden counter and snapped a photograph of the youngest worker holding up a gigantic salmon. The worker was grinning from ear to ear, with three front teeth from the top row missing completely. The salmon, a good forty to fifty pounds, had just been delivered to their doorstep only moments ago.

Then Billy Pigeon made a 180-degree turn and said the following to Julie Sanders:

"Do you mind if I take your picture?"

"Sure, go ahead," said Julie Sanders, "but I look terrible. My hair's soaking wet; my face is all red from the rain and the cold air."

"That's what makes you look so interesting," said Billy with a big old smile.

Billy Pigeon snapped his picture of Julie Sanders, grabbed his bicycle, and he was off, pausing momentarily to smile again at Julie.

"Maybe we'll meet again one day," said Billy.

"You never know," said Julie. "What's your name?"

"Billy," said Billy Pigeon.

"What's your last name?" asked Julie.

"Pigeon," said Billy.

"And what are you going to do when you're all grown up, Billy Pigeon?" asked Julie.

"I'm going to be President of the United States!" said Billy.

Julie Sanders was quiet. She smiled and waved goodbye to Billy. She watched him ride away, his wet, blond curls bouncing on both sides of his baseball cap, his old mountain bike still doing the trick, still hanging in there, still useful. The bike was purchased for the paltry sum of $15, paid for with cash, of course!

Billy Pigeon pedaled hard on his bike pedals, his heart rate increasing again, his heart going beat, beat, beat, beat, beat—really fast—as Billy climbed the six, seven, or eight steep blocks up from the waterfront. Then Billy headed for his shift at McDonald's. The traffic in Seattle was heavy for a Sunday morning.

After work, Billy rode his bike home. He focused his attention on the ground. He spotted, with his two eagle eyes, two quarters and three dimes lying on the sidewalk. He stopped, got off his mountain bike, picked up the coins, and put them in his pocket. His savings account was about to grow by another eighty cents.

Crossing through an empty parking lot, Billy spotted three beer cans by some bushes and a plastic pop bottle lying by itself on the pavement, rolling with the sudden gust of wind. He placed them in a plastic bag he carried and put them in his knapsack on his back. He continued his ride. Along the way, he stopped and took a picture of a big old pair of dirty sneakers dangling from a power line and a black kitty-cat sitting on the very top of a telephone pole. "Interesting," thought Billy Pigeon, "but not as interesting as the big old Husky dog carrying pack bags over its back, the pack bags full of something, the dog proud as punch that it was appreciated, that it was making its master happy, that it was doing something useful, and that it was sharing the load!"

After another long day of slipping on French fry and hamburger grease and pedaling his old mountain bike, Billy Pigeon was home at last. He parked his mountain bike in the garage and put his beer cans and pop bottle in the big old cardboard box with fifty or so other bottles and pop cans all ready to go to the bottle depot.

In his bedroom, Billy took the eighty cents he had in his pants pocket and placed the coins with more coins he had in a small glass bottle; the glass bottle was always half full, never half empty. He would take some of the coins to the bank next week and add them to his savings.

I believe I told you before that Billy had started to save at the age of four when his father gave him his first piggy bank for Christmas. I don't think I said too much about the piggy bank. That was when Billy first heard the jingle-jangle of real money. Other family members, including uncles and aunts, all put coins in Billy's piggy bank when they came to visit. The piggy bank was soon full, his first $44.23 soon tucked away at Washington Mutual, and the piggy bank soon started to fill up again, with Walter Pigeon saying the following to Billy: "Every time you fill up your piggy bank, I will donate another $5 to your bank account!"

\* \* \*

Walter also gave a piggy bank to Sarah, but Sarah told her dad she really preferred dolls. Walter got a refund on her piggy bank and used the money to buy her a doll instead.

\* \* \*

And so it began, with Billy Pigeon getting 25 cents from his mother, Sally, when he dried the dishes, with Billy selling Kool-Aid on their front lawn to thirsty neighborhood children, cutting the neighbor's grass, babysitting their children on Friday and Saturday nights, doing everything he could to make a buck, to fill up his piggy bank. Billy saved it all: he put away the twenty dollar bill in the Christmas card; he put away 80 percent of the $50 a month he received from Walter and Sally for his allowance.

\* \* \*

Sarah, at the age of nine, had the largest collection of dolls in Bellevue; at last count she was pushing 93. There were dolls here, there, and everywhere in Sarah's bedroom. She even asked Billy if she could put some of her dolls in his room. Billy said the following to his sister Sarah: "No!"

\* \* \*

"Life without money is not much fun," said Walter to Billy. Billy remembered that phrase; it was the first entry he made in his Scrapbook of Life in Grade 8. The second entry made in his binder was another one that his father had told him. This was Walter's phrase, his Golden Rule: "Nobody needs to know how much money you have or don't have!"

\* \* \*

Billy made a point of that. He said nothing to anybody about his money. His friends at school always thought he was broke. They saw his used clothes he bought at the thrift store; his new shirts were always old shirts. His friends felt sorry for Billy. One kid Billy didn't really like actually gave Billy fifteen dollars to buy a new shirt. The kid's father was rolling in dough; he played linebacker for the Seahawks. I bet you know what Billy bought with his $15. If you said a new shirt, you would be dead wrong. If you said a new used mountain bike, you would be dead right!

\* \* \*

Sarah had a big mouth. Billy's mother, Sally, was soon aware of the fact that a kid at school had given Billy money to buy a new shirt and that Billy had bought a new used mountain bike instead. Sally told Billy that he looked like a ragamuffin; he should break down and get some new clothes, and girls would pay attention to him then.

"Come on, Billy, they're having a big sale at Nordstrom's. Let me replace that raunchy leather jacket of yours. I saw one you'd really like," said Sally.

"I like the one I have," said Billy.

"Come on, Billy, I have room on my credit card. I can get you the best one there!" said Sally.

"I told you, Mom, I'm more than happy with the few things I have. I have a roof over my head, clothes on my back, a bed to sleep on, food to eat, and money in the bank. What else do I really need? I can't take it to my grave!" said Billy Pigeon.

"I give up!" said Sally.

"Good," said Billy.

\* \* \*

About a week after Billy first met Julie, when Billy was having a coffee break at McDonald's, guess who plunked herself down in a seat not too far away from Billy? You guessed it: Julie Sanders, in the flesh!

Finding Billy Pigeon in Seattle wasn't difficult for a smart young lady like Julie. Look for the Pigeons in the phone book, call around to Bellevue High, and ask the following question to the first student you see getting ready to begin the fall semester: "Anybody know Billy Pigeon?"

"Know him, everybody knows Billy Pigeon," said one of the Grade 11 students.

"Any idea where I can find him now?" asked Julie.

"Probably at the McDonald's over that away," said the Grade 11 student.

\* \* \*

"So what's a future president doing working at McDonald's?" asked Julie, after Billy had excused himself from his little group of workers and sat down across from Julie Sanders.

"I'm saving to buy a motor home to take around America," said Billy. "Why, do you want to come with me, be my tour guide, read all the maps, make sure I'm going in the right direction, and maybe be my campaign chairwoman?"

"I'll think about it!" said Julie.

"You do that," said Billy. Hearing his boss calling him back to the kitchen, he said, "Got to go!"

\* \* \*

The next day, the final day of summer holidays, Julie was back at McDonald's. She had called ahead on her cell phone and asked Billy to have coffee with her on his break.

"So, were you serious about me keeping you company on your trip across America? I've been thinking about it a lot," said Julie.

"Dead serious!" said Billy.

"So when are we going?" asked Julie.

"As soon as I complete Grade 12, I'm on the road," said Billy. "I have a little over twelve months before I have to start convincing people to vote for me to defeat President Obama in 2012."

Julie Sanders was quiet. She looked into Billy's blue eyes. Julie was no dummy. It was quiz time; she would ask Billy some skill-testing questions.

"So why would you want to run for president?" asked Julie.

"Because America is a mess, politically, economically and morally; the Republicans and Democrats are in gridlock; nothing is happening in Washington and millions of Americans are unemployed. We need a leader with a plan. We need an outsider, someone who can think out of the box, someone who can give jobs to our unemployed, who will stop spending money we don't have and who can put America on the road to recovery," said Billy.

"And you have a plan?" asked Julie.

"Absolutely!" said Billy.

"I Googled it last night," said Julie. "How old are you?"

"Eighteen next month," said Billy.

"Do you know how old you have to be to run for president?" asked Julie.

"Thirty-five," said Billy.

"Houston, we have a problem!" said Julie.

"Nothing that an amendment to the Constitution can't change," said Billy.

"And how are you going to do that?" asked Julie.

"By putting pressure on the president, Congress, and the Senate to do it," said Billy.

"And how are you going to do that?" asked Julie.

"I don't have to," said Billy. "The people of the United States will do that for me."

"I see," said Julie. "And how are we going to pay for this trip around America?"

"With campaign donations we collect along the way," said Billy.

"And what if we don't get any donations for a month?" asked Julie.

"We get a loan at my bank," said Billy.

"And why would your bank give a loan to a high school student who works part time at McDonald's?" asked Julie.

The questioning was getting into dangerous territory. Billy was about to break his father's Golden Rule! Billy looked into Julie's beautiful brown eyes; his decision was easy.

"Because I have collateral for the loan," said Billy.

"And what would that collateral be?" asked Julie.

"Cash and CDs," said Billy.

"Whose cash and CDs?" asked Julie.

"Mine!" said Billy.

"How much are we talking about?" asked Julie. "We need real money to travel around America for two years."

"How about $12,206.47 in cash, and $35,000 in CDs?" said Billy.

Julie was quiet. She sipped on her coffee and smiled.

"You expect me to believe that you have over $47,000 put away in the bank," said Julie.

"I do," said Billy.

"And where did you get all that money from?" asked Julie.

"I worked for it; I saved it," said Billy. "You don't believe me, do you?"

"I'm not sure," said Julie.

"I appreciate if you could keep our conversation to yourself," said Billy.

"Which part: the president part or the money part?" asked Julie.

"Both!" said Billy.

\*\*\*

Their conversation over, Billy headed back to the kitchen at McDonald's to do more clean-up. Julie was still sitting and still sipping coffee. Thoughts of Billy, of presidents, of cash and CDs were in Julie's mind all the way home in her Jeep Wrangler, with the top down, her long, black hair blowing here, there, and everywhere in the cool Seattle breeze.

So how long can this young woman keep Billy Pigeon's secret? Can Billy really trust young Julie Sanders? You'll have to wait and see! Okay, let's not wait long; let's follow Julie as she gets some new textbooks from her locker at Roosevelt High, and then heads home. Let's hear what we can hear. Let's be a fly on the wall at her parents' house for dinner. Her mother, Debra, was a Seattle lawyer; her father was, of all things, a political science professor at the University of Washington! Go figure.

Julie Sanders was no different than most young women in America when it came to keeping secrets. It was impossible! When Julie arrived at her two-story home on a quiet street a few blocks from the U-Dub campus, she parked her Jeep Wrangler, opened the front door and walked inside to the living room and gave her father, Paul, a big old hug, said hi to her mother, Debra, and then went to wash her hands before returning to the dinner table. The main course tonight was fresh northwest shrimp, on a bed of brown rice, with a sauce made by Debra, served with a glass of chilled, Californian white wine.

"So what did you do all day?" asked Debra.

"I met a boy," said Julie.

"Really!" said Debra. "Go on, we're listening."

"His name is Billy Pigeon. He's going into Grade 12 at Bellevue High. He has a summer job at McDonald's and plans to run for president," said Julie.

"President of student council, that's nice," said Debra. "I was student council president in high school, too. I bet you didn't know that!"

"That's not the president I was talking about!" said Julie. Her father's eyes suddenly perked up and he put his glass of white wine down on the large, oak, dining room table.

"He's going to run against Barack Obama in the 2012 presidential campaign!"

"Really!" said Paul Sanders, his curiosity peaking. Paul Sanders was all ears now. "Don't you think he's a little young for the job?"

"He knows his stuff, Dad; he realizes you have to be thirty-five to be president," said Julie.

"And how's he going to get around that?" asked Paul, his curiosity *really* peaking, reaching for his glass of wine and taking a sip.

"He says all he has to do is to get a constitutional amendment," said Julie.

"Really!" interjected Debra. "And he believes he can just call up the president in Washington and have him tell the Congress and the Senate that he wants the Constitution amended so a teenager can run against him in 2012. Good luck with that one!"

"He says the people of America will force the government to amend the constitution to allow him to become president," said Julie.

"Really!" said Paul.

"So what's he like, other than wanting to be our next president?" asked Debra.

"Tall, blond, handsome, and he saves money like crazy," said Julie.

"That's different!" said Paul.

"I was teasing him and told him there were better summer jobs in Seattle for students than working at McDonald's. Guess what he said?" asked Julie.

"What?" asked Debra.

"He said it's not how much you make, but how much you save," said Julie.

"Smart boy!" said Paul.

"He also said that he was writing his valedictorian address for his high school graduation," said Julie. "He said his speech would shock America."

"I thought you said he just finished Grade 11," said Debra.

"That's exactly what I said," said Julie.

"Pretty cocky guy!" said Paul.

"He's special—he's unique—he's confident—he's unlike any other boy I've ever met," said Julie.

"Sounds like it," said Debra.

"And he's going to tour America in a motor home in 2011 and 2012, leading all the way up to the election in November. And guess what else?" said Julie.

"What?" asked Debra.

"He asked me if I'd like to come along with him, to be his tour guide and campaign chairwoman," said Julie.

"And what did you say to that?" asked Paul.

"I don't remember. I was *shocked*. I don't believe I said anything," said Julie.

"And how's he going to pay to travel around America for two years in a motor home?" asked Paul. "I did it in my teens. I hitchhiked and believe me, it costs money, lots of it!"

"It sure does," said Debra.

"That's the same question I asked him," said Julie.

"And what did he say?" asked Paul.

"He told me, and he told me not to tell anybody else, that he has $12,206.47 in cash and $35,000 in CDs at his bank," said Julie. "He would get a loan for the trip and use his cash and CDs as collateral."

"Really!" said Paul.

"And you believe that?" asked Debra.

"I don't know what to believe," said Julie. "That's why I'm telling you this."

Julie paused. Her parents were quiet. Julie said, "Help!"

Debra looked at Paul, their eyes interlocking. They both shook their heads at the same time, both amazed at their daughter's incredible story.

"I remember something President Ronald Reagan once said," said Paul.

"And what's that?" asked Julie.

"Trust, but verify!"

\* \* \*

Billy Pigeon was in his bedroom. He added another quote to his Scrapbook of Life, a quote he heard at the car wash when he dropped by to say hi to Willy Reid. This is what Billy heard someone say to Willy: "Politicians and diapers have to be changed for the same reason!"

# 7

# I Need a Tylenol

After Billy Pigeon added the car wash quote to his Scrapbook of Life, he stretched out on his single bed, his mind going here, there, and everywhere, really fast! What had he done; why did he let the cat out of the bag? Why did he tell Julie Sanders—a girl he hardly knew—about how much money he had and that he was running for president of the U. S. of A. in 2012? Why did he invite her on his trip around America?

"What was I thinking…what was I thinking…what was I thinking?" asked Billy Pigeon to himself.

Billy got off his bed, walked to his desk, and turned on his old, old, 12-inch black and white TV. He returned to his bed, stretched out again, his head resting on two pillows and watched TV. He would try to take his mind off Julie Sanders. He listened to a retired Colorado senator on MSNBC complain about the legacy his generation was about to leave to Billy Pigeon's generation, catching Billy's attention big time. The complaint went something like this: "Not only do we have a Federal government debt of 13 trillion dollars and counting, but we have another 37 trillion dollars in unfunded liabilities like pension funds for public service sector employees. The problem with democracy is that people in charge of democracies do a poor job of saying *no!* They're good at collecting money and doling it out, but have a difficult time making tough decisions, of being fiscally responsible."

When the retired Colorado senator was all said and done, Billy got up and switched the TV to CNN, which was playing an interview with Donald Trump. The Donald, a real estate tycoon based in New York City, with his own reality TV show, was someone the Republicans were thinking about for president one day. This is what The Donald had to say to anyone who would listen: "America has two big problems. We should not be paying OPEC $100 a barrel for oil and we should not be shipping our manufacturing jobs overseas where they have cheaper labor. We should be focusing our energies on rebuilding the American manufacturing sector. We need to start making things again. We should be the world leader in business. We should unleash our entrepreneurial spirit once more."

"Great stuff, Donald, great stuff!" thought Billy Pigeon. "But what you and the rest of the world don't know is that I'm already ten steps ahead of you, my friend. I'm ready to rock and roll, to kick some Asian and Oriental butt!"

Billy's mind was starting to hurt. The problems of America were weighing heavily on their new potential president. The challenges were mind boggling and the solutions complicated enough to cause a migraine! Billy got up, turned off the TV, returned to his bed, punched his two pillows, found a comfortable spot for his head and stretched out again. Try as he may, he could not focus on Billy's World tonight; the sketches, diagrams, and 250-page written proposal were on hold for the time being. Billy's mind was totally preoccupied on the boner comments he had made to Julie Sanders—how he had risked everything for the sake of one gorgeous smile and a set of beautiful brown eyes.

Julie Sanders lay on her bed, too, also unable to sleep, her head also spinning. "Trust but verify" was on her mind, and Billy Pigeon was the center of her attention. She couldn't get her mind off Billy. She was excited about getting in a motor home and exploring America, and about being Billy's tour guide and his campaign chairwoman.

"This is crazy," thought Julie Sanders, "absolutely crazy!"

# 8

# Bring Your Savings Book

It was the dawn of another day in America.

"What are you up to?" asked Debra Sanders.

"I'm going to see Billy," said Julie.

"Why don't you call him—save yourself a trip across Seattle and see if he's available to see you," said Debra.

"Billy doesn't have a cell phone. He thinks they're a waste of money and bad for your health," said Julie.

"I like our new president already!" joked Paul Sanders, his eyes buried in the *Seattle Times* business section, with Boeing telling Wall Street that there would be another delay in Dreamliner parts from an overseas production unit. Paul said the following to his pretty wife Debra: "Our Boeing stock is about to take another big hit!"

"What else is new?" asked Debra.

"Mom, can I invite Billy over for dinner with us on Saturday night?" asked Julie.

"What do you think Paul?" asked Debra.

"Sure, why not, I mean how often do we get to dine with the President? I'm looking forward to it," said Paul.

"Trust, but verify!" said Julie.

"Trust, but verify!" said Paul.

"Trust me!" said Debra. "Your father and I will know in ten minutes whether or not your Billy Pigeon is presidential material!"

"Thank you, Mom, thank you Dad," said Julie.

\*\*\*

Meanwhile, back over at the Pigeon household, on *Morning Joe,* Billy was captivated by the comments of one of the commentators saying that youth unemployment will be the biggest issue facing governments around the world in the twenty-first century, that according to Sir Bob Geldof and One Young World, 77.7 million kids in the world are without a job right now.

*Tell me something I don't know!* thought Billy Pigeon.

\*\*\*

It didn't take Julie long to whip through Seattle and find Billy hard at work after school at McDonald's. She knew exactly when he would be on coffee break. She was excited about inviting Billy to her home for dinner with her parents. Billy was excited, too, when he saw Julie sitting all alone at a table, his heart going beat, beat, beat, beat, beat—really fast!

"What are you doing here?" asked Billy.

"I came to see you. I thought about you all night long," said Julie.

"I thought about you, too," said Billy.

"I'm glad," said Julie.

"I'm glad you're glad!" said Billy. "So what's up?"

"I'd like you to come to dinner tomorrow tonight, to meet my parents," said Julie.

"Really!" said Billy.

"Really!" said Julie.

"I would be honored to have dinner with your parents," said Billy.

"I'll pick you up after work," said Julie.

"I'll be here," said Billy.

"I have one more favor," said Julie.

"And what's that?" asked Billy.

"When we stop by your house so you can change clothes, I would like to meet your family, too. I want you to get your savings book and a recent statement of your CDs to show my parents!" said Julie.

Billy was quiet. He looked into Julie's beautiful brown eyes and said the following: "I can do that!"

\*\*\*

Billy was in the kitchen of McDonald's. He listened with interest as George Bell, the manager, flew off the handle with two new employees who spent their time laughing and talking instead of working.

"If assholes could fly, this place would be an airport!" screamed George Bell.

Billy loved the comment and would add it to his Scrapbook of Life when he got home!

\*\*\*

The next evening, after work, Walter, Sally, and Sarah were shocked to see Billy show up at the front door and say the following: "Mom, Dad, Sis, I'd like to introduce Julie Sanders!"

Why was everyone in the Pigeon household so shocked? Because, in Billy's seventeen years on the planet Earth, he had never once said anything about girls, had never once been seen in public with one, and had certainly never brought one home to meet his parents!

"It's nice to meet you," said Julie. "I've heard so much about you."

"All good, I hope!" said Walter.

"Of course!" said Julie.

"Come in, come in," said Sally. "You'll have to excuse the mess!"

Billy and Julie entered the living room. Walter was still in his moping clothes.

"I'm going upstairs to grab a quick shower and change," said Billy. "Julie is taking me to her mom and dad's house for dinner."

"Where do you live?" asked Sally Pigeon.

"By the university," said Julie.

"Hmmm!" said Walter.

\*\*\*

Billy was in his bedroom. He showered, changed into his clean pair of blue jeans, put on some underarm deodorant, put on his white short-sleeved shirt, a pair of white socks, his dark brown, leather belt, and slipped into his leather moccasins. The leather moccasins were dark brown, too, matching his belt. He combed his wet hair, put on some aftershave, reached into his desk drawer, grinning from ear to ear, as he grabbed his savings book and his latest CD statement from his bank. He folded it neatly and placed it inside his savings book, which he placed in his shirt pocket before he headed downstairs.

"That was quick," said Julie. "You look awesome!"

"Thank you!" said Billy.

And they were off. Walter, Sally, and Sarah were still in shock, with Walter telling Sally that the next time Julie came over, he wouldn't be wearing his moping clothes. Walter was on the road to recovery for sure. Julie was in total control of her Jeep Wrangler as she raced through Seattle, her long black hair blowing in the wind once more. Billy Pigeon kicked back in the passenger seat, his life about to jump into high gear!

\*\*\*

"Are you nervous?" asked Julie.

"Who me—nervous—are you kidding?" said Billy with a grin.

It didn't take long for Julie to get home, whip her Jeep Wrangler into her driveway and park behind her dad's silver BMW.

"Nice car," said Billy.

"That it is," said Julie. "He's worked hard all his life for that car."

"I bet he did," said Billy.

Paul and Debra Sanders were standing in their living room when Julie and Billy entered the front door. Billy was about to conduct his first press conference as president, knowing full well that the future of America was at stake and that the next few minutes of his life could possibly determine the future of his presidency.

*Perception is everything; perception and follow-up actions are even better!* thought Billy. *Let's get this show on the road!*

Debra Sanders broke the ice; she broke it with a real big sledge hammer!

"Welcome to our home, Mr. President!"

"That's a little premature, don't you think?" asked Billy.

"Is it?" asked Paul Sanders. "We just thought we'd like to meet the young man from Bellevue High with such lofty goals in life, the young man who wants to take on Obama in 2012, who wants to take our daughter on a two-year motor home trip around America!"

"That would be me," said Billy Pigeon, "and trust me, I fully understand your concerns!"

"I'm glad we all agree on that!" said Paul Sanders.

"Come in, come in, have a seat," said Debra, with Billy and Julie crossing a beautiful hardwood floor, and then sitting side by side on a brown leather couch. The press conference continued.

"So, Billy, why would you want to run for president at such a young age?" asked Paul Sanders, his curiosity killing him.

"Because America is a mess, sir!" said Billy Pigeon.

"I agree with you on that point, but why couldn't you wait like everybody else, go to college, drink a few beers, see some Husky football, and get your undergraduate degree first?" asked Paul Sanders.

"With all due respect, sir, I've read the great philosopher Plato. I've studied the theories of Adam Smith and John Kenneth Galbraith. I know all about Pavlov's dog. I've read Macbeth, Moby Dick, The Old Man and the Sea, The Grapes of Wrath, and the Bible. I know all about the American Revolution. I've read the American Constitution from front cover to back cover. I know Einstein's Theory of Relativity. I love calculus. I've read *Computer Organization and Programming* by Professor William Gear in the Department of Computer Science at the University of Illinois. My favorite American author is Kurt Vonnegut. I still use a dictionary. I can write a three hundred-word essay by hand; my writing is legible. I know how to Google any information I want.

I can list all the stats of Warren Moon when he played quarterback for the Washington Huskies before he went to Canada and played with the Edmonton Eskimos in the CFL, before he was a star in the NFL with Bum Phillips and the Houston Oilers, and I prefer a glass of red wine to a pitcher of beer! I'm a people person. I'm going to give my graduation speech at Bellevue High in ten short months. I'm going to tell the world I'm running for President in 2012, and then I have to get on the road. Americans can't wait any longer. They need me; they need my ideas, my vision, and my plan for America. They need Billy's World. They need a president who will shake up Washington, not just with words, but with actions, not a Democrat like President Obama or a Republican like Mitt Romney, but an Independent candidate from a new party—a party with a real plan to put all our unemployed workers back to work, to give our young people hope, to change the moral fabric of our society, to put the words yes sir and yes ma'am and thank you sir and thank you ma'am back in the vocabulary of our youth, to get Americans to save money and then spend it on things they really need or things they wanted to own after a lifetime of hard work, like BMWs, not just spend and spend for the sake of spending. I want to be the president who gets rid of our 13 trillion dollar federal debt. I want to draw a line in the sand. I want to end deficit spending and balance the budget. I want to start a Rainy Day Account for the people of America—maybe two of them. I want to regain respect for Americans in other countries. I want to return America to its rightful position in the world. I want to bring our troops home, put an end to the unnecessary bloodshed, put them to work at Billy's World, and have enough of them ready to help a neighbor or chase foreign boots off our soil. I need to start now, not when I'm thirty-five!" said Billy Pigeon.

Paul Sanders was quiet. He looked at his wife, Debra, smiled at Julie and spoke.

"Debra, would you get our president a glass of wine?"

"I'd love to!" said Debra Sanders. "Any special red, Mr. President?"

"I prefer a merlot," said Billy Pigeon.

"A merlot it shall be!" said Debra Sanders.

\* \* \*

On the way back to Billy's home in Bellevue, Julie told Billy how proud she was of him, how impressed her parents were with him, and that he had done a fantastic job of being the president at his first press conference. She told Billy that her parents were blown away when he showed them his savings book and his CD statement, told them about his three shirts and two pairs of pants, and his initial comments about Billy's World. They understood how complex the problem was, that there were so many moving parts, that there were lots of dots to connect before he could announce it to the world, before he could blow the socks off President Obama and whoever, and before he walked his only used suitcase through the front door of the White House.

"I have to be impressive!" said Billy Pigeon.

"And why's that?" asked Julie.

"Because I have a lot more people to impress before we move into our new home in Washington!" said Billy.

"You haven't even held my hand or given me our first kiss and we're already moving into the White House!" said Julie.

"That's right," said Billy, "as a newlywed couple!"

Julie shook her head; she couldn't believe the stuff coming out of Billy's mouth. "You never cease to amaze me, Billy!" said Julie.

"I know!" said Billy.

\* \* \*

Julie reached over with her right hand, steering her Jeep Wrangler with her left hand. She placed her right hand in Billy's hand. Billy squeezed it. He held Julie's hand all the way home.

In front of Billy's house, in the dark, Julie pushed herself across the Jeep. Billy kissed her gently on her cheek, then her lips.

"When can I see you again?" asked Julie.

"Whenever you like," said Billy.

# 9

## 5,000 Dormitories

Billy Pigeon was reading the *Seattle Times* business section. He was reading about the PIIGS, a condescending acronym for Portugal, Ireland, Italy, Greece, and Spain. Billy read with great interest that those five members of the European Economic Union were having major money problems, that all five countries had borrowed heavily to maintain their government programs, be it social or economic, and that their debt loads were becoming an issue for the rest of the countries of the European Economic Union, countries like the Netherlands, Germany, and France, which had enough problems of their own to worry about and which might have to fork out their own money or put up collateral to put together a big bail-out package for those governments and their banking institutions.

*Holy crap!* thought Billy Pigeon. *Is there anybody in the world unaffected by debt?* "Yes there is," said Billy Pigeon, "and that person would be me!"

All kidding aside, Billy Pigeon had a right to be concerned. America needed a strong and viable Europe to buy its manufactured goods, not a wishy-washy Europe with all kinds of economic woes. Billy was also smart enough to realize that we were all living in a global economy in the twenty-first century, a fact that a future president should always keep in the back of his crowded mind.

\*\*\*

Billy was mentally exhausted from all the diagrams, the new sketches, the add-on notations. He would take a break from Billy's World, do something else as a change of pace, but still make good use of his time. He flipped through his Scrapbook of Life. He read some of the famous one-liners he had collected over the years: some old, some not so old, some ultra-modern. He needed a really good one for his presidency, one that would be an eye-popper, a show-stopper, one that historians would record for the world to remember. Billy read out loud, one word at a time; he wanted to get a feel for a really top-notch one-liner.

"Ask not what your country can do for you, but what you can do for your country."
"Life is like a box of chocolates."
"I have a dream."
"Go ahead; make my day!"
"That's one small step for man, one giant leap for mankind."
"I didn't have sexual relations with that woman!"
"A man has to believe in something. I believe I'll have another beer!"
"Gentlemen, start your engines!"
"If you find a path with no obstacles, it probably doesn't lead anywhere."
"The Fonz was here!"
"Life is like a roll of toilet paper, the closer it gets to the end, the faster it goes!"
"Sit on it!"
"And here's Johnny!"
"Try not to become a person of success, but a person of value."
"The truth will set you free, but first it will piss you off!"
"This day will go down in infamy!"
"Give peace a chance."
"Frankly, my dear, I don't give a damn!"
"The worst loneliness is not being comfortable with yourself."
"What's up, Doc?"
"Stick it where the sun don't shine!"
"Money often costs too much."
"Eat shit, asshole!"
"Don't bring a woman to do a man's job!"
"You always see your cup half empty, never half full."
"Shut the fuck up!"
"Let's get ready to rumble!"
"Don't mess with Texas!"
"It ain't over till the fat lady sings."
"Life is not measured by the number of breaths we take, but by the moments that take our breath away."
"If I wanted to hear from an asshole, I'd fart!"

"Life is like a grindstone, whether it grinds you down or polishes you up, depends on what you're made of."

"We are made wise, not by the recollection of our past, but by the responsibility for our future."

Billy really like that last one by George Bernard Shaw, the references to the past and future, two big words in Billy's vocabulary, certainly two words he could use in his historic phrase.

"How about:: 13 trillion in the past, 0 trillion in the future!"

"How about:: Without a past, we have no future."

"How about:: Focus on the future, not the past."

"How about: Let us reflect thoughtfully on our past as we deal with the present and gaze into the future."

"How about:: Past, present, future, who gives a rat's ass?"

\* \* \*

Billy called Julie on her cell, told her to tell her mom and dad not to worry about any hanky-panky going on in their motor home on their two-year trip across America. Tell them that his dad would be joining them as their campaign finance director, and he would be counting all their campaign contributions and depositing them in the bank after he had written out all the receipts. He also had eagle eyes and didn't miss a trick!

"I'll tell them that for sure. I'm positive they'll be thrilled," said Julie.

"Good, I just wanted to make sure we have all our ducks in a row!" said Billy. "And you're good to go with my father in tow?"

"Not a problem," said Julie. "Maybe my mom can come along, too, handle the media, take care of any legal issues, and brush up on the constitutional amendment you're going to need. She always wanted to travel around America, but was always too busy to do it."

"Now there's an idea," said Billy. "And I think we should tow your little Jeep, too, just in case we get a flat tire and have to go get help."

"Or if you and I have to get away to a quiet place for some hanky-panky!" said Julie.

"That too!" said Billy.

\* \* \*

Billy Pigeon was in his bedroom again; time was flying by. This time he was at his study desk, working on the third draft of his 250 page written proposal for Billy's World to go along with the eighty-five and counting Scotch-taped pages containing his sketches and diagrams, with Billy running out of colors. He was still trying to connect the dots, to have a logical A to B to C to D process, still trying to tie all the pieces of the puzzle together, changing this, modifying that, taking out a whole piece of paper with his pocket knife (the wooden floor of his bedroom full of knife cuts), replacing it with another piece of paper, taping the paper back into place, and starting all over again. The process was extremely fluid—a mental challenge of gargantuan proportions!

Billy wanted his initial sketches and diagrams and his 250-page written proposal ready for the architects and engineers before he left Seattle, before he presented it to the public at the Presidential Debate in 2012. He had no desire for his plan to be prepared by a government committee, especially a committee of government bureaucrats working 9–5 after he was elected president. The work had to be done now!

He had thought originally of having a manufacturing hub in each state, but the idea of having to duplicate something fifty times in fifty locations spread out all over hell's half acre, all across America, soon lost its appeal. Some states had more unemployment than others; some had bigger environmental issues. The hubs would probably have to vary in size and shape. The thought of modifying his original drawings to meet different needs was mind-boggling and would be almost impossible!

Better to have one General in charge of one location, than have fifty Generals in charge of fifty locations; there would be more hands-on, more immediate control. Better to pick one big flat piece of land to build his five thousand dormitories in the five thousand hubs, each dormitory capable of sleeping four thousand workers, with a short walk from each dormitory to the adjacent single-level factory, with another short walk to the shopping mall and another short walk from there to the one thousand room, 5-star hotel. The dormitory, factory, mall, and hotel made up each manufacturing hub, with five thousand of these hubs to build in total. Each shopping mall would contain its own banks, its wide assortment of stores, its theaters, its gigantic Apple store, its pharmacy, its post office, its restaurants, and its video-game rooms. The shopping mall would be big enough to accommodate the needs of the four thousand factory workers in each hub.

Each dormitory for the four thousand workers would be ten stories high, each floor housing four hundred workers, one one-hundred-person room facing east, one west, one north, and one south, with ten elevators, side by side in the center of the four rectangular rooms. The ten elevators all would go up and down to the gigantic underground kitchen and dining hall below each four thousand person dormitory, each dining hall capable of feeding four thousand workers at one time, with kick-ass, hot, healthy meals, no junk food allowed. The kitchen under each hub would be connected by a massive series of underground tunnels to the other 4,999 hubs in Billy's World, with a ten-lane tunnel going into an incredible food distribution center on the other side of the twenty-mile-long runway, with forklifts running on propane and driven by military personnel, moving fresh food and garbage to and from the five thousand hubs, 24/7, 365 days a year. The garbage would be towed in large, covered containers on wheels to the state-of-the-art, green garbage-burning units, with all the heat and smoke creating energy to be used in Billy's World, the burners running 24/7, 365 days a year. Breakfast would be served from 7:00 a.m. each morning, the workers given a bag lunch to take to their factory, then dinner served at 5:00 p.m. precisely. They would work five days a week, forty hours a week from 8:00 a.m. to 4:00 p.m. each day, with Saturday and Sunday off for rest and relaxation. They could have a nap in their dormitory, go to their mall to shop, or go to the biggest recreation center ever built by man, which was connected to the five thousand hubs by bus and mass transit trains running 24/7, 365 days a year. The recreation center would be open 24/7, 365 days a year, with workers at each hub also allowed to go to their one thousand-room, 5-star hotel to visit their parents, go for a swim in the pool, sip a Bud in the lounge if they were age twenty-one, have some hanky-panky with a condom with a fellow worker in one of the hotel rooms if you were lucky enough to get a room booked in advance, with mass transit trains and buses also dropping off and picking up, not just at the rec center, but also connecting to the other 4,999 hubs at Billy's World, with bicycles free for the taking at each bus stop or mass transit train station, the bicycles to be put back where they came from at the end of your stay.

*Now we're cooking!* thought Billy Pigeon, now focusing his attention on the gigantic runway in the middle of Billy's World. The runway would be twenty miles long, with twenty miles of empty land at each end of the runway and five miles of empty land on each side of the runway. There would be four gigantic airports, with incredibly high control towers and mass transit trains and buses connecting from all four gigantic airports to the five thousand manufacturing hubs. Factory workers would be able to fly home at any time on free military flights going in the same direction if there was a family emergency, with train station terminals and truck stop terminals hooked up to the gigantic airports to pick up finished factory orders and fly them on massive Boeing 747 cargo jets to any destination on the planet earth. The massive airports would be cities by themselves, each airport run as a separate business, the profits going to Billy Pigeon, and running 24/7, 365 days a year, with planes here, there and everywhere on the massive runway, some landing, some taking off, some heading to the gigantic airplane hangars on the other side of the runway for some TLC. Planes would arrive each minute of the day with new military personnel and F-16 pilots doing their day to day combat drills to keep them sharp in case they had to go to war. There would be a massive top-gun training center at the far end of the fourth airport. Other planes would bring in the new factory workers to begin their five-year stint at their war on jobs. Parents would arrive, too, seven days a week to visit their kids and stay in the 5-star motels, blown away by what they were seeing.

Billy Pigeon totally focused on another issue: whether to go with one big service center for snow removal vehicles, if it ever snowed, for the road maintenance vehicles, the buses, the trucks, the trains, for the forklifts lifting the food and pulling the garbage containers on wheels. Billy knew that the military would want their own service center for their own vehicles. The planes had their own service center attached to the gigantic hangars, so it probably made a lot more sense for the trains, trucks, buses, and all the other vehicles to have their own service centers, too. Billy taped in more pieces of paper, with arrows going here, there, and everywhere, Each service center had its own kitchen and dining hall, its own dormitory, and its own shopping mall. *So why am I doing this for everybody? I only need that for the military inside. The people who service our complex will stay in their own service city—a city of one or two million service workers who will live outside Billy's World, coming to work each morning through military checkpoints in their buses and mass transit trains. The service workers carry their own bag lunches, having slept in their own beds, having purchased food in their own shopping malls. That makes it a little easier, but I have a whole new city to design, too, after I finish with Billy's World!*

Switching his mind again, Billy started to focus in on the massive administration building, forty stories high, with the top general on the top floor, the rest of the floors filled with other lower ranked generals, military staff, secretaries, accountants, private-sector executives from each of the five thousand corporations on board filling all the factory orders from the American companies contracted to Billy's World. The companies no longer had to go overseas to get their products manufactured, with new orders coming into the administration building by e-mail 24 hours a day, with those e-mails going to the smaller Admin offices assigned to each factory in each hub, Billy knew full well that companies like Verizon would want to get in on the action, too, that some factories would end up being call-centers, that having call-centers in India was a pain in the ass to American companies like Sprint and American Express, and that Americans were getting tired of having to listen to East Indians and other Asian workers telling them to smarten up and pay their overdue cell-phone bills or overdue credit card bills. They really wanted a North American voice on the other end—someone they could understand!

This was an easy conversion to make for Billy at each factory. The only addition would be all the extra wiring. There would be added pressure on the computer and software center, and the computer server center, with more bandwidth required. The extra attention of computer experts was an absolute must in the architectural and engineering phase, with Billy making a note to the side for the extra attention to detail needed in the design of those factories.

Billy was big on green technology at Billy's World. Green technology in the twenty-first century definitely meant solar panels, stretching for hundreds and hundreds and hundreds of miles to power the complex. The place he ultimately selected to build would have to have lots of sunshine and lots of wind to harness for the thousands and thousands and thousands of wind turbines on site. Certainly Nevada, Arizona, and New Mexico would have to get a good look-over during his two year tour of America, with thousands and thousands of back-up diesel generators in place in case of power outages or terrorist attacks, backing up a gigantic twenty-second century, state-of-the-art, nuclear power station, the main source of power at Billy's World.

So far, so good, with 20 million factory workers, five thousand dormitories, five thousand factories with their own training centers and raw material warehouses, five thousand shopping malls, five thousand 5-star hotels, four airports, four gigantic train stations, four gigantic bus stops, separate service centers for each mode of transportation, a food distribution center, a recreation center, a garbage disposal facility, a military base, a city outside the complex to house and feed and provide all the needs of one or two million service workers, and Billy Pigeon's mind in need of another Tylenol!

He would call it a night. Tomorrow, he would refocus on the parts distribution system, the water and sewer system, the fencing, the security checkpoints, the five hundred gigantic hospitals, the attached dental centers, with the Federal government in Washington committing 2.5 trillion dollars for food, clothing, lodging, and military wages, which they would have had to pay anyway, and the private sector kicking in 2.5 trillion for the factories, the airports, the runway, and everything else. Millions and millions of unemployed Americans soon would be employed constructing Billy's World over a four year period, all working their butts off for Billy Pigeon, all tucking their big, fat paychecks away in their banks to feed all the hungry mouths back home, with 20 million more young Americans waking up in five short years after construction was finished with $50,000 cash in their bank accounts, financial equality amongst America's youth, all ready to go home, have a leg up on the American Dream, with a new save-don't-spend attitude in the homes of America, young Americans with a new code of conduct, a new moral attitude, members of a new Independent political party, controlled by no one—the way it should be!

*Go to bed, Billy; that's enough for one night!*

*One more thing!* thought Billy Pigeon, as he jumped out of bed, switched on his light, and made another entry in his notebook. "The factories have to be large, modern, and comfortable to work in, with lots of light, state-of-the-art washrooms, comfortable staffrooms for coffee breaks, first-aid stations, and fantastic, ice-cold air conditioning on really hot days! There will be no sweat shops in America for my young American factory workers. They will all have the comforts of home!"

That's a good line for my speech at the Presidential Debate. I'll have to write that one down for sure!

*Good night, Billy; now go to bed, shut off that mind of yours, and go to sleep!*

\* \* \*

It was 3:00 a.m. Billy was up again; his mind was on fire!

Can you imagine the excitement in America? His project was the next big thing. Imagine the excitement of the lucky governor in the lucky state chosen to build Billy's World, a state full of happy campers, the governor raking in the bucks in state taxes, the governor one big happy, happy camper, sitting at his desk with his cowboy boots way up in the air next to his laptop, watching all the activity out through his window. The economic spin-off to America was unreal: all the steel, plastic, aluminum, copper, and lumber needed, with all the construction, paving, and fencing companies all lining up in big long lines for contracts. The Donald probably wanted to build all the five thousand hotels all by himself. Wall Street was on fire, with airplane, bus, truck, and train stocks going through the roof. President Pigeon was sitting on his chair in the Oval Office with his feet kicked up, just like the lucky governor, with Julie ready and waiting in the president's private residence for some hanky-panky without a condom, with Secret Service agents guarding all the doors—no need to take off and hide out somewhere in Julie's Jeep Wrangler!

*Go to sleep, Billy!*

I will…I will…I will…I promise!

I think I'll arrive for the grand opening of Billy's World on Air Force One. Julie and I can take the royal tour, stay at one of the 5-star hotels and have some more hanky-panky without a condom. How cool would that be?

*Go to sleep, Billy!*

Maybe even have a president's residence built; I could call it White House #2!

*Goddamn it, Billy, go to sleep!*

Yes sir, my plan is bold, audacious, inspirational, American ingenuity at its finest; it will knock the socks off everyone in America!

*Billy, please go to sleep!*

Obama is toast, so is Romney; can you believe it? I'm going to be President. I'm going to live in the White House, work in the Oval Office every day!

*For Christ's sake, Billy, you need your sleep; you have a long road ahead of you!*

# 10

# Mr. President, I'm Speechless!

Grade 12 was well underway; Billy Pigeon had his eyes focused on graduation day and Julie did the same at her high school across town.

"Are you going to quit your job at McDonald's and focus on the task ahead?" asked Julie.

"Absolutely not!" said Billy. "I have a chance to add three or four thousand more to my savings account, and I certainly don't want to let my manager down. He keeps patting me on the shoulder and saying that good help is hard to find these days!

"But I have to say, and I'm happy to say it, that I'm pretty well finished with my diagrams, my 250 page report is good to go, and my speech to my graduating class is ready to rock and roll, too. Life is good!"

"When are you going to go to the bank and get your bank loan for our motor home, for the money we need on our trip?" asked Julie.

"Soon," said Billy. "Actually, there's a really good motor home for sale on a lawn not too far away from our house. An older couple owns it. They've used it forever; they said it was in mint condition—only has about 185,000 miles on it."

"How much are they asking for it?" asked Julie.

"They're asking $4,500, but we can probably get it for around four," said Billy.

"How old is it?" asked Julie.

"1981," said Billy.

"So when are you going to tell the world what we're up to?" asked Julie.

"At my high school graduation," said Billy.

"If you're anything like me, you must be itching to get mobile," said Julie.

"I am, I am," said Billy, "but our time will come. Let's get through Grade 12 first. I've still got a few loose ends to tie up; everything else will fall into place."

"How's your dad making out?" asked Julie.

"Actually, he's onto something with an insurance company, but it's not his cup of tea. It'll pay the bills, though, keep us afloat, and tide us over till we hit the road. I'm almost positive he'll jump on the bandwagon with us when I ask him," said Billy.

"I hope so," said Julie.

"What if we can't make it to a motel for the night, have you figured out the sleeping accommodations?" asked Julie.

"Yep. Me and my dad up top, you and your mom sleep on the folded down table," said Billy.

"That'll work," said Julie.

"I hope so," said Billy.

"Me too," said Julie.

\* \* \*

The bank was only a short walk from where Julie finally found a parking spot for her Jeep Wrangler. Julie tagged along with Billy. She listened as Billy and Mrs. Larson, the personal loans manager, got it on.

"So how old are you?" asked Mrs. Larson.

"I just turned eighteen," said Billy.

"And how much money are you looking for?" asked Mrs. Larson.

"$48,000," said Billy.

"And what are you going to do with all that money if I give it to you?" asked Mrs. Larson.

"Julie and I are going to buy a motor home. We're going to take a two-year trip around the states," said a confident Billy.

"I see," said Mrs. Larson. "And what are you going to give me as collateral for your loan? Are your parents willing to co-sign for you?"

"They don't have to," said Billy.

"And why's that?" asked Mrs. Larson.

"Because I have money in your bank," said Billy.

"And exactly how much do you have on deposit with us, Billy?" asked Mrs. Larson.

"The last time I looked, it was close to $48,000; it'll be over that when I deposit my next check from McDonald's," said Billy.

"How much did you say?" asked Mrs. Larson.

"Close to $48,000," said Billy, "in cash and CDs."

"That's what I thought you said," said Mrs. Larson. "And how did a young man like you come up with that much money?"

"He earned it," said Julie. "He's saved almost every last penny he earned since he was four!" Julie was as proud as punch of her Billy.

"I see," said Mrs. Larson. "Billy, do you have any debt, any vehicle loans?"

"No I don't, ma'am. I have an American Express card with a zero balance; that's about it," said Billy.

"I see," said Mrs. Larson. She paused for a second, put her pen and paper aside, and spoke again.

"So here's the deal, Billy. Instead of me giving you, say, a five-year loan, I'm just going to authorize a low-interest line of credit for you for $50,000, secured by your cash and investment bonds. I'm sure you'll make up the difference between your 48 and my 50 real soon!" said Mrs. Larson.

"Not a problem," said Billy. "I'm working part-time after school at McDonald's and full-time there on the weekends!"

"You can draw up to $50,000 anytime, any place, at any one of our branches across America. I'll give you a debit card for that if you're not using one of our checks, and you can pay interest only every month if you'd like!" said Mrs. Larson.

"Sounds good to me," said Billy. "I will be very frugal with my spending."

"I'm sure you will!" said Mrs. Larson as she stood up and extended her hand. Billy Pigeon gave her hand a big old shake. "Come back tomorrow, and I'll have all the paperwork ready to sign. I'll give you some temporary checks and your debit card."

"Thank you, ma'am," said Billy.

"You're welcome," said Mrs. Larson.

\* \* \*

"That wasn't very hard," said Julie.

"Life is easy when you have money," said Billy. "Now I just have to teach that to the rest of America!"

\* \* \*

"Billy, remember when you talked about those sleeping arrangements in our motor home," said Julie.

"No, sweetie, my mother and your father will not let my father and your mother sleep together!" said Billy.

\* \* \*

"How about: Our future is now; our worries are a thing of the past."

\* \* \*

Billy watched an interview on CNN with Bill Gross, one of the bigwigs at PIMCO, a big investment bond company. He is a man with a great deal of knowledge, a man people listened to when he spoke.

"I would say that the United States, if you look at all the future liabilities we are committed to, is closer to 70 trillion in debt, not the 37 to 45 trillion that most people are talking about."

"Yikes!" said Billy Pigeon.

"We have a big problem," said Bill Gross.

"No, no, I have a big problem!" said Billy Pigeon.

\*\*\*

Billy was back in his notebook. He was finalizing a contract with his 20 million young workers at Billy's World.

> Minimum wage, no unions, no overtime, free medical and dental, no pensions, nothing else except your paycheck on payday, minus the normal government deductions, and then you have to agree to put 80 percent of your paycheck into the bank on every payday during your five-year Pledge of Allegiance to Billy's World and our war on jobs. The other 20 percent you can spend as you like anywhere you want to on anything you want. And if you want to save more than 80 percent, you have that option. You could be in line to win one million dollars, the prize I'm giving to the worker who saves the most money over a five-year period at Billy's World.
>
> In return for all your hard work and dedication to task at saving money and making made in America products in our five thousand factories, I will be giving you free housing, free food, free clothing (three shirts and two pairs of pants), free transportation, and free access to the recreation center at Billy's World. I want you to save, save, save, not spend, spend, spend!

"I like it. I like it a lot!" said Billy Pigeon to himself. "Now I still have to focus on the discipline part, some rules for my 20 million young workers on site, get that Code of Conduct completed, get it signed off by someone."

\*\*\*

Bill Gross was still on Billy's mind. "We have got to slay that 70 trillion dollar dragon!" thought Billy. "Or else, our country will go down the drain in a hurry. We really have to draw a line in the sand with my generation, not just have it as an objective. There will be no more deficits, no more debt. We will tear up the government credit card. We are way past our limit. Someone will be calling us soon; we will be their puppet on a string.

"Americans have to start working and saving so much money that my generation of Americans will not need our government to give us Social Security, unemployment benefits, Medicare, or Medicaid.

"Our generation does not need the stress of this generation, thank you very much. We will be pro-active; we will take care of ourselves!"

\*\*\*

"How about: the past is for historians, the present doesn't matter, and the future is for rock stars like me!"

"Nah, that would never fly; people would think I had an ego problem!" said Billy Pigeon to himself.

\* \* \*

Billy and Julie cuddled together on Paul and Debra's big, brown leather couch. They munched on a big old bowl of popcorn. They watched a really old movie on TV, starring Ben Kingsley in the title role of Gandhi. The movie won an Oscar; Billy was impressed.

"You need only a pair of sandals, a little rice, some clothes, a place to sleep and show kindness toward your fellow man," said Gandhi.

"Now there's my kind of guy!" said Billy Pigeon.

\* \* \*

After the movie was over, Billy switched the TV to CNN. Billy had all kinds of problems operating the big fancy TV channel changer device! He watched an interviewer on CNN carry on an interesting discussion with Rand Paul of Tea Party fame. Rand is the son of Ron Paul, a prominent Republican in Washington and a presidential candidate in 2008.

"We want to pay down government debt, balance the budget, and change the way Washington conducts its business," said Rand Paul.

"I like it; I like it!" said Billy Pigeon. "The Tea Party folks are going to start tracking my dragon, start telling the dragon that someone will be coming after him with a great big sword, the biggest sword that dragon has ever seen, that someone will take that great big sword and chop the head off that dragon with three mighty swings—that someone will be me!"

\* \* \*

Billy was on Google. He Googled American manufacturing, with all kinds of titles about manufacturing popping up on Billy's laptop. Billy zeroed in and read an article, five pages long, on the demise of American manufacturing from the February 2006 Trumpet Print Edition, with the article making powerful comments like these:

> For over half a century, American manufacturing has dominated the globe. It turned the tide in World War II and hastened the defeat of Nazi Germany. It subsequently helped rebuild Europe and Japan; it enabled the United States to outlast the Soviet Empire in the Cold War. At the same time, it met all the material needs of the American people. ...However, manufacturing as a share of the economy has been plummeting. In 1965, manufacturing accounted for 53 percent of the economy, by 1988 it only accounted for 39 percent, and in 2004 it accounted for just 9 percent. The United States has lost 3 million manufacturing jobs since 1998. Manufacturing loss is occurring because of globalization and outsourcing. Globalization is the increased mobility of goods, services, labor, technology, and capital throughout the world; outsourcing is the performance of a production activity in another country that was previously done by a domestic firm or plant. At the dawn of globalization, the elimination of trade barriers opened up access to foreign markets for American

manufacturers in return for building factories abroad. In due course, more and more manufacturers set up shop overseas, producing goods to be sold to Americans. Today, the trend is so severe, analysts predict that in some industries, a quarter to a half of all jobs are likely to migrate. India alone may have 700,000 outsourced jobs. China has also received hundreds of thousands of outsourced jobs. If America does not manufacture and sell goods, then money only leaves the country. This has resulted in a trade deficit that has ballooned to $800 billion. Every time an American manufacturer closes and then reopens elsewhere, the foreign country gains American technology. Not having to spend resources developing technology, foreigners can focus on improving it or beating it. Next year China will produce 3.3 million university graduates, 3.1 in India; in engineering alone China 600,000, India 350,000, and America 70,000…Many Americans did not take notice in the beginning because it was only the low paying manufacturing workers making toys, shoes, and clothing that lost their jobs to cheap foreign competition. But next to go were the higher-paid ship builders and steel producers; now it is auto workers and others…America as a whole will eventually become poorer, so be prepared to downgrade your standard of living. As progressively more manufacturers move abroad, the flow of money out of the country will exceed the benefits of cheap imports. At some point, America's trade imbalance will overwhelm us. If this trend continues, eventually Americans will not be producing enough to pay for the standard of living that post-World War II America has been used to…If you are not among the rich and you rely on a job, prepare yourself for job security issues. In plain language, if you work in the manufacturing industry, don't expect raises and don't be shocked if your job gets outsourced.

This is what Billy Pigeon said after he read the article: "China, India, Vietnam, Indonesia, Taiwan, the Philippines, Thailand, Malaysia, Bangladesh, Mexico, and Central America: do I ever have a surprise for you!"

\* \* \*

Julie also read the article. She was sharp as a whip, enjoyed an intelligent conversation and was an *A* student, too. She had listened to all the discussions between her mother, Debra, and her father, Paul, over the years about the economy, the stock market, freeways, Boeing, Microsoft, computers in general and what they were doing to the world, the ramifications of the Internet, gay rights, abortion, the environment, social media—you name it, Paul and Debra had discussed it in front of their daughter, Julie. Debra had a bias always to the right, Paul to the left; it was a mini House of Congress at the dinner table.

"So, if you move all the manufacturing jobs back to America, then what about all the poor people who are going to lose their jobs in the other countries?" asked Julie.

"It's a war!" said Billy Pigeon. "It's either them or us. War is not pretty!"

\*\*\*

"I can't worry about every person on the planet, sweetie," said Billy.

"And why not?" asked Julie. "John Evans did in your *Birdman* book: one government for one world."

"I can't, not right now," said Billy Pigeon. "My head is hurting enough already!"

"But you will later?" asked Julie.

"We'll see," said Billy.

\*\*\*

Billy signed on the dotted line. Mrs. Larson gave Billy a book of temporary checks and his own debit card with his own PIN number. She told him to expect his checks in the mail in a couple of weeks.

"Good luck with your future endeavors; you're an amazing young man!" said Mrs. Larson.

"Thank you, ma'am," said Billy. "Who knows, maybe I'll be our president one day!"

"Well, if you ever run for president when you're all grown up, you'll have my vote!" said Mrs. Larson.

"Thank you," said Billy.

\*\*\*

"I know why we only graduate 70,000 engineers a year in America," said Billy.

"And why's that?" asked Julie.

"Because American students are too busy with their credit cards and too busy having a *P-A-R-T-Y.* This sex-drugs-rock-and-roll culture is getting out of control in America. It's destroying our discipline and getting our focus off hard work and real study habits. Our students see a difficult course like calculus in engineering and they run for the hills, switch majors, take sociology and geography instead, something they can pass in their sleep, to give them lots of time to party, not burning the midnight oil with their eyes focused on their textbooks. No wonder the Chinese laugh at us in their TV commercials," said Billy.

"I suppose you're going to fix that problem, too," said Julie.

"Absolutely!" said Billy. "Nothing that some elbow grease and a good kick in the behind won't fix!"

"And don't forget my poor workers in other countries after you've taken their jobs!" said Julie.

\*\*\*

Billy was reading another article in the *Seattle Times*, an interesting article about China. The article said that China sells one billion dollars of stuff to the

United States every day. This is what Billy Pigeon said about that: "Enjoy it while you can, boys!"

Still on the topic of the Chinese, Billy also read an article on the Internet which said that Chinese workers call in sick the most, more than any other workers in the world.

"What do you expect when you only get $200 a month in wages and you have to pack your own lunch!" said Billy Pigeon.

\*\*\*

Billy was having one of those midnight-oil nights. The school year was getting on and Billy was checking and re-checking. He flipped to the cost analysis pages in his 250-page report and calculated his numbers one more time. He wanted to make sure he hadn't missed any zeros, that all his *T*s were crossed and all his *I*s dotted. He talked to himself out loud.

"So if I have 20,000,000 workers at my complex and they eat an average of $10 a day in food, that's $200,000,000 a day times 7 days in a week which equals $1,400,000,000 per week times 52 weeks which equals $62,400,000,000 per year. If I have the food prepared and cooked by military chefs in my five thousand kitchens, and their wages are already covered in the Pentagon budget, then I'm good to go. That's great; I was a little worried about that cost!"

\*\*\*

"How about: Forget about your past; take a trip with me into the future!"

\*\*\*

"Nah, we can't squeeze more than four of us into the motor home!" said Billy to himself.

\*\*\*

On his old, old twelve-inch black-and-white TV, the midnight oil still burning, while Billy was walking in his room, stretching his legs, he saw the National Debt Clock on CNN for the gazillionth time. He watched the American federal debt go up and up and up and up, over $1,000 per second, to be exact, now closing in on $14,000,000,000,000!

"Holy crap!" shouted Billy Pigeon to himself. "I'd better take my driving lessons, ASAP!"

\*\*\*

Billy had stretched long enough. He turned off the TV. He crunched some more numbers, his head spinning with the thought of more zeros on his sheet of white paper inside of his binder. Billy was certainly a candidate for the engineering faculty at U-Dub!

I'm at $100,000,000 per dormitory, so if I multiply that by five thousand dormitories, that's a grand total of $500,000,000,000 for the dormitories. Billy's little calculator was unable to handle all the zeros. Billy had to do all the calculations by hand.

The factories, training centers, and the raw material warehouses should be about half of that because they only have concrete floors, steel framing, and aluminum siding and we're only building one level. Let's say $50,000,000 per factory, five thousand factories, so that's another $250,000,000,000, the malls are at $500,000,000,000, too. The hotels are going to be more expensive because of all the carpets, bathroom fixtures, beds, mirrors, curtains, lamps, TV tables, and the 5,000,000 Gideon Bibles for the 5,000,000 hotel rooms in the five thousand hotels, but the Bibles should be free. So a plain-Jane dormitory comes in at $100,000,000 for ten stories and a total of forty dorms. If the hotel is also ten stories high at one hundred rooms per floor, for a total of one thousand rooms, with the lounge and the big pool and the restaurants on top of that, then I'd better double the costs for the hotel to be on the safe side. So let's say $1,000,000,000,000,000—no that's wrong. I've got too many zeros for 1 trillion. It should be $1,000,000,000, but that means I have too many zeros in my other numbers, too, or do I? Ah-screw-it, I can't handle any more zeros tonight. My head is starting to hurt again. Let's KISS it: Keep It Simple Stupid.

DORMS= .50 trillion

FACTORIES= .25 trillion

MALLS=. 50 trillion

HOTELS= 1.00 trillion

So that's a grand total of 2.25 trillion, which means I still have 2.75 trillion left for everything else!

Piece of cake, walk in the park, nothing to it, it's certainly doable! Man, the U. S. economy is going to be on fire, with a 5 trillion dollar injection of capital into Billy's World. I love it, I love it, I love it!

Billy's butt was sore again; his old wooden chair was hard as a rock. He stretched his entire body, touched his replica of the space shuttle Columbia, made it fly back and forth on his ceiling, and then returned to his chair for more agony. He talked to himself again.

"And the land will be state land, leased by the state of my choice for all the taxes I'm going to pay them. The cost of my lease will be one dollar per year, and I'll maybe have to buy up a few small one-horse towns along the way, and we'll give the farmers and the ranchers the option of selling or staying where they're at, but I'll make them all happy campers; you can take that to the bank. So in the grand scheme of things, it shouldn't be that much; the total land cost should be close to diddlysquat!

"I know I can get each corporation I bring on board to fork out for their own factory, training center, and raw material warehouse, but that will still be part of the private sector 2.5 trillion anyway, so I'm not really saving anything there. If I can come up with any cost savings, I should maybe put up a few more hubs for foreign kids because they're sure as shit going to want to get in on the action: maybe ten hubs for the Canadians, ten hubs for the Brits, ten hubs for the French, and the list goes on. Maybe if I made this thing big enough, I could give a job to everyone on the planet. That would certainly make Julie happy, but then we would probably have spies in amongst the foreign workers trying to steal our secrets, so screw that. Jobs for Americans only—end of story—maybe!"

Billy Pigeon stood up. He was dancing a jig after he crunched all the numbers, when he realized that Billy's World was doable and would not be laughed off as some childish prank, some idiotic, idealistic idea with no legs. His objectives were sound; his plan was in place. He would roll the dice now, take his chances, put everything on the line, and be a risk-taker. He would call on Paul Sanders—Professor Paul Sanders—the liberal professor of political science at the University of Washington, and ask him for his expert opinion and analysis and see where the wind blew him.

If the professor laughed at him, gave the thumbs down signal, made a mockery of Billy's World, thought that his idea to change America politically, economically and morally, all at once, with one stroke of his pen in the Oval Office was preposterous, out to lunch, absurd, ridiculous, foolish, stupid, ludicrous, farcical, risible, insane, outrageous, crazy, or comical, then Billy would pack up his dream of being president, burn his pages and pages of diagrams, save his 250-page report to read when he was an old man, get on the blower with the University of Washington, fill out the application, get ready to go to school again, try to impress more teachers, take another crack at Macbeth, and maybe even take one of Paul's classes in political science—you never know!

\*\*\*

"My father is hard-core, Billy. Trust me, if he doesn't like your ideas, he'll tell you so, in no uncertain terms. His students are scared to death of him. They are in agony for a week when they hand in their assignments. They go for days and days on pins and needles; they go 'Sleepless in Seattle!'" said Julie.

\*\*\*

Billy was falling in love with Julie. He pulled out his Scrapbook of Life and searched through the hundreds and hundreds of pages, the pages in the biggest binder he'd ever seen, the binder given to him by a high school friend whose father was a construction foreman. Billy finally found what he was looking for. He read out loud a quote by Albert Einstein. It went something like this:

"Put your hand on a hot stove for a minute, and it seems like an hour. Sit with a pretty girl for an hour and it seems like a minute."

"I know exactly what you mean, Mr. Einstein," said Billy Pigeon.

\* \* \*

For three more nights running, Billy read and reread his 250-page proposal. He put the finishing touches on Billy's World. He cleaned up the pencil marks on his diagrams, triple checked his cost analysis, covered all his original objectives of having zero unemployment in America, the 20 million young Americans with $50,000 in their blue jeans after five years, the 5 trillion in government and private sector funding, the net results of this mass injection of capital into a stagnant American economy, the bringing home of our boots from foreign lands, all the construction contracts tendered out to down and out American companies, the rejuvenation of the American manufacturing sector, the young people of America ready to leave after five years with a trade, ready to go to Boeing in Everett to work in the really big Boeing plant, or to hook on with Caterpillar, or to even stay at Billy's World for another five years, to come out with $100,000 in their blue jeans, a new attitude to work, an new attitude to everything, physically fit, off of drugs, and the list goes on. You get the point: a new generation of Americans who save and spend their money wisely, no longer depending on governments for handouts, the line being drawn in the sand on the 70 trillion dollar debt, with the profits from Billy's World all going to pay down the federal debt, the debt to be at zero in twenty-four years, America back on track politically, economically, and morally, three birds killed with one stone, America *numero uno* in the world once more—the way it should be!

\* \* \*

Billy was on the basement floor of his Bellevue home on his knees, his quilt of many colors ready to be assembled. The finished diagram for Billy's World was 24 feet long, 14 feet wide, using over 280 sheets of 8 ½ by 14 inch copier paper. Billy had eight massive 6 by 7 foot colored diagrams of Billy's World all ready to be taped together. Billy started with two of the diagrams to form the southern border. He taped those together in the middle, rolled them almost to the top, then added two more, rolled them up, then two more, rolled them up, then added two more, rolled them up, then added the final two 6 by 7 foot diagrams. All rolled up, his roll was 14 feet wide! No way could Julie's

Jeep carry that. Using every inch of the basement floor, he unrolled Billy's World once more, folded it in half, flattened his paper out in the middle, and started to roll Billy's World up again. This time the roll was seven feet wide, with six big strong elastic bands holding his roll in place. He carried Billy's World to his bedroom for safe-keeping!

\* \* \*

*You know,* thought Billy Pigeon, *I wouldn't be doing due diligence if I didn't try to come up with a better name for my military, industrial, and manufacturing complex than Billy's World. I'm going to take the next half-hour to brainstorm and see where the wind blows me.*

Billy brainstormed:

"Job America, Work City, Savings Central, Innovation Under Wrap, Welcome to New America, America Reborn, Twenty-Five Thousand Buildings, Pigeon's Pride, Discipline City, My Way or the Highway, Hotel California, Land of the Free, Easy Money, Asia's Worst Nightmare, America's Last Stand, Try This On For Size, Eat Your Heart Out, Land of the Hard Workers, Factory City, and Workageddon!"

There were some good ones in his list. He kind of liked Job America, Pigeon's Pride, Asia's Worst Nightmare and Workageddon, but they really didn't stand out, and didn't have the world-wide franchising possibilities like Billy's World, so Billy's World it would be—no ifs, ands, or buts. Billy Pigeon took his black felt marker and drew a 5 by 5 inch sign on a piece of white paper taped to the binder, with a one-legged pigeon sitting on the top right hand corner of the sign. The sign looked like this:

```
┌─────────────────┐
│   WELCOME TO    │
│  BILLY'S WORLD  │
└─────────────────┘
```

\* \* \*

"Are you nervous?" asked Julie.

"A little," said Billy.

"How long did you say your proposal was?" asked Julie.

"About 250 pages, 252 if you count the cover page and the table of contents," said Billy.

"That should take Dad about six hours," said Julie. "And how big is your diagram?"

"It's 24 by 14 feet," said Billy, the diagram resting on the dash of Julie's Jeep and on top of the back seat, the last bit hanging out over the small door at the rear of the Jeep.

"Holy crap!" said Julie.

\* \* \*

Billy Pigeon was excited and nervous. He had done all he could do. He could only sit tight, wait for the results, and hope to God everything worked out! Billy now knew how the Wright Brothers felt at Kitty Hawk, how Marconi felt at Signal Hill, what Edison went through watching his first bulb light up, and what Neil Armstrong and Buzz Aldrin probably said to each other as they got ready for lift-off from the moon.

"Please, Lord, make this engine work; we've got a long way to go to get home!"

\* \* \*

Debra Sanders welcomed Billy into their home one more time. She was quiet. She sat in amazement as Billy took the elastic bands off his diagram. The diagram soon filled their entire living room and more, her coffee table pulled to the side by Julie.

"My God!" said Debra.

When Debra recovered, she asked Billy if he would like a glass of merlot. Billy said, "No, not now, maybe later."

"He's in his study," said Debra. "He's waiting for you."

"Go on, give him your proposal; he won't bite!" said Julie.

\* \* \*

Billy entered Paul's study and walked toward Paul. The fate of America was about to be in the hands of one hard-core liberal professor from U-Dub. Billy passed his proposal in his brand new binder to Paul.

"Well, sir, this is it. I appreciate you taking the time to read it," said Billy.

"You're welcome, Billy," said Paul, as he reached out his hand and took the binder from Billy. "Give me five or six hours; then we'll talk.

"Take your time, sir. I'm in no rush," said Billy Pigeon. "Oh, by the way, the corresponding diagram to go with the proposal is sitting on your living room floor!"

\* \* \*

"Let's take a long walk, go tour the campus, watch the Huskies practice, and then grab lunch," said Julie. "It'll get your mind off my father!"

"Good idea," said Billy, "let's do that."

After a brisk walk to the U-Dub campus, with Julie squeezing Billy's hand and Billy still quiet and deep in thought, Julie began a conversation.

"So what do you think of U-Dub? Pretty impressive, isn't it?" asked Julie.

"It sure is," said Billy.

"Are you sure you want us to go all the way across the country to live at the White House?" asked Julie.

"It's not a matter of wanting," said Billy. "I have no choice. I *have* to go; my country is calling out to me!"

Well said, Billy. Billy and Julie were now inside at the far end of Huskies Stadium. The purple and gold were in full gear. The coach was pushing them big time. The players were exhausted from all the wind sprints.

"Won't you miss going to college, too?" asked Billy.

"Not if I'm with you!" said Julie, her left hand squeezing Billy's right hand even more. "Look at the bright side."

"And what's that?" asked Billy.

"We can always enroll after you finish your eight years as president," said Julie.

"Now there's an idea!" said Billy.

\* \* \*

Time always goes by quickly when you're having fun. From the Husky practice, Billy and Julie toured the library. Billy said *hi* to Kurt Vonnegut as he stood in front of his collection of books in the library.

"Read him sometime; his world is crazier than mine!" said Billy.

"I will, I promise," said Julie.

From the library, they stopped in at the campus restaurant, had a late lunch, and held each other's hands as they ate. Billy's left hand was holding Julie's right hand. Julie ate her chicken stir-fry with her left hand; Billy ate his with his right. It was magic!

After lunch and touring a couple more buildings on campus, it was time to head home. All the students of U-Dub had no idea that greatness was in their midst or that greatness would soon find out how really great he was, or whether he was another one of those power-hitters who couldn't touch a curve ball, his fate in the minors a foregone conclusion!

Only a few more steps, along a sidewalk, cut across a street, another sidewalk, another street, another step up, a left turn and they were walking up Paul and Debra's driveway, with Billy's heart going beat, beat, beat, beat, beat—really fast. Julie's heart was going beat, beat, beat, beat, beat——really fast, too. Debra was standing at the open front door with another glass of red wine for Billy. Paul Sanders was standing still in the living room. The diagram was all rolled up again and sitting on Paul and Debra's big oak dining room table. Paul had Billy's binder tucked under his arm.

Billy and Julie entered the living room. Billy's two eagle-eyes focused on the hard-core liberal professor from U-Dub. Paul Sanders looked at Billy; this is what he said: "Mr. President, I don't know what to say, or how to say it. I'm absolutely speechless!"

\* \* \*

"I don't know where to start," said Paul, a Democrat, a supporter of President Obama. Paul's President Obama was getting raked over the coals on the economy. His president was doing the best he could fighting off the two-headed monster of deficit reduction and providing jobs. The pressure on him was enormous, his hair getting grayer with each passing day.

"Well, am I or am I not going on my trip around America?" asked Julie.

"You most certainly *are* going on your trip, young lady, and your mother, too!" said Paul. Julie jumped up and down in the air for joy and hugged Debra, then her father, Paul, and then Billy.

"Oh my God, oh my God, oh my God!" yelled Julie.

"God's got nothing to do with it!" said Paul. "This is all about your Billy."

When everyone calmed down, Debra, Billy, and Julie sat on the comfortable, leather furniture. Paul continued to stand as he spoke again.

"Billy, this proposal of yours is beyond words. Your military, industrial, manufacturing complex, your Billy's World, is so American, so big, on such a grand scale, your goals so admirable, to change America politically, economically, and morally, with one stroke of your pen in the Oval Office, to instantly set our economy on fire, to have zero unemployment, to give 20 million young Americans hope for the future after the construction phase is finished, no lost generation of young Americans, to have financial equality amongst America's youth, every one of the 20 million kids at Billy's World leaving with $50,000 cash to build their futures, all with an equal opportunity in life, and all with a trade. Then you want to foster the goals of hard work and personal and financial discipline in these 20 million young Americans, to change their culture, to go from an immoral generation of out of control spenders to a moral generation of savers is brilliant. It is so simple, yet so eloquent, and so needed. Your 5 trillion dollar outlay, half from the private sector and half from the government is ingenious, as is your use of green technology, your plan to bring 95 percent of our troops home, to not have boots on foreign lands, to use our technology to fight wars, to let our military guard your fence line and train and provide a service at Billy's World, to always be prepared for battle if we absolutely need them, to protect our shores from invaders, to go to bat for a friend in time of need. Your contract with young America, your Pledge of Allegiance, your war on jobs—what brilliance—your five thousand contracts with corporate America, your forced savings plan, your 80 percent, 20 percent concept, your desire to take all the profits from Billy's World to pay off the 70 trillion dollar federal debt in 24 years, to actually do something with the problem is simply amazing. Your Billy's World, if we can ever pull this vision of yours off, will save America, I'm absolutely convinced of it!"

Paul reached down on a small end table, grabbed his glass and sipped on his scotch and water.

"Billy, I've seen a lot in my lifetime. I've read thousands of books, lectured to more students than you'll ever talk to, marked more papers than you'll ever write, but I have never, in my whole life, seen anything like this! I am absolutely stunned! And I've never done this before, ever, but I'm going to give your proposal and your little diagram an $A^{+++++}$, two notches better than you would ever get from Standard & Poor's, or Moody's, or Fitch! I will also be the first one to vote for you in 2012!"

\* \* \*

Paul picked up his glass. He asked Debra and Julie to stand, to toast Billy Pigeon, the next President of the United States.

"To Billy!" said Paul.

"To Billy!" said Debra and Julie together.

Billy smiled; he felt somewhat overwhelmed.

"I only have two questions for you," said Paul.

"And what are they?" asked Billy.

"Where the hell is Osoyoos, and why is a one-legged pigeon standing on the entrance sign to Billy's World?" asked Paul.

Billy Pigeon felt the weight of the world off his shoulders. He broke into laughter; he sipped on more red wine.

"I'll tell you in two years when I get to the White House," said Billy.

"I can't wait two years!" said Paul.

"All right, if you insist," said Billy.

"I insist," said Paul.

\* \* \*

"Osoyoos is a small tourist town just across the border in Canada, just a few minutes drive from Oroville, Washington," said Billy.

"I didn't know that," said Paul.

"There you go!" said Billy.

"And the one-legged pigeon?" asked Paul.

"One of the main characters in a novel I found in a tiny, used bookstore in Osoyoos," said Billy. "I was there a couple of summers ago."

"Really!" said Paul. "And what was the name of the novel?"

"*Birdman of 24 Sussex*," said Billy.

"Never heard of it," said Paul.

"You will one day," said Billy. "From what I found out later, there were only ever four hundred copies of the book, self-published by the author; those copies went like hotcakes."

"Who was the author?" asked Paul.

"A writer by the name of David H. E. Smith from Penticton, a town of about 30,000 people, just up the road from Osoyoos," said Billy.

"Never heard of him!" said Paul.

"You will one day," said Billy. "He's a very private person, just like his father in Gander, Newfoundland. He even had his back turned in the picture on the back cover of the book. I know it's symbolic of something: maybe the loneliness of a writer, maybe the privacy he's requesting in his life. I'm not sure; maybe only he can see something we can't!"

"Fascinating!" said Paul.

"And he writes his books in a beautiful cedar cabin way up in the bush, on a little lake called Headwaters," said Billy.

"And how do you know all that?" asked Paul.

"I read *Birdman,* word by word, cover to cover. As a matter of fact, I've read it three times. I was so blown away by his ability to think out of the box, to come up with solutions to pressing problems, some of them serious, some of them funny as hell, that I took a trip by bus to meet him.

"I found him at his cabin, by his wood box, cutting splits. He asked me to come inside. We talked for hours about his main character in *Birdman,* Mr. John Evans. We talked about the bird, the one-legged pigeon in the book. That's the pigeon I put on my Billy's World sign," said Billy.

"I'll be damned!" said Paul.

"So now you know the rest of the story!" said Billy Pigeon.

\* \* \*

When Julie gave Billy a ride home to Bellevue, his binder and diagram stored safely in the Jeep, she had a little surprise for Billy. She reached under the diagram, opened up her glove box and pulled out a CD. She inserted it in her CD player on the dash of the Jeep. It was a tape of recorded music by Willie Nelson, an American original.

This is what the first song on the CD sounded like:

"On the road again,

Just can't wait,

To get on the road again!"

# 11

# Barack, Barack, Get Out Here, Quick

Emanating confidence, Billy Pigeon broke the news to Walter, Sally and Sarah. They were in total shock and awe when Billy told them he was running for president in 2012, that he had the blessings of Paul and Debra Sanders, that Debra was coming along for the ride, that he had a line of credit from the bank for $50,000 to pay for a motor home and the two-year trip around the states, that a nice old couple just down the street were delivering the motor home tomorrow, that his driving lessons were all set for next week, that Professor Paul had signed off on the concept drawings and written proposal for Billy's World, that his two magnetic Billy Pigeon For President signs were being manufactured as we speak by a local company in Seattle, that they would be ready to stick and screw on after his graduation speech, that a four-foot statue of a one-legged pigeon was being carved out of wood in a Seattle artist's studio. The guy was great with wood—totem poles his specialty. Birds such as eagles and ravens were his usual bird of choice, but he was intrigued by a one-legged pigeon. The wood would be painted the colors of a real live pigeon. Billy's pigeon would look "larger than life." Even though the pigeon only had one leg, that leg would be mounted by bolts to the top of the motor home and it should be able to withstand the rigors of two years on the road: wind, rain, sun, snow, and sleet. Four coats of shellac were going on top of the pigeon paint, and three strong wires—wires as strong as cables—were going from the pigeon's shoulders to the top of the motor home, too. Billy's graduation speech was completed and he was all set to go. He had said his goodbyes at work and across the street at the car wash, and he only had one more piece of the puzzle to put together.

"And what's that?" asked his sister Sarah.

"I want Mom's permission to take Dad along for the ride. I want him to be my campaign finance chairman, to collect, count, and deposit in the bank all our campaign donations, write out tax receipts and keep track of all our campaign expenses," said Billy Pigeon. "He'll be hired on contract at $100,000 per year!"

"I'll do it; I'll do it!" shouted Walter Pigeon. "When do I start?"

\* \* \*

The graduation ceremony at Bellevue High was one of those moments in time: a momentous occasion for young Billy Pigeon, for America, and for the world! Billy was at the microphone; the audience was quiet. They had no idea that history was about to be made, at this very moment. Billy Pigeon read from a prepared statement.

"Principal Brown, teachers, fellow graduating students, parents, other members of the audience, my name is Billy Pigeon. I would like to pretend that I'm excited about high school graduation, that I'm looking forward to entering the next phase of my life, that my classmates are excited, too.

"Well, we're not!" yelled Billy Pigeon, with Principal Brown raising his eyebrows, with all the teachers on the stage raising their eyebrows, too, with a sudden hush coming over the audience, with students knowing they were going to be in for a treat, with students pulling out their iPhones, switching their iPhones to video mode and recording a high-definition, 720P video of Billy Pigeon. His classmates were about to record history in the making!

"America is a mess!" yelled Billy Pigeon. "We have lost the respect of people from all over the world with our bully tactics, our big stick. Our economic engine is sputtering on all cylinders, big time, our government in Washington is in gridlock, our two major political parties are locking horns on every issue presented to them for consideration, our politicians are owned by lobbyists, and our federal deficits and debt are eating away at our future prosperity. We are closing in on 70 trillion in actual federal liabilities, not the almost 14 trillion showing on our national debt clock. We are also up to our ears in personal debt. We spend way more than we save. We are obese, lazy, and addicted to sex, drugs, and rock and roll. We are teetering on the edge of the abyss, politically, economically, and morally. We are fighting needless wars in Iraq and Afghanistan; our soldiers are dying for no good reason. The American Dream is about to become a nightmare!"

Billy Pigeon reached for a glass of water. Julie was smiling; fellow classmates knew something big was happening, with Billy Pigeon already on YouTube, his speech already getting hits. Billy Pigeon was ready to speak again.

"My fellow Americans, I have a plan for America. Learn from the past, deal with the present, and the future will take care of itself! I would like to announce tonight, here at Bellevue High, in the great city of Bellevue, in front of my mother, Sally, my father, Walter, my sister, Sarah, my girlfriend, Julie, her parents, Paul and Debra, that I, Billy Pigeon, age 18, representing a new generation of young Americans, will be running for President of the United States in the 2012 Presidential Campaign Against President Barack Obama!"

The audience was shocked. More students were standing with their iPhones; they were tweeting on their BlackBerries. Billy Pigeon was about to go viral, his speech captured in its entirety on all the popular social media channels and then sent all over the world. Billy Pigeon was about to be on CNN Breaking News, with Wolf Blitzer driving to his TV studio, running to get his makeup on, to get his beard and hair combed, to get his tie and jacket on as we speak, with Principal Brown and all the teachers on stage shaking their heads in disbelief, with Billy Pigeon's classmates not one bit surprised! Billy continued his speech.

"I will be leaving Bellevue bright and early in the morning to tour America in my motor home. I will head east on Interstate 90, with my girlfriend, Julie, my father, Walter, and Julie's mother, Debra. We will tell America slowly but surely, one step at a time, my plan to change America. We will be guided on our journey by a four-foot-tall, carved, one-legged pigeon. I will see you in the White House in two short years!

"To my teachers, to my classmates, to Principal Brown, I will always cherish our time together, but now I have to say goodbye. I have an obligation to fulfill. I have work to do; my place in history awaits!"

Principal Brown turned to Mr. Yates, the District Superintendent of Schools. Mr. Yates was just arriving on the stage, having been hung up in a traffic jam. Mr. Yates listened to Billy Pigeon's entire speech from the back of the room. This is what Principal Brown said to Mr. Yates: "I told you to expect the unexpected. I told you this kid was special!"

"Jesus, Jack, you never told me he was *this* special!" said Mr. Yates.

\*\*\*

Michelle Obama was in her bed at the White House, her eyes focused on her flat-screen TV. Michelle had just watched the Breaking News on CNN, her mouth ajar, with President Obama in the bathroom brushing his teeth.

"Barack, Barack, get out here, quick; you're not going to believe this!"

\*\*\*

Mrs. Larson, the bank lady who gave Billy Pigeon his $50,000 line of credit, was in her living room when the Breaking News on CNN hit the TV. This is what Mrs. Larson said: "I knew it, I knew it, I knew it!"

# 12

## On the Road Again

When Billy Pigeon backed the motor home out of his driveway, the Billy Pigeon For President magnetic signs now screwed in place on both sides of their old beater motor home, a large American flag painted on the rear of the vehicle, the four-foot-tall, carved, one-legged pigeon all mounted and looking good, the one leg bolted down just above the center of the front windshield, the three guy wires in place, he had no idea that there were forty cars and trucks full of friends from Bellevue High all ready and waiting to escort him through Seattle and out onto Interstate 90, with the press all over Billy's front lawn, their cameras trying for a close-up, their microphones in place for any last minute comments, with CNN reporters having taken the red-eye overnight flight from the East Coast to the West Coast, their rental vans ready and waiting to begin the chase, to report all the excitement to the rest of the world, to chase Billy Pigeon here, there, and everywhere around America, to see what their future president was up to, to find out why an eighteen-year-old boy from Bellevue, fresh out of high school, would want to run for the highest office in the country, to see how he would clear all the hurdles in front of him. From a media's perspective, this was huge, the biggest story to hit the wires since 9/11; the press wanted to be all over it, to not miss one Billy Pigeon heartbeat!

\* \* \*

"What's your plan for America, Billy?" yelled John King from *John King USA* fame, with Billy Pigeon more focused on properly backing out of his driveway than any reporters' questions. Billy passed Sally's rose bushes—

thank God—waving to all his friends gathered on his lawn and now starting to run to their cars and trucks to get a move on, with Billy waving to the TV cameras, then yelling the following to John King from CNN: "Call Debra; she might let me give you an exclusive on my plan, tell you where we're going, what we're up to, why I'm running for President. Right now, I have to focus on my driving; it's only my second day behind the wheel of my own vehicle!"

"What's her last name?" asked John King.

"Sanders, Debra Sanders!" yelled Billy.

\* \* \*

"What the hell is that kid up to?" asked President Obama, watching on TV as Billy backed his old beater motor home out of his driveway and headed out of town! "This has got to be some kind of joke. Someone in this town knows what the kid is doing. I want you to find out who! And what is this plan for America he keeps talking about? You have the FBI open a file on him, on his family, on all his close friends, on the people with him in the motor home. Tell them to watch his every move, to keep me posted!"

"Yes, Mr. President, I'm all over it!" said the president's press secretary.

\* \* \*

"We need a name for our motor home," said Billy. "I'm too tired; someone else do the thinking!"

"How about the Birdmobile?" asked Julie.

"I like it; I like it a lot!" said Billy Pigeon. "The Birdmobile it shall be!"

\* \* \*

Paul Sanders called Debra on her cell and asked her how they were making out.

"We're still in Seattle. Billy is doing great; we're cruising along right at the speed limit. There are about fifteen to twenty vehicles in front of us blowing their horns like crazy and another twenty or thirty or more behind us. The highway is lined on both sides with people yelling at us, wishing us well, waving little American flags; there must be a good ten to fifteen TV trucks and vans after us. It's exciting. It's incredible!" said Debra.

"You guys be safe," said Paul.

"We will, sweetie, I promise," said Debra.

"Before I forget it, and don't tell Billy yet, I've contacted Tim Hickman from the engineering faculty to see if he would help, and he said yes. He's contacting a couple of architect friends of his to get some initial drawings of Billy's complex going. I told him it was absolutely crucial that they not say a word to anyone; he assured me they wouldn't. And is he ever pumped! You should have seen the look on his face when I brought in Billy's 24 by 14 foot drawing, told him what Billy was up to, why we had to get him elected in 2012, and that we needed something on real draft paper in a couple of months!"

"What did he say to that?" asked Debra.

"It'll be done!" said Paul.

"Excellent!" said Debra. "And I've got a couple of lawyers in our firm working on a list of American corporations getting products manufactured elsewhere, companies building factories overseas, and companies who are outsourcing jobs. We're also working on a generic contract that Billy can use to sign up his five thousand corporations and also a letter of intent when we need it down the road."

"What about the constitutional amendment?" asked Paul.

"That's a tough one," said Debra. "We're getting legal opinions from everyone we know. People are even calling me, if you can believe it!" said Debra.

"Great stuff!" said Paul. "Keep me posted."

"I will, sweetie," said Debra. "By the way, this is so exciting. I never ever thought I would be doing something like this at my age. I really appreciate you letting me go!"

"You're welcome," said Paul.

"Don't forget to water my fern!" said Debra.

"I won't," said Paul.

\* \* \*

On the outskirts of Seattle, before they headed into the mountains, Billy stopped the Birdmobile for a pee break. He pulled the motor home into a truck stop, his old beater motor home slowly coming to a halt. People rushed up to the Birdmobile and handed Billy Pigeon money: some cash, others personal checks made out to Billy Pigeon. Many of the campaign contributors wanted to personally shake Billy's hand and wish him well on his journey.

Billy's mind was not on shaking hands at this very moment. His bladder was about to burst; he had to get to a urinal ASAP! Billy gave the cash and checks to Julie, told her to get Walter to write out tax receipts, told his crowd of well-wishers that he wasn't trying to be rude, but he had to go pee! They all understood. One nice lady from Kansas said the following to Billy: "Already been there and done that!"

\* \* \*

"What's the total so far?" asked Julie.

"Over $2,000 and counting!" said Walter Pigeon, excited as hell to have a real banker's job!

"That's fantastic!" said Julie.

\*\*\*

Tim Hickman called Paul and told him that this project of Billy's was really big. He asked Paul how much money he had in the budget to work with.

"Five trillion!" said Paul.

"We're going to start with one of the four-thousand-bed dormitories. We want to see how Billy's estimate of $100,000,000 pans out," said Tim.

"The kid's pretty sharp!" said Paul.

"He might be," said Tim, "but costs change from month to month and contractors can get greedy if they think they're onto something big. If this thing ever gets past the drawing stage, it's going to be some shot in the arm for the U.S. economy!"

"That's his plan," said Paul. "We're got 28 or 29 months; he wants to put a shovel in the ground the first day of his presidency."

"If that's the case, we've got one hell of a lot of work to do!" said Tim.

"Tell me about it," said Paul.

"What about the land?" asked Tim.

"He's talking flat land, lots of it, in a warm climate, maybe somewhere in Nevada, New Mexico, or Arizona. I'm not sure where," said Paul.

"He might need more land than he thinks, especially if you take into account all the solar panels and wind turbines he's got in there for power to help run the place," said Tim.

"I know," said Paul. "It's huge!"

"And we have to have one hell of a water source, too," said Tim. "And be fairly close to natural gas reserves, and major rail lines and roadways; there's a lot to consider when he chooses a final site."

"I know, I know," said Paul. "This thing can give you a headache, real quick!"

"Tell me about it!" said Tim. "But you know, when push comes to shove, how lucky can we be, two old farts from U-Dub about to participate in the greatest construction project the world has ever seen, about to test the metal of American technology and innovation like it's never been tested before, to show the world what America is all about. It's absolutely incredible, this Billy's World!"

"You're starting to sound like Billy himself!" said Paul.

"I can't help it!" said Tim. "The whole concept is so ingenious, it's beyond words. I'm speechless!"

"Exactly what I said!" said Paul.

\*\*\*

Billy had just returned from his pee break. He fired up the Birdmobile and they started to roll out of the small truck stop. Julie had an old cassette tape she found in a secondhand store in Seattle. She pushed the tape into the ancient cassette player in the old beater motor home. The music began:

"On the road again,

Just can't wait to,

Get on the road again!"

\* \* \*

Billy Pigeon laughed.
"You're bad!" said Billy.
"I know!" said Julie. "Don't you just love it?"

\* \* \*

Paul Sanders got on the blower to Terry Delaney, a high school buddy who was high up in the food chain at Microsoft.

"So, old buddy, old friend, what if I told you I could have all your software, all your computer stuff, all your video-game stuff, built in the good old US of A, built by contented American workers getting paid minimum wage to produce quality Made in America products—what would you say to that?"

"I would say you were full of shit!" said Terry Delaney.

"Seriously, if I could do that for you, what would you say?" asked Paul.

"I'd say bring it on!" said Terry Delaney.

\* \* \*

Billy chitchatted with his father, Walter.

"Dad, if we have a week or two or three like this, and the money keeps rolling in, I could put away my checkbook, maybe pay off the motor home, be back to zero on my line of credit!" said Billy.

"Absolutely!" said Walter.

"Good!" said Billy. "I hate the thought of owing anything to anybody!"

\* \* \*

And speaking of money, Walter's cell phone rang again; it was Sally, with Sarah screaming in the background!

"Walter, people are lining up at the front door with donations for Billy. The line goes all the way down to Mr. Carter's house!" said Sally.

"Unbelievable!" said Walter.

"Unbelievable is right!" said Sally. "Here, Sarah wants to speak to you!"

"Dad, Dad you won't believe it! All the kids in Seattle are dropping by on their way to school. They have money from their parents, too. I did a quick count; I have over $50,000 in cash, another $35,000 in checks and it's still coming in like crazy!" said Sarah. "And it's not stopping! Our phone is ring-ing off the hook with people from all over the states who want to know if we have a bank account set up yet to collect donations!"

"I'm working on it as fast as I can. Billy wants me to deal with his bank, a Mrs. Larson. She's all over it, but we're all a little overwhelmed right now!" said Walter.

"Tell me about it!" said Sarah.

\* \* \*

"So what's happening, Dad?" asked Billy.

"Your mother and sister are going nuts; that's what's happening!" said Walter.

"They have over $85,000 collected for your campaign already, and it's only the first day!" said Walter.

Billy was quiet for a moment. He gave his dad the thumbs up, and then he spoke again. This is what he said: "Eat your heart out, Obama!"

\* \* \*

Tim Hickman, our engineer friend, was e-mailing his son Jim in Afghanistan. Jim has a wife and two kids to feed in Seattle, and is on his third tour overseas; the first two were in Iraq. Tim Hickman asked his son if he would be interested in a military job in the United States, maybe driving a big old Humvee around a military, industrial, manufacturing complex somewhere in the southern states where the weather was always great, working a day shift with his weekends off because of his seniority on the job, to spend the weekends at home in a townhouse at a military base where he had no rent to pay, lots of time to kick back and watch TV, and plan his trips to Seattle to see the wife and kids. What would you say to that?

This is what Jim Hickman e-mailed back to his father, Tim: "Beam me home, Scottie!"

\* \* \*

Debra made the announcement to Billy, Walter, and Julie.

"Our new campaign phone is activated; we're good to go!"

"Awesome!" said Billy Pigeon.

\* \* \*

Sarah was on the phone again to Walter. "We're up to $120,000 and the lineups are getting longer! Mom says we should hire a couple of security guards, ASAP, to keep the peace, to do crowd control!"

"Do it," said Walter, "but make sure you put their bill in a box in my study. Mark Billy Pigeon, Campaign Expenses on the side of the box!"

"Will do, Dad; sorry, got to go! Mom is yelling at me again!" said Sarah.

\*\*\*

"Pull over the next chance you get," said Debra.

"What's up?" asked Billy.

"I want to stick on a couple of new decals," said Debra.

Debra was out of the Birdmobile, with Walter right behind with his cordless drill and a handful of metal screws, the twenty or so vehicles behind Billy blowing their horns as Debra duct-taped a new decal on the plastic rear window of Julie's Jeep Wrangler, as Walter screwed a screw into each of the four corners of the second magnetic decal on the rear of the Birdmobile just above the American flag, just below the back window. This is what Billy's new campaign phone number looked like:

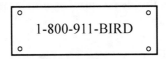

\*\*\*

Debra Sanders wasn't even back to her seat and relaxed when her new cell phone rang.

"That was quick!" said Debra.

It was David Gregory from *Meet the Press*. He was wondering when Billy would be on the East Coast, so that he and Billy could hook up for a one-on-one, TV interview.

"Probably in a month or two," said Debra. "We're in no rush. We're taking our time. We're going where the wind blows us!"

\*\*\*

Debra's phone rang again. It was Sarah Sanford, a reporter from the Washington Post. She was wondering when Billy would be releasing information about his plan for America.

"He's not exactly sure yet," said Debra. "We're still fine-tuning a few details."

"Here's my e-mail address; what's yours?" asked Sarah Sanford.

"We don't have one yet," said Debra. "I'll let you know as soon as it's up and running."

\*\*\*

*I should take care of that right now,* thought Debra. She challenged Billy, Julie, and Walter to come up with something really creative, really catchy, with Julie jumping to the pump immediately.

"How about admin@billybird.com?" said Julie.

Debra was astounded. She told Julie that her creation was perfect, that it was the cat's meow!

"That's my girl!" said Billy.

"I like it; I like it a lot!" said Walter. Walter was not one to get too excited about anything, except counting all the money they were raking in!

Debra was on the blower again. She was talking to her computer guy in Seattle. She told him she wanted their new e-mail address activated, ASAP. Within the hour, she received another phone call. It was her computer guy. This is what he said: "Done!"

\* \* \*

Now Debra was talking to her decal guy again. She ordered two more magnetic signs. She told the decal guy her new e-mail address and said the following: "We're only a few miles out of town. You'll catch up to us when we pull over to sleep. I'll let you know where. And e-mail me a copy of your bill for Walter; he's really fussy!"

"Will do!" said the decal guy.

\* \* \*

Tim Hickman was on the blower, too. He was talking to JJ—Jacob Jack—a local building contractor, one of the biggest and best in the Seattle area.

"Give me a ballpark price on a ten-story dormitory, with four rooms on each floor, one facing north, one south, one east, and one west, each room able to sleep one hundred people, with ten elevators in the middle, keep it plain-Jane, concrete, steel, glass windows," said Tim Hickman.

"What do you want with each room?" asked JJ.

"A room with 12-inch square tiles, one hundred pit areas, big enough for a single bed, a footlocker and a three-drawer desk built into the wall, with washrooms and showers, a washer and dryer room, and beneath the whole structure, I want a kitchen, dining room big enough to feed four thousand people all at the same time, with the ten elevators stopping in the center of the dining hall," said Tim Hickman.

"Do you want a ballpark for the land, too?" asked JJ.

"Nope, just the building," said Tim Hickman.

"So what's going on—something at the University, something I can get in on?" asked JJ.

"I can't talk about it now," said Tim Hickman, "but get me the price, and if the project's a go, I'll get you in, I promise," said Tim Hickman.

"Sounds good to me!" said JJ.

\* \* \*

Ring, ring, ring...

"Hi, this is Debra Sanders; can I help you?"

"Please hold for a call from the White House!" said a female voice.

"Billy, you're not going to believe this; guess who's on the phone?" said Debra.

"Who?" asked Billy.

"The White House!" said Debra.

"All right!" said Billy. Debra and Billy high-fived each other, knowing that their little drive was already garnering attention from the right people.

"Hi Debra, this is Barack Obama, President of the United States!" said the president.

"I know who you are; what can I do for you?" asked Debra.

"You're kidding me, right?" asked Barack Obama.

"I kid you not!" said Debra. "We're dead serious."

"Well, if that's the case, I can only wish your Billy Pigeon the best," said Barack Obama.

"Thank you, Mr. President. I'll pass your comments on to Billy. I'm sure he'll be pleased as punch to know that you've called, that you've taken time out of your busy schedule to notice the start of our campaign. Would you like to talk to him in person?" asked Debra.

"No, that's okay. I'll see him at the Presidential Debate," said Barack Obama.

"He'll be there!" said Debra, the conversation coming to an end.

"Ya, right!" said Barack Obama, the president, with the last word, as usual!

\* \* \*

"Quick, look in your side mirror; there has to be a hundred or more vehicles following us!" yelled Billy Pigeon.

"And look at all the people up ahead," said Julie. "They're standing by their vehicles on both sides of the highway and waving!"

"Ka-ching, ka-ching, ka-ching!" said Walter.

\* \* \*

Paul Sanders picked up his phone at his university office. It was Tim Hickman, fresh off the phone with JJ.

"I've got your quote on the dormitory costs," said Tim.

"What is it?" asked Paul.

"$99,999,999.99, plus tax!" said Tim Hickman.

"I told you that kid was sharp!" said Paul.

\* \* \*

"Look, look!" yelled Billy Pigeon once more. "Two Washington State Troopers are pulling up in front of the line. They've got their lights flashing and their four-ways on; they're going to give us a police escort!"

"Awesome!" said Julie.

"That's too cool!" said Debra.

"My God, listen to all the people yelling at us!" yelled Billy. "They're desperate for change in America!"

\* \* \*

Ryan Smith, a high school buddy of Billy's, in the fifth car behind the Birdmobile, looked at his brother, Jeff, who had a cold Bud between his legs and eagle eyes for any more State Troopers pulling up from behind!

"Piss on it, this is too exciting. I'm not going back to work. I'm following Billy all the way to the Montana border!" said Ryan Smith.

"Right on, dude!" said his brother, Jeff.

\* \* \*

Julie was on Billy's new Twitter account; she was looking at all the Tweets to Billy.

"It's unreal, Billy; you're getting Tweets from all over the world. This is simply amazing!" said Julie.

"I know, I know," said Billy. "My mind is racing here, there, and everywhere; it won't slow down. I've got to start relaxing, put on some Eagles, maybe some James Taylor, or some Dixie Chicks for sure!"

\* \* \*

Ring, ring, ring…

"Hi, Debra Sanders speaking; what can I do for you?"

"Hi Debra, this is Bob Agar from *Time* magazine. We'd like to hook up with you in Chicago, have an in-depth interview with Billy, find out what makes him tick, find out why an eighteen-year-old boy would want to run for president, and ask him how he's going to overcome the many obstacles in his way."

"That sounds like an interesting proposition," said Debra. "I'll talk to Billy; we'll get back to you, I promise."

"Sounds good to me," said Bob Agar. "Oh, by the way, some of our researchers were searching for his line 'Learn from the past, deal with the present and the future will take care of itself.'"

"What about it?" asked Debra.

"They're curious where he plucked that one from!" said Bob Agar.

\*\*\*

"I say we visit the Colonel tonight in Ellensburg" said Julie.
"The bucket or the three-box?" asked Debra.
"The bucket is cheaper!" said Walter. "You get the fries, and two choices of salad."
"And a two-liter drink of your choice," said Julie. "What about you, Billy?"
"I've got to get America off junk food. You guys go ahead. I'm going to stick with my ham and cheese sandwich in the fridge and have an orange juice with it!" said Billy.

\*\*\*

When they finally found a KFC, Walter said the following to Julie: "Don't forget the receipt!"

\*\*\*

"How's my Jeep doing?" asked Julie.
"So far, so good," said Billy.
"Want to stop and go for a ride?" asked Julie.
"Not now, sweetie, I've got too much on my mind!" said Billy.

\*\*\*

One of the things really bothering Billy—a real noose tightening around him, a noose he had to avoid at all costs—was all the sudden fame, being treated like a rock star, all the money Walter was collecting, and the buckets of KFC chicken at their beck and call. Bottom line: the key to the success of Billy's World was to convince 20,000,000 young Americans to be frugal, to save 80 percent of what they would be taking in in wages, to only spend 20 percent, to cut junk food out of their diets completely, and to be happy with their three shirts and two pairs of pants, good hot healthy food, a single bed to sleep on, and a roof over their heads!

Billy had to set the example. He had to be a leader. He had to start with Julie, Debra, and Walter. They would all have to get on the same page. He would have that discussion with them later on in the evening. He would start by finding them a plain-Jane motel: one for $35, $40, or $50 max. All they really needed was a shower, a toilet, a sink, a mirror for the women, not the Waldorf, or the Hilton, certainly not the Trump Tower!

\*\*\*

"What's the latest back at the house, Dad?" asked Billy.

"A Gong Show!" said Walter.

\* \* \*

Billy was still focused on that noose thing again, thinking about the way he looked, the way he presented himself in public. Three shirts, two pairs of pants—I have to *be* that man, no matter what, even at the Presidential Debate—white shirt, blue jeans, white socks, dark brown leather belt and dark brown leather moccasins.

*Just like Steve Jobs from Apple,* thought Billy Pigeon, *only with a different colored shirt!*

\* \* \*

Billy had the motor home radio on. He listened to a commentator on a local radio news segment say that America had a total federal debt, including unfunded liabilities, of 61 trillion dollars. Billy had also heard the number 50 trillion kicked around, too, plus the 70 trillion dollar number he was going by.

*So which number is it? Doesn't anyone in America know what the real bottom line is? Hello, I need it for my projections so 'the future can take care of itself!'* thought Billy Pigeon.

\* \* \*

On the same broadcast, it was reported for the first time that The Donald was contemplating running for president in 2012.

*You can't do that, Mr. Trump. I was counting on you to develop my five thousand hotels, to at least act as a consultant, to get all of your real-estate developer buddies involved!* thought Billy Pigeon.

\* \* \*

It had been a long day on the campaign trail. Billy Pigeon was pooped! They were past the college town of Ellensburg, closing in on Moses Lake and Ritzville, more than halfway across the state of Washington, their bucket of KFC chicken was toast. Billy was craving some good healthy Thai wraps to get some vegetables in his diet!

"Why don't we call it a day and look for a motel," said Billy.

"Sounds like a plan," said Walter. "I could use some shut-eye, too!"

\* \* \*

"There's a motel!" said Billy. "I'm going to pull over."

Billy had Julie run inside. One of the two State Troopers watching their every move took the time to grab a couple of coffees and have a little downtime from the busy Interstate 90 highway. Julie was back at the Birdmobile with the bad news.

"They want $85 for the night!"

"That's way too much," said Billy Pigeon. "Let's keep on trucking!"

\*\*\*

Further along the highway, there was another motel.

"$65," said Julie.

"We can do better than that!" said Billy

\*\*\*

A half hour later, with the deer feeding on the edge of the highway, with Billy's eyes like two piss-holes in the snow, with Walter asleep on the bunk over Billy's head, there was another motel, this one dingy looking, the parking lot with potholes, the paint peeling big-time!

"Now we're talking!" said Billy.

"$34.95!" said Julie.

"I like it, I like it. We'll take it. Let's shut her down!" yelled Billy. "Get four rooms. Dad, wake up; we need some cash!"

"I'm up, I'm up!" said Walter.

"I'll pay for it," said Julie.

"Don't forget the receipt!" said Walter.

\*\*\*

What a bonus for the motel owners, Bob and Ethel Frank. It was their first full season operating their run-down motel, the first time a presidential candidate had ever graced their humble abode, at least that they were aware of, their twenty-five rooms soon filled with tired State Troopers, exhausted TV camera people and reporters, the students from Seattle only with food and gas money, their credit cards maxed out, the high school students crashing in their vehicles, the students determined to follow Billy Pigeon all the way to the Montana border, come hell or high water!

\*\*\*

An hour after the lights were turned out, with everyone in all the motel rooms sound asleep, a loud scream came from Debra's room. The two State Troopers outside their motel room in their bare feet and their boxer shorts, with their hand guns drawn, locked and loaded, ready for bear, and Billy in his boxer shorts, too, came running and knocking on Debra's door. Her face was white as a ghost when she opened the motel door in her pajamas.

"What's wrong; what's wrong?" asked Billy.

"A spider—a big one—over there, on my bed!" shouted Debra.

"Show me!" said Billy.

"Right there—look on the pillow!" said Debra, shaking like a leaf.

Billy went to her tiny bathroom, looked inside, grabbed a pile of toilet paper, and then walked over to Debra's bed.

"What are you doing?" asked Debra.

"I'm going to squish your spider!" said Billy. "There, all done!"

"Yuk," said Debra. "That is so gross!"

Billy walked to the bathroom. He flushed the toilet paper and the big old spider down the drain.

"Now go to sleep!" said Billy.

\* \* \*

Billy said good night to Walter for the second time, and then gave Julie a kiss on the cheek.

"Want to come to my room?" asked Julie.

"Not tonight, sweetie, too many sets of eyes around!"

Billy was in his room, finally, the lights out one more time, the blanket over his shoulders, and his head on the really soft pillow. Billy was exhausted!

*This is hard work!* thought Billy as he closed his eyes and was out like a light!

Half an hour later, there was another blood curdling scream, this one louder than the first!

"What now?" asked Billy.

He was up again, the two State Troopers were up again, all three of them still in their boxer shorts, and the State Troopers with their handguns drawn watching as Billy knocked again on Debra's motel door. Once more, the door opened. Debra was terrified.

"Another spider, Billy, bigger than the first one; it crawled right up my arm. It's in my bed somewhere. I can't sleep in this room. I can't...I can't...I'm sorry!" said Debra.

"Get your stuff. We'll put you in with Julie for the night," said Billy.

"Thank you!" said Debra.

"You're welcome," said Billy.

\* \* \*

Daylight came early, way too early for Billy. There was a knock on Billy's motel door. It was Julie.

"What now?" asked Billy.

"Come quick; you have got to see this!" said Julie.

"Not another spider!" said Billy.

"No, no, Mom's okay; it's something else," said Julie.

Outside, in the parking lot, in the morning mist, on top of the Birdmobile, sitting on the shoulder of the four-foot-tall, carved, one-legged pigeon were four other *real* pigeons, all talking up a storm, all looking down at Billy.

"Isn't that something?" asked Julie.

"It sure is," said Billy, as he grabbed his old Kodak instamatic camera from his motel room and took a picture for his Scrapbook of Life.

"How about making us a cup of coffee?" said Billy.
"Already did!" said Julie.

\*\*\*

"On the road again,

Just can't wait to

Get on the road again!"

With Billy Pigeon singing and sounding their battle cry, with Walter complaining about his bed sagging big-time in the middle, his back sore as hell, with Debra still fussing about how big the second spider was, with Julie still in awe of the four pigeons—the four pigeons coming along for the ride—Billy was behind the wheel of the Birdmobile. Despite Walter complaining about the high gas prices, the Birdmobile was all fueled up and their presidential motorcade all ready to hit the road. The two State Troopers got on the highway first, then the twenty or so vehicles full of tired and hung-over students, then Billy, then more students, and then the TV trucks and vans, with lights flashing and horns blowing and cameras rolling. Billy Pigeon was sipping on his second cup of Morning Joe, missing his old buddy Joe Scarborough and his lovely lady friend Mika.

"Where are we exactly?" asked Julie.

"I have no idea," said Billy. "All I can tell you is that we're heading east!"

\*\*\*

"Do you want me to Google us up on my cell, see where we're at on the GPS?" asked Julie.

"No, it's more fun this way," said Billy. "We have two whole years, I want to take my time, get a feel for our country, take time to smell the roses, talk to people, go back in time, imagine what it was like for the early settlers on their horses and in their covered wagons, feel the cool morning air, smell the prairie grass, relax, and chill out!"

"And how are we going to do that when we've got people in tow and every Tom, Dick, and Harry in the U. S. of A. and around the world on CNN watching our every move?" asked Julie.

"I'm not sure yet," said Billy. "Maybe we'll have to have two hours a day in your Jeep with the top down, just you and me and Bobby McGee!"

"I like that idea," said Julie.

"I knew you would!" said Billy.

\*\*\*

"Sometimes technology and all the information it spews out can be a little overwhelming," said Billy.

"Well said," said Walter.

"IPhones, voice mail, e-mails, Twitter Tweets, Facebook pages, videos, music, news, stock quotes—you need a balance in your life," said Billy.

"Well said, Mr. President," said Debra.

"That's why we're going to have a daily routine: be up at seven, breakfast, on the road from nine till noon, have a relaxing lunch, back on the road till four, get our spiderless motel for the night, have dinner, and then we get to relax, go for a walk, take a nap, read a book, watch a little TV, and plan for the next day," said Billy.

"And don't forget the Jeep ride!" said Julie.

"That, too!" said Billy. "Maybe we'll stay put on Sundays, go to church, get some brownie points from the Religious Right, or kick back and watch football, some baseball, some college basketball, do sweet bugger all. Bottom Line: we have to control what is happening around us, or it will control us!"

"I couldn't agree with you more," said Debra.

"Me too," said Julie.

"Me three," said Walter.

\* \* \*

"And while we're on the topic of mapping out our plan of attack, I want to discuss expenses," said Billy. "I'll be running a campaign of frugality, of saving money, not spending it just because you have it.

"Our campaign donations are rolling in, but I want to keep the costs down big time! Sure it would be nice to go and get one of those big comfortable diesel motor homes that a singer like Allan Jackson takes on the road, or someone like Sarah Palin takes on the road with her family, with fancy showers, bathrooms, bedrooms, TVs, microwave ovens, big fridges, and all the other bells and whistles, but I want none of that for us.

"I want a full accounting, to the penny, on a daily basis, in an old-fashioned ledger book which can't be hacked into, of all our revenues and expenses. I want to be able to say to the press and the American people at the end of our road trip that I took in $50 million, that I spent $1 million, and that the other $49 million I'm going to plunk down as my first payment against our $70 trillion debt.

"Don't get me wrong; we don't have to be so cheap that we never treat ourselves every now and then. I, myself, want to have a big sirloin steak when I get to Chicago, cooked in our motor home. I want to have a fabulous lobster dinner when we hit the ocean, cooked in our motor home, and I'll treat all of you occasionally, too, all cooked in our motor home!

"I really want to cut out the fast food, the KFC, the Big Macs, the tacos and the pizzas. I want the press to videotape us pulling up in supermarket parking lots and coming out with shopping carts full of good, healthy food, then showing all of that to America and the world on their nightly broadcasts. We're going to make our own sandwiches, drink fresh milk and lots of juice, have chicken and fish, lots of fish, we're going to make our own salads, keep it all in the motor home fridge, and if we don't have enough room, we put some ice in our big old cooler!

"If we're pulling an all-nighter, black coffee and vegetarian pizza is okay for a treat, but we don't buy it. The State Troopers will go up ahead and get it for us. Bottom Line: we are going to stay the course; we are going to lead by example, no ifs, ands, or buts!"

\* \* \*

"I know I speak for all three of us Mr. President, when I say that we agree with you whole-heartedly," said Debra.

"Here, here!" said Walter.

"Me too!" said Julie.

Debra Sanders could see Mr. President written all over Billy Pigeon, even at the tender age of eighteen. She knew now why Paul had been so impressed, why he would let Billy take his wife and daughter on a two-year road trip, never question their motives, and agree to stay in Seattle and water her fern for two whole years!

Billy Pigeon had a plan for America. He was gifted intellectually. He was disciplined. He had the work ethic to pull it off. He could take the bull by the horns when he had to. He knew exactly what he was up to and which direction he was headed. Enough said.

\* \* \*

Bob Agar from *Time* magazine was on the blower again wanting to know exactly when Billy would be in Chicago. He had planning to do, a room to book, a plane flight to set up, and he had to meet certain deadline expectations.

"We get there when we get there," said Debra.

"What do you mean by that?" asked Bob Agar.

"Two, three, four months—I can't predict how long it will take Billy to cross America," said Debra. "He's the boss; we're just along for the ride!"

"For Christ's sake, I can't wait four months for that interview," said Bob Agar. "That's not the way we do it in the print media!"

"Sorry, but that's the way we do it with this president!" said Debra Sanders.

"Screw it; I'll come and find you!" said Bob Agar.

"Whatever you like," said Debra Sanders.

\* \* \*

Ring, ring, ring...

"Hello, Debra Sanders speaking."

"Hi, Debra, this is Jay Leno."

"Mr. Leno, what can I do for you?" asked Debra Sanders.

"I'd like to have a corporate jet fly up, pick Billy up at the nearest airport, fly him to L. A., have him as my only guest for the whole hour, fly him back, and catch up to you in a rented limo; he'll be gone for twenty-four hours max. What do you say to that offer?" asked Jay Leno.

\*\*\*

"Let me check with Billy," said Debra.

"Hey, Billy, do you want to fly down to L. A. in a corporate jet and be on *The Tonight Show* with Jay Leno?" asked Debra.

"Not really," said Billy. "Tell him thanks, but no thanks. Tell him I'm going fly-fishing in the morning at the crack of dawn, and I need my sleep!"

\*\*\*

"Sorry, but he's going fly-fishing," said Debra. "He said thanks, but no thanks!"

"You're kidding me, right?" said Jay Leno.

"I kid you not!" said Debra Sanders.

\*\*\*

"Debra Sanders speaking."

"Hi, Debra, this is Mary Morgan from the *Oprah Show*. Oprah says she'll pay big money to Billy Pigeon to be on her show!"

"We'll think about it," said Debra. I'll talk to Billy when he gets back from fly-fishing and see what he has to say."

\*\*\*

Ring, ring, ring...

"Debra Sanders speaking."

"Hi Debra, this is Conan O'Brien."

"The answer is no!" said Debra.

\*\*\*

Ring, ring, ring...

"Debra Sanders speaking."

"Hi, Debra, this is Mary Morgan again from the *Oprah Show*. Did you get a chance to talk to Billy?" asked Mary Morgan.

"I did," said Debra.

"And what did he say?" asked Mary Morgan.

"He said he'd take a pass on that one, that he wanted to make his money the old-fashioned way; he wanted to earn it!" said Debra Sanders.

\*\*\*

"So, Billy, where would you invest your money today if you had a million dollars to burn—a million dollars to risk anywhere you wanted?" asked Walter.

"I saw a guy on one of the business channels not too long ago. He said Mexico was a good bet and that they only have half the debt we do. He also said Chavez in Venezuela is paying 14 percent on Venezuelan bonds: a little hard-core, but he's got all that oil to back him up. They say the Australian dollar is good, also the Swiss franc and Canadian oil and gas stocks. So where are we going with this?" asked Billy Pigeon.

"Well, to be perfectly honest, we are accumulating a lot of money rather quickly," said Walter. "Your mother says she has another $75,000 collected this morning, and it's not even noon. The banks are hardly paying anything in interest right now."

"And how would it look if I became president and was investing my money in foreign countries? It wouldn't show that I had that much confidence in my own country, would it?" asked Billy.

"You're probably right," said Walter.

"No, we keep our money in safe CDs backed up by the Federal Deposit Insurance Fund. When we get over that limit, we buy guaranteed U. S. Treasuries. I'm not risking a dime of the taxpayers' money," said Billy.

\*\*\*

Billy Pigeon glanced in his side mirror. He could see a courier truck passing the long line of vehicles behind him, with the courier truck flashing its headlights from low beam to high beam, then back to low beam, then back to high beam, trying to catch the attention of someone. That someone was Billy Pigeon, with the courier truck and the Birdmobile on a long straight stretch of highway. When the courier truck was parallel to the Birdmobile, the passenger window of the courier truck rolled all the way down, and the young driver of the courier truck—maybe twenty, maybe twenty-one years old—shouted the following to Billy Pigeon at the top of his lungs:

"Pull over, pull over Mr. President; I have your e-mail address decals!"

Billy pulled the Birdmobile to the shoulder of the highway. The courier driver squeezed in behind Billy. Debra got out, walked up to the young courier driver and said, "You're late!"

"Sorry, ma'am, we had issues. I don't have time to explain!" said the young courier driver.

"Well at least you got them here!" said Debra.

"Don't forget the bill!" yelled Julie.

"Good girl!" said Walter.

\* \* \*

Walter was outside the motor home again with his portable Makita drill and a Robertson screw-driver bit all set to go. He drove home four screws into the corners of each magnetic sign. The two new decals were now in place, the eight screws as tight as a bug in a rug! This is what the new decals looked like:

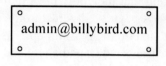

\* \* \*

With the two decals in place right above the *Billy Pigeon for President* signs, our presidential motorcade was off and running again, but only after one of the Washington State Troopers issued a ticket to the young courier driver for speeding. The young courier driver tried his best to plead his case.

"I was only trying to serve my president!" said the young courier driver.

"I understand," said the Washington State Trooper. "It's not a real ticket. It's only a warning, but if I ever see you speeding again, I'll throw the book at you!"

"Thank you, thank you, sir!" said the young courier driver.

\* \* \*

Ring, ring, ring…

"Debra Sanders speaking."

"Hi, Debra, this is Lorne Michaels from *Saturday Night Live!* We'd love to have the *real* Billy Pigeon guest host one of our shows, not a pretend Billy Pigeon dressed up in a pigeon costume! We'd like him to sit at the president's desk in a replica Oval Office, pretend he's the actual president and tell a few good Bill Clinton jokes. We were thinking of having a Monica Lewinski lookalike sitting on the edge of Billy Pigeon's desk, her lips all full of red lipstick, the chick looking hot—think of all the fun we could have on national TV. What do you think?"

"Sorry, but the answer is *no!*" said Debra Sanders, with extra emphasis on the "no" part.

"And why not?" asked Lorne Michaels. "We're talking *Saturday Night Live,* the most watched late night show in America. Look at all the publicity he'd get. It would be a real opportunity for all of America to get to know Billy."

"Or make him look like a buffoon!" said Debra Sanders. "Sorry, but Billy is not a flash in the pan. We're dead serious about running for president in 2012; this is no laughing matter. Goodbye!"

\*\*\*

Ring, ring, ring…

"Debra Sanders speaking."

"Hi, Debra, this is Bill O'Reilly. We'd like to get Billy on our TV show on Fox and see what he's made of!" said the one and only Bill O'Reilly.

"Maybe one of these days," said Debra. "I do have one thing to say to you, though, before I end this conversation."

"And what's that?" asked Bill O'Reilly.

"Be careful what you wish for!" said Debra.

"And why's that?" asked Bill O'Reilly.

"Because he'll eat you for breakfast, that's why!" said Debra.

"And what makes you think that?" asked Bill O'Reilly.

"Because he hates soccer!" said Debra Sanders.

\*\*\*

Ring, ring, ring…

"Debra Sanders speaking."

"Hi, Debra, this is Ed Schultz from *The Ed Show!*"

"I know who you are! I'll call you in five or six days when I have something substantial to say, something you can bite your teeth into, something provocative for your left-wing friends and colleagues," said Debra Sanders.

\*\*\*

Bill O'Reilly was sipping on black coffee, his thoughts going here, there, and everywhere, with soccer balls on his mind! He called his buddy Merv at Fox News and told him about his conversation with Debra Sanders. He told him he couldn't figure out her soccer line.

"What do you do in soccer?" asked his buddy Merv.

"You kick a ball around the field," said Bill O'Reilly.

"And what do politicians do all the time when it comes to difficult decisions on tough issues?" asked his buddy Merv.

"I don't make the connection," said Bill O'Reilly.

"They kick the can down the road; soccer ball, can, what's the difference? They hate making tough decisions. They run for cover. They form another committee to study the issue. They cover their behinds to get re-elected!" said his buddy Merv.

"So that's what she meant!" said Bill O'Reilly, shaking his head in amazement.

"Exactly!" said his buddy Merv.

"She's a smart lady!" said Bill O'Reilly.

"And I'd be careful around her if I were you!" said his buddy Merv.

\* \* \*

Ring, ring, ring…

"Debra Sanders speaking."

"Hi, Debra, this is Tom Moore from the *Seattle Times*."

"Hi, Tom, what can I do for you?" asked Debra.

"I'm doing a story with a local flavor about Billy—you know the routine—local boy does good. We've interviewed his fellow students and his teachers. We're just zeroing in on what makes him tick, where his political leanings are: left, right, center, left of center, right of center, that sort of thing. Could you help me on this one?" asked Tom Moore.

"I'd like to, Tom, but I'm real busy right now. I'll tell you what, though; I'll talk to you about it in five or six days, I promise," said Debra.

"Sounds good to me. I'll hold off on the story till then," said Tom Moore.

"I'd really appreciate it," said Debra.

\* \* \*

"When was the last time you looked on the motor home?" asked Julie.

"This morning," said Billy. "Why are you asking?"

"I was just out there. We've got over thirty-five pigeons going along for the ride!" said Julie.

"You're kidding me," said Billy.

"Cross my heart!" said Julie.

\* \* \*

"Paul, this is Tim. We went through all the drawings and schematics on that diagram of his; we went over every word of his written proposal," said Tim.

"Keep going," said Paul.

"I know big problems have to have big solutions, but Jesus H Christ, this thing is huge; it's a monster. I hope we can get a handle on it!" said Tim.

"Like I told you before, we've got two years to get it done!" said Paul.

"Have you seen it all? Have you really studied it, looked at some of the engineering issues?" asked Tim.

"Sort of," said Paul.

"I mean we're talking five thousand manufacturing hubs, with five thousand dormitories, five thousand factories, five thousand hotels, five thousand malls: that's 20,000 buildings in the top part of his complex alone. Christ Almighty, do you have any idea how much concrete, steel, plastic pipe, aluminum siding, copper wire, and telephone and computer cable we're going to need for this?" asked Tim.

"You tell me," said Paul. "You're the expert! All I know is that there's enough going on here to revive the entire economy of the U. S. A., to put all

19 million people who are unemployed back to work right now: 6 million workers to build it, 13 million more to work in all the plants and factories across the country to provide all the products they're going to need to build it, no ifs, ands, or buts!"

"And below those 20,000 buildings and the five hundred hospitals and dental centers, he's got a twenty-mile-long runway with approach lights on both ends, four massive airports, sixteen cross-runways, gigantic train and bus and truck terminals, all connected to the five thousand hubs, not to mention the fence line and all the security posts, the vehicle service centers, the airplane hangars, the food distribution center the size of Seattle, with underground tunnels connected to all the hubs. Then he's got a fuel depot, a waste water treatment plant, a water filtration plant, a green garbage incinerator, an administration building that would put anything in New York City to shame, and solar panels and wind turbines and nuclear power plants and a thousand more things that I can't even think about right now!" said an exasperated Tim.

"And don't forget the military base and the tent cities for construction spread out all around the perimeter and the service city you're going to have to design outside the complex itself for all the service workers," said Paul.

"Have you seen the size of that military base and the stuff we have to put in there?" asked Tim.

"I can only imagine!" said Paul.

"Did you know he has five thousand smaller admin buildings as well?" asked Tim.

"I thought there was just the one big one," said Paul.

"Hell no, he's got one of them at each of the five thousand manufacturing hubs," said Tim. "And did you see that recreation center; did you see all the stuff he's planned for that place, the weight rooms, his pool for 20 million people, all the saunas, the fitness rooms with mirrors?"

"I know it's big!" said Paul.

"It's bigger than big," said Tim. "It's enormous, colossal, massive, gargantuan, titanic, and humungous; it's the biggest bloody building I've ever been asked to design. Then you've got all the outside stuff: the baseball, football, and soccer fields, and tennis courts. Honest to Christ, Paul, this thing is beyond comprehension. Old Charlie Porter in the English Department would call it Brobdingnagian in scope and scale. I call it Billybrobdingnagian, with Billy Pigeon walking in the land of five thousand corporate giants. This Billy's World is beyond what your imagination can imagine! And you put all the buildings in Billy's World together in one big package. Do you have any idea of the number of computers it will take to run this place?" asked Tim.

"I'm sure Dell and Apple will be happy!" said Paul.

"I don't know about you, but we are going to need every architect and every engineer in the country gathered under one big roof during the construction phase; we'll need every construction company we can come up with, every worker we can find, every portable toilet on the planet Earth, and every tent the military and Walmart can provide. This will be insane; this will be a logistical nightmare of epic proportions!" said Tim.

"That's the plan, Stan; that's what our new president wants and that's what we're going to give him. The economic engine of America will fire on all cylinders and then some. We will stretch our imagination like it's never been stretched before, test our ingenuity like it's never been tested before, display our technology to the world like it's never been displayed before, and show the world what America is really made of—make America proud!" said Paul.

"So who's speaking now—is it you or Billy?" asked Tim.

"Both of us!" said Paul. "And like I said before, we've got to keep this quiet! Can you imagine if Obama or Romney ever got wind of this? They'd draw up a modified version before you could say Charlie Brown. They'd call it their Vision for America in the twenty-first century. They would take the credit, right now, to save their own hides. Billy wouldn't get a sniff!

"We start to make it public, a little bit at a time. We keep them guessing. We slowly add the pieces all together, and then we blow their socks off at the Presidential Debate in 2012."

"So who knows about it now?" asked Tim.

"Just you and two other architects, and then there's me, Debra, Julie, and Billy. His father, Walter, doesn't even know. Once we start releasing information and getting more people involved, we'll have the venture capital people and maybe some of the hedge funds take a look at it, or we might just decide to keep it in house with the $2.5 trillion from the corporations and the $2.5 trillion from the government. We'll have to really think that one out.

"Billy is not a fan of doing things by committee, but he did say he would have a Board of Directors after the construction stage. He prefers to run his own show, not to get too many people involved in the major decision making, but he did tell me to tell you that he was only a dreamer, an idealist with good ideas, that you were the engineer, that he would respect your decisions with regard to analysis and final design, and that he would go with the flow!

"All I know is that as soon as he's elected president, this country is going to explode with activity. Billy's World will be built, come hell or high water, and all because of the sheer brilliance of one young American boy," said Paul Sanders.

"He should have his own Secret Service people," said Tim Hickman. "We've got to watch him like a hawk, protect him at all costs; you never know who's tapping into conversations these days!"

"I agree," said Paul, "and we're already ten steps ahead of you. His security detail is being arranged as we speak, we have four Suburbans, twenty security personnel, the finest that money can buy in the Pacific Northwest, complete with radios, semiautomatic rifles, handguns, you name it. They're the best of the best; they'll be all over him 24/7, 365 days of the year! We're paying for their services out of Billy's campaign donations."

"You can do that already?" asked Tim Hickman.

"Do it? Billy could own Bill and Melinda Gate's home in Bellevue tomorrow, put down a cash deposit, and pay off the mortgage in another month!" said Paul.

"He's bringing in that much?" asked Tim Hickman.

"His parents can't keep up to it," said Paul. "They've hired a secretary now, just to write out receipts in Billy's home."

"What about the architects' bill?" asked Tim.

"Send it to me; they won't even have to wait thirty days!" said Paul.

"Unreal!" said Tim.

"Unreal is right!" said Paul.

# 13

# Pigeon Poop

Another long, slow day, lots of starts and stops, lots of handshakes, another dingy motel in the state of Washington, more sagging beds, no spiders, thank God, but the water smelled like sulfur, and the taste in your mouth after brushing your teeth was God-awful.

"Deal with it!" said Billy Pigeon. "No, we are not going to another motel!"

\* \* \*

Billy was awake; the pigeons on top of the Birdmobile were talking like crazy. The sun was slowly crawling over the rolling hills to the east; the air was still cold, still damp and sent a shiver down your spine.

"On the road again

Just can't wait to

Get on the road again!"

\* \* \*

Once everyone was settled in with their second cup of Morning Joe, the State Troopers still leading the way, the students from Seattle still hanging in there, their night long, cold and uncomfortable, in spite of it being summer, still determined to make it to the Montana border, Debra Sanders began her 9:00 a.m. briefing to the president.

"We have to have an important conversation this morning, Mr. President; we have to have a serious discussion. I don't care how long it takes—one, two, three, four, five days, all night long, too, if necessary—but we have got to decide where we are on the all-important political spectrum. Whether we're on the left, on the right, in the center, to the left of center, to the right of center, we have to know what we are. We have to put out a statement to the press. It has to carry us to our goal. I'm getting hounded by the media looking for answers," said Debra.

Remember how I told you Billy was special, one of those rare birds and one of a kind who came along once in a hundred years? Remember the Preface to our book? Check this out, with Billy Pigeon responding to Debra's justified concerns:

"The name of my new political party will be the RPA, the Reality Party of America—real people with real solutions to real problems! We will have no affiliation with big business to the right, or the union movement to the left. We will make no deals with any Liberals, Conservatives from the center, anyone from the left of center, or the right of center.

"We, all members of the RPA, will be an Independent Party looking for solutions to the problems of all Americans. We will run a full slate of candidates in all fifty states for the office of governor, for state legislatures, for the House and the Senate, as well as president; the president of course will be me!

"All our candidates will be nineteen years old or younger—no younger than ten. They will live and learn the art of government from their president. They will represent a new generation of Americans drawing a line in the sand with our past, a morally sound generation, a frugal generation, a generation of young Americans who will save more than they spend, who will only carry one credit card, who will have three shirts and two pairs of pants, who will pay off our $70 trillion debt in twenty-four short years, who will never, ever, allow America to get in the mess it is in now. They will learn from the past, deal with the present, and the future will take care of itself—end of story!" said Billy Pigeon.

\* \* \*

Debra Sanders was flabbergasted. She knew she would have a good sleep tonight, even if there were spiders. She would not have to burn the midnight oil, drink black coffee and eat vegetarian pizzas. She would not have to put off any more tough political questions. All she had to do now was to make some sense out of her notes she kept of Billy's comments, to get it into a legible and coherent statement, pass the news on to the rest of the world, and maybe even have a bubble bath tonight at the next motel!

\* \* \*

Walter was just off the phone to Sally in Bellevue. This is what he said to Debra: "We need another secretary!"

\* \* \*

Debra e-mailed Billy's statement about his new RPA to Tom Moore at the *Seattle Times*. She started her e-mail with the following words: "So, you wanted a scoop, did you?"

\* \* \*

Within minutes, Debra received an e-mail from Tom Moore. This is what that e-mail said: "Holy Shit!"

\* \* \*

Tom Moore ran his story about Billy Pigeon, the eighteen-year-old high school graduate from Bellevue High who was running for president. He told the country and the world about the RPA, the Reality Party of America—real people with real solutions to real problems. The *Seattle Times* article was picked up by print media in all fifty states and then it was all over the social media, TV and cable; CNN had more breaking news for their worldwide audience. The world was amazed!

\* \* \*

President Barack Obama read about the RPA in the Washington Post. This is what he said to a close colleague in Washington: "I wish I were ten again. I wish I could start all over, with a clean plate, be beholden to nobody, but I can't!"

\* \* \*

Debra was on the blower to the decal company in Seattle one more time. She ordered four RPA circular decals, twelve inches in diameter, black letters against a white background with a black border; she put a rush on her four decals.

"Do a good job on these four, get them to me by morning and you'll probably get an order of a million more when the election campaign really heats up!" said Debra.

"Where are you guys now?" asked Dave Brown, the owner of the decal company back in Seattle.

"We're heading toward Spokane. Billy is fly-fishing in the morning; we'll be here for awhile!" said Debra

"Good," said Dave Brown, "we'll get them out to you tonight while you're sleeping. Do you have any idea where you're going to stay?"

"Not a clue," said Debra. "You can't miss us. We'll be in a roadside motel; just look for the two State Trooper cars in the parking lot, the twenty-one-foot motor home with the big four-foot-tall, carved, one-legged pigeon on top and all the press vans!"

"Don't worry, we'll find you!" said Dave Brown.

Walter took the cell from Debra's hand and this is what he said: "Don't forget to send the bill!"

\* \* \*

Rupert Murdoch was on the blower to his son James who was halfway around the world. He told his son James to stop what he was doing, catch the next flight to Washington, and get a new newspaper up and running there. He could utilize some of the existing staff at the Washington Post for starters and focus the news stories in their newspaper on issues of young people around the world, keeping a special eye on the travels of one young Billy Pigeon. He should call their newspaper the Washington Real News!

\* \* \*

Bill O'Reilly made an unusual phone call. He began a conversation with his archrival Ed Schultz.

"If that boy gets elected, you and I are both going to be out of a job!" said Bill O'Reilly.

"I agree," said Ed Schultz. "So what do we do about it?"

"Bottom line, the boy has got to go!" said Bill O'Reilly. "I don't know how yet, but we'll figure something out!"

\* \* \*

President Obama finished his own briefing with his own press secretary. You could see that Billy Pigeon was starting to get under the president's skin. He went to his private residence in the White House. He walked into his bathroom and swallowed a Tylenol for his headache. He said the following to his wonderful wife, Michelle: "I can handle being $14 trillion in debt. I can handle a shitty economy. I can handle political gridlock in government. I can handle wars in Iraq and Afghanistan. I can even handle a hurricane, an earthquake, and a major flood all at the same time, but I sure as hell can't handle 20 million kids and the second American Revolution on my plate, too!"

\* \* \*

Ed Schultz was on the phone to Bill O'Reilly again.

"So what did you mean when you said the boy has got to go?" asked Ed Schultz.

"You know *exactly* what I mean!" said Bill O'Reilly.

"You're not talking about what I think you're talking about, are you?" asked Ed Schultz.

"I am so!" said Bill O'Reilly. "Just like the Mafia did to your Kennedy guy!"

"So where are you getting these ideas from?" asked Ed Schultz.

"A whole bunch of us," said Bill O'Reilly. "We don't need any young people revolting and taking over our government and country!"

"So it's going to be Kill Bill!" said Ed Schultz.

"Right on, brother, just like in the movie!" said Bill O'Reilly. "And we'd like your support. It's your country, too, that's in peril!"

\* \* \*

President Obama was talking to his press secretary again, his headache not going away anytime soon.

"We've got to get the kid on *The Ed Show*, have Ed rip him apart, tear a strip out of him, and find out some of his real solutions to real problems!" said the president.

\* \* \*

In Mitt Romney's campaign office, this is what Mitt Romney said to his campaign chairman, "We've got to get him on the *Bill O'Reilly Show*, have Bill do a number on him and show the world what they're really getting for a president—that you can't send a boy to do a man's job!"

\* \* \*

Debra e-mailed her friend Tom Moore at the *Seattle Times*. She told Tom that she had another exclusive story he could write about Billy Pigeon—a real scoop of pigeon poop. She told Tom about Billy holding a big political rally at Central Park in New York City, that he was hoping that over a million Americans between the ages of ten and nineteen would show up, all of them single, all of them wanting to commit their time and energies to the RPA and sign on the dotted line. That signature would guarantee them a job in Billy's World. The ten-year-olds would be sixteen and ready to go to Billy's war on jobs when Billy's World was completely built. They could easily get in two tours of duty. The nineteen-year-olds would be twenty-five and would still be able to do their five years before they reached the age of thirty. IDs would be checked, and you had to have two pieces of identification: one picture, a driver's license, a birth certificate, a library card with a photo, the other a Social Security card, a medical card, a debit card, a credit card, a fishing or hunting license or something like that!

\* \* \*

Tom Moore e-mailed Debra, thanked her for the latest scoop of pigeon poop, said he would get the story out tonight, and that it would be in the paper tomorrow.

\* \* \*

Debra e-mailed Tom again, gave him some really good info to add to his story, told Tom that Billy hoped to have 20 million young RPA members all signed up by the end of his two-year trip around America: 20 million young workers all set to work at a new place in America called Billy's World!

"Tell me more about Billy's World!" said Tom Moore in a follow-up e-mail.

"Sorry, not yet!" said Debra.

\* \* \*

Glenn Beck was on his TV show. This is what he said when he heard about the big RPA rally at Central Park in New York City: "Doesn't that smell like the Hitler Youth Movement, that maybe Billy Pigeon is Hitler reincarnated? Just think about it! No jobs, a depressed economy, what a time for a new leader to waltz right in and take over the whole country, lock, stock and barrel, to get their own Gestapo going with the pitch black uniforms and the black RPA arm decal, to march en masse, all twenty million of them into Washington, with their AK-47 assault rifles, in their heavy black marching boots, to incite a brand new Nazi movement in America, to have a swastika on their other arm, all ready to dominate the world, and take us into World War III!"

\* \* \*

Rush Limbaugh was on his radio show. This is what he said about Glenn Beck's new assertion about Billy Pigeon: "I think he's bang-on for once in his life!"

\* \* \*

This is what Bill O'Reilly said: "I agree with Rush!"

\* \* \*

"Keep your eye open for a decent-sized supermarket," said Julie.
"What for?" asked Billy.
"I want to get a couple of boxes of those crunchy croutons that you put in a Caesar salad," said Julie.
"I love Caesar salads!" said Billy.
"They're not for you," said Julie.
"So who are they for?" asked Billy.
"Who do you think?" asked Julie.

\* \* \*

With the Birdmobile through the mountains and on rolling land again, Billy relaxed. The drive was not so onerous, the open expanse of highway gave him time to look around, see all the sights, carry on longer conversations, and take in the big picture, with all his sudden fame, his adoring fans waving American flags on the side of the highway, all the thumbs-up, and all the political campaign donations that were rolling in on a daily basis.

"It wasn't always this way, was it, Dad?" said Billy.

"No it wasn't, Billy, but you survived. It made you into the young man you are today; it gave you the motivation to succeed," said Walter.

"So what are you guys talking about? Let us in on your little secret," said Debra.

"Yes, do tell!" said Julie.

"It was the Pigeon name," said Billy. "From my first day in kindergarten, all the way through elementary school, the Pigeon jokes were flying. The kids even stuck notes on my desk. I remember them all. Would you like a worm? Go lay an egg—go find a pole to sit on—pick up your feathers—sing me a Pigeon song—go sit in your nest—fly, fly away—watch out for Pigeon poop—throw him some bread crumbs—cat got your tongue—go take a birdbath—watch your back, the big black cat is coming—hop, hop, hop along—flock-off, Pigeon—watch out for the car—bye-bye birdie—hope you hit a window!"

"That's awful!" said Julie. "How could kids be that mean?"

"They could and they would, something like all the bullying going on in schools today. It's no different," said Billy. "So I went underground. I spent a lot of time by myself. I read. I worked my butt off. I saved my money. I didn't want to be around kids. It all changed after elementary school. The boys got into girls, the girls got into boys, and they forgot about me. The Pigeon jokes came to an end. I started coming out of my shell and the rest is history!" said Billy.

"Who'da thunk it!" said Debra.

"Wow!" said Julie.

"It's all true," said Walter.

"That's one of the reasons the one-legged pigeon is on our roof right now," said Billy. "To me, the one-legged pigeon symbolizes the struggle I went through in my youth, the struggle a real one-legged pigeon would have to go through in life just to survive on a daily basis; he's my inspiration!" said Billy Pigeon.

"That's beautiful, Billy," said Julie.

"It truly is," said Debra.

"I agree," said Walter.

"So now you know the rest of the story!" said Billy.

\* \* \*

In her motel room that night, in her pajamas, with the motel door locked, Debra Sanders e-mailed Tom Moore from the *Seattle Times*. This is what her e-mail said: "No more scoops of pigeon poop!"

\* \* \*

Tom Moore e-mailed back to Debra right away. This is what his e-mail said: "Does that mean I'm cut off, that I'm getting no more stories? Please reply."

\* \* \*

"No, that doesn't mean I'm cutting you off. I'm just putting an end to the pigeon poop comments. I don't want them going around your office. I certainly don't want the late night boys like Letterman or Conan or Leno or Lorne or Stewart and Colbert to get started down that road, too. Billy has enough issues to deal with as it is."

"Too late for that; Leno started last night!"

"That's too bad. He's probably still pissed that Billy didn't want to go on his show."

"Do I detect a weakness in our future president—a character flaw, maybe a little sensitivity?"

"Not at all. He's the strongest person I've ever met in my life."

"So why all the fuss?"

"He had a rough childhood with the Pigeon name. I bet you never had that in your first story. I bet you the school kids you interviewed never told you about all the Pigeon jokes, how he was treated like crap in elementary school."

"No they didn't, not a word."

"Well at least we know now that they've all grown up. I guess that's a good thing."

"Billy's all grown up, too. He'll roll with the punches; it'll go in one ear and out the other. This is more about me. I don't want to be one of those elementary school kids sticking Pigeon joke notes on his desk."

"I understand."

"Thanks, you're a good man, Charlie Brown!"

\* \* \*

Debra turned off her laptop. She started looking under her sheets and under her pillow. Everything looked promising, for now! She would try to get some sleep and get her mind off pigeon poop and gigantic spiders!

# 14

## The Midnight Train

The old floating compass on the dash of the Birdmobile said they were definitely heading northeast. Hopefully, they would find another cheap motel on the other side of Spokane when they stopped for dinner. Then it was only a hop, skip, and a jump across a little bit of Idaho, and then Montana.

Ah Montana, God's country, the fly-fishing was supposed to be out of this world. Billy was looking forward to finding a sports shop, getting some streamers, some really good dry-flies, some nymphs, and then wading down a stream or a river, looking for some real trout—not the little piddly-assed ones in the mountain streams that he was mostly unable to catch, the ones that he did catch could hardly be called a meal!

At every gas station, at every truck stop, Americans continued to come up to the Birdmobile to shake Billy Pigeon's hand, to wish him well, and then make a donation to Julie who passed it on to Walter. One old geezer, with a big old beard and a flat felt hat said the following to Billy Pigeon: "Get rid of them all, Billy, the whole goddamn works of them. They're nothing but a bunch of corrupt bastards lining their own pockets and the pockets of their business friends. They're goddamn parasites; they're a bunch of God-damn useless tits. They're sucking the life out of the country!"

"I'll do the best I can, sir!" said Billy.

"I want you to do better than your best. I want you to stick it to them; stick it to them where the sun don't shine!" said the old geezer.

\*\*\*

More Americans came up to the Birdmobile, took lots of pictures of the Billy Pigeon For President signs, the 1–800–911-BIRD signs, the admin@billybird.com signs, the brand new RPA decals, and the Birdmobile standing out like a sore thumb from all the other trucks, campers, motor homes, and cars in the parking lot, with the four-foot-tall, carved, one-legged pigeon and all his feathery friends keeping a watchful eye over everybody!

The scene was like something out of a movie, with people running here, there, and everywhere, with people wanting their pictures snapped with their arm around Billy's shoulder, with more and more donations coming in, and with Julie and Debra writing receipts along with Walter. The scene was chaotic!

The old geezer with the big old beard and the flat hat came up to Billy again. He gave Billy a crisp one hundred dollar bill for the cause.

"Would you like a receipt?" asked Billy Pigeon.

"Hell no!" said the old geezer. "I wouldn't declare income and pay taxes to those goddamn assholes if my life depended on it!"

"Would you pay taxes if I were president?" asked Billy Pigeon.

"It all depends," said the old geezer.

"Depends on what?" asked Billy.

"On what you do with my one hundred dollars!" said the old geezer.

\* \* \*

At Spokane, our four travelers in the Birdmobile were joined by their new security detail, with the two State Troopers still leading the way, then two black Suburbans, then the Birdmobile, then two more black Suburbans, and then hundreds and hundreds of cars and trucks full of students from Seattle and Spokane. The new students from Spokane were full of piss and vinegar, happy to be out of school, yelling "Go, Billy, Go," with their cars and trucks decorated with red, white and blue balloons. The new students were leaning on their horns to beat the band!

\* \* \*

"What's with all the extra security?" asked Billy. "Are we expecting trouble?"

"No, not at all," said Debra. "We just want to be proactive. We want you to look presidential. Just pretend you're President Bill Clinton in his presidential motorcade going into Chicago from O'Hare Airport! Get used to it, Billy; this is what presidents do. It'll be this way for the next ten years of your life! It was Paul's idea; he's my husband and I do what I'm told—most of the time, anyway!"

\* \* \*

"So when Julie and I go fly-fishing in Montana, are they coming with us?" asked Billy.

"Absolutely!" said Debra.

"Mom!" said Julie. "I strongly object!"
"Objection noted!" said Debra.

\* \* \*

Billy still had the old geezer's one hundred dollar bill in his pants pocket when they checked into a motel for the night. Billy told his father, Walter, that this one hundred dollar bill was special, that it wasn't going in the bank, that it was going on his desk in the Oval Office when he became president, that he might even have the FBI track down the old geezer, put him on a plane and bring him to the White House to have a coffee with the president in the Oval Office. Hopefully, if the old geezer was still alive in 2016, Billy would have him on hand for the grand opening of Billy's World, maybe even bring him to the White House for a sleepover—who knows?

\* \* \*

"I'll get your one hundred dollar bill put in a glass frame the next time we see a Walmart!" said Julie.

"What did the old geezer say to you?" asked Debra. "He certainly made an impression."

"Nothing much, just a couple of comments about politicians in Washington, nothing you'd want to say to your grandchildren!" said Billy Pigeon.

\* \* \*

President Obama met with the Director of the FBI. They were alone in the Oval Office. They chatted about Billy Pigeon.

"He's squeaky clean, Mr. President: no drugs, no alcohol, just a sociable drink of red wine. He gave the graduation speech you saw on TV. He has just one line of credit at the bank for $50,000 secured by $49,000 in cash and CDs. He's only used the line once to buy that old beater motor home they're driving around the country in. He has one American Express credit card with a zero balance, and that's about it. Oh, he usually rides around Seattle on a mountain bike he bought at a thrift store for $15. Anybody in America would be proud to have him as their son!" said the FBI Director.

\* \* \*

"And you have twenty-four-hour surveillance on him?" asked the president.

"Yes, sir, we do," said the FBI Director.

"I'd be interested to know if any radical, home-grown terrorist groups have infiltrated his inner circle, or if he has any ties to al Qaeda, the Ku Klux Klan, the Nazi movement in America, or a group that I don't even know about yet that you probably have information on," said President Obama.

"We're all over him like a dirty shirt, sir!" said the FBI Director. "We have a team of Special Forces in the air as we speak; we have them on the ground, too. We have FBI agents in the rear of his presidential motorcade mixed in with the press. We'll be all over him, sir, like shit to a fly!"

"That's good to hear," said the president. "This has got to be some sort of extremist right-wing plot to draw our attention away from Washington, to keep us unaware of what is happening right here, right now, right under our noses!"

"We're in daily communication with the CIA, the Secret Service and Homeland Security. If something's afoot, we'll find out about it, sir!" said the FBI Director. "We've got your back covered!"

"Can we listen in on their phones if we have to?" asked the president.

"Absolutely, and we can justify it under the Patriot Act. We have the software capability to tap into their server network in Seattle, to listen to them at the source—not in their vehicles—to listen to every word they say on their cell phones. Just say when. We can even get a bug into their motor home if we have to. And their motel rooms, too, if need be," said the FBI Director.

"Sounds good!" said the president. "I'll keep you posted."

"Very good, sir!" said the FBI Director. "Oh, there is one more thing I forgot to tell you. The husband of his media director is a professor of political science at the University of Washington in Seattle."

"Really!" said the president. "Maybe we should pay him a visit, see what he's all about, and see if he's stirring up the student base on campus."

"I agree with you, sir. I don't think we should leave any stone unturned. I'll make that happen," said the FBI Director.

\* \* \*

President Obama paced the Oval Office after the FBI Director left the room. He spoke out loud to himself.

"Something is up; I just know it, but what? It's a free country. The kid hasn't done anything wrong. He can go around the country for twenty years if he wants to, telling anyone who'll listen that he's the second coming of Jesus Christ or that he's running for president against me in 2012. It's called free speech; it's a right he has under our constitution. What to do, what to do, what to do?"

The president paced the Oval Office some more. He scratched the side of his face; he scratched just below his nose. He called his personal secretary and told her to get the FBI Director on the phone again. He told the FBI Director to hold off on the University of Washington professor for now, to watch and observe him. He didn't want to tip Billy Pigeon off that he was being investigated, that he was being watched 24/7!

"Yes, Mr. President," said the FBI Director. "I'll call them off right away."

"Thank you," said the president.

\*\*\*

Jeff and Ryan Smith, Billy's high school buddies, were completely baffled. They were befuddled.

"What the hell are we doing in Idaho? I thought Montana was the next state after Washington!" said Jeff Smith, their case of Bud gone, gone, gone, their credit cards maxed, their used car just about on empty.

"How the hell do we get back to Seattle?" asked Ryan Smith. "We've got $10 left to our names!"

"We'll have to be creative, siphon some gas, hook up with a fat, ugly girl, one with big old thunder thighs, tell her she looks like Madonna, and get her to open up her big fat wallet!" said Jeff Smith.

When the Birdmobile reached Kellogg, Idaho, two hundred screaming kids were on the side of the highway. They were all under the age of nineteen and were carrying their hand-made Billy Pigeon for President placards, their red, white, and blue balloons, and their American flags. They shouted in unison "RPA, RPA, RPA," like one of their favorite wrestlers on *Monday Night Raw*. They continued their "RPA, RPA, RPA" chants as the Birdmobile came to a halt at a nearby gas station.

The screaming kids ran toward the motor home. They were kept in a straight line by Billy's security detail from Spokane. The security detail looked impressive as hell in their black suits with white shirts and black ties. They wore dark sunglasses and had earpieces in their ears for communication in noisy crowds. One of the security detail walked up to the Birdmobile, escorted Billy to the two hundred screaming kids from Kellogg, and Billy Pigeon shook the hand of each and every one of the young Americans. He chatted with them about everything under the sun including Billy's World. A bunch of them were thinking seriously about enlisting in Billy's War on Jobs. Billy high-fived them and signed his name on pieces of paper, on baseball caps, and on footballs. It was amazing. The entire frantic scene was captured live by the press, which sent pictures of Billy and all his happy campers all over the world. The scene was repeated in Wallace, Idaho, in St. Regis, Idaho, in Deer Lodge, Montana, not too far from Butte. The Smith brothers looked here, there, and everywhere for fat ugly girls to take on their trip back to Seattle, to give them a night on the town!

Billy Pigeon was pooped. He said goodbye to the Smith brothers. The back seat of their used car was now filled with fat ugly girls, who were already treating them to pizza and pop, the way it should be! In spite of all the people, all the hand shaking and all the signing of autographs, Billy was still excited. He expressed his excitement as he exited the Birdmobile after dinner for another really cheap motel room.

"I'm in Montana—I'm in Montana—I'm in Montana. Julie, can you believe it? I want to fly-fish for really big trout!" said Billy Pigeon.

"Then fly-fishing it shall be!" said Julie, proud as punch of her Billy.

\* \* \*

Billy Pigeon visited his Montana sports shop. It was one of the most incredible sports shops he had ever seen, with waders, fly-rods, nets, fishing vests, hats, and trout flies. Billy was in fly-fisherman's heaven, purchasing some streamers, dry flies, and nymphs and hiring a local guide to take him fishing for the day. Billy paid for his flies and his little fly box and his guide for the day with his American Express card, not from the piles and piles of cash piling up inside the Birdmobile.

"I could have easily included that in my expense sheet, Billy. The president has to have some R&R, a little downtime on your way to Washington," said Walter.

"Probably so," said Billy, "but it's a gray area. I feel better putting it on my own card; that way, no one can second-guess us. Just make a note for me to pay on the credit card in two weeks at a bank along the way."

"No problem," said Walter, making a note in his day planner. Billy already had a big old plastic bag of beer cans and pop bottles he had collected on the trip so far. He had enough cans and bottles to pay for his trout flies and fly box. He would collect more bottles and cans on his trip around America, pay off the fishing guide expense, and top up his savings account once more!

\* \* \*

"Can I take your Scrapbook of Life with me to read while you fish?" asked Julie. "I was glancing at it this morning; you've collected some really interesting stuff."

"Sure, go ahead," said Billy, "but don't lose it. I've been collecting in that binder since I was ten."

"I'll take good care of it, I promise," said Julie.

\* \* \*

While Billy was fly-fishing the large Montana stream, accompanied by five members of his security detail from Spokane, Julie sat on a lawn chair. She read from Billy's Scrapbook of Life, a scrapbook full of newspaper clippings, jokes, some clean and some dirty, quotations from everywhere and everybody, bumper stickers, cute one-liners, a treasure trove of Americana in one big old construction binder, all the stuff that made Billy's fertile mind think the way it did. Julie felt privileged as she pored through the pages, eight years of Billy Pigeon finding stuff here, there and everywhere: stuff that provoked the human mind. One article in particular caught Julie's attention. She read the entire article. This is what Julie read:

And You Call This Progress...

The Internet is a vast, uncharted territory that has the sublime mixed with the ridiculous. The real test for the explorers venturing into the territory is deciding which is which. The following is a message for us all:

The paradox of our time is that we have taller buildings, but shorter tempers, wider freeways, but narrower viewpoints. We spend more, but have less. We buy more, but enjoy it less. We have bigger houses and smaller families; more conveniences, but less time. We have more degrees, but less sense; more knowledge, but less judgment; more experts, but more problems; more medicine, but less wellness. We drink too much, smoke too much, spend too recklessly, laugh too little, drive too fast, get too angry too quickly, stay up too late, get too tired, read too seldom, watch TV too much, and pray too seldom. We have multiplied our possessions, but reduced our values.

We talk too much, love too seldom, and hate too often. We've learned how to make a living, but not a life. We added years to our life, not life to our years. We've been all the way to the moon and back, but have trouble crossing the street to meet a new neighbor. We have conquered outer space, but not inner space.

We cleaned up the air, but polluted the soul. We've split the atom, but not our prejudice. We've learned to rush, but not to wait. These are the times of fast food, but slow digestion, tall men and short character, steep profits and shallow relationships. These are the days of two incomes, but more divorce, of fancier houses, but broken homes.

These are the days of quick trips, disposable diapers, throw-away morality, one-night stands, overweight bodies and pills that do everything from cheer, to quiet, to kill.

It is a time when there is much in the show window and nothing in the stockroom, a time when technology can bring this letter to you, and a time when you can share this insight or press delete.

* * *

Billy Pigeon caught and kept four magnificent trout that glorious day in Montana. They were big trout. They devoured the fly, buckled his rod, and took off down the stream, with Billy in tow. They were no easy pickin's; they struggled to the very end, putting up one heck of a fight.

Billy had Debra fry up all four for dinner. She boiled some potatoes, corn and green peas. It was a meal fit for a king. The trout were superb, so tender, so tasty, the bright orange meat melting in your mouth.

"This was probably one of the best days of my life," said Billy Pigeon. He laughed after dinner; he talked about his guide, how he knew exactly where to place what fly by which rock in the gentle current. He knew where the fish were hiding and where they would rise for the fly. He also had great stories, even a few fishing jokes. Here is one of those jokes that Billy told, that he recorded in his Scrapbook of Life.

"What do fish say when they hit a concrete wall? Dam!"

\* \* \*

Julie asked Billy where he found the article "And You Call This Progress?" Billy told Julie that it was in the Penticton Herald he read when he went to visit David H. E. Smith, the author of *Birdman of 24 Sussex*.

"No kidding," said Julie. "Whoever wrote the article is one perceptive cookie."

"I agree," said Billy.

\* \* \*

The next few days took the Birdmobile through Butte and Billings, then to Little Bighorn Battlefield National Park. This was sacred ground in America's short history and deserved Billy Pigeon's utmost attention. Billy didn't disappoint. Billy and Julie went for a long walk. They read the plaque on the stone monument telling about the great battle between General Custer and the Indians. Billy and Julie sat down on the grass on the exact spot where Custer circled the wagons, where he met his Waterloo, where he got his butt kicked by the local Indians, big-time!

Billy Pigeon sat on the grass for hours, Julie at his side, with his security detail watching him with binoculars, giving him lots of space to contemplate, to breathe in the history, to see the ghosts of Indians and American soldiers battling one more time for Billy. Julie knew exactly what was going through Billy's mind and squeezed his hand.

"History was made here on these battlefields," said Billy Pigeon.

"I know," said Julie. "You can feel the place is special. To actually be here, to be sitting on the same ground, to smell the grass, to feel the wind, to read everything on the stone monuments sends shivers down my spine."

"This is where I will make my last stand, too," said Billy Pigeon. "If I have to, I will set up a revolutionary government right here. We will challenge the legitimacy of Washington if it ever comes to that. I will die here like Custer; he will be at my side!"

"You're serious, aren't you?" asked Julie.

"Dead serious," replied Billy. "It will be so symbolic; it will be the right place and the right time for my generation to take a stand against this lunacy that is America!"

"Let's get back to the motor home," said Julie, "the wind is making me cold."

\* \* \*

Billy Pigeon really appreciated the time spent at the Little Bighorn Battlefield National Park. He thought even more of Julie for sitting there so long when he knew she was cold, with Billy really not wanting to go that much further before the sun went down. He would stay in the area, meet some of the locals, and do a little campaigning. Their motel for the night was on the Indian reservation; it was run by the local natives. The rooms were better than average. The price was only $19 per night, the cheapest so far, by a long shot. There was even a little store at the end of the motel where Indians came and bought groceries, cigarettes, and liquor—lots of liquor!

"Are you sure you want to stay here, Billy?" asked Debra.

"We are surrounded by Indians," said Julie.

"Now you know what Custer felt like!" said Walter.

"But these Indians don't have guns. They seem friendly enough. They look okay to me. They actually seem intrigued by the four-foot-high, carved, one-legged pigeon on top of our motor home," said Billy. "And how can you beat $19?"

While Julie paid cash for their rooms for the night, Walter walked up to the counter in the little store. He spoke to a nice, but rather chunky, Indian lady.

"You wouldn't happen to have a map of the Custer Battlefield that I could buy?" asked Walter.

"You don't need a map of the battlefield," said a big old Indian standing by the counter. He was about six feet three inches tall, with a huge beer belly and long black hair all the way down his back to his waist.

"And why's that?" asked Walter.

"All you have to remember is that *we* won!" said the big old Indian.

\*\*\*

It had been a long day. Everyone was tired, but the thought of Indians and Custer and lots of liquor at the store next to them kept everyone of our sleepers on edge. Debra told the security detail from Spokane to have five of them pull an all-nighter, to keep an eye on the Birdmobile; there were a lot of valuables inside, including all the laptops, and all the cash and checks that Walter had ready for their next bank deposit. By eleven, it was lights out for Debra, Walter, Julie, and Billy, their thoughts about Indians and Custer long gone, in their warm beds with their comfortable pillows. They were soon in La-La Land!

At twelve midnight, three locomotives heading east, and pulling 315 box and freight cars entered the Indian Reservation, their horns blowing loudly as they crossed the only road into town, as they headed for Billy Pigeon's $19 motel room, the train tracks only twelve feet behind their motel rooms, with all of the motel rooms starting to shake, with glasses, cups, and plates in their little kitchen units starting to shake, rattle, and roll as the big old train inched closer. The shaking and the rattling woke up Debra and Julie first, then Walter, then Billy, with Debra screaming and yelling at the top of her lungs: "I told you—I told you—the Indians are coming—the Indians are coming!"

The three locomotives passed behind the $19 motel first. The metal to metal sound of the train and the tracks meeting gave an eerie screeching, grinding sound, the bump, bump, bump, bump, bump of the 315 cars in tow seemed to last forever and ever, the room still shaking big-time, with Debra, Julie, Walter, and Billy and the two State Troopers and the security detail and all the TV people wide awake, their sleep for the night all but toast. Julie, Walter, and Debra, especially Debra, shook their heads and beat on their walls in disgust, with Billy Pigeon laughing his head off, the cars in tow still going bump, bump, bump, bump, bump, then the final box car, then the caboose, then the sounds in the distance fading, fading, fading, soon replaced by the sound of two drunk Indians in the parking lot screaming and yelling at each other. The five members of the security detail from Spokane were wide awake, too, and approached the two Indians with caution, telling the two Indians to bugger off, that the future president of the United States was trying to sleep!

They were all back to bed, tossing and turning, finally asleep again, when a west-bound freight train approached the Indian Reservation at 2:00 a.m. The train was longer than the first, with the shaking, the rattling and the rolling starting all over again as the freight train approached their $19 motel. Debra, Julie, and Walter were wide awake again, with Billy cracking up, laughing even more than the first time. The 4:00 a.m. east-bound train was right on schedule, and the 6:00 a.m. west-bound train was the longest yet, with Billy on the ground of the parking lot laughing as Julie banged on one of his walls, and Debra banged on the other wall on the other side of his room. Billy was on his back on the parking lot busting a gut, laughing so much that his gut was hurting, tears were rolling down his eyes, with one of the security detail from Spokane saying the following to Billy Pigeon: "Mr. President, we're getting worried about you; are you okay?"

# 15

## Save A Spot For Me

"On the road again,

Just can't wait to

Get on the road again!"

Debra started the day off saying the following to Billy Pigeon: "Trust me; I'll be picking out our next motel!"

\* \* \*

Billy Pigeon was still laughing as he glanced at the floating compass on the dash of the Birdmobile, telling him that they were headed south into Wyoming. The Birdmobile was in the Granite Pass now, elevation 9,033 feet. Huffing and puffing, the automatic transmission changed gears like crazy, the Birdmobile an inspiration to all on board.

"They don't make 'em like this anymore," said Walter, as he tapped the dash of the Birdmobile. The Birdmobile soldiered on, through Buffalo, Gillette, and Sundance—Robert Redford's hangout for his once-a-year film festival—then Deadwood, and Sturgis, home of the biggest yearly motorcycle ride on the planet Earth. Billy and the Birdmobile were now in South Dakota.

"We have to turn on Highway 97. I want to spend all day at Mount Rushmore National Park," said Billy, looking at Julie as he continued to speak. "I'm going to be up there one of those days, me and my one-legged pigeon; you just wait and see!"

"I believe you, Billy," said Julie.

"Me, too," said Debra.

"Me, three," said Walter.

\* \* \*

The tourists at Mount Rushmore went ballistic when Billy's presidential motorcade pulled into the national historic site, and they actually saw Billy Pigeon in the flesh. Billy spent hours and hours speaking to older Americans. He gave all of them the time of day, telling them that he was running for president to make America a better place, to give hope to his generation of Americans, to give hope to the world, too, to make the world a better place. Julie smiled, appreciating Billy's comment about the world. Billy signed more autographs, with hundreds of cameras flashing. Billy took in a pot full of donations, taking time to look up and see the faces of George Washington, Thomas Jefferson, Theodore Roosevelt, and Abraham Lincoln, and to read the details of the construction of Mount Rushmore by Gutzon Borglum and his son Lincoln. He read about all their trials and tribulations, a history lesson itself, in clutching victory from the jaws of defeat. Billy Pigeon was dog-tired at the end of another long day, with the press all over him like a dirty shirt. Billy at Mount Rushmore was the lead story on all the evening news broadcasts, with Billy Pigeon making his historic gesture with his finger that day, not his middle finger, but the first finger next to his thumb on his right hand. Billy Pigeon pointed his arm straight up at the mountain, with his finger leading the way, and confident as ever he said the following to John King from CNN: "Save a spot for me!"

\* \* \*

President Obama was watching CNN news. He saw Billy Pigeon pointing his finger on his right hand, making his historic-moment-in-time gesture. The president shook his head in disgust and disbelief at the same time, saying the following to himself: "That kid is getting to be a real pain in the ass!"

\* \* \*

Debra Sanders could not let go of their night at Custer's Last Stand, the night with all the trains. She complained bitterly of continual headaches and of a sore neck from all the rattling and shaking.

"So what's worse, the trains for one night in your life or enduring what General Custer had to go through? I'll take the trains anytime!" said Billy Pigeon. Walter tapped Billy on the shoulder, proud as punch of his son, and said the following to Debra and Julie: "Now that's how you turn a negative into a positive!"

# 16

## Chicago, My Kind of Town

They were in South Dakota: the prairies, the rolling hills, the miles and miles of flat land, then more rolling hills, then more flat land, the hawks swooping through the air, catching an air pocket, then diving for their prey, a field mouse or a small rabbit, the field mouse and the small rabbit seeing nothing but a big old shadow before being lifted off the ground. Life was getting back to normal, with Julie spotting the first Wall Drug sign on the side of the Interstate 90, then the second, then the third, then the fourth, then the fifth and the sixth and the seventh and the eighth and the ninth and the tenth and the eleventh and the twelfth and the thirteenth and the fourteenth and the fifteenth and the sixteenth and the seventeenth and the eighteenth and the nineteenth and the twentieth—I'm sure you get the point. Julie started to count all the gigantic billboards leading into the town of Wall, South Dakota, with Wall Drug their big draw. The Birdmobile pulled into the Wall Drug parking lot to see what all the fuss was about, to see why hundreds of other tourists were stopping their vans, campers, and motor homes there, too, Wall Drug was in the middle of nowhere, with stores full of western paintings, lots of cowboy clothes, bubble gum, cotton candy, carvings, jelly beans, jade trinkets, ice cream, Indian art, beef jerky, hunting knives, popcorn, leather belts, native moccasins, beads, cowboy boots and hats—a tourists' delight. Billy walked through all the stores with the wooden floors and wooden sidewalks, gawking at all the prices of all the merchandise. He was *so* tempted to pull out his American Express card and be an impulsive shopper; the trout flies were superb in their originality and authenticity, the deer hair extraordinary, Billy was *so* tempted to buy something special for Julie, but there were eyes everywhere. It wasn't like the deal he cut for his fishing guide in the back office of the Montana sport shop. This was different; the press had their cameras rolling. They were all watching for frugal Billy to slip up, to make a wasteful purchase, to buy something he really didn't need. Billy wanted to change America from a spending nation to a saving nation. Wall Drug was not the place to be, for sure. Billy Pigeon said the following to his sweetie pie, Julie: "Time to go, dear!"

"Aren't you going to buy something?" asked Julie.

"There's nothing here I really need," said Billy.

"Aw!" said Julie, her eyes glancing here, there, and everywhere, really fast!

* * *

"This is a hell of a place to put Billy's World. I'll keep it in the back of my mind," thought Billy Pigeon, as he continued to move eastward across the vast expanse of nothing. "I wonder if they have snow."

Billy recorded his thoughts in his notebook. He recorded possible snowplows, with mountains of sand and salt under covered tent-like structures. He added them to his Plan B notes.

* * *

They traveled through Kadoka, past Presto, then Chamberlain, Mitchell, and then into Minnesota, the land of a million lakes. Billy took more time to rent a boat to go fishing, to relax before they hit the road again, with more stops at gas stations and truck stops and town halls all through Minnesota. Billy greeted Americans in Worthington, Jackson, Fairmont, Blue Earth, Albert Lea, Austin, and La Crescent. Billy crossed into Wisconsin, the home of cows and cheese-heads and the Green Bay Packers football team, the only professional football team owned by their fans—their fans their shareholders—with Green Bay Packer paraphernalia for sale everywhere, at all the tourist shops, at all the restaurants, and at all the truck stops. Billy and the Birdmobile passed through Tomah, Wisconsin Dells, and Portage before stopping for a hero's welcome in Madison.

Julie was all over the big Walmart store in Madison. She loaded up on crunchy croutons for her pigeons. Her pigeons from the west were now joined by pigeons from the east, with the pigeons from the west talking up a storm with the new pigeons from the east, with Julie pleased as punch when all the pigeons flew down together to the parking lot pavement and devoured a whole bag of crunchy croutons in one massive eating session!

Billy left Madison and headed toward Chicago, the land of big shoulders. The open spaces between the towns of Minnesota were gone, gone, gone, with the traffic intensifying, with the big rigs on the road—one really big rig had over a hundred tires—with Billy soon approaching the ten or fifteen lanes all leading into a whole bunch of tollbooths west of Chicago. The tollbooth collector, a big husky, black man with a smile revealing one big old gold tooth, said the following to Billy as Billy exited the Birdmobile and grabbed a Pepsi can on the cement sidewalk by the side of the small tollbooth building: "We've all been watching for you, Mr. President. We were all told to tell you that this one is on the house, compliments of the Mayor of Chicago and the Governor of the State of Illinois. They both told us to tell you, 'Welcome to Chicago!'"

"No, no" said Billy Pigeon, "we don't do freebies; we're paying your toll just like everyone else in America!"

\*\*\*

"Billy, the Mayor of Chicago wants to talk to you!" said Debra.
"Really!" said Billy.
"Really!" said Debra.

\*\*\*

"Hello, Billy Pigeon speaking; what can I do for you?"
"Hi, Billy, I'm the Mayor of Chicago," said a big old husky voice.
"What's up?" asked Billy.
"I hope they gave you the royal treatment at the tollbooth," said the mayor.
"They did," said Billy.

"Anyway, to make a long story short, I hear you're in town for three or four days. I hope you don't mind, but we have rooms booked for you at the best hotel in Chicago. I have tickets for you at the Cubs' game at Wrigley, tickets for you at a pre-season Bears game at Soldier Field, and the governor heard that you were into fly-fishing, so he's arranged a flight in a float plane into a private lake we take all our good friends to on a regular basis. There's a private lodge with incredible meals and the fishing is fantastic!" said the mayor of Chicago.

"Wow," said Billy, "that's a lot!"

"Don't ever say we don't know how to treat a future president in Chicago!" said the mayor.

"I appreciate your offer, sir, I really do," said Billy Pigeon, "especially the fishing part! But I'm going to take a pass. We're probably going to pull our motor home over in a mall parking lot somewhere to sleep. I'm going to buy my own tickets to the Cubs' and the Bears' games and I'm sort of fished out right now!"

\*\*\*

"Good for you, Billy!" said Debra Sanders.

\*\*\*

The mayor of Chicago got on the blower to the governor of Illinois. This is what he said: "The kid's pretty shrewd; he's going to be no pushover if he ever makes it to the Oval Office!"

\* \* \*

Debra Sanders sent an e-mail to Bob Agar from *Time* magazine: "We kept waiting for you to show up, but you never came."

"Sorry about that, but I was stressed out. The stars didn't line up. I had to go out on another story."

"I understand. Anyway, we're going to be in Chicago for four days. We're going to a Cubs' game at Wrigley Field. We have an extra seat on the upper deck way out in left field if you'd like to come and talk to Billy and hopefully get his picture on the front cover of Time."

"I'll be there. I'll fly up tonight!"

"Give me a call when you get into town."

"I most certainly will!"

\* \* \*

Debra also received a call from Mary Morgan, the lady from the Oprah show.

"Yes, Billy will go on your show," said Debra, "but he doesn't want to be paid for it," said Debra.

"I understand," said Mary Morgan. "And I'm sorry if I offended you the last time we talked."

"Apology accepted," said Debra.

\* \* \*

The Cubs lost another baseball game; the popcorn was great. Bob Agar interviewed Billy for *Time* magazine. He really pushed Billy on his plan for America. Billy told Bob Agar to stop pushing, that he didn't like being pushed into a corner, and that he might have to start pushing back, like ending their conversation right now. Bob Agar backed off, and Billy told him that he would be releasing more information at his Central Park speech in New York City.

Billy signed autographs. Walter, Julie, and Debra collected campaign donations like crazy in a big old paper bag. The atmosphere at the game was electric. Billy even went to the press booth and led the crowd at the seventh-inning stretch. This is what Billy Pigeon sang for America: "Take me out to the ball game!"

\* \* \*

Oprah's TV ratings went through the roof when Billy appeared on her show. The ratings were better than any other guest, better even than Tom

Cruise! One young girl in the audience had a "Marry Me Billy" sign hanging over her shoulders. Julie gave her the evil eye!

Billy sat on Oprah's leather chair. He talked to Oprah about growing up in the Seattle area, about Americans turning their focus from spending money to saving money, about not buying things you don't need and can't afford, that the personal debt that all Americans were carrying and all the debt that the federal government was carrying for the country was like a giant noose about to strangle everyone in America, that the noose was tightening every day, and that something had to be done to cut that noose real soon.

Billy also brought his old Kodak instamatic camera on stage. He asked his sweetheart, Julie, to come up and take a bow and take a picture of Billy and Oprah, a picture he wanted to put in his Scrapbook of Life. Oprah was delighted. She put her arms around Billy and gave him a big old squeeze. Billy had to admit to himself that her big old breasts felt awful good pushing into his chest!

Billy turned his attention to Central Park in New York City. He told his audience all over America that he would really open up to them there, that he would tell young Americans what he was really going to do for them as their president, that he was also going to take care of Oprah's generation, too, and that he was going to draw a line in the sand on any more federal government debt. Waxing poetic, he said the flames of debt burning all around America would extinguish themselves with the passing of time, that he would pay off all 70 trillion dollars of debt in twenty-four short years, that he had a plan for America, that debt would become a dirty word in America, just like the F-word, and that savings would become the new normal!

"I don't know if they're going to like you at Macy's or Target or JC Penney or Walmart!" said Oprah.

"They'll like me," said Billy Pigeon. "They'll realize that having an economy with a zero unemployment rate, with zero debt and standing on a sound financial footing, and having customers with lots of room to spend on their one credit card, with oodles and oodles of cash in their savings account, is a much better scenario than we have now, where shoppers are forced to stop spending because they're maxed out, because they don't have a job, because their future looks bleak, because they don't know where their next dollar is coming from, and store managers are tearing their hair out trying to decide how much inventory to carry.

"The Macy's and the Targets and the JC Penney's and the Walmarts of the world have no idea what's in store for them, what I have coming down the pipe, or that they just have to hang in there with zero or little growth in the economy for two more short years!

"My generation of Americans, my RPA followers, will help me change America. Our country will become the envy of the world; you just wait and see!" said Billy Pigeon.

"I believe you, Billy, I believe you!" shouted Oprah, giving Billy another big old bear hug, with Billy enjoying every second of it, with the audience giving Billy a five minute standing ovation, with the young girl in the audience wearing the "Marry Me Billy" sign running up on stage, the young girl wanting to get her claws around Billy just like Oprah did, to give him another big old hug on national TV, to promote her modeling career, with the young girl with the misguided intentions held back by four of Billy's security detail from Spokane, with Julie running up to the young girl and saying the following: "Sorry, sweetie, but he's already spoken for!"

\* \* \*

Back in the Birdmobile over a hot cup of coffee and a good healthy granola bar, Debra said the following to Billy: "That was one hell of a speech, Billy. I know I told you to tease our competition, to throw them a few bread crumbs, but my God, you're going to drive them stir crazy! I love it, I love it, I love it!" said Debra.

\* \* \*

Billy Pigeon was on the front cover of *Time* magazine. The picture they chose, from the many they took, was the one with Billy throwing out the first pitch at Wrigley Field, zinging the ball into the catcher's mitt! The Time article written by Bob Agar was superb. The article was a little premature, full of assumptions, full of *what ifs,* and lacking meat on the bone, with another picture of Billy, Julie, Debra, and Walter on the inside of Time, our four travelers all standing by the door of the Birdmobile, smiling for the camera, with the west coast and the east coast pigeons and the four-foot-tall, carved, one-legged pigeon up top. The Birdmobile was parked in a big old mall parking lot for the night, motel and hotel rooms in Chicago way too expensive for Billy's liking, the motor home guarded by Illinois State Troopers and the twenty-member security detail from Spokane.

As a really long mass transit train went zooming by on a raised track bed just above the mall parking lot, and directly above the Birdmobile, Debra said the following to Billy, Julie, and Walter as they entered the motor home for the night: "Why me, lord, why me, lord; you have got to be kidding!"

# 17

## Don't Do It in Dallas

"Quick!" said Billy, "get your notebook!"
"What for?" asked Julie.
"The bumper sticker I just saw before I forget it!" said Billy.
"What did it say; I'm ready!" said Julie.
"I used to be indecisive; now I'm not sure!" said Billy.
"That's funny!" said Julie.
"Tell me about it!" said Billy. "Write it in my Scrapbook of Life after supper."
"Our Scrapbook of Life!" said Julie.

\* \* \*

The Big Apple was just around the corner, with David Letterman all over it, still hurting from Debra's rebuff, finding out, too, about Conan's rebuff and Jay's rebuff and Lorne's rebuff, and fighting back like only David Letterman could. David Letterman had a live pigeon on his desk, tied by one leg to a hook screwed into his desk. David Letterman gave live Birdmobile sightings, starting every monologue with the latest pigeon joke his writers could churn out for him, determined to put Billy Pigeon in his proper place. David Letterman would be the Big Bad Wolf. This 18-year-old punk kid from Bellevue, had no business being in New York City, telling the world that he wanted to be president of the United States, and especially telling sophisticated New Yorkers, living in the home of Wall Street, the *New York Times*, the *New Yorker* Magazine, the Empire State Building, the Statue of Liberty, Saturday Night Live, Times Square, Broadway, the United Nations, and of course, the one and only David Letterman Show. David Letterman told the world how God-awful pigeon poop looked and smelled. He said, "Do you know that white stuff on pigeon poop, that's pigeon poop, too. Did you know that all of the buildings in New York are all covered with pigeon poop!" David Letterman was absolutely disgusted with the real live pigeon on David Letterman's desk squeezing out some pigeon poop of its own, David Letterman was all riled up, getting New Yorkers all riled up too, his national audience riled up big-time, all waiting in anticipation for the Birdmobile to pull into town, with the four-foot-tall, carved, one-legged pigeon on top, with all the pigeons on top of the Birdmobile, with that punk kid from Seattle, that punk kid with the idiot name, that punk kid known as Billy Pigeon!

\*\*\*

They drove through Indiana, home of another famous bird named Larry, then into Ohio, past Toledo, past Cleveland, the drive along Lake Erie breathtaking, with the awesome smell of the Great Lakes and the sighting of the occasional seagull. Walter sang a verse for the seagulls:

"Seagulls, seagulls,

Sit on the sand,

It's never good weather,

When you're on the land!"

\*\*\*

Then it was across Pennsylvania, into the state of New York, with crappy highways, more tollbooths—lots and lots of tollbooths—the cheap motels getting harder and harder to find, the people all wound up, the litter all along the grass on the shoulders of the highways, past Rochester, then Syracuse, with the traffic intensifying big-time. Billy had no time to think, no time to collect bumper stickers. The traffic got even worse through Albany, then Highway 84 into New York City. The New York State Troopers were now leading the way, Billy Pigeon having no idea how they would ever find Central Park. He would just follow the flashing lights; the traffic was *C-R-A-Z-Y*. What a mess, what a mess, what a mess, with roads going here, there, and everywhere. Billy's armpits were starting to sweat, with cars and trucks and boats and planes and trains going in all directions—organized chaos. Billy Pigeon held onto his steering wheel for dear life, with his eyes glancing to the left and to the right, with police cars flying by, their sirens howling, their lights flashing, with ambulances and fire trucks flying by, too, with a left turn and a right turn, another left turn. The traffic was insane and the drivers were full of road rage. Billy Pigeon was pooped, his eyes worse than two pissholes in the snow again. Even more cars and trucks and boats and planes and trains passed by, the cars and trucks whipping onto off-ramps, over bridges and driving through tunnels, with Billy Pigeon needing a good two days R&R before he hit Broadway!

*　*　*

David Letterman had a contest going for a week now; he challenged all of New York City to find him a *real* live one-legged pigeon. He didn't want someone to go out and cut a real live two-legged pigeon's leg off and then bring it into the studio as a real live one-legged pigeon. He wanted the real McCoy!

All of New York City searched; there was no such pigeon to be found!

"I'll be damned!" said David Letterman.

"Only in Canada, eh!" said his piano player Paul, a Canadian. Paul was one of the lucky ones to have read a copy of *Birdman of 24 Sussex,* one of the original four hundred copies given to him to read by a friend of a friend of a friend of a friend!

"A great read!" said Paul, the piano man. "Mr. Evans as the Mayor of Penticton, then the Premier of British Columbia, then the Prime Minister of Canada, the $L = P^2/M$ formula at the end of the book made me piss my pants, made me bust a gut! If he read that book, Billy Pigeon has a shot at becoming our new president in 2012!"

"Ya right!" exclaimed David Letterman. "And how's he going to get past that age thirty-five part?"

"He'll figure it out; you watch and see!" said Paul, the piano man. "He had a great teacher!"

*　*　*

Walter and Billy got into it about a motel room.

"We can leave the motor home in Central Park till your big rally with the kids. We can have some of the security detail from Spokane watch over it. We can find a nice motel room. I can pour a hot bath and smoke a cigar!" said Walter. "We're in New York City. We have to pay New York City prices, son. Don't worry about it; we have the money. We can handle it, no sweat!"

"You're missing the point, Dad," said Billy Pigeon. "We're in the Big Apple; we're on center stage. There are millions and millions of sets of eyes in the naked city. What better place in America to show America that I mean business, that we are going to change a culture, to get people to save money, not spend it. We are going to sleep in the park in our motor home by the stage, at no cost to us. It will be so symbolic; the press will eat it up. I'll tell them exactly why we're doing it and what we are up to."

"I agree with Billy," said Debra. "Perception in politics is everything. Why change now?"

"It will be fun sleeping in Central Park!" said Julie.

\*\*\*

And so it was, with the New York State Troopers leading the way, with Debra Sanders on her cell, telling the State Troopers that they were going to sleep in Central Park with the pigeons, that they weren't going to try and look for a cheap motel, with the security detail from Spokane on high alert, with thousands of New York pigeons hovering over the Birdmobile as it crawled through traffic, the scene surreal, the scene putting Alfred Hitchcock to shame. Billy Pigeon got a hero's welcome in New York City, with young Americans and old Americans raining down confetti and ticker tape on Billy and the Birdmobile, the city going bananas, a spectacle rivaling the return of Alvin York from World War I in Europe, the return of Charles Lindbergh, the return of Neil Armstrong and Buzz Aldrin and Michael Collins from the moon, the first Stanley Cup win for the Rangers in fifty years, or another Yankees World Series!

"Holy crap," said Billy Pigeon, "am I really this popular?"

\*\*\*

"No, you're not!" screamed David Letterman on his next late night broadcast. "I made you. I turned you into the celebrity you are. Give credit where credit is due!"

\*\*\*

"Letterman's full of it!" said Debra Sanders. "He hasn't done jack-shit to make you a star on Broadway. You did it all by yourself with your gutsy decision to run for president, your RPA party, your real people with real solutions to real problems slogan resonating through the world of politics. The world of politics realizes that you are a different bird, a rare politician who won't be bought or sold down the river, a politician with a plan for America, not the bunch of crap that is spewing out of Washington on a daily basis. You're the man, Billy. Now you've got to walk the walk, starting here in Central Park and finishing up at the Presidential Debate. You will rock their socks!" said Debra.

\*\*\*

Billy Pigeon was pumped. He read the news on his laptop. Obama's approval rating was beginning to decline; soon it would sink like the Titanic. Soon Obama would have to leave Washington, take a ride in his own motor home, a big black one, made in Canada, not made in America, start out on the campaign trail, shake hands, talk to people, try to hit a nerve with something, blame all the negativity on the Republican Congress, and hope that he could bullshit his way back to the White House for another four years. Billy Pigeon was only one good sleep away from delivering a telling blow before the big knock-out punch in Washington in 2012!

\*\*\*

For some strange reason, Debra had comedians on her mind. She could handle Letterman; he was just full of hot air. She could handle Jay and Conan and Lorne. Conan was too busy trying to keep his hair stuck up in place. Jay was in La-La Land. Lorne had already been dealt with, but Debra had concerns about the two new boys: Stephen Colbert and that raving lunatic Jon Stewart, who amassed big old protest crowds at the Washington monument, who went make-believe nuts on TV to prove a point, who yelled and screamed at the world, and who used the F-word on a daily basis. She had to be proactive with those two boys; those two were dangerous. They were also very smart—no they were smarter than smart—they were intelligent. They were cutting-edge when it came to the world of comedy and politics. Old Stephen Colbert even put a live chicken in a big old potato sack on national TV, ready to catch a hobo train to look for his next job in a shitty economy. These two would know trouble if it were headed their way. You would never pull the wool over their eyes, never be able to control them. So if you can't control them, why not join them? Now there's an idea. What would happen if I gave them the opportunity of a lifetime, if I told those two clowns that they could ride the Birdmobile all the way to the Oval Office, become our biggest supporters, get them on our side, have a running feud with Letterman, Conan, Leno, and Lorne, the Hatfields versus the McCoys, the new boys against the old boys. Wouldn't that be fun to watch: the new boys for real change in America, supporting Billy Pigeon, the new boys on lawn chairs on top of the Birdmobile, hooked on with safety hooks to the three guy wires on the four-foot statue of the one-legged pigeon, doing their show live from Central Park. Debra, you are just too smart!

Now how do I approach them, get them on our side, and get them to really know Billy like I do? Maybe they could be my way of getting the other comedians to cut Billy some slack and take him seriously as a candidate. Maybe Stephen and Jon could put them on the run; wouldn't that be something?

\*\*\*

"Just call them," said Walter.

\*\*\*

Julie was in Billy's Scrapbook of Life again. She read the following by an old, old comedian by the name of Dick Cavett. This is what he said: "If your parents never had children, chances are you won't either!"

"That is too funny!" thought Julie.

She read another comment Billy had highlighted.

"Always carry jam; you never know when you'll be toast!"

And one more.

"Always be the lead dog. The view is a lot better from the front!"

Julie was cracking up, she continued to read: "When I was kidnapped, my parents snapped into action. They rented out my room!"

Finally Julie read a grace before dinner; she busted a gut:

"Rub a dub dub,

Here comes the grub,

Go, God, go!"

"Where do you get all this stuff, Billy?" asked Julie.

"Here, there, and everywhere!" said Billy Pigeon.

\* \* \*

Billy, with the blessing of the mayor of New York City, set up camp in Central Park. Out came four lawn chairs, the small Hibachi barbecue, the wieners and hotdog buns, the ketchup, relish and mustard, the paper plates, the plastic cups for the cold lemonade, and the paper towels.

"This is fun!" said Julie, as hoards and hoards of New Yorkers descended upon Central Park to meet and greet a possible future president: New Yorkers of all ages, all shapes and sizes, all ethnic backgrounds. Billy's security detail from Spokane was getting a little nervous, and rightly so. They requested some New York City barricades; they were delivered immediately by New York City workers. The Birdmobile was cordoned off, giving Billy and friends a fifty-foot space all around their decked-out motor home.

"Could we get some Porta-Potties, too?" asked the security detail from Spokane. "Maybe get us some of that really soft toilet paper, the heavy duty stuff. Their butts were still sore from sitting all those long days in their black Suburbans and sitting all night on their lawn chairs guarding their president!

"Thanks a million, man!" said one of the security detail from Spokane when the Porta-Potties were delivered; the rolls of toilet paper were exactly what the doctor had ordered!

\* \* \*

Billy Pigeon waded out to the edge of the crowd. He had a veggie-dog going, with mustard along the edges of his mouth. The smell of all the hot briquettes and the sizzling wiener juices splattering on the hot coals below made the crowd hungry, also made them antsy.

"Make me a hot dog, Mr. President; they smell fantastic. I'll pay you $10 for it!" yelled one of Billy's admirers, a cute brunette in her late teens.

"Don't worry about the $10!" said Billy, as he told Walter to bring him a real hotdog with the works.

Billy smiled some more, shook hands, collected more campaign donations, and signed autographs on paper napkins, paper plates, Frisbees, baseball caps, and plastic beach balls. The scene in front of the Birdmobile was festive, but the security detail from Spokane was still nervous, still on their toes, all eagle eyes, with some really strange dudes showing up in the park. The security detail knew full-well that all it took was for one bad apple in the Big Apple to spoil the party and to put an end to the Reality Party of America before it even began. The security detail from Spokane was not letting their guard down, not one little bit—the way it should be!

\* \* \*

President Obama was watching CNN; he also watched Billy Pigeon schmooze the crowd, doing what a good politician does best.

"He's good; I'll give him that!" said the president.

Billy was all over the local news. David Letterman was at home, glued to the TV.

"Look at all the pigeons in the park!" said David Letterman. "Get some of our guys over there. Surely to God we can find one pigeon with one leg!"

\* \* \*

Debra was on the blower to Stephen Colbert and Jon Stewart; they did a conference call. Debra apologized for not returning their earlier calls and said she was really busy; there had been so much happening the first few days on the road. Debra told Stephen Colbert and Jon Stewart that Billy Pigeon was the real deal, that she had seen his plan for America, that it would knock the socks off everybody when it came to fruition, especially the Chinese, and that she wanted Stephen and Jon on their side. She asked them to cut Billy some slack, to come and get to know Billy on a personal, business, and political level, to sit on top of the Birdmobile all the way to the White House, to be part of the Gong Show, to throw crunchy croutons to all the pigeons sitting by their feet, and to sip on piña coladas. She said that their TV ratings would sky-rocket, would go through the stratosphere, that the old boys would be pissed, that America would laugh like they've never laughed before, that they could even bring guests to sit up on top of the Birdmobile with them to do live interviews, that Billy would be their first guest, that they, and *they only,* would have exclusive access to Billy, and that they could feel free to ask him any question they'd like, within reason. Billy didn't want to spill all the beans at once—he wanted to keep people guessing—so they had to play along with him, but as soon as he wanted to tell America something new, he would tip them off first and give them a head start on anyone else in the media world. So what do you think?

Debra knew now what Paul and Art meant by the sound of silence; the silence was deafening, with Debra waiting and waiting and waiting—a good two minutes—until Stephen Colbert finally spoke for himself and his good buddy Jon: "We're in!"

\* \* \*

"So when do we start?" asked Jon Stewart.

"How about tomorrow when he gives his big speech at Central Park?" said Debra.

"We'll be there!" said Jon Stewart.

"We'll have a pancake breakfast ready and waiting, your piña coladas on ice, your lawn chairs, your own special bags to pick up pigeon poop and a big old ladder to climb up on top of the Birdmobile—all ready and waiting!" said Debra Sanders.

"We'll be there, bright and early, with bells on!" said Stephen Colbert.

"Seriously, guys, get to know Billy like I do; treat him like a man and he might even let you in on a few secrets!" said Debra.

"That would be cool!" said Jon Stewart.

\* \* \*

Darkness fell on Central Park; the thousands and thousands of New Yorkers headed home, all happy to have seen their future president in the flesh. Debra and Billy were still sitting outside on their lawn chairs. Walter and Julie were inside and sound asleep, with new money all over the Birdmobile, on the counter in a big old glass bottle, in a cardboard box under Julie's folded-down table, in plastic containers in the ice box in the fridge, and in their empty cooler sitting on the floor. Walter and Julie were wiped from counting all the new money, from writing tax receipts, and from putting their money away for safe keeping!

\* \* \*

"Time for a strategy session," said Debra.

"Shoot!" said Billy.

Before she began, Debra told Billy that Stephen Colbert and Jon Stewart were showing up in the morning, bright and early, to show support for his campaign, to sit up on top of the Birdmobile with all the pigeons, and to do a live show for all of America to see.

"That is so cool!" said Billy Pigeon. "Those two guys rock! How did you manage to pull that off?"

"Magic!" said Debra, pausing for a sip of her martini. She continued.

"Anyway, Paul and I have been talking since Chicago. We both feel that we should hold off on the details of the military, industrial, manufacturing complex and the five thousand contracts with corporate America. You can still tease them with Billy's World like you did on Oprah, but you should only talk about your 20 million workers tomorrow—tell them that you'll have a job for them in six short years," said Debra.

"And why's that?" asked Billy. "I thought we were going to let the whole cat out of the bag."

"Because we still want to keep them guessing. We want to drive them stir-crazy and have them pull their hair out. We want to save it for a critical point in the campaign when our backs are against the wall. We don't want them trying to screw up our five thousand contracts with corporate America; corporate America doesn't even know yet that they'll be participating. We want to take it one step at a time and get all our ducks in a row. And trust me, if you think for a moment that the Washington establishment on the left and on the right are going to go down without a fight, then you're mistaken! They will do anything and everything they can do to keep us from crossing the Potomac River and driving right up to the White House lawn!" said Debra Sanders. "We hold the military, industrial, manufacturing complex and everything involved with it as our big smoking gun, our ace in the hole, our straw that broke the camel's back, and when we fire, we'll hit them so hard that they'll fall over like flies!"

"I like it!" said Billy Pigeon. "I like it a lot. So when do I get to fire that big smoking gun?"

"We're thinking the Debate in 2012; hopefully, we'll have clear sailing till then!" said Debra.

"I hope so, too!" said Billy.

\*\*\*

Billy's mind was on fire; his thoughts were going here, there, and everywhere, really fast! Debra could sense Billy's wandering mind. She knew he had changes to make to his speech tomorrow to the one million young Americans already packing their knapsacks for their big day in Central Park. She would give Billy the space he needed.

"Go to sleep, Mr. President. We have a long day tomorrow. Tomorrow will be one of the most important days in your life. I want you to stay away from my daughter, Julie. I want you to be fresh as a daisy!" said Debra.

"Yes, Mommy!" replied Billy. "Goodnight!"

"Goodnight, Billy, don't mind me. I'm going to stay up for a while, sip on my martini, have a cigarette, look up at the stars, listen to New York City, and try to come down a bit," said Debra.

"Watch out for the pigeon poop dropping from the sky!" said Billy.

"Goodnight, Billy!" shouted Debra.

\*\*\*

While Walter and Julie slept, Billy was still wide awake, the changes to his speech tomorrow still dancing in his head. While Debra gazed at the stars in

New York City, at a secret location in Washington on the outskirts of town, the Gang of 11 was meeting.

This was a real hush-hush meeting, by invitation only, so it would only be fair that we keep the names of the gang members secret, too, but I can't do that. I'll spill the beans a little bit. I'll carry on this incredible conversation using people's initials to at least give you a clue as to who was in attendance, who was saying what to whom. You just have to promise to keep it really quiet, after all, it was a hush-hush meeting in a secret location: with K. R. there, with B. O. there, with R. L. there, with G. B. there, with another G. B. there, with D. C. there, with D. R. there, with R. P. there, with P. R. there, with J. B. there, with G. W. there—all eleven men. See, I just gave you another clue—all eleven men sitting around on comfortable chairs and sofas. They were only beginning their night, their chinwag over scotch and Kentucky bourbon and Canadian whiskey and beer and wine, a chinwag that would go on into the wee hours of the morning. Their conversation went something like this: "That little fucker has got to go!" screamed G. B.

"I agree," said K. R., "but we have to be a little more subtle in our approach!"

"Why?" asked G. B. "I say we take him out right now, him and his stupid fucking one-legged wooden pigeon, blow that fucking motor home right out of the water, do it with a fucking military drone when he gets on the road again, one shot, boom, the mother fucker is toast!"

"And how are we going to get our hands on a military drone?" asked the other G. B. "Obama would have to authorize that."

"Fuck Obama!" said B. O. "We have all the contacts; we could put together our own hit team, and everyone would think it was the Democrats doing it from the White House. They would have to duck for cover, explain to the American people why it wasn't them who did it. "

"I agree," said D. C. "We could call my buddies at Halliburton, get the private drone contractor and CIA involved like Ollie did. It would be a piece of cake to do if we talk to the right people."

"We have to do what it takes to protect the political right," said R. P.

"I agree," said D. R.

"Real people with real solutions to real problems: what a crock of shit!" said P. R.

"Someone, somewhere, is feeding the kid with all this crap, orchestrating his every move; no 18-year-old kid is capable of doing this by himself," said J. B.

"But who?" asked R. L. "Who would want to take down our political system as we know it?"

"Maybe it's Wall Street; maybe they've got some new cock-eyed bubble they want to inflate," said G. W., "but I'm sure we would have heard about it by now."

"No bloody way!" said G. B. "Those bastards are so beholden to me after we bailed them out in 2008, they'd never want another stick shoved up their assholes again. They wouldn't have the goddamn nerve!"

"Maybe it's al Qaeda," said D. C.

"That makes a lot more sense," said K. R. "They could easily be financing his campaign. They could be keeping all the campaign donations to fund terrorist activity right here under our noses, have people in the States who are sympathetic to their cause and who hate Washington."

"Or it could be a local radical group that is out to get us all, that is just fed up with the fucking government," said G. B.

"That's what I just said, you idiot!" said K. R.

"Maybe it's the fucking Russians or their fucking commie friends in China!" said R. L.

"It doesn't matter who it is; we've got to do something about it now," said D. C. "I think we all agree on that point."

"Have we really pissed that many people off?" asked G. B.

"I didn't even mention the Iranians or the Pakistanis or the North Koreans," said R. L.

"I say we wait a few days, see what the kid is going to say in Central Park tomorrow," said a relaxed G. W.

"I agree," said D. R.

"Me, too," said P. R.

"Maybe then we might get a few more clues about what the kid's up to," said R. P.

"Fuck you guys!" shouted GB. "I know it's the Nazis. I say we do a number on him tonight, right in fucking Central Park. The little mother fucker won't know what hit him!"

"Shut the fuck up!" yelled K. R. "Man, you are fucking nuts! Now calm down, for Christ's sake! He's on a two-year trip around America; we can pick him off anywhere we like, any time we like, any way we like."

"Don't do it in Dallas!" said G. B.

# 18

# Let the Games Begin

Julie was up and about first. She saw the new green garbage bag full of pop cans and plastic water bottles that Billy had collected after all the people left Central Park the previous evening. The new garbage bag was left by her Jeep Wrangler. Billy didn't want to ask Julie for the key to her Jeep when he went to bed, while she was sleeping.

She opened the Jeep and put the bag inside with six other bulging bags; there was no room left, except on her driver's seat. This was ridiculous! She would get on Billy's case when they left New York City and get him to find a bottle depot to get rid of his bottles and cans!

\*\*\*

After she put Billy's new bag of returnable bottles and cans away, Julie focused on her pigeons. She handed out her last bag of crunchy croutons. She would have to reload. There were New York pigeons here, there, and everywhere. There was pigeon poop on all four lawn chairs, which should have been folded up and slid under the motor home, but they weren't. One pigeon was doing it to a smaller pigeon on top of the motor home, with Stephen Colbert and Jon Stewart arriving, climbing up their ladder, their camera man climbing up, too. Stephen and Jon were now back on the air, together again, the way it should be. Stephen Colbert spoke to America; this is what he said: "Good morning, America. Welcome to New York City; welcome to Central Park; welcome to the top of the Birdmobile. Say hello to the four-foot-tall, carved, one-legged pigeon, and all his fine feathery friends. Eat your heart out, David Letterman!"

"Ditto!" said Jon Stewart.

***

Billy was up; he had an okay sleep, not that great, but he would survive. He sipped on a cup of Julie's freshly brewed Morning Joe. He was all decked out in his white, short-sleeved shirt, his blue jeans, his white socks, his dark brown, leather belt, and his moccasins for his moment on the big stage, his moment in time. He said the following to Julie as he stepped outside the Birdmobile: "Look at all the pigeons in the park!"

Billy Pigeon stretched his sore back, his sore arms, his sore everything from sleeping on the same overhead bunk with his father, Walter, who was tossing and turning all night long. His father was snoring, dreaming endlessly of a hot bath in a comfortable New York motel or hotel, of smoking a big old cigar. New York city police and private security firms were at the entry points to Central Park, checking for two pieces of ID, making sure that all the young Americans entering the park for the big rally were nineteen and under, with Stephen Colbert and Jon Stewart interviewing Billy and then introducing Debra Sanders to the world. Bill O'Reilly and Glenn Beck were watching TV at the same time, with Bill O'Reilly calling Glenn Beck on the telephone and saying the following: "That's the bitch running his campaign!"

The scene in and around Central Park was unbelievable, with busloads and busloads of young Americans arriving from New Jersey, Buffalo, Boston, and Philadelphia. The young Americans were all messed up, from broken marriages, from homes with both parents working, with no direction in their lives, with no discipline, and with crappy grades at school. The youth of America were searching for Mr. and Mrs. Walton and John-Boy, searching for someone to give them hope, keep them on the straight and narrow, give them a job in their future, teach them how to save money, and get their screwed-up lives in order. All these young Americans were flooding Central Park to see and hear Billy Pigeon, to see if he was their messiah, and to see history in the making. Hopefully, he was more than a one-hit wonder, a flash in the pan. The one million and counting young Americans, from ten to nineteen, were living for the moment, and the moment was just about here, with TV crews from all over the world focused on Central Park, on the stage, with no wind storm in sight, no chance of a stage collapsing on Billy Pigeon, with FBI agents on the perimeter, with special forces in the air, with the mayor of New York and the governor of the state of New York on the stage. The mayor of New York never once offered Billy Pigeon the key to the city. He knew exactly what Billy would tell him to do with his key. Billy was finally being escorted to the stage by ten members of his security detail from Spokane, with chants of "RPA, RPA, RPA, RPA, RPA" coming from the young people in the audience. The crowd was enthusiastic, boisterous, inventive, with a gigantic red, white, and blue beach ball, over forty feet in diameter, being tossed here, there, and everywhere by the crowd. The one million and counting young Americans realized that this was one of those special, really special moments in time that we all remember, like Woodstock, like the Beatles playing Shea Stadium, like Watergate, like the Iran/Contra hearings, or like Bill Clinton having to justify his hanky-panky moment. Shouts of "Billy, Billy, Billy" electrified the audience.

President Obama was glued to his TV set; the Gang of 11 all tuned in, and every other political figure in the U. S. of A. , whether they be municipal, state, or federal, were all looking in, too. All of America and the world watching on CNN focused on Billy Pigeon, watching with interest, wanting to see if Billy would deliver the goods, would walk the walk. The old geezer from Washington was especially interested, wanting to see what he was really getting for his $100 bill!

*　*　*

Billy Pigeon silenced the crowd with both arms and with both hands. The crowd was quiet; you suddenly could hear a pin drop, hear the pigeons talking to each other, and hear Jon Stewart cutting a big old fart on top of the Birdmobile! Billy Pigeon spoke to the world.

> My fellow Americans, I have a plan for America. Learn from the past, deal with the present and the future will take care of itself. Good morning America, my name is Billy Pigeon. I am 18 years old, I am single, for now, I'm from Bellevue, Washington, and I'm running for the office of president of the United States of America in 2012!

The crowd cheered; the crowd screamed "Billy, Billy, Billy." Stephen Colbert said the following to Jon Stewart: "What a ballsy kid!"

Billy continued his speech.

> The Constitution of the United States, written way back when, by our Founding Fathers, states very clearly that I have to be thirty-five to run for president. Our party, the RPA, the Reality Party of America, will be demanding a constitutional amendment from our current government in Washington. I will ask President Obama to instruct the Congress and the Senate to write up a new bill allowing me, Billy Pigeon, to run for president in 2012.

> I cannot wait seventeen more years to be your president. Our country cannot wait another seventeen years, but more importantly, you, all one million of you, cannot wait another seventeen years. I was unemployed once; I know what it feels like to be without a job, to have no hope. I'm one of the lucky ones. I come from a caring, loving family, but I know hundreds and hundreds of young people in Bellevue who have no direction, who come from broken homes, who get no support with both parents working, parents who are too tired to talk to you about your future plans—what you want to do with your

life. So you wonder the streets of America, all alone, you join gangs, you do drugs, you drink till you drop, you P-A-R-T-Y all night long, and you sleep in till noon the next day. Nobody understands how you feel, what you feel, that you just want to be a useful part of society, not riot in the streets or throw Molotov cocktails at the police. You just want a job; you want a piece of the American Pie. You want your mom and dad to get together again, to become a family once more. You want your mom to stop working, to be there when you get home and talk to you about your issues at school and cook you a good, hot, healthy supper, not have her stuff another frozen pizza in front of your face, tell you to nuke it in the microwave as she heads back to work a second job to pay the bills mounting up on the kitchen table!

Trust me, I understand; I know the mess America is in. I know how tough it is to make a living in our country, to keep families together, to raise children. I know how complex our problem is, how it changes every day, but this is America. I will be your president, and I have a plan to fix all of this, to give you hope, to put all of America on the path to prosperity, to restore America to its rightful position in the world—*Numero Uno,* Number One—the way it should be!

And my Plan for America is based entirely on you, all one million of you, all 39 more million of you watching me on TV today wherever you may be across this great country we call America, I will be calling on you, all of you, 40 million of you, to join me, to join the Reality Party of America, to go to war with me in my War on Jobs, to sign up by e-mail on admin@billybird.com, to start when I'm finished talking.

I have three shirts and two pairs of pants to my name. I ride a mountain bike everywhere I go. I've worked hard all my life. I have been saving money since I was four years old. I have $49,000 in my bank account. I have one American Express credit card, with a zero balance. I have a $50,000 line of credit, secured by my cash. I just paid off my only purchase last week; my credit line is now at zero, too.

I have no debt. I feel strong, really strong, financially. When I walk into my bank, I feel proud; I feel confident! I feel no stress whatsoever. I want all of the members of the RPA to feel that exact same way. I want you to feel like you're dancing on easy street!

In two short years, when I'm president, I am going to begin construction of Billy's World. It will be the largest construction project ever built by man. I will employ every American without a job now to build it. It will take them four years to build, and then, six short years from now, for those of you who are ten, you'll be sixteen and old enough to go to war if you have both your parents' signatures; those of you who are nineteen, you'll be twenty-four by then and you'll be able to sign up for one five-year Tour of Duty if you're still single. You will all go to work for me at Billy's World. I will guarantee you a job as soon as you sign on the dotted line. You will make a Pledge of Allegiance to your country, America. Your pledge will be for five years. I will ask you to leave home, to go to war with me, to say good-bye to your mom and dad, wherever they may be, to get on a plane or a train or a bus and come to Billy's World. You will not, and I emphasize this, you will *not* have to go to war in Iraq or Afghanistan or Iran or Russia or Pakistan or North Korea or China. You will not have to come home in a wooden casket, get buried in a place called Arlington, go to Walter Reid Hospital in Washington to have a new leg or a new arm put on. You just have to come and work for me!

I am going to put a roof over your head, give you a bed to sleep on, a footlocker to hang your two other shirts and one pair of pants, a chair and a desk and three drawers to give you a spot to store your savings book, your underwear and your socks, and write letters to your mom and dad at home, or to your sweetheart. I will also feed you good, hot, healthy food every day. There will be no junk food at Billy's World. None of you will be allowed to look like Porky Pig! You will not be allowed to do drugs. You will only be allowed to drink alcohol in a bar or tavern or lounge if you're twenty-one. Smoking will only be allowed in designated areas. I will do my best to wean you off cigarettes, too. Porn will only be watched under a blanket with a flashlight. If you are caught, you will be in big trouble!

You will exercise one hour a day. You will be watched by a man or woman carrying a really big stick. You will conduct yourselves under a four-strikes-and-you're-out policy. You will get your hair all chopped off; you will look like you would if you were going to a real war!

You will all work a forty-hour week. You will wear a pair of uniformed coveralls assigned to you for work. You will look sharp; you will wear an American flag on your chest. You will look like and feel part of a well-oiled working machine. You will all be happy campers, with your nights off and weekends off to go for a drive in your used car or truck, take a swim, play tennis, or just kick back and read a good BATMAN and ROBIN comic book. You will all get up at 6:30 a.m.; you will dress and eat, work from 8:00 a.m. to 4:00 p.m., have dinner, then exercise. Lights will be out at 10:00 p.m. on Monday, Tuesday, Wednesday, and Thursday. Friday night, Saturday, and Sunday will be yours; you're back at it on Monday morning, bright and early. I will teach you manners, how to get along with people, to respect little old ladies, and to respect other people's property. I will put discipline back into your lives, big-time!

And I will teach you how to save money, just like me. You will all feel the same strength I do when I walk into a bank. I don't want to spoil you, so you will not get a big fat paycheck of $4,000 a month, or a big bonus like they pay out on Wall Street here in New York City, or a big old $100 million, five-year contract like they give out to football and baseball players and basketball stars.

You will all receive minimum wage for your work. You will get paid every two weeks; 80 percent of your wages will stay in the bank. You will be able to take the other 20 percent, approximately $200 per month, and spend it at Billy's World. In five short years of being at war, all of you will walk away with $50,000 in your blue jeans. If you want to do a second tour of duty and commit for another five years at Billy's World, you will end up with over $100,000 in your pockets, money you can use to go to college, as a down payment on a new home, or to just leave in the bank making interest, to let it grow at compounding interest rates over a long period of time. Your $50,000 will make you a millionaire when you retire.

I have a plan; my plan is Billy's World. We will all have loads of fun. I even have lots of big hotels for your mom and dad to come and visit you on weekends. You can even go for airplane and train and bus rides, take a bicycle around to visit your friends, and eat some popcorn, but not too much. You will have the time of your life!

Remember, you only have two short years to sign up before construction begins. I have 20 million beds to fill. It will be first come, first served. Go online to admin@billybird.com, fill out your application, sign on the dotted line, and I will save a bed for you! America is a mess. We are politically, economically, and morally corrupt. My generation of young Americans will change America, so help me God! We will restore its greatness. Our country will once more be the envy of the world. We will draw a line in the sand. We will run no more federal government deficits. We will pay off the $70 trillion obligation of previous generations of Americans in twenty-four short years by using the profits I make at Billy's World. Our generation will have no debt; we will pay our bills on time and our pockets will be lined with cold, hard cash. We will buy only what we really need at Walmart and Target—what we can afford. We will not own three houses and six vehicles. We will be a frugal generation. We will be the most disciplined generation America has ever seen. We will make climate change a priority in Washington. I will not kowtow to special interest groups. Our Congress and Senate and state governments will live by the same golden rule.

In conclusion, I would like to thank you all for coming out to Central Park this morning. I would urge you all to join the RPA, the Reality Party of America, to make a commitment of five years to my War on Jobs, to sign on the dotted line at admin@billybird.com, to wait six more years, to help me change America, to revive the American Dream, Billy's World will rock your socks, set fire to the American economy, provide work for every unemployed American, and will be the catalyst that all Americans are so desperately searching and hoping for. Trust me, I have learned from our past; I will deal with the present, and the future will take care of itself!

God bless you, and God bless the United States of America!

\*\*\*

When Billy's audience of one million, and counting, young Americans started to applaud and stamp their feet and jump up and down in the air, all at the same time, the Birdmobile began to shake, rattle, and roll, with Stephen Colbert and Jon Stewart clipping their safety harnesses to the guy wires on the four-foot-tall, carved statue of the one-legged pigeon. Disney shares on Wall Street tumbled 20 percent in the first five minutes after Billy's historic speech, with McDonald's, Papa John's and all the other fast food stocks tanking, too. Hugh Heffner was glad he had taken Playboy private. Little old ladies and property owners e-mailed Billy thanking him and wrote their feelings on thank-you cards. The thank-you card businesses all across America were on fire. The old geezer in Washington State said the following to another old geezer at their favorite coffee shop: "Fucking 'A' Billy!"

\*\*\*

President Obama turned off his TV. This is what he said to his wonderful wife Michelle: "I can't even create one new job, and he's going to have zero unemployment and then 20 million young Americans are going to go and work and play at Billy's World! Give me a break!"

\*\*\*

"Where the fuck is he going to get the money to finance Billy's World?" asked Glenn Beck "I can't even get an extra five grand from my own fucking bank to redo my own bathroom!"

\*\*\*

Jimmy Joseph from Baltimore, age 14, talked with David Jones from Boston, age 13, before they got on their respective buses outside Central Park.

"I like the idea of $50,000; I might even go for the $100,000," said Jeremy Joseph, "but don't you think the rules are a little harsh?"

"Nothing different than our parents and teachers would say, if we had real parents and real teachers!" said David Jones.

\*\*\*

"Great speech, Billy, with no notes; I don't know how you do it!" said Debra.

\*\*\*

"Way to go, son!" said Walter.
"I love you, Billy!" said Julie.
"Un-fucking-real!" yelled Jon Stewart.
"Ditto!" said Stephen Colbert.

\*\*\*

"I hope you slip on your ass in pigeon shit!" said David Letterman.

# 19

## I'm with the FBI

Bob Iger, the top dog at Disney, called his good friend, David, who was lying by his pool in sunny Burbank.

"Did you hear the latest, that an 18-year-old kid by the name of Billy Pigeon is running for president against Obama in 2012 and how he's going to build a brand new theme park called Billy's World?" said Bob Iger.

"I did, and I hear it's big," said his good friend David.

"Big, are you kidding me?" said Bob Iger. "He says 20 million kids are going to work there!"

"Really!" said his good friend David. "And how's he going to pull something like that off, especially in this recession?"

"I have no idea!" said Bob Iger. "It's got to be Chinese money; they're into everything else in the country these days!"

"Or else his head is in the cloud, like all the Internet generation!" said his good friend David.

"That's really funny!" said Bob Iger.

"I thought you'd like it!" said his good friend David.

\*\*\*

Julie was on her laptop; she saw all the applications piling up.

"Billy, look at this application for a job at Billy's World," said Julie.

"What's the big deal?" asked Billy.

"Check out the last name," said Julie.

"What is it?" asked Billy.

"Pigeon!" said Julie.

"You're kidding me!" said Billy.

"She's from Bellevue. She says she wants to get some financial discipline in her life. She wants to save $50,000, maybe even $100,000. She wants to open her own sewing business when she finishes up at Billy's World and use some of her money as a down-payment on a small business loan," said Julie.

"What's her first name?" asked Billy.

"Sarah!" said Julie.

"I'll be going to hell!" said Billy. Billy passed the good news onto his father, Walter, who said the following to his son, Billy:

"I'll be damned; good for her!"

\* \* \*

Holy Cow, Batman, with all of America raving over Billy's Central Park speech, with millions of young Americans on admin@billybird.com to fill out their application forms to work at Billy's World, to book a bed, to make some sense out of their screwed-up lives, with the applications pouring in to beat the band, with Billy and the Birdmobile and Julie's Jeep Wrangler headed to Ocean City for a three-week holiday, Billy Pigeon was wiped from the Chicago to the New York City part of his two-year trip around America. The traffic was still nasty, with the Birdmobile heading down the New Jersey Turnpike toward Philadelphia, with Walter driving, with Billy and Julie catching up on their Scrapbook of Life entries.

"Did you see the kid in the front row with the long red hair?" asked Julie.

"The one with the beads?" said Billy.

"That's the one," said Julie, flipping through the pages in her little notebook. "Did you see what he had written on his T-shirt?"

"No, I didn't," said Billy. "I was too focused on my speech. What did it say?"

"It said, 'I have gone to find myself. If I get back before I return, keep me here!'" said Julie.

"That is definitely Scrapbook of Life material," said Billy.

"I agree," said Julie.

\* \* \*

Billy found a bottle depot. He took all the plastic bags of pop and beer bottles and pop and beer cans from Julie's Jeep. He received $62.45. Billy was elated!

\* \* \*

"Spray my Jeep with air freshener!" yelled Julie.

\* \* \*

Walter pulled the Birdmobile in for gas at a truck stop close to Philadelphia, the tank showing less than a quarter, the windshield full of bugs.

Billy went in for a cup of coffee and was instantly recognized by one of the truckers sitting in a booth next to the till. The booth was spacious, with its own card-operated telephone.

"You're the kid running for president, aren't you?" asked one of the truckers, wearing a dirty, oil-stained baseball cap.

"I am," said Billy Pigeon. "I'm on a two-year campaign tour of all the states."

"There are only two states in America," said another trucker sitting in the same booth.

"Really!" said Billy Pigeon. "And what are they?"

"Drunk and sober!" said the other trucker.

One of the truckers then told Billy that he had seen his speech in New York on TV, that he wished he was sixteen again, and single, and could go work at Billy's World and come out with $50,000 in his blue jeans after five years.

"Trust me," said Billy Pigeon, "I'll be keeping your trucks busy for a long, long time during and after the construction phase!"

"So this place you're building sounds big," said another trucker.

"It's bigger than big," said Billy Pigeon.

"So where are you building it?" asked another trucker.

"Not sure yet," said Billy. "We're looking for a spot right now. When I find it, I'll let you know."

"All I can say is good luck, kid," said the same trucker. "At least you're doing something about our unemployment problem, not blowing smoke up our ass!"

"Thank you for the compliment," said Billy. "I won't let you down."

* * *

"Julie, Julie, I have a great joke for our Scrapbook of Life; you're going to crack up!" said Billy Pigeon.

"And I've got one for you, too!" said Julie. "It's not a joke, but I think it's a great bumper sticker. Did you see it on the white van from Florida?"

"No, I missed that one. What did it say?" asked Billy.

"It said, 'If a man is talking in the forest and his wife is not there to hear him, is he still wrong?'"

"I saw a good one, too, when I was cleaning off the bugs," said Walter.

"What was that?" asked Billy.

"It said, 'It's Adam and Eve, not Adam and Steve!'"

"My turn," said Debra. "I saw mine in the women's washroom.

"What was it?" asked Billy.

"It said, 'Sex is like pizza. Sex when it is good is very good; sex when it is bad is still good!'"

"I saw one in the bathroom, too!" said Billy.

"What was that?" asked Debra.

"It said, 'I used up all my sick days, so I called in dead!'"

\* \* \*

As Billy and the Birdmobile cruised through Philadelphia, the conversation got a little more serious. There was plenty of time to fill Billy's Scrapbook of Life in Ocean City. Ocean City was only a hop, skip, and a jump away from Philadelphia, the crowds still waving at the Birdmobile, their American flags still flying, the money continuing to roll in at every stop they made.

"Let's play Devil's Advocate," said Debra. Devil's Advocate was a favorite game of Debra's on their trip around America.

"Suppose you're at the Presidential Debate and the moderator asks you the following question: 'Billy Pigeon, you say you want to stop spending and start saving, but the first thing you're going to do the day you become president is to spend $2.5 trillion of taxpayers' money building Billy's World. Do you have an answer for that?'"

"I do so, sir," said Billy Pigeon. "That's money—$625 billion per year—I already have budgeted for 2013, 2014, 2015, and 2016, money I'm going to save from bringing all our troops home, from closing all those unnecessary foreign bases, from not having to pay out unemployment insurance to the unemployed who will all be working at either constructing Billy's World or building all the products we need to make Billy's World, building those products at all kinds of factories and plants all across America. All the extra payroll taxes and income taxes paid by all those hard-working Americans and construction workers will come to me, too, so I don't see an issue at all, especially when I'm not going to be paying as much interest on our federal debt when I draw that line in the sand, when I cap federal spending, when I pay off China, and when I start kicking the crap out of our $70 trillion credit card balance. Oh, I forgot, I'm also going to be raking in all that corporate income tax coming in from all the construction companies who will be working like crazy to get Billy's World built on time and on budget, plus 20 million Americans will be employed by those companies in America making Made in America products, paying more payroll and income taxes. The five thousand corporations will be paying more income tax, too, not hiding it in off-shore accounts like the Cayman Islands or Switzerland or other places where they keep their money. I rest my case, Mr. Moderator!"

"You win again!" said Debra.

\* \* \*

The Birdmobile was past Salisbury; you could smell the ocean. Billy had his window down, feeling the fresh ocean breeze. The west coast and east coast pigeons were all gone, gone, gone, and now replaced by beautiful white and gray seagulls. Billy Pigeon was walking on the beach, already planning his lobster dinner, the lobsters all set to go in a big old pot of boiling hot water, with hot butter and big old white buns and white wine. President Obama was wiped, too. The real president was heading out to Martha's Vineyard for his own vacation, to hide from the press, to take no more RPA questions, no more Billy Pigeon questions, no more Billy's World questions, no more job questions, and to just get the hell out of Dodge!

Billy walked the beaches with Julie, his mind totally off work. Debra had no more Devil's Advocate questions. Billy's mind was totally on Julie, her beautiful smile, her brown eyes, and her long black hair. Billy was thinking about hanky-panky and filling his green garbage bag again. Wet kisses and rolling in the sand were top priority, the way it should be for every 18-year-old American boy, even one who was closing in on the presidency, really fast!

\*\*\*

"Don't get mad, get naked!"

\*\*\*

"Don't forget the receipt!" said Walter.

\*\*\*

"People who claim they never let things bother them have never slept with a mosquito!"

\*\*\*

"Need some more time alone, try washing dishes!"

\*\*\*

"Get back there and get that receipt," yelled Walter.
"Sorry," said Billy.
"It was my fault!" said Julie.
"I don't care whose fault it was; just go back and get me my receipt!" yelled Walter.

\*\*\*

"How are a Texas tornado and a Tennessee divorce the same? Someone's going to lose a trailer!"

\*\*\*

"Bite off more than you can chew, and chew it well!"

\*\*\*

"Julie, have I ever told you that you have beautiful eyes?" asked Billy.
"You have beautiful eyes, too!" said Julie.

\*\*\*

"Lost, wife and dog,
$500 reward for return of dog!"

\* \* \*

"If you two forget one more friggin' receipt, I'm going to bite your butts!" said Walter.
"Lighten up," said Debra, "they're on holidays; they're in love!"

\* \* \*

Dear Lord,
I pray for wisdom to understand a man, love to forgive him, and patience for his moods. Because, Lord, if I pray for strength, I'll just beat him to death!"

\* \* \*

"I love you, Billy," said Julie.
"I love you, Julie," said Billy.

\* \* \*

"You can't save your face and your ass at the same time!"

\* \* \*

"Where's your receipt, Walter?" asked Debra.
"Oh shit!" said Walter.

\* \* \*

"Drink till he's cute!"

\* \* \*

"You won't tell Billy and Julie?" asked Walter.
"What's in it for me?" asked Debra.

\* \* \*

"Life is all about *ass,*
You're either covering it,
Laughing it off,
Kissing it,
Kicking it,
Busting it,
Trying to get a piece of it,
Behaving like one,
Or you live with one!"

\* \* \*

Billy was on Google; he read that the population of the world will be 9 billion by 2050!
"Yikes," said Billy, "that's a lot of unemployed kids!"

\* \* \*

Billy was on a different Google site. He was thinking about recessions and depressions. He Googled The Great Depression. He saw a big old sign tacked on the side of a downtown building in Anywhere, America. This is what the sign looked like:

> JOBLESS MEN,
> KEEP GOING,
> WE CAN'T EVEN
> TAKE CARE OF
> OUR OWN JOBLESS.
> CHAMBER OF COMMERCE

"Wow!" said Billy Pigeon to himself.

\* \* \*

Billy Pigeon went to the local library; he found a copy of *The Grapes of Wrath* by the great American writer, John Steinbeck. He laid his head on Julie's lap on the beach. He read the book out loud to Julie over a six-day period. This is what Julie said when Billy read the last word of the last paragraph on the last page: "My God!"

\* \* \*

Billy had also read the book three years ago in Bellevue. The book had a lot more meaning today.

"Do you think people will ever live like that again in America?" asked Julie.

"If I don't become president, they will," said Billy.

"I think we've taken enough of a holiday. I think we should get on the road again," said Julie.

"I agree," said Billy.

"Me, too," said Walter.

"Me, three," said Debra.

\* \* \*

"Billy, we need some new blank pages for our Scrapbook of Life," said Julie.

"I know," said Billy. "It's been a busy book these last three weeks."

\* \* \*

"And don't forget your three bags of bottles and cans," said Julie.

"I won't," said Billy.

\* \* \*

Vacation was over, all done with for another summer, with Billy at the wheel of the Birdmobile again, singing once more to his girlfriend, Julie.

"We owe, we owe,

So off to work we go!"

\* \* \*

Billy Pigeon bypassed Washington, D. C. He did not stop at Go; he did not collect $200. He would spend enough time there as president. He wanted to get out on the road and meet real people, with the Birdmobile cruising through Richmond, Virginia, with the Willie Nelson tape switched to southern music, with Alabama the group of choice, with Billy singing the words out loud:

"Roll on highway,

Roll on along!"

The Birdmobile was now heading for Raleigh, North Carolina, with Debra setting up another press conference, with Billy fielding lots of really good questions, with the press itching to know where Billy's World was going to be built, and what all the unemployed workers were going to build in two short years. The unemployed in America wanted to know what Billy Pigeon really had up his sleeve, whether he was serious or just whistling Dixie and was just another politician from Washington full of hot air and promises, looking for their vote!

The debate went on all across America while Billy Pigeon was cruising down the highway, with people in taverns, at the race tracks, in casinos, in supermarket lineups, in offices, in unemployed lineups at job fairs, on TV sets, and talk show hosts getting their 50 cents worth in:

"Let's see some actual details of Billy's World," said Bill O'Reilly.

"All he's done so far is to give a bunch of pigeons a ride across America," said Ed Schultz, "all talk and no substance!"

\* \* \*

The real Robert Redford was on the telephone talking to the real Dustin Hoffman.

"Did you see the kid in Central Park?" asked Robert Redford. "The one running for president?"

"I sure did," said Dustin Hoffman. "I was standing right next to a young girl he made a hotdog for!"

"What an idea for a new movie," said Robert Redford. "We should call up Hollywood, get all the boys going again, revive our Woodward and Bernstein characters, get them out on the road to check out the kid for the Washington Post, see what he's really up to."

"Great minds think alike," said Dustin Hoffman. "I already did that. They said they would start on a script right away, told me to start growing my hair really long again!"

"I like it. I like it a lot. I think it's got legs!" said Robert Redford.

"I do, too!" said Dustin Hoffman.

\* \* \*

John McBain, the real news editor of the real Washington Post, was in a closed-door meeting with Terry Porter, one of his sharpest and most reliable reporters.

"This kid is really something!" said John McBain. "He keeps teasing us, first with his Reality Party of America, real people with real solutions to real problems, and now a job in two years for every unemployed American building Billy's World, the largest construction project the world has ever seen. Honest to Christ, the fucking kid is driving me crazy!"

John McBain lit a cigarette, he listened to Terry Porter.

"He's either one real sharp cookie, or he's got some brilliant minds behind the scenes planning his every move. That speech to those one million naïve kids in Central Park was ingenious. Kids all over the country are getting worked up. Even my brother's son in Detroit has registered to go to work for him. Can you believe it? Either this lad is the real deal or this whole affair is nothing but a bunch of bullshit!"

"I agree," said John McBain, "and the crazy thing is that nobody knows nothing!"

"I know; I can't believe it myself," said Terry Porter.

"Grab Harvey White, you guys get on the road and start turning over fucking stones. I don't give a shit how much it costs, just find out what that kid is up to and get me a story I can sink my teeth into," said a pissed-off John McBain, a veteran of the Washington political scene, a man not used to the unknown.

\* \* \*

Terry Delaney from Microsoft put in a call to Paul Saunders.

"I was waiting for your call," said Paul Sanders.

"This is all about Billy Pigeon, isn't it," said Terry Delaney. "Microsoft is going to hook up with Billy's World, that's what you have in mind. Billy's World has bugger all to do with Disney."

"Terry, old buddy, old friend, now we know why they pay you the big bucks! Come over to my house tonight; I'll fill you in. But you say nothing to nobody about anything. There's less than ten people in America right now who know what's going on with Billy Pigeon and Billy's World. Billy could be in a lot of danger if the wrong people find out," said Paul Sanders.

"Hey, don't worry, you can trust me," said Terry Delaney.

\* \* \*

It had been a long day at the University of Washington campus. Paul Sanders was looking forward to going home, taking his shoes off, kicking back and having a drink of scotch, maybe even call Debra. Debra was somewhere in Georgia the last time they talked.

Paul had no sooner hung up the phone with Terry Delaney from Microsoft when he heard a loud knock on his office door.

"Exam results will be posted in the morning!" screamed Paul Sanders through his solid wood office door.

Another round of knocking, this time even louder!

Paul Sanders got up from his old wooden chair on wheels, he walked a few steps, and then opened the door.

"Paul Sanders?" asked one of the two tall men in suits.

"I'm Paul Sanders; what can I do for you?" said Paul.

"I'm FBI agent McSwain; this is FBI agent McGill," both FBI agents showed their ID badges. "We'd like to have a talk with you about your relationship with Billy Pigeon!" said FBI agent McSwain.

\* \* \*

After the FBI agents left his office, Paul Sanders called his wife, Debra. This is what he said: "It's time to go fly-fishing again!"

\* \* \*

Julie was reading a poem in their Scrapbook of Life. The poem was "Ode to a Woodpecker." Julie read out loud; it went something like this:

>Wily, wily woodpecker
>
>Come to my house,
>
>Land on my window ledge,
>
>Be quiet as a mouse.
>
>Let me load my pellet gun,
>
>Watch me as I aim,
>
>I'm going to shoot your heart out,
>
>You have no one else to blame!
>
>Go away, go away,
>
>Drop like a fly,

> I hope the ants eat you up,
>
> And you suffer when you die!
>
> When you get to heaven,
>
> Don't hammer on a thing,
>
> Cause Jehovah and I both believe,
>
> That birds should only sing!

"Where did you get the woodpecker poem from?" asked Julie, with Walter still laughing, and Debra busting a gut!

"David H. E. Smith wrote that poem," said Billy. "It was in one of his other books called *Moustafa and Me in World War III.* I have a copy in my bedroom in Bellevue. He wrote the entire manuscript for one person: his best friend Ron. The book is funny as hell!"

\* \* \*

Debra waved to Billy, Walter, and Julie, told them to stop the motor home, and that they had to go for a walk. On the walk, Debra told everybody about Paul getting a visit from the FBI, and that the FBI was probably tapping into their cell phones as we speak, that their motor home was probably bugged, too, and that there would certainly be eyes in the skies for sure!

Debra told them that she and Paul already had a contingency plan all set to go, that they had already set it in motion, that they had a bunch of code words ready that they would change periodically if they were discussing anything to do with Billy's World, that the code words right now had to do with fly-fishing, that anything they had to say about Billy's World when they were on their cell phones, in the Birdmobile and even in their motel rooms, had to be spoken about in a fly-fishing context.

"I love it already!" said Billy.

"We knew you would, Mr. President!" said Debra.

\* \* \*

When Terry Delaney arrived at Paul's house later on that evening, Paul let him in the door. He put his finger to his lips and motioned for Terry to be quiet. He gave Terry a written note. This is what the note said: "I had a visit today from the FBI. Billy is being investigated. There are ears everywhere. He could be in trouble. We're going to go shoot some hoops and we'll talk there."

\* \* \*

Billy Pigeon gave it a week. He checked his e-mail; he was really curious. Eight million young Americans between the ages of ten and nineteen had already signed up to go to war with Billy, with their names signed on the dotted line.

"All right!" said Billy Pigeon to himself.

Billy was pumped; he wanted to share his excitement with Julie, Walter, and Debra. He would try some fly-fishing talk—give it a go.

"I'm really excited about my trout fly collection," said Billy. "I've got eight trout flies from various states already, all colors of flies, all patterns, all shapes and sizes. I told you that I had room in my fly box for twenty flies. I only need 12 more, and my fly-box will be full."

"When do you want to try and find another trout fly, Billy?" asked Debra.

"Let's look for another fly-fishing store in another week or so and see how many more flies I can add to my collection. We should really look hard here in the southern states; see if I can reel me in some big old catfish down here!" said Billy.

"That's a great idea, Billy!" said Debra.

"Will you fry them up for me again?" asked Billy.

"Absolutely," said Debra, "but you'll be the one doing all the cleaning!"

\* \* \*

When Billy Pigeon and the Birdmobile reached Miami, Billy Pigeon said the following to Julie, Walter, and Debra: "My fly box is full. I have 20 trout flies. I don't have to go into any more fishing stores!"

\* \* \*

"How can that be? He hasn't been in a fishing store since Minnesota!" said Tim Jones, an FBI agent from sunny California, from La-La Land.

"Maybe he's been picking up his trout flies at the gas stations and the truck stops and the convenience stores," said FBI agent Sammy Saunders, also from La-La Land.

"But they don't have trout down here in the southern states. It's mostly bass and crappies—those kinds of fish," said Tim Jones.

"Maybe he lucked out, had horse shoes up his butt, got them all from one store that ordered them by mistake, were getting rid of them in a fire sale, who knows, who cares!" said Sammy Saunders.

\* \* \*

Debra called Paul in Seattle and gave him the good news. She told Paul that Billy was stoked, that he had found all twenty trout flies he was looking for, that his fly box was full, that he could forget about fishing right now, that he wanted to try another sport, that he was ready for a new challenge, that it was probably the most difficult sport out there, that he would have to meet that challenge head on, that he wanted to try and master golf, that he was up for the mental challenge of the game, and that he figured he should hit five thousand golf balls before he was ready to go on the course by himself!

"Tell Billy that I've lined up four people who want to play golf with him, who are treading carefully, who haven't played that much golf, but are willing to give it a try, maybe even get some tips from Billy, and that they too are up to the challenges that the great game of golf presents!" said Paul.

\* \* \*

"Do you think I look old?" asked Robert Redford.

"Hell no!" said Dustin Hoffman. "A few wrinkles, some loose skin, but you still have a full head of hair, and you still look good in a sports jacket with patches and your tie loosened up!"

\* \* \*

"I think seagulls are almost as pretty as pigeons!" said Julie.

\* \* \*

Billy was in Tampa, Florida, when he played his first round of golf. He was rock solid. He was joined on the first tee by—surprise, surprise—Steve Ballmer from Microsoft! Billy and Steve dueled all the way to the eighteenth hole. There were ears and eyes everywhere. They talked a lot about Billy's World in code, how golf was a worldwide game, more now than ever before, that there were good players and great golf courses sprouting up everywhere, especially in Asia, but if he had his druthers, he would still like to play in America, not have to get on a big old plane and travel all across the world, that it was expensive to do that, that he would like to relax when he played golf, not have to worry about someone from Asia he didn't know stealing one of his golf clubs when he was busy with someone else trying to learn a new language, that in America, in his own golf and country club, he could lock all his clubs in his own locker, never have to worry about them being stolen.

"That makes a whole lot of sense to me," said Billy Pigeon.

\* \* \*

On the eighteenth hole, Billy hit a sand-wedge out of bounds into the bushes. Steve Ballmer laughed as he hit a nine iron to the green, the golf ball finally stopping three feet or so from the cup. Steve Ballmer tapped the short putt into the bottom of the cup with ease. Steve Ballmer pocketed $20 of Billy Pigeon's hard-earned bottle and can money!

"Just what you need, more money!" said Billy Pigeon.

"It all adds up!" said Steve Ballmer.

"I couldn't have said it any better myself," said Billy Pigeon.

Steve Ballmer and Billy Pigeon laughed all the way to the clubhouse. The Florida press were all over it and asked Mr. Ballmer how his and Billy's golf game was.

"For a couple of novice golfers, I'd say it wasn't bad, not bad at all. We got a lot accomplished; we're going to team up again one day, maybe play another round," said Steve Ballmer.

\* \* \*

Billy took the Birdmobile north on Highway 75, then hung a left on Highway 10, passing through Chattahoochee, De Funiak Springs, Crestview, Milton, and Pensacola. The crowds along the way were boisterous, waving flags, wishing Billy Pigeon a safe journey. Billy came out of the Birdmobile once more and talked to lots of little old ladies. One little old lady told Billy that he was one smart bird for an eighteen-year-old.

"I would have thought I was a strange bird," said Billy Pigeon.

"No, my dear," said the little old lady. "A smart bird, not a strange bird!"

\* \* \*

In Pensacola, Billy Pigeon played golf with Tom Cruise. Tom and his wife, Katie Holmes, were in town on vacation, their kids on the beach playing with the other kids, careful not to step on any tar balls.

Billy told Tom Cruise that he really enjoyed his movie *Top Gun,* that the kiss scene with Kelly McGillis was pretty good, especially when all you could see in the shadows were their two tongues going here, there, and everywhere, that if he ever was going to do a new movie, and if he had another kiss scene, that he, Billy Pigeon, had invented a better kiss than the French kiss, and if he weren't running for president, he would probably have a patent put on his new kiss. His new kiss still involved the tongue; the new kiss was called the Newfoundland kiss, not the French kiss. Julie really liked it, and if his run for the presidency failed, maybe he could give Tom first crack at the new kiss in *Top Gun 2.* Tom Cruise told Billy Pigeon that he could make a lot of money with that patent, that the kiss on the lips and the French kiss were *B-O-R-I-N-G,* that he could probably sell a hundred million copies of the new movie just on the new kiss alone, that he would prefer to call the new movie *The Newfoundland Kiss,* or just *The Kiss,* and Oprah would come absolutely unglued if she knew he had a new movie called *The Kiss.* He would leave the actual new kiss right to the very end, drive the audience wild in anticipation; turn them on so much when they saw the new kiss scene that they all would go home and practice all night long on their own beds. What do you think?

"Sounds good to me," said Billy Pigeon.

"So can you give me one little hint? Maybe Katie and I can give it a whirl tonight," said Tom Cruise.

"Nope, I can't do that!" said Billy Pigeon. "All I will say is that it takes a little practice, the tongue changeover is a little tricky, but once you get the hang of it, the sensation will rock your socks!" said Billy Pigeon.

"Sounds like it!" said Tom Cruise.
"Thanks for the golf game," said Billy Pigeon.
"You're welcome!" said Tom Cruise.

\* \* \*

The Florida press and the national press were all over Billy's golf game with Tom Cruise; so was the FBI. The FBI immediately looked for some connection between Billy and the Scientology movement, that maybe Tom had already convinced Billy and his 20 million young Americans to enter their secret world, and that Billy's World was the new home of the Scientology movement in America. What analysis, what a breakthrough! The FBI Director passed the good news onto President Obama!

\* \* \*

In New Orleans, Billy Pigeon played golf with Drew Brees, the fabulous quarterback for the New Orleans Saints football team. Billy thanked Drew Brees for all the community work he was doing. He was proud of the way Drew was helping the citizens of New Orleans cope with the aftermath of Hurricane Katrina. Drew told Billy that he was also proud of Billy, the way Billy was giving hope to all of America's youth, how he was going to put discipline back in their lives, how he was dealing with the porn issue, how all the young Americans at Billy's World could only look at porn under a blanket with a flashlight, that he might send his own kids to Billy's World, too, when they were old enough, so they wouldn't flick on the TV set and see girls in wet T-shirts or watch *Girls Gone Wild,* or watch all that crap on MTV. He had seen enough of that for one lifetime, thank you very much. Sex should be a private act between a man and a woman. Modern sex was degrading; it was commercialized so much in America that it had lost its innocence and its mystique. A simple kiss on the lips should be more than exhilarating if done the right way, if the man was in love with the woman and the woman in love with the man. The rest of the stuff was sinful!

\* \* \*

"Betcha Drew Brees doesn't take his sweetheart wife to see the new movie *The Kiss,* starring Tom Cruise!" thought Billy Pigeon.

\* \* \*

In Lafayette, Billy played five holes of golf with Steve Jobs from Apple. Steve wore his blue jeans and his black, collarless pullover top. Billy wore his blue jeans, too, with his white, short sleeved shirt. Billy and Steve hit it off big time.

"Nice pullover top!" said Billy Pigeon.
"Nice white shirt!" said Steve Jobs.

\* \* \*

Billy and Steve signed autographs and headed for the first tee. Billy was about to have the most important business meeting of his young presidency, with ten of his security detail from Spokane walking with Steve and Billy. Steve and Billy were pulling their own little carts on wheels, with Steve Jobs saying the following to Billy Pigeon: "I'm okay; the exercise will do me good."

\* \* \*

Guaranteed their privacy, with no need for code words, Billy Pigeon began his sales pitch: "I know exactly what you're like, Steve. I know you're a hard-nosed businessman. I know you like to deal with people who come to the table with their act together. I know how hard you have worked all your life to make Apple the success it is today: the biggest corporation in the world, with 25,000 workers in America, with another 450,000 in China building all your Apple computers and iPhones. I know why you have your products made overseas. I wasn't born yesterday!

"So here's the deal. I'm going to be president in two years. I'm going to build Billy's World; it's not a Theme Park. It will be the largest military, industrial, manufacturing complex in the world. I know you saw my speech at Central Park. Steve Ballmer told me you were impressed. I'm going to take care of the youth of America; they are our future. I'm going to give them all an equal chance in life. No one will ever complain again about financial inequality in America. I'm going to put 20 million young Americans to work in five thousand manufacturing hubs. They will be disciplined; they will be a lean, mean working machine. They will work under the watchful eye of the toughest general in the United States. They will train and then work hard in their uniform coveralls in five thousand state-of-the-art factories. Each manufacturing hub will have its own factory, its own four thousand bed dormitory with a four thousand seat dining hall, and its own shopping mall with its own Apple store. Each hub will also have its own one thousand room hotel for visiting parents. The kids will build made in America products. They will revive the American manufacturing sector. Each of the five thousand factories will have its own training center, its own raw material warehouse, and its own Admin Building. The five thousand factories will be connected by train and truck to Boeing747 cargo jets at our 20-mile-long runway, and four gigantic airports, with factory orders flown by plane to any location on the planet Earth, taken by rail and highways to any city and town in America. The 20 million workers will be paid minimum wage. They will be happy campers because 80 percent of their wages will go into their savings accounts. They will leave Billy's World with $50,000 each after they have committed their five-year Pledge of Allegiance to their country. They can sign on for five more years, do another tour of duty in my War on Jobs, and leave with $100,000 in their blue jeans. There will be no unions at Billy's World, no strikes, and no labor disruptions of any kind.

"You do the math! If you bring your 450,000 Chinese jobs to Billy's World, at a cost say of $14,000 a year per worker, which comes to a grand total of $6.3 billion per year in wages you have to pay, plus a $200,000,000 contractual fee per year per hub to Billy's World. Then you have no more Chinese workers, no more theft of corporate secrets. The $6.3 billion in extra wages and the contractual fee per hub is peanuts compared to your annual profits, plus you'll save a ton on shipping costs and not have to send corporate executives to China to keep an eye on your businesses there and to train new workers to set up new product lines to keep China happy.

"I'm investing $2.5 trillion of taxpayers' money into Billy's World. I'm going to ask you and 4,999 other corporate giants to do the same thing, to bring your overseas profits home, to spend the piles and piles of corporate cash you have sitting on the sidelines collecting dust and provide the other $2.5 trillion needed to build Billy's World. It is a $500 million investment per company, per hub, a $5 trillion injection into the U. S. manufacturing sector. The American economy will be on fire during the four-year construction phase, with Apple providing a shit-load of computers to Billy's World. Unemployment will be at zero in America, all the profits of Billy's World will go to pay off—not down, but off—in twenty-four short years, all of our $70-trillion debt. America will be a land of savers, not spenders, with oodles of cash and credit cards and lines of credit at zero to buy your latest version of the iPhone or whatever else you and your creative mind are about to come up with. America will be prosperous and the world leader once more, the way it should be. America will be changed politically, economically, and morally—three birds killed with one stone," said Billy. After he finished talking, Billy hit another sand wedge; the golf ball went out of bounds and into the bushes again!

\* \* \*

Steve Jobs was quiet—really quiet. They were walking slowly back to the clubhouse. Steve Jobs finally spoke. This is what he said: "I'll take twenty hubs to start with. I'll create 80,000 jobs for young Americans. I'll bump it up big-time if your Billy's World is a success; it will give me fantastic leverage with the Chinese! And if you figure out a way to replace the 30,000 Chinese engineers I have working on our products in China, I'll give you those jobs too!"

\* \* \*

Billy was elated. He shook Steve Job's right hand. He said the following: "Work with Debra. She's good at keeping secrets and at surprising people, too—at hitting home runs every time she goes to bat. She's also going to be my vice president!"

"Good choice," said Steve Jobs. "I've talked to her already; she seems to have her shit together. I like that in a person, especially a person I'm going to do business with, to hopefully form a long-term business relationship.

"Mum's the word!" said Billy.

"Mum's the word!" said Steve Jobs.

\* \* \*

"Let's pick a place. Steve and I will gather your other 4,998 CEOs in one room. We'll do it late at night when we won't garner any attention. We won't wear our business shirts. We won't tell them what we're up to. We'll get them in the room, and then it's up to you to do the sell job, just like you sold me on Billy's World," said Steve Jobs.

"Sounds good to me," said Billy. "I couldn't have asked for anything more! I appreciate your commitment to Billy's World, I really do."

"No problem," said Steve Jobs. "America has been good to me, and like my friend Steve Ballmer said, it's time to give back to America, to take care of our young people, to give them an opportunity, to see if they'll change their ways."

\* \* \*

"Billy," said Julie.

"What sweetie?" asked Billy.

"Could we go for a walk? I'd like another one of those Newfoundland kisses," said Julie. "They're really good."

# 20

## Piss on the Alamo

"Dad, if it was the Super Bowl and you were six points down at the two-minute warning and you were at your three yard line, with first and ten, who would you sooner have as your quarterback, Drew Brees or John Elway?" asked Billy Pigeon.

"John Elway," said Walter, "in a heartbeat!"

"Me, too, I feel the same way," said Billy Pigeon.

"Why the question?" asked Walter.

"I was just thinking," said Billy.

\*\*\*

Debra called Paul in Seattle and told him that Billy had played enough golf, that Steve Jobs had bought him 20 brand new golf balls, that they were in the bag, all tucked away, that they were all top-flight, really good balls, that Billy had enough balls now to stop anywhere, to play golf with anybody in America, and that his confidence was at an all-time high!

Debra added some more vital information. "We're going to go to Las Vegas, play the slot-machines, maybe watch a show or two, play some blackjack, and roll some dice, but the real reason Billy wants to go to Vegas is to try a new sport besides fly-fishing and golf. He's now going to try his hand at poker, maybe get in on a hand with Jackie Chan, his poker hero!"

"When are you heading to Las Vegas?" asked Paul.

"Probably in a month or so. Billy wants to spend a lot of the time in the desert, really check out the lay of the land. He's never seen the desert before. He wants to see how well his kite flies, how hot and sunny it gets, photograph some desert dogs, maybe even get a top-notch close-up photo of a big old snake, drive a dune buggy for sure, race Julie in her Jeep Wrangler, do a Baja race of their own at midnight, and have some fun. He said to tell you that all work and no play make Billy a dull boy!" said Debra.

"I think I'll fly out to Vegas when you get there. I could use a break. It will be nice to see you and Julie in the flesh!" said Paul.

"Julie and I would love that. Vegas and in the flesh, it doesn't get any better than that!" said Debra, sharp as a whip with her quick wit. "Love you, sweetie."

"Love you, too!" said Paul.

\* \* \*

"Mr. President, quite frankly, I don't know what to make of it all," said the FBI Director. "One day he's talking about collecting trout flies, then he's into golf. He's mixing with everybody, celebrities like Tom Cruise and Drew Brees and business people like Steve Ballmer and Steve Jobs. He played a round with each of them; they laughed, they kidded around, they all played lousy golf!"

"What did they talk about?" asked President Obama.

"When he played golf with Steve Ballmer, they only talked about golf. He was talking kissing with Tom Cruise and keeping porn away from kids with Drew Brees, and that's about it. We heard nothing when he golfed with Steve Jobs. We even had an FBI caddy all set to carry Steve Jobs' clubs, but Steve Jobs insisted on pulling a little golf bag around on wheels and they were completely surrounded by Billy Pigeon's own security detail from Spokane, and they're good at what they do—really good. They've got to be ex-military, that's for sure," said the FBI Director.

"Anything else?" asked the president.

"Not much; we've sat around and talked about it a lot. We've already mentioned the Scientology Movement possibility. We're analyzing all the data. We think now he's trying to make it look like he's rounding up investors for Billy's World, but he doesn't have a pot to piss in. I can tell you, though, he's up to $200 million and counting in his campaign war chest, but $200 million won't build piss all, especially if he's talking about the largest construction project on the planet Earth.

"To be honest, we think that this is the biggest con job ever pulled on American soil. It would put Paul Newman and Robert Redford's con in the movie *The Sting* to shame, big-time, that a whole lot of people are involved besides Billy Pigeon, and that this is all about collecting campaign donations. How'd you like to be on a motor home pretending to be a presidential candidate and all you have to do is smile, look good on TV, give a few speeches to rally the troops and the money just keeps rolling in, and pretty soon, when you reach that magic number, whatever it is, you will say, "Thank you very much, suckers. It was a slice; see you later, alligator!" said the FBI Director.

President Obama paced the Oval Office. He thanked the FBI director for all the hard work he was putting into the Billy Pigeon file and for his frank assessments and analysis. He told the FBI Director to keep on listening, and that they might get their big break soon.

\* \* \*

"I wouldn't mind heading up to Dallas, maybe having a chitchat with Jerry Jones, see his new digs for the Dallas Cowboys, and see if he's still dancing with the devil!" said Billy Pigeon.

"Forget it, Mr. President; you are not going to Dallas. Forget it—don't even think about it!" said Debra Sanders.

"Well, let's head west, then. I want to take a drive in that dune buggy, take a look at the land, take those photos I wanted to take, and go to some college basketball games in New Mexico, Arizona, and Nevada," said Billy Pigeon.

\* \* \*

"Jesus Christ, now he's into college basketball!" said the FBI Director.

\* \* \*

"Billy, the seagulls are all gone," said Julie. "The four-foot-tall, carved, one-legged pigeon is all alone!"

\* \* \*

"Don't forget your receipt!" yelled Walter.

\* \* \*

"My Jeep's starting to fill up again!" said Julie. "Find another bottle depot!"

\* \* \*

"Jesus loves you, but everyone else thinks you're an asshole!"

\* \* \*

"Weekends: brought to you by the Labor Movement."

\* \* \*

"Billy, I'd like another Newfoundland kiss!" said Julie.

\* \* \*

"He who laughs last, laughs the slowest!"

\* \* \*

"There's a big old hawk circling the motor home. I think he's going to land. No, he just took a look; he's gone again!" said Julie.

\* \* \*

"Attitude is everything!"

\* \* \*

"Did anyone see the receipt I had on the counter? I know I left it there. Would someone help me, please!" yelled Walter.

\* \* \*

"Unlike the mall, I bare it all!"

\* \* \*

"Billy, let's go for another walk. It's a beautiful sunset!" said Julie.

\* \* \*

"Why do men fart more than women? Because women talk so much that their mouths are never closed long enough to build up pressure!" said Billy. Debra busted a gut, with Walter also busting a gut big-time.

\* \* \*

"It's better to die on your face than live on your knees!"

\* \* \*

"If it weren't for the last minute, nothing would get done!"

\* \* \*

"Stop, quick, stop!" yelled Walter. "My receipt just blew out the goddamn window!" Debra was busting a gut again.

\* \* \*

"Grow your own dope;
Plant a man!"

\* \* \*

"People sure speak their mind in this neck of the woods!" said Julie.
"Tell me about it!" said Billy Pigeon. "I hope you're getting it all down on paper."
"Every last word, sweetie!" said Julie.

\* \* \*

"Goddamn it!" yelled Walter.
"What's wrong now?" asked Billy.
"A receipt just went down between the dash and the bloody windshield!" said Walter, with Debra busting a gut again.
"It's a good thing you're not my wife!" said Walter, with Debra busting a gut even more!

\* \* \*

The Birdmobile kept on Highway 10 from Houston to San Antonio, all across Texas to El Paso.
"Texas is huge!" said Billy Pigeon. "No wonder the Mexicans can find places to hide!"

"Tell me about it!" said Walter, still counting money, the campaign donations still rolling in, the total now over $300 million and counting. Mrs. Larson from Billy's bank was on the blower to Billy to tell him that he was now a member of the prestigious 300 Million Club, that as of this very moment, the interest rate he was paying on his line of credit was being lowered even more, and that she could bump up his $50,000 line of credit to any number he wanted, as long as it was below 300 million!

"That's okay," said Billy Pigeon. "I'm more than happy with my $50,000 line. I'll let you know if I ever want it bumped up!"

\* \* \*

From Highway 10, Billy and the Birdmobile hooked into Highway 25 to Albuquerque. Billy totally focused on the landscape, the lay of the land.

"I like it; I like it a lot," said Billy Pigeon. "We could build Billy's World here for sure!"

\* \* \*

The Birdmobile hung another left at Albuquerque, got on Highway 40 and headed west through Arizona, with Billy catching a college basketball game in Phoenix. The University of Arizona played the Runnin' Rebels from Las Vegas, the game going down to the last shot, a win for the home team. The University of Arizona basketball team presented a signed basketball to Billy Pigeon, with the home team and everyone in the packed stadium cheering on Billy, the college kids telling Billy that if they weren't registered in college, they would certainly go to war and sign up at Billy's World for a five-year tour of duty.

Billy thanked them for their comments, telling the college kids that Billy's World wasn't for everybody, with different strokes for different folks, and that he was only taking in 20 million of the 40 million kids between ten and nineteen. America still needed doctors, lawyers, accountants, teachers, research scientists, and engineers—lots of engineers—he understood that fully. He was focused on helping all the young Americans who couldn't help themselves: the ones who weren't motivated in school, who came from broken homes and families, families who didn't have the disposable income to send their kids to college, poor kids and messed up kids with little direction in their lives, kids who spent their nights wandering the streets of America and getting themselves in a heap of trouble, kids who needed discipline and guidance and hope in their lives.

The college kids from the University of Arizona had an even greater appreciation of their future president when he left the campus, when he was ready to, in the immortal words of that iconic rock band Steppenwolf:

"Get your motor runnin'

Head out on the highway

Lookin' for adventure

And whatever comes our way."

    Billy continued to drive to the White House in 2012. God bless you, Billy Pigeon, God speed. Hope you have a safe and productive trip around America, you and your one-legged pigeon!

    "Oh, by the way," said David Turner, a fourth-year nursing student, "it doesn't seem fair that after four years of college, I'll owe $50,000 in student loans, and a graduate of Billy's World ends up with $50,000 cash in his or her blue jeans, and no debt. Could you fix that disparity, Mr. President?"

    "I'll work on it," said Billy Pigeon. "What's your e-mail address?"

\* \* \*

    The highway was full of traffic, with Arizona State Troopers now leading the way. The sun was pelting into the old Birdmobile and the temperature was rising; their old Chevy motor home had nothing but Mexican air conditioning, with every window in the old girl rolled down and pulled across for fresh air. Walter had a big old flat rock sitting on top of his day-old receipts on the motor home table; the receipts were slated to be filed in a big old box in their next motel room. Debra and Julie's long black hair was blowing in the wind. Walter was smoking a big old cigar, and he kicked back, sucking on a Bud Lite, with his receipts safe as a bug in a rug, loving every moment of the trip!

    "Arizona has potential," thought Billy Pigeon, "lots of sun for the solar panels, plenty of wind for the wind turbines, great roads and railway lines, and lots of wide open spaces!"

\* \* \*

    "We've just got to see the Grand Canyon!" said Julie.

    "I agree," said Billy Pigeon, hooking a right at Williams and getting on Highway 64 for the drive to Grand Canyon Village, and then the canyon itself.

    "Wow!" said Julie.

    "Wow!" said Billy.

    "Wow!" said Walter.

    "Wow!" said Debra.

\* \* \*

    Once that was out of their systems, the Birdmobile headed north, up Highway 89, then Highway 9, then southwest on Highway 15 toward Las Vegas.

"How much time do we have?" asked Billy.

"Another week," said Debra. Billy turned the Birdmobile north, with three beautiful hawks now riding up top with the four-foot-tall, carved, one-legged pigeon. Julie was pleased as punch, wondering if her hawks would want road kill or if crunchy croutons would still do the trick!

"Road kill!" said Walter.

"Road kill!" said Billy.

"Road kill!" said Debra.

Julie had a weak stomach. She thought of David H. E. Smith's disgusting woodpecker poem, with all the ants crawling all over and eating that suffering woodpecker. She thought of all the poor rabbits getting creamed by all the big trucks and cars ripping by on the open highway—the poor rabbits done like dinner—and Julie having to stoop down and pick up a dead rabbit or a dead skunk or a dead desert dog and walk up on the ladder and having to feed it to the hawks, with the brains sticking out and all the guts and intestines dragging on the ground, with the three hawks ripping and ripping at the road kill in Julie's outstretched hand!

"Yuk!" said Julie.

\* \* \*

"I like what I see," said Billy Pigeon. "I really like what I see in Nevada; this is the place to build Billy's World. This is why I had to take my trip, to get a first hand look. Billy and the Birdmobile cut all the way across the state to Reno, the expanse of desert immense, all the sand and the sagebrush, the coyotes howling at night over their prey, and the wind swirling and gusting. Billy was all excited, all wound up, tighter than a popcorn fart, with the Birdmobile zipping all the way down to Las Vegas again, this time along the Californian border.

"Nevada it is!" thought Billy Pigeon. "If they can build Las Vegas from nothing, then I can do the same thing, only much, much, much bigger, on a grander scale, maybe even get some Vegas money to help finance my service city outside the fence around Billy's World!"

Billy couldn't help but notice all the Mexicans living and working in this part of the country.

"Good thing I'm going to have Billy's World surrounded by a big old high fence guarded 24/7 by U. S. soldiers with guns!" thought Billy Pigeon.

\* \* \*

"Shit!" screamed Billy Pigeon. "We forgot to go to the Alamo when we were in Texas!"

"Piss on the Alamo!" said Walter. "Did you know that Davy Crockett was my hero when I was a boy? Did you know I saw all of his movies on Walt

Disney Presents on Sunday nights, and the thought of having to go to the place where all those goddamn Mexicans killed my Davy Crockett and his buddy James Bowie, the guy with the big Jesus Bowie knife, is enough to make me want to puke. That's why I don't want to see any more goddamn Mexicans on this trip. I've seen more Mexicans than I can stomach for one lifetime, thank you very much!"

# 21

## Religious Meeting in Progress

Debra and Steve Jobs were bang-on in their assessment when they selected Las Vegas as the place for Billy Pigeon to meet the corporate elite of American business. The town was *so* busy. There were planes coming and buses going, buses coming and planes going, people racing everywhere at breakneck speed, all in a hurry to get somewhere, to meet someone, to do something, to find their fortune somehow, someway in Sin City. Not a person in Las Vegas had any idea that Steve Jobs from Apple and Steve Ballmer from Microsoft had gathered 4,998 other American business leaders with the click of their fingers, with a little arm-twisting—not much, mind you—and that all five thousand business leaders were dispersed throughout the city, amongst the throngs of happy and sad campers staying in motels and hotels all over town. They had left their corporate jets at home and had all flown commercial in regular coach with all the regular Joes of the world and all the regular Joannes of the world. They had left their suits and ties at home, too, with no large gathering of corporate executives at their side, walking with them, barking out every step they were to take. There was none of that stuff. Nobody in America had a clue what was going on in Las Vegas that day. It was so covert, so perfect; the CIA would have been proud of Debra and Steve Jobs for pulling this off and for Debra's attention to little details.

Billy, Julie, Walter, and Debra stayed in a little plain-Jane motel Billy found on the outskirts of town. The beds were squeaky as hell, having had years of humping and pumping; the bed springs were tired as hell, too!

"You can do it, Mr. President!" said Debra. "I have all the confidence in the world in you. Your five thousand letters of intent will be there, all five thousand of them. We just need their John Hancocks and we're good to go, like pre-selling condos before they're built!"

All the corporate CEOs were well-versed in the routine, with the e-mails sent for their eyes only. Steve Jobs told them to slip into the Sands Convention Center at the Venetian at midnight, that it was an historic meeting in American business, that they had to be there for America, to wear shorts and sandals and Hawaiian shorts, to look like beach bums, not James Bond at the Casino Royale, to carry no briefcases, to have their dark sunglasses on and wear a baseball cap or a big old straw hat, to be creative, that there was even a bottle of 50-year-old scotch for the best outfit, to bring no iPhones or BlackBerries, maybe hit the slot machines, play a little bingo or blackjack before slipping past the two security guards in purple sports jackets, white shirts, purple ties and gray pants, and the passwords to get in were Marilyn Monroe. Billy Pigeon looked like a tourist in his motel room as he listened to Julie say the following: "Can I please have one more Newfoundland kiss?"

\* \* \*

Billy and Julie took a cab to the Venetian at 11:00 p.m. precisely; Walter and Debra had gone hours earlier to set up the convention center. The FBI was all over Billy and Julie.

"What's he up to now?"

"I have no idea."

"Follow that cab."

"They're heading into town."

"Probably going to play some poker."

"Or take in a show."

"At this time of night?"

"The lights are on 24/7 in this town!"

"They're pulling into the Venetian."

"Follow their every move."

"Yes, sir!"

The five thousand corporate CEOs began slipping into the Sands Convention Center at 11:30 p.m., the majority surprised—no, totally shocked—to see so many of their pals in business all gathering in one room, with the CEOs all getting a kick out of all the colorful shirts and shorts and T-shirts and dresses and skirts and hats on display. All of them were eagerly awaiting their guest speaker, who had been divulged to no one. It had to be someone special: maybe President Obama, maybe the Pope, maybe the leader of Russia or China, maybe Warren Buffett from Berkshire Hathaway, or maybe Ben Bernanke from the Fed. Who knows? The CEOs were never stopped by anyone in Las Vegas and never asked what they were doing here. The CEOs were just part of the crowd. The Venetian was rocking on a Saturday night, with thousands and thousands of people laughing and shouting and yelling and walking and running here, there, and everywhere. Billy Pigeon was on the move at 11:53 p.m., followed closely by the two FBI agents in suits—the two FBI agents in suits stood out like a sore thumb. Billy got through security easily. The big sign on the double door entrance to the convention center said the following:

> RELIGIOUS
> MEETING
> IN PROGRESS

\* \* \*

The two FBI agents came to a grinding halt, as if stuck in the mud.
"The passwords, please," said one of the security detail from Spokane.
"Jesus Saves!" said one of the FBI agents.
"Sorry, try again!" said the security man.
"Angels from heaven!" said the other FBI agent.
"Sorry, you guys are shit out of luck!" said the security man.
"Do you mind if we wait here, sit over there in those two chairs?" asked one of the FBI agents.
"Go ahead, be my guest, the more the merrier!" said the security man.
"So what's with the meeting?" asked one of the FBI agents.
"Have no idea!" said the security man.

\* \* \*

Billy Pigeon walked directly to the stage. He was soon sitting on his chair, his dark sunglasses placed on top of his straw golf hat, with Steve Jobs to his left, and Steve Ballmer to his right. The 4,998 other business CEOs were in shock and awe, talking to themselves:
"It's the kid running for president!"
"That's Billy Pigeon!"
"Holy Crap!"
"I saw him on TV in Central Park!"
"What a treat!"
"Can you believe this?"
"Unreal!"
"This should be something!"
Steve Jobs stood up; he looked good in his dark gray collarless pullover and blue jeans. Billy looked equally as good in his white, short-sleeved shirt, and his blue jeans!

Steve Jobs thanked all the CEOs for coming. He was a businessman and wasted little time on pleasantries. He exerted very little energy; he handed the microphone to Billy Pigeon.

"Nice to see all of you tonight," said Billy Pigeon, "and I must say you all look fabulous!" Billy dropped the 18-year-old boy from Bellevue routine, the "rah-rah-rah" approach he used in Central Park. He was dealing with five thousand of the sharpest minds in America, possibly the world. Billy was all business.

The audience laughed at Billy's opening line; they were quiet again.

> I want to welcome all of you to an historic event in American business. You are America! I know for a fact that young people in America are getting ready to protest big-time. I know why you are taking your manufacturing jobs overseas, why you are outsourcing, why you have the majority of your manufactured products you sell in America and around the world produced in China, India, Japan, Mexico, and dozens of other foreign countries. I understand we are a global economy, why GM would build a plant in China to build cars for a new foreign market, why they would want to be producing cars there and not in America. I say fill your boots; do what you have to do to be competitive. But we don't have to build everything overseas. We also have an obligation to America—to its youth. We have to give them hope; without our youth, America will have no future. We have to put them on an equal footing, give them an opportunity at their own American Dream, let them lead the world in the twenty-first century, not riot in the streets, express their disgust at the capitalist system, feel that their concerns are never taken seriously by government, and that they will never ever have a job.
>
> America once produced almost 50 percent of our goods in America. We stamped our goods with our Made in America label; now less than 10 percent of our manufactured goods are produced in our own country. That's a shame. Who do we blame?
>
> I know you are taxed to the max by our bloated federal government in Washington. I know you are regulated to death by agencies like the EPA; even more regulations are coming down the pipe from Washington because of the recent financial crisis on Wall Street. I know how tough credit is to get for large and small businesses in America, how much pressure is being put on our financial institutions to be adequately capitalized, how much of the blame they are taking for the financial crisis. There's enough blame to go around: the lenders, the government pushing the lenders to lend, to give everyone in America an opportunity to buy a home, the buyers who signed on the dotted line when they knew that they had no business signing on the dotted line in the first place. We can play the blame game all night long. I'm not here tonight to do any of that. I want to learn from the past, deal with the present, and the future will take care of itself!

I know for a fact that federal government spending is out of control, that Washington politicians spend all of our tax money for all the wrong reasons, that there is no end to government spending, with money poured down the drain on desperate stimulus packages for infrastructure projects to get the party in power through the next election—all temporary projects with no real solutions to the real problems of the American economy. The government in Washington is in gridlock, our federal debt at $70 trillion and counting, with Washington playing political games with our deficits and debt, kicking the can down the road for future generations of Americans to deal with, with no real plan to stop spending, to get rid of the deficit, to cap spending, to actually slay the dragon of debt breathing down our backs. Our country is on the verge of economic collapse, similar to that of Russia, with desperate Democrats offering business tax breaks and payroll tax holidays, with no clue whatsoever that money has to come from somewhere to pay for these tax reductions, the money having to come from business and ordinary taxpayers when the smoke settles and reality takes over.

I am forming my own political party, the Reality Party of America—real people with real solutions to real problems! I will answer to no one except the American people. I will not be bought or sold by big business or the labor movement. I will do what is right for America. I will fix what is wrong in our economy.

I know your cost to produce goods in the United States is outrageous. I know some of you are paying over $75 an hour, and probably more, to produce products in America to feed an appetite for material things brought on by access to credit that Americans never, ever had when they lived within their means, paid their bills on time, and saved money for a rainy day. Abuse of credit has produced serious, even fatal results for American consumers. The American consumer is up to his or her ying-yang in debt, looking to all five thousand of you to bail them out, to pay them way more money than they are worth, and if you don't pay them what they want, they have work slowdowns, call in sick, disrupt the flow of goods in a fast moving economy, and they go on strike!

I know that union demands and non-union demands are killing you, that wages and benefits and health care costs and pension plans are affecting your bottom line big-time, forcing you to move entire production facilities overseas, to go find workers in other countries who will produce your products for a lot less—a hell of a lot less than your American workers—forcing you to pay for extra-shipping costs, for extra everything costs. Your profits are left overseas so you don't have to pay more taxes, to be double-taxed by our bloated federal government in Washington, with all kinds of corporate cash sitting in your bank accounts collecting dust. I know how vital it is that we do it right this time around, that we rebuild our manufacturing sector, that we provide jobs to every American who is unemployed right now—over 19 million of them—that we revive our ailing economy, that we get the economic engine of America firing again on all cylinders, and that we revive the American Dream.

As your president, I am committed to rebuilding America, politically, economically, and morally. I have a plan, but I need you to help—all five thousand of you tonight in this room! I would really appreciate it if we stick to the old adage, 'What happens in Vegas stays in Vegas.'

The laughter began again, and then there was total silence.

If I don't become president, then all of this is for nothing. That is why we had the cloud of secrecy over tonight's meeting. I will present my plan for America at the Presidential Debate in Washington in 2012; if word of what I'm about to tell you leaks out before then, I'm toast! The future of America is on your shoulders, right here, right now. I'm a risk-taker. I am risking my presidency, but to me the risk is worth it. I'm sick and tired of all the political bullshit in America. We, all 5,001 of us, are going to fix America, starting right here, right now! So here we go; hold onto your shorts, because I'm about to take you all on a wild ride!

My plan for America is called Billy's World, the design of which is well underway. The diagrams and cost analysis are with the architects and engineers as we speak; we are 90 percent complete, with some minor adjustments to go—I hope!

I have 20 million young Americans, between the ages of ten and nineteen, signed, sealed, and delivered to work at Billy's World in six short years, to change the culture of spending in America and actually save money—a new generation of Americans ready to draw a line in the sand—a new generation of Americans who will pay off our federal debt of $70 trillion in twenty-four years with the profits of Billy's World—a new generation of Americans who are committed to my values of discipline, hard work, and family values—not sex, drugs, and rock and roll, and calling in sick so they can sleep till noon.

I need you—all five thousand of you—to give them a place to work. As your president, the day I am elected, I will unleash the power of America like it's never been unleashed before. We will showcase American ingenuity and technical know-how like it's never been showcased before! I plan to start building, on the first day of my presidency, the largest military, industrial, manufacturing complex ever build by man; it will be named Billy's World.

I will kick in, over a four-year period, $2.5 trillion of taxpayers' money to house, feed, and clothe those 20 million workers, and I want you to match that. I want you, the leaders of corporate America, to unleash another $2.5 trillion of your money, which I know you have sitting on the sidelines. I need $500 million from each of you. I want you to invest that money in America. I want each of you to put up your own state-of-the-art factory, with a training center teaching applicable trades for each factory and a raw material storage facility, all to employ these 20 million young Americans to produce Made in America products.

And here's the really good part! Billy's World will have five thousand manufacturing hubs, each hub will have a factory and a ten-story dormitory to house four thousand workers; beneath each dormitory will be a massive dining hall and kitchen. There will also be a shopping mall and a one thousand room, five-star motel for visitors and guests.

The 20 million kids will be motivated to work. They will be under the command of the toughest general I can find in America—the toughest son of a bitch in the land. All 20 million young Americans will sign a Pledge of Allegiance to go to my War on Jobs at Billy's World for five years. They will all leave Billy's World happy campers. They will all have $50,000 in their blue jeans to give them an equal jump on the rest of their lives. There will be no more financial inequality in America—the way it should be. I will be putting 80 percent of their money into a savings account; the other 20 percent they can budget and spend at Billy's World. They will be paid minimum wage. Your wage cost per worker per year will be roughly $14,000—that's it!

They will all have their regular taxes taken out like all other American workers. There will be no overtime. They will work forty hours a week, from 8:00 a.m. to 4:00 p.m., with their nights and weekends off. They will never say the word *union* or the words *you owe me a pension plan!* I will have five hundred hospitals at Billy's World, as well as attached dental centers to take care of their medical and dental at no cost to you.

My 20 million workers will quickly, and I mean quickly, be made into lean, mean, working machines. They will fight our War on Jobs here in America. There will be no drugs at Billy's World. They will have their hair cut like they were in a real army. They will wear a uniform when they're not working, and a pair of uniform coveralls to work in, with an American flag on their chest; they will look impressive! They will exercise nightly for an hour under their military commander. There will only be alcohol served at Billy's World at taverns and bars and lounges. They will only be served liquor in those establishments if they are twenty-one. Smoking will be tolerated in designated smoking areas. We will try and wean them off cigarettes completely. There will be no junk food allowed. Pornography will not be tolerated in any way, shape, or form. The 20 million kids will say *excuse me, yes sir, yes ma'am, what can I do for you next!* We will provide them with the largest recreation center ever built by man. We will produce a new generation of Americans at Billy's World—no ifs, ands or buts. You will have workers who will compete with any foreign worker you can find to put up against them. This I will guarantee!

We will have the best plane, train, and trucking system to ship your raw materials in and to ship your finished products out. We will have accommodations for your company executives and your company training staff on site. We are bringing our troops home, especially our boots. They will oversee and secure all of Billy's World from terrorists and illegal immigrants, to make sure our five trillion dollar investment is protected and not put in harm's way. The military will have their own military base. They will control all access to and from the site. They will also train to help a neighbor and a friend overseas in their time of need, and to deal with any foreign boots coming on our soil. I have so much more I could tell you about Billy's World, it would take the whole night. I will save it for the Presidential Debate with my power point presentation. I think you get my point!

Maybe you can go to China and get a baseball cap made for 93 cents and sell it for $22.95 in New York City, but I'm asking you not to do that anymore. Steve Jobs from Apple has signed up for 20 hubs already; he will now employ 80,000 young American workers at Billy's World, with a verbal commitment to hire more American kids if I can produce a first-class facility, a facility to produce quality Apple products in six short years! At $14,000 per worker, your labor costs are peanuts. If it works for Apple, it should certainly work for you. Thank you, Steve Jobs, you are a visionary. You are a real American business icon. I salute you here tonight, as well as Steve Ballmer from Microsoft. Microsoft also signed on the dotted line. What a fantastic start to Billy's World! Thank you, Mr. Ballmer; you, too, are a visionary. You, too, can see the forest for the trees!

I'm asking all of you in the audience tonight, here in the fabulous city of Las Vegas, to make a similar commitment: to commit to me, to the future of America, and to America's youth who need a helping hand in today's difficult and complex world. I want you to give a lot to get a lot. I will create for you a new generation of American workers who will make America proud!

If we do this right—and I know we can, and we will—the American economy will be on fire! With one stroke of my pen in two short years from now, at the Oval Office, I will unleash six thousand construction companies to build Billy's World. They will immediately employ 6 million unemployed Americans; the other 13 million unemployed people will go to work in your factories and your plants all over America making all the concrete, steel, plastic pipe, building blocks, aluminum siding, copper tubing, electrical wiring, and millwork products we need just for the buildings. We also need the fencing, the roadways, the train tracks, the airports, and the list goes on a mile long. We need planes, trucks, buses, and trains built; we need uniforms made, and computers built. We need to do it all over again at the military base and the 2 million person service city outside Billy's World. You get the point: this thing is gigantic! The orders for materials will be huge; it will boggle your mind. We will build Billy's World in four years. During that time, America will prosper; American companies will prosper like they never have prospered before. Wall Street will explode, but don't buy your stocks for another two years, please!"

There was more laughter, then silence.

Americans will have money again—money to spend on your products. Unemployment will be at zero. Our 20 million young workers will be itching to go to work, running to their factories to begin making Made in America products; China will be pissed! All the Asian countries will be pissed! We will have to put NORAD on high alert for incoming nuclear weapons aimed at Billy's World, but the Air Force will handle that bullshit; I have total faith in them!

War is not pretty! You have winners—you have losers. The winner will be America; the winner will be you! In five years, each manufacturing hub will produce four thousand skilled and trained workers for your plants and factories all over America. You'll have the pick of the litter: workers with discipline, without a desire for two houses and six cars and four flat-screen TVs, with quality of life more important than quantity of life, workers happy with a sixteen-dollar-an-hour job, with lots of room to give them appreciated raises, workers who will be fiscally responsible, who will make America proud, who will buy Made in America products at stores all across the land. You can all keep your corporate secrets at home, all safe and tucked away in your corporate offices. You can still do your R&D here, too. All I want is an opportunity to build your products in America, to have those products built right here in the good old U. S. of A. by a new generation of Americans who will never, ever again stress out on debt, who will never again be so in debt that they stop spending and put us in recession again, a new generation of Americans who will never, ever again let government in Washington run deficits and build up another gigantic debt causing even more recessions. We need a leader in Washington who will restore confidence in America, who will lead by example, who will be a risk taker: that leader is me. My name is Billy Pigeon!

Under my leadership, the economic engine of America will run as smooth as silk, with no sputtering, no stops and starts, an economic engine you can count on whenever you turn the key!

God bless you and God bless the United States of America!

\* \* \*

Wow! Was that a speech, or what!

\* \* \*

Billy Pigeon reached for a glass of water. He watched and listened as five thousand of the sharpest minds in America all stood up and gave Billy Pigeon a standing ovation that lasted for over ten minutes, with chants filling the convention room: "Sign me up—sign me up—sign me up!"

\* \* \*

"Here we go!" said one of the FBI agents sitting outside the convention center door. "They're all headed to the front of the room. God is going to make them better and heal every ailment they have. I hate that part about religion!"

"Me too. It's such a farce, a real turn-off; it really is!" said the second FBI agent.

\* \* \*

Billy Pigeon left the convention center just after 3:00 a.m., with one large cardboard box filled with five thousand signed letters of intent. The letters of intent would be followed in a week by an actual contract after board ratifications. Billy put the box on a dolly and rolled it through the double doors into the lobby. The box was full of letters of intent from Apple, Microsoft, GM, Ford, Chrysler, Arctic Cat, IBM, Dell, Oracle, Hewlett-Packard, Maytag, Levi Strauss, Delphi, Sara Lee Corporation, Amazon, Goodrich Corporation, John Deere, Coach, MasterCard, 3M, American Express, Visa, Baker-Hughes, Xerox, Biogen, Caterpillar, Hershey, Kraft, General Electric, Windstream, AT&T, Verizon, Goodyear Tire, Sprint, Harley-Davidson, First Solar, International Paper, GlaxoSmithKline, DuPont, Colgate-Palmolive, Microchip Technologies, Jabil Circuit, Cisco Systems, Gillette, Johnson & Johnson, Merck, Boston Scientific, Hawkins Chemical, Nike, Proctor & Gamble, Chubb, Electronic Arts, Winchester, Corning, Peterbuilt, Rubbermaid, Remington, Campbell Soup, Boeing, Cummings, Tellabs, Tupperware, Mattel, Kellogg, Westinghouse, Dow Chemical, Rockwell International, General Dynamics, Coca-Cola, PepsiCo, United Technologies, Emerson Electric, Coors, PetSmart and 4,926 other American corporations. All the hubs were spoken for, the smallest of the corporations splitting a factory and a dormitory, the biggest corporations taking multiple hubs, Billy's World was all sold out!

Billy Pigeon took the time to shake the hand of every CEO in the convention center. He shook their hands as they left the eight tables on the stage set up by Debra to sign their letters of intent. The letters of intent were all produced at Apple with one push of a finger. Now that the five thousand letters of intent were all signed, sealed, and delivered, Billy Pigeon headed back to the casino to find his sweetheart, Julie, to have a little fun pulling handles!

As Billy left the room and passed the two security guards from Spokane, he stopped the dolly, raised both arms in the air, and yelled the following: "Praise the Lord—Praise the Lord!"

As Billy passed the two FBI agents sitting on their chairs and watching Billy Pigeon's every move, watching him "Praise the Lord," one of the FBI agents said the following to Billy: "What's in the box?"

"Bibles, sir, Bibles—would you like one?" asked Billy.

"No thanks!" said the FBI agent.

As Billy walked toward the casino to hook up with Julie, one of the FBI agents spoke again. This is what he said: "What a fucking idiot!"

Then the other FBI agent spoke. This is what he said: "Can you imagine that asshole being our president?"

\* \* \*

"How was the gambling?" asked Paul, who was still in Seattle, grounded because of a baggage handler's strike and a whole bunch of Pacific Ocean fog!

"Billy was amazing; he won $5,000!"

"Fantastic!" said Paul.

\* \* \*

"All I know, Mr. President, is that he spent over three hours at some religious gathering. He came out with a box of Bibles and told everyone in the lobby to Praise the Lord, Praise the Lord! Quite frankly, I think he's going off the deep end. We think the rigors of the campaign trail might be getting to him. We think he might pack it in any day, take the money he's got, and fly the coop!" said the FBI Director.

\* \* \*

Julie was excited in the morning as she boarded the Birdmobile for the next part of their journey around America.

"We're going to Disneyland; we're going to Disneyland for Christmas!"

Billy selected an old cassette by a great American band, one of the greatest American bands ever: the Eagles. Billy listened in reverence as they sang from their American classic: "I get a peaceful, easy feeling!"

"Me, too," said Billy, "I get the same feeling."

"Great job in Las Vegas, Mr. President!" said Debra.

"Roll up the goddamn window! It's bloody cold in here!" shouted Walter.

"That's too bad about Dad," said Julie.

"Shit happens!" said Debra.

# 22

## I Have a Plan

"Dad, they say Elvis is alive, that they faked his death, that Priscilla goes to visit him once a week," said Billy.

"He's dead son; trust me, he's dead!" said Walter.

\* \* \*

From the bright lights of Las Vegas, the Birdmobile headed southwest with Billy driving. Everyone on board was savoring the moment; the five thousand letters of intent with corporate America were tucked away in the big old box on the floor of their only closet in the motor home. Everyone was all pumped up as Billy crossed the Nevada/California border and they made their way to more bright lights, as they closed in on Tinseltown!

"Stop the motorcade!" yelled Billy on his cell phone to the Californian State Trooper leading the way.

"Why are we stopping, Mr. President?" asked the Californian State Trooper.

"There's a bunch of beer cans in this truck pullover; shit, there's a whole case of them!" yelled Billy Pigeon.

\* \* \*

Billy would ride Highway 15 all the way into L. A. The excitement in California was building as the Birdmobile headed further west, with five hawks and two black crows and three bald eagles now along for the ride. The birds were all listening to Julie, behaving themselves and eating road kill out of her hand, the way it should be. The road kill and the big rig traffic were intensifying, with Billy really having to focus on his driving once more. The two California State Troopers were leading the way, then the security detail from Spokane, then the Birdmobile, then more of the security detail, then a good 300 or more vehicles with California plates in tow, all blowing their horns, all waving American flags out their windows. The sounds of the horns were deafening. Billy had 3M earplugs stuffed in his ears, his Eagles tape pulled from the cassette tape player half way through "Hotel California," his favorite Eagles' song!

\* \* \*

"Gas prices are going up again!" yelled Walter.

\* \* \*

"Billy, can I have another Newfoundland kiss? They're really good!"
"Not now, sweetie, maybe later!" said Billy.

\* \* \*

"Billy?"
"What now?"
"Your shirts are starting to look ragged around the edges again!" said Julie.
"I agree," said Debra.
"They're right, Billy!" said Walter.

\* \* \*

"Look at the poor deer!" screamed Julie.

Julie had her head out the passenger window. She watched in horror as fifty or so ravens and a couple of big old buzzards were picking the deer carcass clean. The ravens on the outer edges of the feeding frenzy were getting frustrated, hopping around on both legs, and decided instead to hop up on top of the Birdmobile to get a free lunch of road kill from Julie, with the count on top now at six hawks, ten ravens and three golden eagles. With more birds coming in for a landing from the southwest, the landing became difficult, like landing a big old jet fighter on a moving aircraft carrier, with no safety cables across the top of the Birdmobile, with some birds making it, some not, the winds treacherous, some birds smacking right into the side of the Birdmobile, some lifting off at the last moment and making a second approach. Julie begged Billy to slow down to at least give the new birds a fighting chance.

"I can't slow down!" screamed Billy. "The traffic is a mess; the Suburbans are right up my butt. Your birds are on their own!"

\* \* \*

"Maybe you're right about the traffic, but I need more crunchy croutons. I'm down to my last bowl," said Julie.

"I thought you were feeding them road kill," said Billy.

"She's been sneaking them croutons on the side!" said Debra.

"Mother, no one asked you!" said Julie. Walter was busting a gut and puffing away on his big old cigar.

\* \* \*

"Dad, did you hear that Al Gore broke up with Tipper, his high school sweetheart?" said Billy.

"Now he can go spend all that money he made buying Google shares!" said Walter.

"Or she can go spend it," said Billy.

"Whatever!" said Walter.

\* \* \*

Billy was having another pee break at a big old Californian truck stop; the big old Bear of California flag was flying proudly on the roof. Billy made sure he washed his hands with soap and hot water before he greeted more well-wishers in the parking lot.

"Have a Merry Christmas, Mr. President!"

"Hope you enjoy California."

"Sorry about all the traffic!"

"Can you do something about the Dodgers?"

"Are you going on Leno? He wants to sit on top of the Birdmobile, too!"

"Don't forget to give Snow White a big old hug for me!"

"Go visit the redwood trees!"

"Do you have your face masks for all the smog?"

"Can you get us an NFL football team again?"

"Watch out for the crazies!"

"Would you sell me some of your sperm? I have a test tube in my car!"

\* \* \*

Billy sang as he drove.

> "Jingle bells, jingle bells,
>
> Jingle all the way,
>
> Oh what fun it is to ride,
>
> A motor home into L. A.!"

\* \* \*

L. A., Tinseltown, La-La Land was just around the corner. The lights were coming on; the traffic was a mess!

"How do we find a motel in this sea of humanity?" asked Walter.

"I don't know," said Billy, "I can't even look sideways!" Julie was all excited, turning on the motor home AM stations, settling for ZZ Top. ZZ Top was on fire, their electric guitar electric, and the drummer pumping out the tunes. Walter yelled the following to Julie: "Turn that shit off; it's Christmas, for Christ's sake!"

"Just drive, Billy; a motel will show up somewhere!" said Debra.

"Where are we now?" asked Julie.

"I have no idea; call ahead to the lead Trooper and have him take us to Disneyland. Screw the motel. We'll suck it up and sleep by the front gate. We'll wait till they open up in the morning!" said Billy.

"I agree," said Debra. "They probably charge an arm and a leg around here anyway!"

"How about two arms and two legs!" said Billy Pigeon.

"We've got lots of money; we can afford it!" said Walter.

"Dad, we went through all that in New York City," said Billy.

"But you're not giving a big speech here; we're just passing through. A hot bath would feel good for my tired, aching back," said Walter.

"Dad, don't even go there. You know the rules!" said Billy.

"Billy's right," said Debra. "Suck it up and quit your whining!"

"Mom, you shouldn't talk to Walter like that," said Julie.

"Mind your own business!" said Debra.

"Calm down, everybody, calm down; it's Christmas!" said Billy.

"I'm sorry, Mom," said Julie.

"I'm sorry too," said Debra.

"I'm sorry, three," said Walter.

"Good," said Billy. "I'm glad that's all settled!"

\* \* \*

Billy began to sing again.

"Silent night, holy night,

All is calm, all is bright!"

"You're right about the bright part!" said Julie.

\* \* \*

Debra was on the phone to Paul in Seattle.

"How's the big painting doing, dear?" asked Debra.

"It's getting there, but it's tough sledding, really tough. There's more to this painting than meets the eye. Actually, I'm painting by numbers right now. I hope to give it a go and try to paint on a bigger canvas in about three more months," said Paul.

"Three more months sounds good to me," said Debra.

"Oh, I just remembered. Two friends of ours who bring us papers all the time from their trips brought me over a bottle of wine and a copy of the Washington Post. I really didn't care too much for the question and answer session on the business page all about Billy's World," said Paul.

"I'm sure I wouldn't have enjoyed the discussion either," said Debra.

"I find the Washington Post rather aggressive in their assumptions; sometimes I'm not sure in what direction they're headed in their analysis," said Paul.

"I can relate to that," said Debra.

\* \* \*

"I'm thinking about dying my hair—getting it real black again," said Dustin Hoffman.

"If you do that, you'll have to get a facelift, too!" said Robert Redford. "I think we should stay *au naturale*."

"You're probably right," said Dustin Hoffman.

\* \* \*

Billy sang again as he drove.

"Dashing through the snow,

In a one horse open sleigh!"

"There's no snow here!" yelled Julie.

\* \* \*

Disneyland was chaos. Billy's behind was killing him from all the driving in the Birdmobile; the rides at Disneyland didn't help one bit! Mickey Mouse was no big deal and Goofy was the same. Snow White was cute. Billy was dragging his behind from all the walking, the hand shakes, the autographs, and the greasy veggie-burgers were giving him a gut ache, big-time!

"Why don't we drop down to Mexico, have a few Coronas, and eat some hot, spicy Mexican food?" said Julie.

"No way Jose!" said Debra. "Our president is not crossing the Mexican border in a motor home. Forget it!"

"You know how I feel about Mexico," said Walter.

"So let's blow this one horse town. I've seen enough of L. A. for one lifetime!" said Billy Pigeon.

"Me too!" said Julie.

"Me three!" said Debra.

"Me four!" said Walter.

\* \* \*

Ring, ring, ring...

"Debra Sanders speaking."

"Hi, Debra, this is Jay Leno. Remember me? What's this I hear about you guys hitting the road again? You just got here! I really wanted to get Billy on

The Tonight Show, maybe even sit up on top of the Birdmobile like Jon Stewart and Stephen Colbert did, that was so cool!"

"Why, so you can tell some more pigeon jokes to his face," said Debra. "Forget it!"

\* \* \*

"She's a fucking bitch!" said Jay Leno to his producer, Murray.

"Who are you talking about?" asked Murray.

"That bitch running Billy Pigeon's campaign! She's nothing but a pain in the ass to deal with!" said Jay Leno.

"Haven't I heard that line before?" asked his producer, Murray.

"I just don't get it. Me and Conan and Lorne and Letterman don't get a sniff and Colbert and Stewart have her wrapped around their fingers. Go figure," said Jay Leno.

\* \* \*

"On the road again,

Just can't wait

To get on the road again!"

\* \* \*

"What's the count today?" asked Billy Pigeon.

"Four hawks, fifteen crows, three bald eagles, twenty-five pigeons and a partridge in a pear tree!" said Julie.

"You know, Julie Sanders, you are one real smart ass!" said Billy Pigeon.

"I know; don't you just love it!" said Julie.

\* \* \*

With the tunes cranked up and the Dixie Chicks leading the way, Walter tried to communicate with Billy.

"So what's your plan, Billy? Where are we heading next?" asked Walter.

"I have no plan!" yelled Billy Pigeon at the top of his lungs.

Billy Pigeon did have a plan. It was a real good plan, but he would keep it secret till show time. Right now, he was headed to Kansas—to the heartland of America. He wanted to see the Kansas Jayhawks play the North Carolina Tar Heels in person, not on a TV in far away Bellevue. He wanted to kick back, stretch out his legs, have a front seat, and pig out on plain-Jane popcorn, without the butter!

\* \* \*

"I have to see you, Mr. President," said the FBI Director. "It's real important!"

"Come on over, I'll put a pot of coffee on," said President Obama.

\*\*\*

"Dad, it felt really good when Oprah gave me those big hugs back in Chicago," said Billy.

"It does with all women, Billy!" said Walter.

\*\*\*

"What's up?" asked President Obama.

"We've had our ears on; we have their motor home bugged. We heard the kid yell I have no plan!" said the FBI Director.

"So!" said the president who was not having one of his best days.

"So our people think they're talking code inside their motor home, that all the fishing crap and the golf talk and the poker games and the painting lessons are all part of one big con job."

"You told me that before!" said the president.

"We're absolutely convinced now that the code words are just to get us all worked up, to keep us guessing, that they really *are* playing us for fools. They're going around the country talking about their great plan for America. They're calling their plan Billy's World. They've got 20 million kids all worked up when America is down and out on its luck, when the economy is struggling. So guess what the kid yells in the motor home today?" said the FBI Director.

"What?" asked the president.

"He yells I have no plan!" said the FBI Director.

"You're kidding!" said President Obama.

"I'm not kidding, Mr. President. "Not one bit! They go around pretending to run for president, collecting all these campaign donations and writing out tax receipts, when they know—everyone of them—that it is just one big elaborate hoax!" said the FBI Director.

"So if I hear you correctly, the Reality Party of America is nonsense; the real people with real solutions to real problems is a bunch of bullshit. Billy's World is a crock. The 20 million kids are being suckered as we speak, and this is just about the money. He has no plan!" said President Obama.

"That's what I'm telling you, sir: 300 million and counting, as of a few days ago, all tucked away, all safe and secure. Here today, gone tomorrow to some foreign country and playing us for suckers, just like the 20 million kids," said the FBI Director.

"Incredible!" said President Obama.

"The decision you have to make, sir, is whether or not you call their bluff!" said the FBI Director.

\*\*\*

That evening, with a cool wind blowing and an open campfire burning in a small gravel pit near the main highway, Billy Pigeon said the following to Debra Sanders: "You are just too smart!"

"Well thank you, Mr. President; you're a pretty smart guy yourself," said Debra.

"So do you think they'll take the bait?" asked Billy.

"I'm not certain," said Debra, "but it will certainly play some head games with them, keep them second-guessing what we're up to."

"You want to bet?" asked Billy.

"You're on!" said Debra.

\* \* \*

President Obama paced the Oval Office. The pressure on him was intense: to get the economy going again, to pass even one bill in Congress to create jobs, to deal with the deficit and debt issue, to hang onto the White House for another four years after the present term expires, and to deal with Billy Pigeon and his gang of thieves!

"What to do—what to do—what to do?" thought the president.

\* \* \*

Ed Schultz was on the blower to Bill O'Reilly. This is what Ed Schultz said: "I have it from a reliable source that the kid has no plan. The kid is a fraud; he's just blowing hot air. He has no intention whatsoever of running for president.

"You're shitting me!" said Bill O'Reilly.

"I shit you not, my friend!" said Ed Schultz.

"So what do we do now?" asked Bill O'Reilly.

"We're going to shut him out, give him the cold shoulder, and not mention his name on TV. We don't give him a sniff. We stop being played for the fools we are!" said Ed Schultz.

"What are your friends in the media saying?" asked Bill O'Reilly.

"They're too busy celebrating to say anything," said Ed Schultz. "We stop the publicity gravy train, the campaign donations slow down to a trickle, the kid and his band of fraudsters pack it in, leave town and we're back to normal, with no Billy Pigeon—just you against me, the way it should be!"

"I'd better pass the word to our side, too," said Bill O'Reilly. "We'll shut him out as well, pretend he doesn't even exist!"

\* \* \*

"That fucking kid is something else!" screamed Glenn Beck. "We're on the fucking air 24/7, every hour of the day, telling people all over the country where he is, what he's up to, promoting the shit out of the RPA, talking about the 20 million kids, talking about Billy's World, trying to guess what he's building, and the whole country is pumped. They're going to have a new president with a plan for America, maybe a brand new theme park one thousand times that size of Disneyland, and he's going to employ all the unemployed in America to build the fucking place. We keep pumping this shit out and the money keeps rolling in and he's probably sitting under a big fucking tree right now, with his goddamn friends. They're all probably counting their money all the way to the fucking bank! Well fuck that shit—no more, no way—the kid is toast. I will never utter the name Billy Pigeon again, not over my dead fucking body!"

\* \* \*

Actually, if the truth be known, Billy Pigeon was under a tree. He was under a big old tree with Julie. They were wrapped around each other inside a blanket, practicing their Newfoundland kisses, the wind picking up, and the air still cold.

\* \* \*

"Roll up the window," said Walter, "it's so goddamn cold my nipples could cut glass!" Debra was busting a gut!

\* \* \*

*This is worse than high-stakes poker on TV,* thought President Obama. The president, in his mind of course, was rolling poker chips from one finger to the other, back and forth, back and forth, his face Stone Cold, his eyes motionless.

"Do I make the call, or do I not make the call?" said the president to himself.

The president almost made the call; he chickened out and threw in his cards. He called a Cabinet meeting instead. He told all of his Cabinet to be there; he told everyone to show up in two hours—no ifs, ands, or buts!

\* \* \*

"I could easily be a truck driver!" said Billy Pigeon.

"But then you wouldn't be home to keep me all warm and cuddly all night long!" said Julie.

"You're right; I wouldn't!" said Billy Pigeon.

\* \* \*

"I have great jeans, don't I, Dad?" said Billy.

"You come from a great family, Billy; our family has a long history of great genes," said Walter.

"Those aren't the jeans I'm talking about!" said Billy.

\* \* \*

"Dad what do you think of *Jersey Shore?* I saw you watching it on TV last night," said Billy.

"Ask me another question!" said Walter.

\* \* \*

The special Cabinet meeting began, with everyone present and accounted for.

"We're going to be talking about Billy Pigeon," said President Obama.

There was total silence in the room as the president informed the Cabinet of his meeting with the FBI Director and told them exactly what was said at the meeting: Billy Pigeon was pulling a gigantic con on the American people, he had no plan, and it was all about the money—over 300 million and counting!

"This is probably the most important decision of my presidency. If I make the call, and I'm right, then Billy Pigeon is toast. If I make the wrong call, then I'm toast!" said President Obama.

\* \* \*

"So are we getting good intelligence?" asked the Secretary of State. "I'd like to remind you all that we've been down that road before!"

\* \* \*

Billy Pigeon was also headed down the road—Highway 5 towards Bakersfield to be exact. The engine of their old motor home was purring like a kitten. Everyone on board was laughing, counting more money, and waving to the crowds. The crowds were all bundled up along the side of the highway. Everyone on board was totally relaxed, not a care in the world.

"I'm pulling over," said Walter. "You drive, Billy. I've got to go to the bathroom big time; it's so close, it's almost touching cloth!" Debra busted a gut once more.

\* \* \*

"Before I ask for a head count," said President Obama, "I would like to remind you, if I go down, we all go down. We'll all look like a bunch of clowns!"

The president asked his Cabinet for a simple show of hands. They were split—dead even. The ball was back in the President's court. The President walked toward the window. He saw a group of pigeons on the White House lawn; they all had two legs! He made up his mind. This is what the president said: "We hold off. I don't want him to know we know he has no plan. We continue to shut off the press, and if he's still around in 2012, we crucify him at the Presidential Debate. There's no such thing as a one-legged pigeon!"

\* \* \*

When Billy pulled the Birdmobile over for the evening at another cheap motel, he went for a pee break, and then he ate supper with Julie in the motel restaurant. They had a fabulous meal of spaghetti and meatballs, and a delicious cup of black coffee.

Debra and Walter were glued to the TV set. They watched the news on six or seven different channels. Billy Pigeon didn't get a sniff: the FOX network was talking about the war in Iraq and Afghanistan and the possible drawdown of troops; MSNBC was focusing their attention on the tough time states were having paying their bills, the lousy job Republican governors were doing across the country, with all their cuts to state governments to try to balance their budgets, and how the Republican governors were done like dinner in the next election, none of them with their poop in a group!

\* \* \*

Stephen Colbert and Jon Stewart gave Billy a plug, mentioning that he had snubbed their buddy Jay Leno once more. Jon Stewart told Jay Leno that you can catch more mice if you offer them cheese, not continue to bring in the big black cat!

\* \* \*

The president's press secretary told the country that the president was taking the weekend off, that he was headed to Camp David for some much deserved R&R, but that it was a working weekend: he and his economic advisors were working on some package of new initiatives to get the American economy on track again. They hoped to have something concrete after Congress and the Senate returned from their well-earned Christmas vacations. From Camp David, the president and his family were heading out in Air Force One to Hawaii again, for some sun and sand, and to play a little golf. He should have something to say to the country on his economic initiatives no later than January 20, 2011, early in the new year.

\* \* \*

"You owe me $20!" said Debra.

"Best $20 I ever spent!" said Billy Pigeon.

\* \* \*

"Dad, would you eat road kill?" asked Billy.

"Depends on how hungry I was," said Walter.

"Dad, would you eat me if you were the only survivor in a plane crash?" asked Billy.

"I'd eat your mother first!" said Walter.

"You are so bad!" said Debra busting a gut again. Walter had a big old smile!

# 23

## Hanky-Panky

    The year 2011 was starting off with a bang for Billy Pigeon. He had accomplished so much in six short months on the road since they backed the Birdmobile out of their driveway that first morning in Bellevue. The state of Nevada was all picked out for their construction site, with the architect drawings coming along just fine, thank you very much. The 20 million kids were all signed up and raring to go in six short years, and the five thousand letters of intent with corporate America were all hidden away in a box in the closet of the Birdmobile. There were still some private land issues to deal with in the state of Nevada. The list of construction companies available to construct Billy's World was getting longer and longer with each passing day, and that was about it. With another year and a half before their trip was over, all the parts of the puzzle were coming along just nicely, a lot better than was originally expected, and of course there was the $300 million and counting campaign donations already tucked away with Mrs. Larson, the bank in Seattle giving Walter a real good interest rate on their CDs, although their Treasuries were paying them a little less than expected!

    Life was good for our four merry travelers as they continued to saunter around America, one mile at a time, their spirits high. Billy's Scrapbook of Life was being added to every day. Debra and Billy were now focusing on their speech for the Presidential Debate in 2012, as they awaited the Republican candidate for president to win his or her own nomination to step upon the grand election stage. There were rumors circulating that the Democrats might even have someone run against Obama, maybe Hillary Clinton; wouldn't that be something!

Billy was gearing up for Obama, however. He wanted to face Obama head on, no holds barred—the great orator, Mr. B. S. himself, the one with the gift of gab. The Republican cupboard was essentially bare so far, with a few reruns signing on, a couple of has-beens, nothing to get too excited about, no Ronald Reagan for sure, as far as the eye could see!

Billy took time to visit all the little towns, read the sign posts and plaques on the town monuments, browse through the books of the local writers in the quaint little gift shops, see if there was a rare bird to be found on the store shelves, maybe a book covered in dust, maybe another *Birdman of 24 Sussex* ready to leap into literary libraries all over America, a rare writer who thought out of the box, who created unbelievable characters, who pleased the average folk, not just the intelligentsia, an Ernest Hemingway, a Norman Mailer, a John Steinbeck, a Kurt Vonnegut, a Margaret Atwood, an Erika Jong, a Robert Frost, or even a singer/songwriter like Paul Simon or Neil Diamond or James Taylor or Johnny Cash or Leonard Cohen, their lyrics magical, or maybe even some obscure writer tired of rejected manuscripts, tired of being told you have to have an agent, tired of the agent saying we're not taking any more submissions by new writers, try again next year, the writer spending the time to self-publish his or her own material, edit the lines himself or herself, be proud as punch to have that first book in their hot little greasy hands, to say I know one person who thinks this book is a really good book.

Billy Pigeon took time to chitchat with ordinary Americans, to sit on more lawn chairs, to sit at night and listen to more stories, to hear the birds chirp on top of the Birdmobile, to hear more frogs croak, to look up at the full moon and see the circular indentations on the moon's surface, to watch a shooting star, to gaze out into the Milky Way, to ask why no alien has ever stepped foot on the planet Earth from another planet, to taste the ice-cold water of a mountain stream in January, to stand for hours on top of a high mountain pass and stare at the majesty below, to pick up a really prickly cactus, to smell the bark of a really big pine tree, to see the hot air shoot out of the nostrils of a big old elk on an ice-cold morning, to watch a grizzly bear stand up on its two hind legs and scratch the hell out of a big old tree, to see, taste, feel, hear, and smell all of America, to turn off the laptop, to shut off the Internet and the TV for a whole week—and guess what? Ed will still be there; Wolf will still be there; Jay will still be there; David and Oprah will still be there; they'll all still be there. Another day, another dollar; life goes on in America, but take time to smell the roses, to drive within five feet of a gigantic bald eagle protecting its dead rabbit in the middle of the highway, to wait for Mr. Moose as he slowly crosses the dirt road without a care in the world, to see the wily, wily woodpecker pounding into a fully grown poplar tree, because tomorrow the bald eagle will be gone, the moose will be gone, the wily, wily woodpecker will be gone, too, rarely returning to the same place at the same time on any other day.

"Now that is the reason I came on this trip," said Debra.

"Me, too," said Julie.

"I never thought I would ever take the time to drive around my country. I thought I was doomed to the airplane," said Debra. "I feel a spirit in me I've never felt before."

"Me, too," said Billy.

"Ditto," said Walter.

\* \* \*

When President Obama, suddenly, without warning, announced to America that Billy Pigeon had earned the right to sit on a stage at Georgetown University and debate him for president, a *pretend* presidential debate, all of America cheered. The President's popularity even soared for a couple of weeks. America thought their president was a really nice guy and was giving the kid a break. The kid was 18 years old—nowhere near 35. The kid got a chance to strut his stuff, to show America why they should listen and take him seriously as a political candidate for president. President Obama was ready to take out Billy Pigeon, to hit him below the belt, to put an end to this gigantic con on the American people, to embarrass the hell out of him, to send him home with his tail between his legs: end of story!

It also stirred up a hornet's nest of political angst in America, especially from the Right!

"Is this pretend debate the real debate without us or just something the president is going to do to kick a kid down a few notches before the real debate when the president will square off with the real Republican nominee nominated at the Republican Convention?"

No sir, Mr. Obama has to learn to share the bounty. We, the Right, are not going to give him a chance to get two kicks at the can on prime-time TV in two presidential debates. No way Jose! The kid should get his chance to debate in a pretend debate; we think that's fair, but we want a strong Republican on that stage, too!

\* \* \*

"And let the games begin!" shouted Debra Sanders, as Debra, Billy, Julie, and Walter watched the *CBS Evening News* in another dingy motel in the middle of nowhere. Obama's bolt from left field caught them off guard. The TV screen was rolling and rolling and rolling; the screen occasionally stopped for a brief moment, and then began to roll again.

\* \* \*

Old Bill O'Reilly got on the bandwagon, too. He said the following on FOX: "The Republican Party of the United States has not reached chopped liver status yet!" GW from the Gang of 11 also led the charge; he told his Gang of 11 that they had to make noise, that they had the right number of guys on the Supreme Court, that they could easily make enough political noise to take their rightful place on the other side of the stage for the pretend debate!

\*\*\*

"You know, Billy, God works in mysterious ways sometimes! This is working out even better than we thought," said Debra Sanders. "We thought they would be quiet and leave us alone, but their egos got the better of them. We don't have to wait now till the real debate; we don't have to do a legal challenge to the Supreme Court. This has walked right into our laps! We're going to get our debate a lot sooner. You might even be able to get your construction workers building Billy's World six months earlier, your 20 million factory workers packing their bags six months earlier, too. This is unbelievable. Thank you, Mr. Obama, hook, line, and sinker: not in my wildest dreams did I ever anticipate this!"

\*\*\*

Glenn Beck got busy, Bill O'Reilly got busy, Rush Limbaugh got busy, the whole right-wing political machine in America got busy. They demanded a seat on the stage at the pretend presidential debate with President Obama and Billy Pigeon. They would definitely make that filing of their own to the Supreme Court. They would argue that what's fair enough for the goose was fair enough for the gander. Speaker Boehner was in his office dialing 1–800–911-BIRD. Debra's cell phone went:

Ring, ring, ring...

"Hello, Debra Sanders speaking. What can I do for you?"

"This is John Boehner from the United States House of Congress."

"I know who you are!" said Debra.

"Now listen here, young lady, we demand a seat at your pretend debate!" said John Boehner.

"But you don't have a nominee yet," said Debra.

"We'll send someone; we just want to be there. We'll go to the Supreme Court if we have to!" said John Boehner.

"That's not necessary. All you had to do was ask," said Debra Sanders.

"Really!" said John Boehner.

"Really!" said Debra.

"You're serious?" said John Boehner.

"Dead serious," said Debra. "You can have as many candidates there as you like. Oh, there is one other thing," said Debra Sanders.

"And what's that?" asked John Boehner.

"You have to get Obama's permission," said Debra.

"Already did that. He said it all depended on you, whether you would go along with it," said John Boehner.

"I say, bring it on, the more the merrier!" said Debra Sanders.

"You mean we can have more than one pretend debater there?" asked John Boehner.

"That's what I just said!" said Debra.

\* \* \*

Speaker Boehner was on a conference call to the Group of 11. This is what he said:

"She's a pussy; she caved into me in thirty seconds!"

"So who do we send to the debate?" asked GB.

"It could be Romney, Palin, Gingrich, Santorum, Cain, Pawlenty, Bachmann, Paul, Hunstman, McColter or Johnson—whoever wants to run for president," said BO.

"Let's send them all. Let's rip the little fucker's eyes out, and give Obama a swift kick in the ass, too!" said GB.

"That's a good idea. So how many do we have so far?" asked BO.

"Eleven," said GB.

"That's a nice number; I like eleven," said BO.

"We forgot about The Donald. And there's rumblings that Rick Perry might get in. That's thirteen!" said GB.

\* \* \*

Ring, ring, ring...

"Debra Sanders speaking."

"This is John Boehner."

"Hi, John, what's up?" asked Debra.

"We have thirteen so far," said John Boehner.

"Great. There's room for thirty on each side of Billy if you'd like. I checked with George Washington University; they said they had lots of chairs!" said Debra.

\* \* \*

Breaking News on CNN.

This is Wolf Blitzer reporting to you live from New York. CNN is first to confirm that the pretend Presidential Debate coming up in early 2012 will include President Obama and Billy Pigeon, along with thirteen candidates from the Republican Party. Those thirteen confirmed are Mitt Romney, Newt Gingrich, Tim Pawlenty, Rick Perry, Donald Trump, Sarah Palin, Michele Bachmann, Ron Paul, Rick Santorum, Herman Cain, Ron Huntsman, Ron Johnson, and Thaddeus McCotter.

An actual date will soon be confirmed, and yours truly, Wolf Blitzer, will be the moderator; we will even sing the National Anthem.

\* \* \*

"Who the hell is Thaddeus McCotter?" asked Billy Pigeon.

"No idea," said Debra.

"Let's do some research on him," said Billy. "I don't want some kid coming up from the minors with a curve ball that I can't touch."

"Julie, would you Google Thaddeus McCotter for us," said Debra.

"Who?" asked Julie.

"Now, will everyone chill, relax, and have a glass of red wine. I still have twelve or thirteen months to go fly-fishing!"

\* \* \*

Ring, ring, ring…

"Debra Sanders speaking."

"Please hold for a call from the president."

"Debra."

"Yes, Mr. President," said Debra.

"Do you mind if I bring a few of my Democratic friends along to the pretend debate?" asked President Obama.

"Who did you have in mind?" asked Debra.

"People like Harry Reid, Bill and Hillary Clinton, Jimmy Carter, Robert Reich, Lawrence O'Donnell, Chris Matthews, the Rev. Al Sharpton, Nancy Pelosi, Al Gore and Ed Schultz," said President Obama.

"You have room for one more; they have thirteen so far," said Debra.

"Okay, let's go with my wife, Michelle, then," said President Obama.

"Perfect, that makes thirteen, too," said Debra.

"Sounds good," said President Obama.

"Sounds good to me, too!" said Debra.

"Oh, there is one other thing, Mr. President," said Debra.

"And what's that?" asked President Obama.

"We have room on your side of Billy for another seventeen!" said Debra.

\* \* \*

Breaking News on CNN.

This is Wolf Blitzer reporting to you live from New York. CNN is first to confirm that the Republicans have thirteen chairs filled to the right of Billy Pigeon and the Democrats now have thirteen chairs filled as well at next year's spring presidential pretend debate to be held at George Washington University, with yours truly, Wolf Blitzer acting as your moderator. Sounds like it's going to be a lot of fun!

\* \* \*

GW was on the blower to the Group of 11 in another conference call.

"So I guess the drone hit is toast!" said GW.

"Looks like it," said DC.
"That's a shame," said GW.
"And why's that?" asked KR.
"It would have been a blast, just like the good old days!" said GW.

\* \* \*

Near San Francisco, the city of love and peace, Billy Pigeon listened to a local radio station. The radio was full of foul-mouth RAP music. The words were spoken so fast you could hardly understand them; the words he did understand were about death, war, rape, AK47s, and suicide: all that good stuff!

Billy didn't need San Francisco radio; he would make up his own song, a song easy on the ears. This is the first verse to Billy's song:

"Hanky-panky in the morning,

Hanky-panky at noon.

You've got to pull your pants down,

To give your bum some room!"

\* \* \*

Debra busted a gut; she couldn't stop laughing.
"Billy, you are so bad!" said Julie.
"I know!" said Billy.
"So get your mind out of the gutter!" said Julie.

The Birdmobile headed east again, taking Interstate 80 inland, with Billy Pigeon crossing Nevada one more time, to get a second look at his location for Billy's World, to really get the lay of the land. Billy drove through Reno, Lovelock, and Winnemucca, stopping to admire the scenery at the Gondola Summit, elevation 5,154 feet. With the Birdmobile climbing again, Julie's Jeep Wrangler was a real weight for the old Chevy motor home. Billy drove through Emigrant Pass, elevation 6,114 feet, then through Carlin, Elko, Wells, and Silverzone Pass to Wendover. They came to a great big lake, with Billy Pigeon saying the following to anyone who would listen:

"Smell the fresh air; there's nothing like Salt Lake City in late February, early March!"

\* \* \*

Billy headed southeast on Highway 40, the Birdmobile and Billy and all his fine feathered friends freezing their butts off. Julie's Jeep Wrangler was full of dirty beer and pop bottles and cans; the outside of her Jeep Wrangler was covered in snow and mud and salt. The State Troopers had their studded snow tires on. The vehicles full of people cheering and blowing their horns behind Billy were now mostly 4 x 4 pickups and SUVs and the drivers were all sipping on cups of hot chocolate. A couple of young girls at a small town along the way cheered Billy and yelled the following: "You're a winner; we're winners. We're all awesome, Charlie!"

\* \* \*

Billy was in another one of his devilish moods; he was ready to let the world hear the second verse to his "Hanky-panky" song:

> "Hanky-panky in the shower,
>
> Hanky-panky on the floor,
>
> The only thing to remember,
>
> Is to close the motel door!"

"Stop that, Billy!" shouted Julie.
"No, go ahead, sing the next verse!" said Debra, still busting a gut.

> "Hanky-panky in the evening.
>
> Hanky-panky at night.
>
> You've got to give your sweetheart,
>
> A sensual delight!"

Debra busted a gut one more time. Julie slapped Billy on the shoulder. "For God's sake, Billy, stop it!" said Julie.

\* \* \*

Billy focused on his work; the silly love songs were a thing of the past, a distant memory, for the moment anyway! He liked RPA, the name he had given to his political party. He was struggling though, with a name for the kids, a name he could run with. The thought process was driving him crazy.

Then one morning, on a stretch of highway between Craig and Steamboat Springs in the Rabbit Ears Pass of Colorado, John Denver's home turf, Billy was singing:

> "Take me home, country roads,
>
> To the place I belong,"

\* \* \*

An inspiration came, not another brain freeze, but one of these rare moments in time when your brain has a whole bunch of stuff mixing around inside and then this wonderful, amazing, incredible idea just pops out from nowhere: the symbol YA in a circle—the symbol for Young America. It was absolutely perfect; it was just what the doctor

ordered. He would have his super sister Sarah sew some simple samples. He would have her design shoulder patches to go on the sleeves of his 20 million young American workers as they walked proudly in their coveralls into their respective factories to begin their work day, their chests pushed out proudly and displaying the American flag. Their uniforms outside the factories looked really sharp, too, with their short-sleeved shirts, beige in color, their YA shoulder patches, their pants dark green, their baseball caps dark green too, their belts and their boots dark brown—his 20 million Young Americans looking really, really sharp!

"HELL YA!" shouted Billy Pigeon.

"HELL YA!"

"HELL YA!"

"HELL YA!" repeated Billy Pigeon.

Billy Pigeon met John Elway in Denver. Billy was in shock and awe. John Elway gave Billy an autographed football. Billy placed the football on the dash of the Birdmobile for the remainder of his journey around America.

\*\*\*

Debra was reading Billy's Scrapbook of Life. This is what she said: "I thought a Hummer was only the name of a truck."

"Me, too!" said Billy.

\*\*\*

The Birdmobile headed southeast on Highway 70. Billy's timing couldn't have been more perfect; his Kansas Jayhawks were on a roll, March Madness was in full swing, and Billy Pigeon was on a beeline to Wichita, turning south on Highway 35.

"Now here's another fantastic idea!" thought Billy Pigeon, one of those dreamers from way back. "When I land at the airport for the Grand Opening of Billy's World aboard Air Force One, I'll have 20 million YA kids all lined up along the edge of the twenty-mile-long runway, the YA kids all wearing their YA uniforms—their dark brown boots, their dark green pants, their dark brown belts, the beige shirts with the YA patches, their dark green baseball caps—Young America on parade, with Billy Pigeon, now the President of the United States, exiting Air Force One and hopping into an open air military Jeep with the top general at Billy's World. The top general and his president drive the entire twenty miles of the runway, past the four gigantic airports, past all the buses and trucks and trains and planes, with twenty million Young Americans quiet as a church mouse, standing straight as a whip, their chests puffed out big-time, all chomping at the bit, waiting for their president to give the signal to get to their dormitories, to change into their work coveralls, to run to their factories, to start their machines, to roll up their sleeves, to kick some ASIAN and ORIENTAL butt, and to start saving their $50,000!"

*I love it—love it—I love it—that is so cool. That's exactly what I'm going to do on opening day!* thought Billy Pigeon.

Billy could hardly hold his excitement; he shared his idea with Julie, Debra, and Walter. Debra summed up all their thoughts into one: "Billy, I don't know where you come up with your ideas, but this one is absolutely brilliant! And trust me," said Debra Sanders, "it takes a lot to impress me!"

\* \* \*

"Don't forget the receipt!" yelled Walter.

\* \* \*

"Dad, speaking of money, how much do we have in our account today?" asked Billy.

"Well," said Walter, "if you count all the coins in the big bottle, the checks in the drawer, and the cash in my suitcase, plus the money in our bank in Seattle, plus our investments, we, young man, have a grand total of $325,464,218. 17!"

"Not bad!" said Billy Pigeon.

"Not bad at all, son," said a proud Walter.

"All in bank CDs and U. S. Treasuries, I hope!" said Billy.

"Absolutely!" said Walter. "And paying us 1.5 percent interest."

"Now that's what I like to hear!" said Billy Pigeon.

\* \* \*

"Do you think April is too early to unhook the Jeep and go fly-fishing?" said Julie.

"It's never too early to go fly-fishing!" said Billy Pigeon.

\* \* \*

Billy had completed the final two verses of the "Hanky-Panky" song; he tried them out for size:

"Hanky-panky in the water,

Hanky-panky in the boat.

Be careful what you wish for,

It could be with a goat!"

"That is so gross, Billy," said Julie, with Debra busting a gut some more, big-time!

"Hanky-panky in the White House,

Hanky-panky on the lawn.

Watch out for the Secret Service,

Make sure they're definitely gone!"

"I like that one better!" said Julie, with Debra still busting a gut from the goat verse!

\* \* \*

It was a slow news day on the road; it was an information day, with Julie a treasure trove of knowledge.

"Did you know that President Obama will turn fifty this year?" asked Julie.

"And he'll soon be taking an early retirement, too!" said Billy.

"Did you know that President George W. Bush took 183 days of vacation during his first term in office?" asked Julie.

"Now you know why he was asleep at the switch!" said Billy.

"Did you know that Coca-Cola is investing four billion dollars in China?" asked Julie.

"The Chinese had better enjoy it while they can!" said Billy.

"Did you know that the stock market is no longer called the new normal; it's called the new flat!" said Julie.

"When I'm finished, it will be called the new, high, high in the sky!" said Billy.

\* \* \*

President Obama's press secretary was talking to him once more in the Oval Office.

"Have you thought about Billy Pigeon and the age thirty-five thing?" asked the press secretary.

"A little bit, not much; if he survives the pretend debate, which he won't, then it might become an issue, but it really won't be a concern of ours," said the president.

"And why's that?" asked the press secretary.

"Because I just know she's got something all worked out!" said the president.

\* \* \*

"So, Billy, where do you want to spend the summer of 2011?" asked Debra. "Where do you want to go on vacation?"

"Somewhere where I can say, 'Here fishy, fishy, fishy, fishy!'" said Billy. "Why are you asking?"

"Because we're all going to take a break soon, to recharge our batteries, to find a nice quiet place to get off the road for awhile, have some down time, and get all ready for the fall. Then 2012 is just around the corner," said Debra.

"The place should definitely have a lake, a stream, a Cabela's Sportshop, and a nice, quiet campsite!" said Billy. "I could go for that."

\* \* \*

With the press still sleeping in their motel rooms, Billy Pigeon and the Birdmobile and the security detail from Spokane slipped away to a secret getaway spot somewhere between Table Rock Lake and the Lake of the Ozarks in Missouri. They found an isolated campsite and tarped over the Birdmobile and the Suburbans. They all wore sunglasses. Billy Pigeon, Julie, Walter, and Debra spent the summer of 2011 there. They slept in every morning, snoozed in the afternoon, picked up bottles and cans on their walk to the general store every day, read newspapers, read books, and made entries into their Scrapbook of Life. Julie and Billy had lots of Newfoundland kisses, and of course, Billy Pigeon fished in the evening, just before dark, when the big ones splashed the surface.

This area of the state was a fisherman's paradise. Billy was in fisherman's heaven barbecuing his fresh fish on his little Hibachi barbecue, knowing something that nobody else in America knew: that Hibachi barbecues would soon be a thing of the past in the U. S. of A. , that pretty soon the barbecues would be called Billy-Bob Barbecues, or Uncle Tom's Barbecues, the way it should be in America—barbecues manufactured at Billy's World, made my YA workers who proudly stamped their Made in America logo to the bottom of each new barbecue they pumped out for sale at Walmart or Sears!

After Billy finished his fish barbecue, he would always climb up on top of the Birdmobile with his plastic pail of fish guts. The birds were all excited whenever they saw Billy coming; it was a bird's delight, with Billy tossing the bowl of fish guts here, there, and everywhere on the Birdmobile roof.

"I appreciate you feeding my birds, Billy, but that is just so gross!" said Julie.

"Relax, sweetie, the rain will wash the leftovers away!" said Billy.

\* \* \*

Debra was on her laptop. She was just about to check in with Paul and catch up on all the latest from Seattle when she heard a familiar sound.

Ring, ring, ring…

"Debra Sanders speaking."

"Hi, Debra, it's John Boehner again."

"What can I do for you?" asked Debra.

"We're up to twenty-five in your pretend debate, I have a lot of pretenders who want to give debating a first shot, to get some exposure on the national stage of public opinion," said John Boehner.

"Just as well to fill up the last five chairs!" said Debra Sanders.

"I was thinking the same thing!" said John Boehner.

\* \* \*

It was August 3, 2011, an interesting day on Wall Street. The Dow Jones average dropped 512 points because Wall Street decided that the U. S. Congress and the U. S. Senate had kicked the bucket on the debt ceiling issue past the 2012 presidential election. They were not making a real effort to deal with their deficit and debt issue and were passing it on to the next generation of Americans to deal with.

The Dow had been dropping for over a week, a slow, drip, drip, drip pool of blood gathering on the floor of the New York Stock Exchange; a full-blown bloodbath was just around the corner. There were European issues as well, especially in Italy, the eighth largest economy in the European Union, where the Italians had also taken on too much debt and didn't have the income to service it or the taxes to pay it down.

This is what Billy Pigeon said when Debra told him what she had read on her laptop: "Hang in there, boys and girls; we'll see you soon!"

\* \* \*

Within hours, Debra was calling Billy again.
"Come and check this out," said Debra.
"Check what out?" asked Billy.

U. S. loses Triple 'A' rating,

Standard and Poor's drops

Rating to '$A^{++}$,' the first time

In history that U. S. debt

Has been downgraded!

This is what Billy Pigeon said to Debra Sanders: "Relax, chill, calm down; it won't take me long to fix that!"

\* \* \*

"Here fishy, fishy, fishy, come to your daddy!" said Billy as a big old bass swallowed his hook and worm, took off across the bottom of the lake, and made three spectacular jumps before landing in Billy's net for dinner.

"Hey, Julie, could you go over to the store and get me some more worms?" asked Billy.

"What's the magic word?" asked Julie.
"Please," said Billy.
"Almost!" said Julie.
"Pretty please!" said Billy.

\* \* \*

"Are you going to keep soldiers in Korea?" asked Walter.
"I haven't thought about that one yet," said Billy.

"I think you should give it some thought," said Walter.

\* \* \*

"Ever hear of *Nope?*" asked Julie.

"Nope," said Billy.

"Not in my backyard!" said Julie.

"I hope the people of Nevada don't feel the same way!" said Billy.

"Don't worry, they won't," said Debra. "I saw the governor on TV the other night. He was begging for new businesses to come to Nevada to enjoy all their tax breaks and to enjoy all their hospitality!"

\* \* \*

"Do you know what Mark Zuckerberg had printed on his first Facebook business card?" asked Billy.

"No idea," said Debra.

"I'm CEO, bitch!" said Billy.

"He must have had a girl problem!" said Debra.

"He must have!" said Billy.

\* \* \*

"Who do you think shot President Kennedy?" asked Billy.

"Why do you ask that?" asked Debra.

"I don't know," said Billy. "I was just thinking. Do you believe Lee Harvey Oswald acted alone?"

"No, I don't," said Debra. "I think the Mafia got him, and then they got his brother, too."

"Why?" asked Billy.

"Because they were the Kennedys and they were after the Mob," said Debra.

"What about the Mexican drug lords?" asked Billy.

"What about them?" asked Debra.

"I was wondering what I should do," said Billy. "We can't continue to let drugs come into America.

"That's your call," said Debra. "Just remember what happened to the Kennedys. Maybe you should pressure the Mexican government to do all the dirty work, certainly more than they're doing right now."

"That a tough one, isn't it?" asked Billy.

"It sure is," said Debra. "Just think about how brave and courageous those young Texas Rangers and border guards are," said Debra.

"And remember the Alamo!" said Walter.

"Exactly," said Debra.

\* \* \*

"What about nuclear weapons?" asked Billy.

"Would you want Iran to be the only country in the world with them?" asked Debra.

"Not really," said Billy.

"What about gay marriage?" asked Billy. "And gays in the military?"

"Equal rights for everyone," said Debra. "We're all equal in the eyes of God, aren't we?"

"Of course we are," said Billy, "but it would be nice if they kept it in the closet."

"You're not the first one to feel that way, Billy, and certainly not the last!" said Debra.

"And speaking of God, what about evolution?" asked Billy.

"Go read Darwin's chapter on the theory of evolution tomorrow and the next day on your Kindle, and then come back and ask me again," said Debra.

\* \* \*

"Billy, when you're famous and you're the president and you get to attend all those state dinners and get to meet beautiful women from all over the world, are you still going to want me with you in the White House?" asked Julie.

"Only if you keep getting me my worms!" said Billy Pigeon.

\* \* \*

"I read Darwin," said Billy.

"So what did you think?" asked Debra.

"I'm kind of mixed up even more," said Billy.

"Welcome to the club!" said Debra.

\* \* \*

"Do you think I'm taller than I was then?" asked Dustin Hoffman.

"Not a chance!" said Robert Redford.

\* \* \*

"Billy, have you ever had real hanky-panky?" asked Julie.

"Nope," said Billy.

"Me neither," said Julie.

"Would you like to have some?" asked Billy.

"Yes, I would," said Julie.

"Me, too," said Billy.

\* \* \*

Billy Pigeon was intrigued by the Standard and Poor's decision to downgrade the U. S. federal debt from Triple A, a rating which had been in place since 1917, an issue that would soon be on his plate. He watched CNN daily; he watched Republicans and Democrats start the blame game, fight and claw at each other like cats and dogs, with Michele Bachmann even wanting Secretary Treasurer Tim Geithner's head served on a platter!

"Keep it up; this will be good practice for our pretend presidential debate in 2012," thought Billy Pigeon.

\* \* \*

Billy was on the Internet; he learned that certain pension funds in the United States would have to, by law, liquidate all their holdings in American treasuries if all three rating agencies, Standard and Poor's, Fitch, and Moody's downgraded at the same time.

"Yikes!" thought Billy Pigeon. "That should get Jim Cramer jumping on *Squawk Box!*"

\* \* \*

All joking aside, Billy Pigeon, at the tender age of eighteen, was smart enough to see the writing on the wall. He could see that the U. S. of A. was at the beginning of the slippery slope—no, they were actually sliding down the slippery slope to Banana Republic territory, to junk bond status.

"Not on my watch—no way, not even remotely!" said Billy Pigeon.

\* \* \*

Walter and Debra sang,

> "Happy Birthday to you,
>
> Happy Birthday to you,
>
> Happy Birthday, dear Billy,
>
> Happy Birthday to you!"

"What's going on?" asked Billy. "My birthday isn't till October."

"We couldn't wait till October; we wanted to give you your birthday present early," said Julie.

\* \* \*

> "Happy Birthday to you,
>
> Happy Birthday to you,
>
> May you live a hundred years,
>
> May you drink a million beers,
>
> Get plastered, you bastard,
>
> Happy Birthday to you!" sang Julie.

"Where on Earth did you ever hear that?" asked Debra.

"At a party I went to at U-Dub!" said Julie.

"I love chocolate cake," said Billy. "Thank you so much. I really appreciate it!"

"Open your present; go on, open it," said Julie. "It's from all three of us!"

Billy opened the cardboard box and pulled out the device inside.

"What is it?" asked Billy.

"A color TV, DVD player for your dash," said Julie. "No more boring days on the road for us!"

"That is so cool!" said Billy. The TV DVD player was installed in the Birdmobile that week, and Billy was all rested and ready to rock and roll in September, when he could finally:

"Get on the road again,

Just can't wait to get

On the road again!"

\* \* \*

"Get the worms; we're going fishing one more time before we 'head out on the highway!'" sang Billy.

"Billy, there has got to be more to life than fishing!" said Julie.

"Does that mean you're not coming?" asked Billy.

"Of course I'm coming!" said Julie.

"And if you're a real good girl, and do exactly what you're told, and don't bother me too much while I'm fishing, we might have some more hanky-panky!" said Billy.

"No, no, sweetie, I control the hanky-panky in this relationship; you remember that!" said Julie.

"Oh!" said Billy.

\* \* \*

"Just so you know, I do love you," said Billy.

"Ah, that is so sweet!" said Julie.

\* \* \*

Billy Pigeon was putting the final touches on Billy's World. He was tweaking this; he was tweaking that. Billy was a stickler for detail. He had a big decision to make. He had 20 million YA kids all confined inside a large, large, large military, industrial, manufacturing complex. His top general had to be a strong leader, had to have a bark that reverberated across the entire length and width of Billy's World when he or she barked, had to have Eisenhower qualities, McArthur qualities, Patton-like qualities, had to be someone who would take the bull by the horns, run a tight ship, carry a big stick, someone who would put the fear of God into young people, and who would chew the ass of those that needed chewing, with pieces of chewed ass left all over Billy's World!

There were several outstanding ex-generals available in America: Wesley Clarke and Colin Powell were at the top of the list. General David Petraeus heading up the troops in Afghanistan was another possibility, but they were not legends in the eyes of Young America. Billy Pigeon needed someone they knew. Billy had his eyes on someone further down the food chain. That someone was Gunnery-Sergeant Highway: Clint Eastwood. He would be promoted to general; he would be Four-Star General Highway!

Billy Pigeon had already talked in length to Clint, who was intrigued by the possibility. He told Billy that he was getting up there in years, that he was actually cutting back on the acting and directing, and that he would sign up for a five-year stint in Billy Pigeon's War on Jobs under the following conditions:

1. He didn't have to buy his cigars!
2. He could run a tab at any bar or tavern or lounge at Billy's World!
3. He got a fully customized, used, 1981, dark green, Chevy 4x4 to drive around Billy's World in, since he found the little military Jeeps somewhat cramped for his big old long legs!
4. He had permission to say whatever he wanted to whomever he wanted, wherever he wanted, however he wanted, whenever he wanted, no questions asked!

"Done deal!" said Billy Pigeon.

"It's *my* way or the *highway!*" said Clint. I don't want to have duct tape across my mouth. If some snot-nosed, foul-mouthed little sixteen-year-old says something I don't like, I'm going to give him shit. I'm going to let him know who's in charge, and he will change his ways. Trust me on that one!"

"Agreed!" said Billy Pigeon.

"There's one other thing," said Clint.

"Shoot!" said Billy Pigeon.

"That's exactly what I'm going to do!" said Clint. "I want to pack my .357 Magnum handgun with me at all times. I want a strong leather belt, a specially-designed holster, and a five-year supply of armor-piercing bullets, so when I fire my big gun into the air, 20 million Young Americans will listen, know I mean business, and run for cover—no ifs, ands, or buts!"

"I don't care how you do it, or what you do," said Billy Pigeon, "just don't start any bar fights!"

\* \* \*

"I'm going to break down and get a facelift!" said Robert Redford.

"Are you sure?" asked Dustin Hoffman.

\* \* \*

"I've also got a cub reporter all set to tag along with me, to make all the notes and do some of my out-of-town interviews," said Dustin Hoffman.

"And who's that?" asked Robert Redford.

"Danny DeVito!" said Dustin Hoffman.

"And why him?" asked Robert Redford.

"Because he's shorter than me!" said Dustin Hoffman.

\* \* \*

"Billy, with all that's happening in the world today, I'm bumping up your daily briefing to two a day," said Debra.

"But I'm still on holidays for another week!" said Billy.

"I don't care," said Debra. "We start tomorrow morning, so get up early, get your breakfast, and be ready to go to work!"

\* \* \*

Billy Pigeon e-mailed Clint; he laid out some ground rules—a Code of Conduct that he expected Clint to enforce.

"Each dormitory room with one hundred kids of the same gender will have one real military person assigned to them. That person will turn on the lights and wake up the kids at 6:30 a.m. Monday through Friday, will inspect them and their beds and footlockers, will take them on a one-hour run after dinner at 6:30 p.m. each night during the week, will tuck them back in their beds at 10:00 p.m., and shut out the lights—good-night, Irene, sweet dreams!

"There will be no junk food, if you want a Dunkin Donut, you'll have to have your parents sneak it to you when they come to visit and stay at the hotel in the hub, but a letter will go out to all parents telling them not to!

"There will be no drugs; no alcohol will be served to minors. If you're twenty-one or older, you can drink and smoke in any bar, tavern, or lounge. There will be no wet T-shirt contests, no Show Me Your Tits, no Girls Gone Wild, no bullying, no hazing, no spring breaks at Fort Lauderdale, no binge drinking, no walking around with open cans of beer, no new tattoos, no pierced earrings, especially the ones hanging from your eyes and nose and lips, no studs in your tongue, and no urinating on the sidewalks. Porn will not be permitted unless you look at it under a blanket with a flashlight, and if you get caught doing that, you're in big trouble with the powers to be. A little bit of hanky-panky with a condom is okay, as long as you book your hotel room in advance, and don't do it on the floor of the laundry room!

"My Young American workers will work from 8:00 a.m. to 4:00 p.m., five days a week, will get their week nights off after they exercise at 6:30 p.m. for an hour. They get their weekends off to come and go anywhere they want to on Billy's World, except the Military Base, and they can't go outside to the service city. Lights are out at 11:00 p.m. on the weekends. You can sleep in on

Saturday or Sunday, but you're back at it at 6:30 a.m. on Monday morning, except on holidays.

"They cannot leave Billy's World for five years, unless they have a family emergency requiring them to do so. They can't just head out to Vegas for the weekend! There will be a strict four-strikes-and-you're-out policy, with confinement to your dormitory without pay for two weeks after three infractions. After the fourth infraction, you're toast; you take the next plane home—no ifs, ands, or buts. General Highway is the boss; it's his way or the highway!"

\* \* \*

Clint sent an e-mail back to Billy Pigeon; this is what he said:
"You just *made my day!*"

# 24

# World War III

Walter turned to Billy; this is what he said:
"What are the first three words in a Mexican cookbook?"
"I don't know," said Billy.
"Steal three eggs!" said Walter.
"That's cute, Dad, real cute!" said Billy, having heard that joke before, but where?

\*\*\*

About an hour later, Walter turned to Debra this time; this is what he said:
"Why does Bill Clinton wear underwear?"
"I don't know," said Debra.
"To keep his ankles warm!" said Walter.
"That's terrible," said Debra, "talking about one of our presidents like that!"
Billy had heard that joke, too, but where?

\*\*\*

Debra had her first 9:00 a.m. briefing with Billy Pigeon in months. The situation in the world was extremely fluid, with so many issues on the president's plate, so many hot spots in the world. The world of politics was so intertwined; the world of economics was intertwined, too. Put them together and you've got one massive headache for any American president, no matter who that president was.

"Mr. President, I hate to inform you of this, but we lost a CH47 Chinook helicopter last night in Afghanistan. There were 38 people killed, 31 of them Americans," said Debra Sanders.

Billy was quiet, his head swimming. This is what Billy finally said to Debra:

"We have got to bring our troops home and get them working and training with Clint. War is a messy business; there's no reason for us to be there now. We can keep an eye on the Taliban from the sky. We can have CIA agents in the field. We can hit our targets with unmanned drones. We can still do selective Special Forces raids to free American citizens who are in danger overseas, just like the Israelis do. We can fire Tomahawk cruise missiles from the sea. Our stealth bombers can do strategic raids at night. We can do economic embargoes. We don't need boots on foreign lands!

"We can have a couple of submarines, a couple of aircraft carriers with fighter jets, and a couple of destroyers carrying U. S. Marines for rescue missions in each of the major oceans of the world. We can certainly cut down big time from the nine hundred or so military bases we have for soldiers and airmen and sailors throughout the world, and we bring everybody else home. They will be based and trained in America to defend America from foreign armies who put their boots on American soil, or to go overseas to help a friend in their time of need, but that's it. We will still have a vibrant defense budget. We will still purchase the best war technology that money can buy. We will still be ready to use force anywhere in the world if need be, but war will no longer fuel the economic engine of America while I'm president—end of story."

"Well said Mr. President," said Debra.

\* \* \*

"Do you think I'm getting a bit of a gut?" asked Robert Redford.

"Not enough to lose sleep over," said Dustin Hoffman.

\* \* \*

"Hi, Billy, this is Tiger Woods. I heard through the grapevine that you'd like to play a round of golf with me. I'm okay with that. I could sure use a friend to practice with these days. Maybe you could give me a tip or two on my driving."

"I appreciate the call," said Billy Pigeon, "but I'm kind of busy right now. Maybe some other time, if all the stars line up!"

\* \* \*

"Billy, there was an owl on the roof of the motor home this morning. I couldn't believe it!" said Julie.

"Maybe someone is trying to tell you something, Billy," said Walter.

"And what's that, Dad?" asked Billy.

"That you're going to be up lots of nights when you get to Washington!" said Walter, grinning from ear to ear.

\*\*\*

"Dad."

"What, Billy?" asked Walter.

"Would you keep 50,000 soldiers in Germany if you were president? We've had them there forever," said Billy.

"The Cold War is over," said Walter.

"That's what I was thinking, too," said Billy.

\*\*\*

Billy read about the unveiling of the Martin Luther King Jr. Memorial statue slated for October 28, 2011 in Washington.

"I have a dream, too!" said Billy Pigeon to himself.

\*\*\*

Billy read China's comments about the Standard & Poor's debt downgrade in the United States. China told the world that the days of the U. S. borrowing themselves out of their own messes are long gone.

"Do I ever have a surprise for you!" said Billy Pigeon. "And you say in your press release we still owe you $1.2 trillion. Don't worry. I'll be taking care of that problem, too, real quick!"

\*\*\*

Glenn Beck also heard about the Chinook helicopter going down in Afghanistan, the Taliban saying that they had shot it down with a hand-held rocket.

"Let's find the assholes who sold them that rocket. We declare war on them; we piss China off, we piss North Korea off, and we piss the Iranians off. We declare war on the whole fucking works of them. We start World War III. We reload our military machine and get hundreds of war factories pumping out all kinds of war equipment. Our economy is booming again, everybody goes back to work, and our problems are solved!" said Glenn Beck.

Glenn Beck received a whole bunch of e-mails. Here is one of them:

"Great idea, Glenn, but where are you going to get the money to build your war factories and fund your war machine? Haven't you heard we're broke? Someone told me you were a dickhead; now I know it for sure!" said John from Miami, Florida.

"What if the rocket was made in Russia?" asked Mary from Portland.

"Open the silos, push the buttons, and release the missiles; goodbye Mother Russia!" said Glenn Beck.

"What if the rocket was made in Pakistan?" asked Tim from Memphis.

"We nuke them, too, those useless fucking rag heads!" shouted Glenn Beck.

"What if the rocket was made in the U. S. of A.?" asked David from Seattle.

There was silence; old Glenn Beck had no answer for that one!

\*\*\*

At his 3:00 p.m. briefing, Debra told Billy that he had better start thinking of someone to be his vice president.

"I've already made up my mind!" said Billy Pigeon.

"You have!" said Debra, who was rarely caught off guard.

"Yes, I have. I've chosen a female!" said Billy.

"We've never had a female vice president, except in the movies," said Debra. "Who did you choose? Not Julie, I hope!"

"No, it's not Julie," said Billy. "Her initials are *DS*," said Billy.

"You mean Diane Sawyer," said Debra. "That would be a very interesting choice, almost like having a mother figure at the White House. She's bright, articulate, well-informed and she knows everybody in Washington."

"No, it's not Diane Sawyer; she's much younger," said Billy Pigeon.

"DS, DS, it's certainly not Donna Summers. It can't be Debbie Wasserman-Schultz; she's a Democrat. Who is it, Billy? You're driving me crazy!" said Debra.

"I'm talking to her!" said Billy Pigeon.

\* \* \*

"Billy, there's a gentleman from Arkansas on the phone for you," said Walter.

"Hello," said Billy.

"Billy Pigeon, this is Ted Thompson. I'm a businessman from Little Rock. I develop real estate. My partner and I have been trying for years to get a piece of property on line for a big housing project—a housing project for the poor—but we can't get it re-zoned properly," said Ted Thompson.

"So what's your point?" asked Billy Pigeon.

"My point is if I gave you a million dollars as a contribution to your campaign as president, would you give our re-zoning issue a little push in the right direction, a push from the White House?" said Ted Thompson.

"Sorry, Mr. Thompson," said Billy Pigeon. "I won't be doing deals like that as your president; neither will any one of my RPA candidates for Congress or Senate or for governor or the state legislatures."

"What if I said two million?" asked Ted Thompson.

"The answer is still *no*," said Billy Pigeon. "Actually, I have a housing project of my own in the works for America's poor."

"How about five million? That's my final offer," said Ted Thompson.

"Sorry, the answer is still no," said Billy.

"Well, young man," said Ted Thompson, "you can kiss my vote goodbye!"

"Mr. Thompson, I don't need your vote, or anyone else like you, for that matter!" said Billy Pigeon.

\* \* \*

Billy thanked Debra for getting him signed up in an anger management course when he arrived back in Seattle in 2012. He said he was this close to telling Ted Thompson what he could do with his vote, where he could shove it and how far!

\* \* \*

Billy was still crunching numbers, asking what if, making sure he was correct, making sure that Billy's World wasn't going to go bankrupt, and it was going to make that huge profit he needed to pay off the $70 trillion debt staring him between his two eyes! He talked out loud to his father, Walter, who listened carefully to each and every word Billy spoke.

"We have $2.5 trillion in government money. We use that money to build the five thousand hubs. The five thousand corporations under contract come on board to build everything else, including the factories in the hubs, with their $2.5 trillion. We have $5 trillion in total to pay for all the construction costs. The factories are all owned by the five thousand companies. They also pay for the training of their employees and the raw materials to run the factories. The factories are really an extension of their existing businesses. I form a holding company for the people of America, owned by the people. We staff and run and collect all the profits from the five thousand hotels. We lease out all the shops in the four gigantic airports and the big recreation center. We collect rent for all the leased-out space in all the stores in the five thousand malls. We lease out all the shops and restaurants in all the bus stops, train stations, and the trucking terminals. We let private entrepreneurs living in the service city outside Billy's World run all the businesses and make their own profit. They're happy; they have 20 million regular customers, plus all the military people, plus all the service people like the janitors, plumbers, and electricians who are going to want to buy a cup of coffee and a snack and a newspaper for their coffee breaks. Then we get to collect all the rent from the 2 million people living in the service city. We get landing fees at the airports. We get our big yearly contractual fee from all the corporations. It's a win-win for everybody including the American people. The 20 million YA workers get paid by the five thousand factory owners. We cover the cost of the food and clothing and Clint's cigars. We pay tax on our profits to the government like any other American business, and we plunk our profits as a payment against our $70 trillion federal debt. We pay the debt off in twenty-four years and 300 million Americans never have to worry again; the future will take care of itself!" said Billy Pigeon. "Have I missed anything?"

"Not that I can think of," said Walter. "The military costs are already covered in your budget. I think you have all your sources of revenue and your expenses. I'd say you're good to go!"

"Me, too," said Julie.

"Me, three," said Vice President Sanders. Walter proposed a toast. He pulled out a brand new bottle of Jack Daniel's Old #7 Brand, paid for by his own money from his own wallet. Walter told Debra, Julie, and Billy that Jack Daniel's, according to the late great Frank Sinatra, was the nectar of the gods. Billy Pigeon proposed a toast to Billy's World, his brilliant plan for getting rid of the $70 trillion federal debt, a debt hanging over America like a bad migraine!

"Cheers!" said Julie.

"Cheers!" said Walter.

"Cheers!" said Debra.

"Cheers!" said Billy.

\* \* \*

"Here fishy, fishy, fishy, fishy; come to Daddy!" said Billy.

\* \* \*

"Do you think they'll still know who we are?" asked Dustin Hoffman.

"I don't know. I hope so!" said Robert Redford.

\* \* \*

"I wonder what's going to happen to the stock market when it opens in the morning, when Wall Street has to deal with the debt downgrade," said Billy Pigeon.

"I don't know, but don't worry," said Walter. "Your $345 million is tucked away safely; you have nothing to worry about."

"I want to get up early and catch the opening bell," said Billy.

"Me, too," said Walter.

\* \* \*

"Have you figured out where most of our donations are coming from?" asked Billy.

"From YA kids," said Walter, "probably about 75 percent of them."

"So if 40 million YA kids kick in $20 apiece, that's $800 million. I could easily hit a billion dollars," said Billy.

"You could," said Walter, "and you probably will."

\* \* \*

It was 3:00 p.m., Eastern Time, on Sunday, August 7, 2011 when one of the richest men in America, Charlie Morris Sr., had one of those light bulb moments. Charlie, like a lot of other wealthy Americans, was pissed with all the gridlock in Washington, was pissed that Standard & Poor's had downgraded the U. S. federal debt.

Charlie Morris Sr. had spent a lifetime dealing with U. S. politicians. He was a staunch Republican supporter. He had made his money the old-fashioned way—he had earned it. He had started as a stock-broker, moved up the ladder, got into all kinds of investments, including mutual funds and pension funds and hedge funds, had a knack for shorting stocks, for going long, too, was always ten steps ahead of his peers, had risen to the top, had obtained the American Dream, was a multi-billionaire, and was one of the wealthiest men in America. Charlie knew all about "a penny saved," watched his money like a hawk, and had a dollar in cash to back up every dollar in debt, not like the Washington crowd who spent money like there was no end to it. He doubted very much if an S&P downgrade would affect their spending habits one iota. All the accumulated federal debt was an embarrassment to Charlie Morris Sr.—his once-proud country falling on tough times, looking to China to lend them money at all the weekly treasury auctions.

Charlie Morris Sr. got a bunch of his really, really wealthy money manager buddies on a conference call; he said the following to them:

"We control the computers. Let's push the right buttons. The other computers will follow big time. Let's get another flash crash going. Let's rock their world. Let's sell our equity portfolios, go down 1,000, 2,000, 3,000, 4,000 points, and let's stay there for a week or two or three. Let's turn our flash crash into a permanent crash; let the media call it black, black Monday, the blackest Monday of all. Let Washington squirm. Let the American people get riled up. Let them take their politicians to task, tell them to get their shit together, and when we see some action, some real action in Washington, we buy back in. I'm pushing my computer button tomorrow. I'm selling. I want you all to do it!" said Charlie Morris Sr.

\* \* \*

It was 4:00 p.m. on Wall Street. "Do you know where your money is?" It was August 8, 2011, with the Dow Jones Industrial Average dropping a staggering 634 points, and gold topping $1,700 an ounce and climbing! It was a wild ride for most investors. President Obama had sweaty armpits as he sat in the Oval Office, and said the following to himself out loud:

"Dear Lord, what have I done to piss you off so much?"

\* \* \*

Remember that really rich guy I was just telling you about: Charlie Morris Sr.? He personally got on the phone with each of his nine investment buddies he had talked to on Sunday afternoon. He spoke to each of them one at a time, starting with Richard Coffee. This is what he said:

"You make me want to puke, you fucking pussy! Coffee, you just ruined a country today—six hundred and thirty four lousy fucking points! It'll be business as usual in a few days, you just watch! You could have pressed the sell button with me. We could have had a monstrous decline, even a 1,000 point drop on the Dow would have helped; 2,000 would have been better, 3,000 would have really gotten their attention, and 4,000 would have rocked their fucking world!

"Six hundred and thirty-four lousy fucking points! You all talk the talk, but no one walks the walk! You blew it! Now we have to put up with this fucking bullshit until hell freezes over!"

\* \* \*

"I watched *Love Story* the other night on cable," said Julie. "Then I saw Ali McGraw on Oprah. My God, she looked old! And then Ryan O'Neil came out on stage. He looked old, too."

"And fat!" said Debra. "I saw the same show."

"Life *does* go on," said Walter.

"We all get old," said Debra. "I watched Mary Tyler Moore and Joan Rivers and that exercise lady—what's her name, it's on the tip of my tongue—Jane Fonda, that's her. My God, they haven't changed one bit in all these years; they've got to be 70, 80 years old!"

"How do they do it?" asked Julie.

"It's called money, sweetie!" said Walter.

"Do you have any idea how much money is spent by American women just trying to stay young looking?" asked Debra.

"More than the GDP of some countries!" said Walter.

"You're probably right!" said Debra.

\* \* \*

Billy returned from fishing. He took out his favorite bowl to clean his fish. The birds on top of the Birdmobile were going nuts!

"So what are we all talking about?" asked Billy.

"Nothing that would interest you," said Debra. "Now go clean your fish!"

\* \* \*

Billy saw that Anderson Cooper was heading out on another road trip, this time to Somalia.

"Oh man, don't tell me I've got to solve their problems, too!" said Billy Pigeon.

\* \* \*

"Jane Fonda is in good shape. She could hop on a flight and go get her activist friends all fired up and show everyone on TV what a shitty job we're doing taking care of the poor people of the world," said Julie.

"Nice thought," said Billy, "but we're all too preoccupied with our own lives to do anything like that!"

# 25

## Kiss My Ass

"Too much information coming at me too fast!" said Billy Pigeon.

"Get used to it," said Debra. "Summer is just about over. I want you focused. I want you to start multitasking. We've got to get on the road soon. I want you reading every newspaper you can get your hands on, to see America from a local perspective. I want you watching Wolf Blitzer on CNN every day in the *Situation Room*. I want you to know what your competition is up to. I want your brain going click, click, click, not stopping for a second. I only want it to stop when we pull over in the afternoon at a cheap motel room, when you're dead tired, when you crash, and you're out like a light!

"The world is moving quickly—too quickly for some. Media and technology have created a very fluid landscape for political planners like me. We're flipping here, there, and everywhere at breakneck speed on our iPhones, our BlackBerries, our laptops, and our TVs. It's not just Big Brother watching these days; it's Big Sister, Big Mother, and Big Father. There are eyes and ears hacking into technology. No one is safe anymore from instant scandal. We're probably being watched right now by satellites in the sky. Modern technology is able to beam in and show you everything you want to see and more. You've seen the movies; it's all true!"

"So someone is watching us right now," said Billy Pigeon.

"You can bet your last dollar on it," said Debra.

"This is serious stuff," said Billy.

"The world is not a safe place anymore," said Debra Sanders.

\*\*\*

When Billy went for a walk with Julie later on in the evening, this is what Billy said: "No more hanky-panky on the beach; we have to find a big old tree to get under!"

\* \* \*

"So those satellites could be American, Russian, or Chinese. They could be people who paid the Americans or the Russians or the Chinese to put a satellite in orbit for them," said Billy.

"Exactly!" said Debra.

"So the Chinese could be watching me right now, at this very moment," said Billy.

"What are you doing?" asked Debra, as Billy dropped his drawers and mooned whoever was watching!

"I'm saying hello to the Chinese!" said Billy Pigeon, the future president of the United States. Then Billy Pigeon proceeded to give the Chinese the finger—the bird, so to speak!

Then Billy Pigeon paid the Chinese a nice, good old American compliment, their due respect. This is what Billy said: "Kiss my ass!"

After Billy pulled up his pants, Debra gave him what for: told him that he shouldn't moon the Chinese, give them the finger, or tell them to kiss my ass! She told Billy that politics was a chess game, that we needed China to sell our manufactured products to, just like we needed the Europeans. We had to be smarter than them.

"Maybe so," said Billy, "but I'm not a regular politician. I'm not going to be manipulated by them; I'm not going to be their puppet on a string. Maybe I have to be careful, maybe it is a chess game, but the fact of the matter still remains that we will always be in an economic war with China, and it's a given fact that China plays unfairly. They manipulate their currency. They control which American companies are getting into their country to do business. They are putting selective tariffs on American imports. They are hacking into our computers and stealing our business secrets. They are using cheap, cheap, cheap, cheap labor to make their products for sale in America, and whether they like it or not, the first thing I'm going to do as president is to cut WFDS in government—waste, fat, duplication and stupidity—to take those savings and pay off our $1.2 trillion obligation to China, to take on no more Chinese debt, to remove that Chinese financial noose around our neck. We're going to cut back, big-time, on the billion dollars a day of products we're buying from China. We're going to bring those Chinese jobs to America for our young American workers, to make all our own products for Walmart and Target—end of story," said Billy Pigeon with a mind like no other. Billy Pigeon would continue to do business with China but on a level playing field, bargaining from a position of strength, the way it should be!

"Fair enough," said Debra.

"Our nation will be strong. We will pay off our federal debt. We will lead the world again, financially and militarily. People will respect us!" said Billy Pigeon.

"I believe you," said Debra. "I believe every word you say!"

\* \* \*

"Billy, you could do a lot in the bully pulpit to help the poor when you become president—the really poor in the world—the really poor who are starved and undernourished," said Julie. "I'd like to see you give it some more thought."

"Let me ask you a question," said Billy.

"Go ahead, shoot!" said Julie.

"How many times since we left Bellevue have you thought about the poor people of the world?" asked Billy.

"Only once," said Julie.

"That's my point," said Billy. "We never talk about it until it pops its ugly head up in the air. Thinking and doing are two different things. If you're going to solve a problem, then you have to immerse yourself in that problem. You have to have all kinds of ideas going here, there, and everywhere, and then you have to direct those ideas toward a final solution. Then you have to actually do something with your solution."

"That makes a lot of sense," said Julie.

"So I've got a great idea," said Billy. "When we finally get to the White House and I'm president, why don't you make it your project, as America's First Lady, to change the way Americans think about starving children, to get the issue at the forefront of our thought process every day, not just when it pops its ugly head up in the air, actually get all of America to do something about it."

\* \* \*

"Don't forget your receipt!" yelled Walter.

\* \* \*

"Billy, I'm going to take you up on that offer," said Julie. "I think it's a great idea. It'll give me something to do at the White House besides digging for worms!"

"And don't forget the pigeons," said Billy. "There'll be lots of pigeons in Washington to feed!"

"So what are you trying to say?" asked Julie.

"I'm just trying to say that you have to make a real commitment to your goal, not just the flavor of the month," said Billy.

"I've been thinking about the problem a lot," said Julie. "And I think I've come up with a really good idea to get the ball rolling."

"And what's your really good idea?" asked Billy.

"You and I are going to adopt two orphaned children from Somalia. We are going to give them a new home in the White House! How's that for starters!" said Julie.

"I just hope you don't end up wanting to solve the homeless problem in America, too!" said Billy Pigeon.

\* \* \*

"Your daughter is one very smart young woman!" said Billy.

"She has excellent genes!" said Debra.

"Did she tell you what she wants to do as First Lady?" asked Billy.

"She did," said Debra.

"And?" said Billy.

"And I think it's an absolutely fantastic idea!" said Debra.

"I figured you would!" said Billy.

\* \* \*

"Do you think I should wear glasses," asked Robert Redford, "or should I let them dangle on my chest?"

"It's more you to let them dangle!" said Dustin Hoffman.

"But if I'm chasing someone in an underground parking lot, it could be an issue," said Robert Redford.

"Better wear them all the time then!" said Dustin Hoffman.

# 26

## A One-Legged Pigeon

"Billy, quick, come and look. Mom, Walter, come out, too; you've got to see this. You won't believe what I'm looking at!" yelled Julie.

Out of the Birdmobile came Billy in his boxer shorts, Walter in his house coat, and Debra in her pajamas.

"What's wrong, Sweetie, what's wrong? What are you yelling at?" asked Debra.

"Look up, way up; look at the *real* one-legged pigeon sitting on the tarp on top of the big one-legged pigeon!" said Julie.

"Oh my God!" said Debra.

"Unreal!" said Billy.

"I'll be—go to hell!" said Walter.

"It's a sign, Billy; it means you're going to be president. I truly believe that, with all my heart!" said Julie, overcome with joy.

"Get your camera, Billy; this is one for the ages!" said Debra.

"I've got it already!" said Billy, with his old Kodak instamatic camera going *click!*

"Do you think he'll stay?" asked Julie.

"Only time will tell," said Billy.

"I hope he comes with us," said Julie.

"Me too," said Billy. "I know one thing."

"And what's that?" asked Julie.

"David Letterman is going to be pissed!" said Billy.

"Maybe we should send him a copy of your picture, by courier!" said Julie.

"Now there's an idea!" said Billy. "Take off the tarp so we can see both birds!"

***

David Letterman had the picture of the real one-legged pigeon standing on top of the big one-legged pigeon on top of the Birdmobile, blown up for all the world to see.

David Letterman went directly to his Top 10 List for the evening—The Top 10 Reasons to be Billy Pigeon!

Number 10: You get the summer off!
Number 9: You get to chitchat at Mount Rushmore!
Number 8: You get to travel around America on the taxpayers' dollar!
Number 7: You get to go fishing whenever you like!
Number 6: You get to play golf with famous celebrities!
Number 5: You get to hold hands with a beautiful young lady!
Number 4: You get time to know and understand your future mother-in-law!
Number 3: You get time to relax and smell the roses!
Number 2: You have a chance to become president.

And drum roll, please, the

Number 1 reason to be Billy Pigeon is that you get to really piss me off!

***

"I told you he would be ticked!" said Billy Pigeon.—"I knew it—I knew it—I knew it!"

David Letterman wasn't the only American pissed off because of the sighting of a real one-legged pigeon. President Obama paced the Oval Office. He saw the real live one-legged pigeon standing on top of the four-foot-tall, carved one-legged pigeon on top of the Birdmobile on his TV. He had committed to the pretend debate; there was no turning back now. This is what President Obama said out loud to his press secretary: "Fuck!"

***

Wolf Blitzer was pissed, too. His CNN reporters were asleep at the switch; they missed the boat. They would have to settle for second place behind CBS. Breaking news on CNN...

> This is Wolf Blitzer reporting to you live from New York. The whole world is in total shock and awe tonight, with an actual sighting of a real live one-legged pigeon sitting on top of the four-foot-tall, carved, one-legged pigeon on top of Billy Pigeon's Birdmobile! Stay tuned to CNN for further developments as they unfold!

***

Clint was on the blower to Billy. He told Billy that the YA kids were really into their action video games with their control joy sticks, *Monday Night Raw* and *Friday Night Smackdown,* Hollywood action movies, and Hardcore UFC fights on TV. The stars of those four forms of entertainment meant more to the YA kids than anyone else on the planet Earth. He was promoting Colonel Nathan Jessep to three-star general. Colonel Jessep was out of military prison. He had served all his time for calling the Code Red in the blockbuster movie, *A Few Good Men.* Jack Nicholson would be the three-star general in charge of the fence line at Billy's World. Jack was adamant that he was the right man for the job, saying, in no uncertain terms, the following to his buddy Clint: "You want me on that wall; you need me on that wall!"

\*\*\*

Clint also told Billy that Arnold was kind of down and out these days, with his wife Maria splitting the sheets, and Arnold out of a job.

"It might be the change he needs," said Clint, "to get him back on his feet again."

Clint also said that Arnold would be out of the country for awhile, but the last thing he said before he left was: "I'll be back!"

\*\*\*

"You're the boss; you bring whoever you want to work alongside you," said Billy Pigeon.

"No, you're the boss!" said Clint.

"I'm glad you remembered that!" said Billy.

"What about Donald Sutherland?" asked Clint. "I know he was born in Canada, but he sure has a great sense of humor; he'll keep everyone loosey-goosey!"

"I saw him in the original Mash movie; he was hilarious. I've got nothing against Canadians. My one-legged pigeon friend statue idea originated in Canada," said Billy.

"What about Tommy Lee Jones? He's getting tired of sitting on the moon all by himself!" said Clint.

"Tommy Lee is cool!" said Billy.

"What about James Garner? He plays a mean game of poker. It would feel like old home week," said Clint.

"I kind of like Chuck Norris myself," said Billy. "He might be able to talk Lee Marvin into giving you a hand, too."

"I'll give him a call. He could see if any of the original *Dirty Dozen* guys are still alive and kicking!" said Clint.

"Charles Bronson is. I know that for a fact," said Billy.

"Can you imagine the look in the eyes of your 20 million YA kids if I show up with General Jessep, Arnold Schwarzenegger, Donald Sutherland, Tommy Lee Jones, James Garner, Chuck Norris, Lee Marvin, and Charles Bronson at your Grand Opening of Billy's World? They'll shit their pants. I'll have my guys dressed to the nines in their spiffy Marine outfits, all of them with brush cuts, and looking like Grumpy Old Men. I'll make sure I've got some wrestlers like Stone Cold and The Rock, some UFC guys like Chuck Lidell and Tito Ortez, and some ex-football players like Dick Butkus and Jack Lambert. We could even have Chuck Norris rip up your 20 mile runway on his dirt bike. You could open up the door of Air Force One, throw down a rope, and old Chuck could climb up your rope into the 747 before it comes to a final stop. That would get the kids excited and get Billy's World off to a great start. The kids would go absolutely bananas. It would give them a real morale boost. They would be on their toes, too, knowing that any one of those mean-looking bastards could be lurking around any corner anywhere inside our fence line. It would be fucking unreal!" said Clint.

"And what are you going to do when you've got all these guys doing all your dirty work for you?" asked Billy Pigeon.

"I'm going to do what all four-star generals do: I'm going to kick back in my chair, put my big old boots up on my wooden desk, suck on my big old Cuban cigar and I'm going to think!" said Clint. "It's a tall order, but I don't see any reason why I can't pull it off for you."

"Great stuff!" said Billy Pigeon. "Give me a call if you need any arm twisting."

\* \* \*

President Obama was on the blower to the FBI director.

"Anything new to report?" asked the president.

"Not that much. We think he's sucking up to the movie stars for donations now. It looks like he's pretending he's going to do a big epic movie at Billy's World, starring Clint Eastwood and all his hardcore buddies from the entertainment world. They're even talking the *Dirty Dozen* guys; it sounds like it's a big war movie!" said the FBI director.

"I'm glad it's not another western!" said the president.

"Me too!" said the FBI director.

\* \* \*

The word was out about the real live one-legged pigeon. Bird watchers all across the U. S. of A. were calling each other, trying to find out where Billy Pigeon was hiding. No luck so far.

"He'll come out of hiding soon," said one bird watcher from Dayton, Ohio.

"That's a trait of a good bird watcher; you have to have lots of patience. If you don't, you should look for another hobby," said another bird watcher from Vero Beach, Florida.

"The one leg—it must be a freak of nature. We have to get a close-up, see if it was born that way or if some cat or coyote ripped it off, trying to get some supper!" said another bird watcher from Jefferson City, Missouri. The bird watcher from Jefferson City had no idea that if a good strong wind came up, he could just about be able to spit on Billy Pigeon and his real, live, one-legged pigeon!

\* \* \*

"Billy, it's Paul. He wants to talk to you. He says it's urgent!" said Debra.

"Hi, Billy," said Paul. "How's your summer been so far?"

"Very relaxing," said Billy. "What's up?"

"That big apple pie you want to bake is so big that we are going to have to go somewhere else to stir up all the ingredients. Good luck in gathering all your supplies," said Paul.

"I understand completely," said Billy. "We'll start looking as soon as we get on the road again."

"Sorry about that," said Paul.

"No worries," said Billy, "it's not your fault. I had a feeling you might be calling."

"So much for having an excuse to fly to Las Vegas on my way to Billy's World!" thought Billy Pigeon. "If not Nevada, where do I go next—where, where, where do I go?"

\* \* \*

"Honest to Christ, the kid is nuts!" said the FBI director. "Right now he's trying to set the Guinness Book of World Records for the largest apple pie ever baked on the planet Earth!"

"How big of an apple pie does he have to beat?" asked the president.

"I have no idea," said the FBI director, moving on to another topic. "So how are you holding out—is everything okay?"

"I'm all right," said the president. "I was just thinking of a strategy for the real presidential debate next year, trying to figure out how to get this economy rolling again, how to get both parties in Congress out of gridlock, and how to make the electorate happy. I've got enough going on to keep me busy. Trust me; I don't have time to think about Billy Pigeon baking a world record apple pie!"

"Well hang in there, sir. No one ever said life in Washington was easy!" said the FBI director.

\* \* \*

"So much for the real one-legged pigeon," said a down-in-the-dumps Julie Sanders. "My pigeon has flown the coop!"

\* \* \*

Breaking news on CNN...

This is Wolf Blitzer reporting to you live from New York. CNN is first to confirm, without a doubt, from a host of reliable sources, that Billy Pigeon's real live, one-legged pigeon is gone, gone, gone. Billy Pigeon has no idea where his bird is at this time!

\* \* \*

"Give him a call. He must be heartbroken. Tell him we're sorry he's lost his bird!" said Stephen Colbert.

"I'll do that," said Jon Stewart.

\* \* \*

Billy Pigeon was amazed when he heard on CBS News that David Letterman had announced a bounty for Billy's bird; the real live, one-legged pigeon was now wanted dead or alive. The bounty was $100,000 American. David Letterman told the world that he would pay the bounty on live television, if he had the bird, dead or alive, in a cage, on his desk, in his New York studio!

\* \* \*

At Debra's insistence, Billy continued to focus on the news and keep himself current on world events. Today was not a good day for the children of the world. Still reeling from the aftermath of all the kids killed in Norway by another raving lunatic terrorist, today Billy found out about the eighteen children killed by NATO forces in Tripoli. The head of the NATO forces said the following: "Sorry, wrong building!"

Then Billy found out that another thirty-four children were killed in Iraq by an IED—an improvised explosive device—at a busy shopping district, with four more children dead in Pakistan from another explosion, and it was also announced that in the last 90 days, over 29,000 children under the age of five had died from starvation and draught and civil war in Somalia.

Now Billy Pigeon knew why Anderson Cooper from CNN was on a flight to Somalia as we speak. He was, in the immortal words of that iconic Canadian rock band Trooper, going to Somalia to "Raise a little hell, to raise a little hell, to raise a little hell!"

\* \* \*

On a lighter note, Peyton Manning had just signed a new $90 million, five-year contract, to quarterback the Indianapolis Colts football team, and Jane Fonda was spotted by an L. A. photographer heading into a plastic surgery center in the same town. She was there for a long, long, long time!

\* \* \*

Billy Pigeon listened to the soothing sounds of the Dixie Chicks; they sang their country classic "Wide Open Spaces."

"That's what I need right now," said Billy Pigeon, "some wide open spaces to bake my apple pie!"

* * *

Debra must have been thinking the same thing that Billy was thinking. She told Billy, Julie, and Walter that they were breaking camp, and they were all going with Billy to find a good place for him to gather all his ingredients, to start stirring, to get his crust all ready to put the cut-up apple pieces on, and put Billy's big apple pie in the oven!

# 27

## Saddle Up, Boys

Breaking news on CNN…

This is Wolf Blitzer reporting to you live from New York. CNN is first to confirm that Billy Pigeon is on the move again. The Birdmobile was spotted on Interstate 70, heading west to Kansas City, with crowds all over the sides of the highway, people blowing their truck and car horns, grandmothers and grandfathers sitting in their lawn chairs and waving American flags as the Birdmobile cruised by. Billy Pigeon was giving the thumbs up sign, with hundreds of young YA kids giving the thumbs up sign right back and shouting in unison: "We want jobs—we want jobs—we want jobs!"

Billy Pigeon wasn't the only one on the move in America. Thousands and thousands of ardent, retired bird watchers were also on the move—in their trucks and campers, in their fifth wheels, in their motor homes—all looking for that illusive, real live, one-legged pigeon, all wanting to be the one cashing in on that big old $100,000 bounty offered by David Letterman!

One old, savvy bird watcher from Iowa spoke for all the other retired bird watchers from all across America when he said the following: "These goddamn gas prices are killing me!"

\* \* \*

Breaking news on CNN…

"This is Wolf Blitzer reporting to you live from New York. CNN is first to confirm, from reliable sources, a sighting of a real live, one-legged pigeon in Broken Bow, Nebraska, the sighting made by a Donald Spalding from Lubbock, Texas. Mr. Spalding is looking for a cage as we speak, to capture the real live one-legged pigeon in. Everyone on site has promised Mr. Spalding first crack at catching the bird. The real live, one-legged pigeon is just sitting on a large six-foot-high rock, in the middle of nowhere. He is completely surrounded by hundreds of people with cameras and iPhones. The real live, one-legged pigeon isn't scared or anything, like he has no intention of ever moving!

\*\*\*

"Find me a cage," shouted David Letterman. "We're going to Broken Bow, Nebraska!"

"Can I come, too?" asked Paul, his piano man.

"Sure, why not!" said David Letterman.

\*\*\*

"So where the hell is Broken Bow, Nebraska?" asked Billy Pigeon.

"We're here," said Julie, as she stuffed a folded-up section of her map of the U. S. of A. in front of Billy's nose. Billy was watching the road and looking at the map all at the same time, multitasking just like Debra wanted!

"We go north at Kansas City, head up Highway 29 to Omaha, then hook a left on Interstate 80, go as far as Grand Aisle, then get on Highway 2 into Broken Bow," said a pumped-up Julie, all excited about seeing her real live, one-legged pigeon again, to rescue him from the dead or alive bounty placed around his poor little neck, to get him inside the Birdmobile in her own cage where she should have had him in the first place!

"So how long do you figure?" asked Billy.

"If we giver river, we'll be there by morning!" said Walter.

"Well, what are we waiting for? Let's giver river!" shouted Billy Pigeon, as he called ahead to the State Troopers by cell phone and got them to pick up the pace, telling them that the real live, one-legged pigeon had been spotted in Broken Bow, Nebraska, and this was an emergency!

Billy also told the lead State Trooper to really get his butt in gear, to go on way ahead, to find a good pizza place, to get enough pizzas for everyone, to get extras they could heat up and chew on during the night, about sixty in all, to get some pepperoni ones, some ham and pineapple ones, eight vegetarian for sure, and lots of those with the works for the security detail from Spokane. The boys from Spokane were hungry enough to eat the asshole out of a skunk!

"And don't forget the coffee, lots of coffee. See if they have those big pour boxes with the spout!" said Billy Pigeon.

"Yes, Mr. President," said the State Trooper, "sixty pizzas to go and lots of hot coffee it is. I'm on my way. I'll put it on my credit card. Walter can pay me back tomorrow with cash. " The big old State Trooper put the pedal to the metal; the big old Ford highway patrol car was soon gone, gone, gone out of sight, his lights a-blazing, and his siren making really loud screaming sounds!

Billy had Walter take over the wheel at his next pee break. He poured a glass of red merlot; he got a couple of chocolate chip cookies from the cupboard, and then kicked back with his map of the U. S. of A.

"You really shouldn't be drinking till you're twenty-one; you shouldn't be drinking while you're working!" said Julie.

"Out of sight, out of mind, a drink is okay every now and then. I'm not driving; my dad doesn't have a problem with it. I'm not peeing on any sidewalks," said Billy.

"What if Big Brother, Big Sister, Big Mother, or Big Father is listening?" asked Julie.

"She's got a point; it's not like we're in my house or your house," said Debra. Billy was enjoying his glass of red merlot as much as Walter enjoyed his Jack Daniel's, his nectar of the gods, and was reluctant to give up his drink, putting his finger to his lips, and then saying the following to Julie: "Shhhhhhh!"

Julie persisted; she talked real low.

"A leader, especially our president, is supposed to set an example for everyone to follow. He certainly shouldn't drink under age!" said Julie.

"Then technically, kids shouldn't have hanky-panky until they're married!" said Billy, with Debra exploding in laughter. Julie's conversation was about to come to a screeching halt, after saying the following to her mother, Debra: "Mom, whose side are you on? I'm your daughter; remember me!"

"Now, I was about to say, before I was so rudely interrupted, what's so special about Broken Bow, Nebraska, why would the bird be sitting on a big old rock there?" asked Billy.

Billy's eyes were all over the map of the U. S. of A., his eyes were going here, there, and everywhere—really fast. Then his heart started to go beat, beat, beat, beat, beat really fast, too, as Billy connected the dots. He said the following to Walter: "Pull over, let's all go outside for a chitchat!"

\* \* \*

"That's one smart bird," said Billy to Julie, Debra, and Walter as they sat at a picnic table near a truck stop along the side of the highway. Billy had his map of the U. S. of A. spread open for all their eyes to see. Billy was using his flashlight.

\* \* \*

"I can't hear a goddamn thing!" said one of the FBI agents.

"That's because they're out of the motor home!" yelled a Special Ops operative hooked into all the listening going on, from high in the sky above the Birdmobile in a big old military helicopter.

"I wonder what they're talking about now," asked another FBI agent on the ground.

"They're probably looking for the next big town to buy Walter some more Jack Daniel's!" said a third FBI agent on the ground.

\* \* \*

"Look at the map," said Billy Pigeon. "The bird's sitting right in the middle of the Great Plains, and look at the major highways all around him: Interstate 70 to the south, Interstate 80 in the middle, Interstate 90 to the north, Highway 29 to the east, Highway 76 from Denver running up to Interstate 80. We'd only have to build one major highway from the Interstate 80 at Chappell straight up to Wall on the Interstate 90 and we'd be completely surrounded by major highways for all the trucks and buses coming into Billy's World. Look at this: there are major rail lines all over the place for us to tap into, and the land is mostly as flat as can be. The airport runway could go here in the middle somewhere. We'd have to be creative with the Interstate 80 and the railway lines cutting across the site itself, but we have the technology and engineering to figure that out. You know, girls and guys, this is doable, it really is. That bird is spot-on. This is absolutely incredible—a lot better than Nevada," said Billy Pigeon, then saying the following to his sweetheart, Julie: "Would you be a sweetie-pie and pour me another glass of red wine?"

"And what are the magic words?" asked Julie.

"Pretty please!" said Billy, with Debra busting a gut once more!

"That bird of ours is something else; he's telling us where to construct Billy's World! I find this whole exercise so amazing. I'm just blown away. I'm lost for words; I don't know what to say!" said Billy Pigeon.

"Say your bird is my bird, too!" said Julie, with Debra busting a gut again!

Billy felt the red wine kicking in. He was inside the Birdmobile. Walter was at the wheel. They would soon have vegetarian pizza—delicious hot pizza with vegetables and cheese, lots of cheese—and hot black coffee. They were getting closer and closer to Broken Bow. Billy began to sing:

> "Home, home on the range,
> 
> Where the deer and the antelope play,
> 
> Where seldom is heard,
> 
> A discouraging word,
> 
> And the skies are not cloudy
> 
> All day!"

"That's it, that's it!" shouted Billy Pigeon. "We can still go with all the solar panels for electricity!"

The wind outside began to howl, with Walter holding on for dear life. The Birdmobile was swerving from left to right on the busy highway. Walter was trying his best to keep the old Chevy motor home from crossing the center median.

"My God," yelled Billy Pigeon, "we can do wind turbines here, too!"

Billy was pumped; he was stoked. The excitement was building as the Birdmobile soldiered on, the 350 cubic inch Chevy engine still purring like a kitten and showing no ill effects whatsoever from sitting all summer long. Julie's Jeep Wrangler was used to get anywhere in Missouri they had to go and was now in tow again. The Jeep was filling up with Billy's beer and pop cans and bottles once more. Julie insisted that Billy give her Jeep a shot of air freshener every now and then, the way it was supposed to be!

\* \* \*

David Letterman was pumped, too, especially when the pretty security lady at JFK groped his testicles at the security gate and gave him a complete body pat-down!

"What time are you off work?" asked David Letterman.

"I'm a married woman!" said the pretty security lady.

"So!" said David Letterman. David Letterman said the following to his piano player Paul: "We've got to grab that pigeon first before someone else does!"

\* \* \*

Clint Eastwood, Jack Nicholson, Arnold Schwarzenegger, Donald Sutherland, Tommy Lee Jones, James Garner, Chuck Norris, Lee Marvin, and Charles Bronson also boarded a Lear jet at LAX. They, too, were on their way to Broken Bow, their horses being saddled as we speak!

\* \* \*

Julie continued to show her sensitive side. Looking at the map of the U. S. of A., she said the following to Billy: "What about all the people living in the little places like Marlin, Winner, Wagner, Dunning, Plainview, and Wahoo? What's going to happen to all those people in all those little places they call home when you construct Billy's World?"

"We'll take care of them, sweetie, don't you worry! We'll meet with them all. We'll explain why we have to do what we're doing. We'll tell them the truth, that if we don't do this, then America will become a vast wasteland, politically, economically, and morally. We'll pay them way more than top dollar for their properties. We'll give them rent-free apartments, condos, townhouses, or homes in the service city outside Billy's World. We'll also put them up in a hotel somewhere during the four-year construction process. We'll also give them first crack at any service job inside Billy's World if they're not ready to kick back and enjoy their retirement. They can fill the jobs at the five hundred hospitals and dental centers, in the big recreation center, in the hotels, in the malls, in the airports, in the bus stops, in the train stations, in the truck terminals—wherever they want to work, for as long as they want to work," said Billy.

"I'm glad you told me all that," said Julie. "Now I feel a whole lot better!"

"Shit," thought Billy Pigeon. "Putting the displaced workers up in hotels during the construction phase, that's going to cut into my profits. I wasn't even thinking of that. I'll have to increase the leases and rentals to offset those costs for sure," said Billy, adding more add-ons to his add-on list in a hardcover book he kept on the dash between John Elway's football and his new TV and DVD player.

As the Birdmobile closed in on Broken Bow, with the sun rising at their backs to the east, Julie said the following to anyone who would listen: "My God, look at all the people, look at all the cars, look at all the TV cameras, and look at all the cowboys on horseback!"

As soon as the Birdmobile came to a complete stop, Julie was out the door. She was running as fast as her little legs could carry her, toward her real live, one-legged pigeon. The pigeon was still standing proudly on top of the six-foot-high rock completely surrounded by nine men on horseback: Clint Eastwood, Jack Nicholson, Arnold Schwarzenegger, Donald Sutherland, Tommy Lee Jones, James Garner, Chuck Norris, Lee Marvin, and Charles Bronson all dressed in cowboy clothes, wearing big old cowboy hats, chewing on small cigars, with 30–30 Winchester rifles across their laps—Clint with his. 357 Magnum in his specially designed holster on his hip—all sitting on top of really big horses, with stone-cold faces!

Our nine horsemen had just dealt with David Letterman, who with his metal cage was just about to climb up on the big old rock and grab the real live, one-legged pigeon.

"Go ahead, make my day!" shouted Clint, his .357 Magnum out of its holster and pointing directly at David Letterman's nose. David Letterman came to a screeching halt. Donald Spalding from Lubbock, Texas, asked David Letterman for the $100,000 for finding the real live, one-legged pigeon. David Letterman said the following to Donald Spalding: "Go fuck yourself; I said in a cage, on my desk, in my New York studio!"

"I'm going to sue your ass!" said David Spalding.

"Go ahead. You won't be the first, and you certainly won't be the last!" said David Letterman.

\* \* \*

Clint and Jack moved their really big horses; they let Julie through to go see her pigeon still sitting on the big old rock. Her pigeon was starting to talk, happy as a lark to see Julie and to eat some crunchy croutons!

Julie put out her arm. The one-legged pigeon jumped from the top of the rock, its wings fluttered, its one leg doing the best it could to push off, to get airborne, landing safely on Julie's outstretched arm, with Julie saying the following to her feathery friend: "Come to mommy, sweetie; let's go home to the Birdmobile!"

People clapped their hands and said, "Way to go, Julie!" People took all kinds of pictures. Even Charles Bronson cracked a really small grin from underneath his big old cowboy hat. Julie and Billy walked hand in hand back to the Birdmobile. One of the little old ladies in the crowd said the following to Billy as he passed by: "You've got a good woman there, Mr. President. I'd hang onto her if I were you!"

\* \* \*

"So what do we do now?" asked Julie.

"Let's have some Newfoundland kisses and some really good hanky-panky!" said Billy.

"That can't happen here," said Julie.

"And why's that?" asked Billy.

"Because there isn't a tree in sight!" said Julie.

\* \* \*

Billy was on the blower to Paul in Seattle. This is what he said to Paul: "Julie has the real live, one-legged pigeon with her in the motor home. We're going to start baking our apple pie right here in Broken Bow!"

"Fantastic!" said Paul. "I want to be there when you eat the first piece!"

\* \* \*

The FBI director called President Obama in the Oval Office.

"It's just what I figured. More PR stuff—they're really pushing that Guinness World Record for the largest apple pie!" said the FBI director.

"That's it," said the president

"There is one more thing," said the FBI director.

"And what's that?" asked the president.

"We were wrong on the war movie. Clint's definitely doing another cowboy movie!" said the FBI director.

\* \* \*

"You know, we should definitely think about putting some of our $435 million into solar power and wind stocks," said Walter.

"Nope, we keep it in bank CDs and Treasuries," said Billy. "I don't want any insider trading issues on my plate, none whatsoever!"

"Never thought of that," said Walter.

* * *

"On the road again,

Just can't wait to get

On the road again!"

Debra Sanders gave Billy Pigeon more information to chew on in their 9:00 a.m. briefing.

"We have young people in Israel demonstrating because they have no jobs and because house prices and rental costs are soaring. We have over 1,700 people killed in Syria since rebellions have broken out. We have twenty-six police injured when young people rioted in London after police shot a man for no apparent reason. Market watchers say the financial system in the world is on the brink of collapse!"

"Anything else?" asked Billy.

"The NBA is probably going to go out on strike."

"Anything else?"

"Another air traffic controller was found sleeping on the job."

"Anything else?"

"California is looking for more money from the federal government in Washington."

"Anything else?"

"Obesity has reached an all-time high in America."

"Anything else?"

"Another NATO bomb missed its target in Libya."

"Anything else?"

"The number of cases of diabetes is sky-rocketing in the world."

"Anything else?"

"North Korea is rattling its sabers again."

"Anything else?"

"Authorities in Japan are predicting another major earthquake soon."

"Anything else?"

"Scientists are worried now that polar bears will soon be extinct."

"Anything else?"

"We've had another big high school shooting."

"Anything else?"

"Another big hurricane is brewing in the Gulf—a really big one!"

"Anything else?"

"Seventy federal sites have been infiltrated by hackers."

"Anything else?"

"American hikers in Iran are still waiting for a verdict from the court."

"Anything else?"

"The American Cancer Society is concerned about the increasing rate of prostate cancer in men."

"Anything else?"

"Food prices are on the rise again, economists are getting concerned about inflation and its effect on the economy."

"Anything else?"

"Two more states are talking recall."

"Anything else?"

"Tiger Woods just missed another cut!"

"Anything else?"

"A whole bunch of environmentalists are gearing up for a two or three week protest at the postcard zone in front of the White House over the big Keystone XL pipeline coming down from the tar sands in Alberta, Canada. They say this is a really big project, a really big issue; they want to gather everyone together and protest vigorously!"

"Anything else?"

"That should just about do it for this morning!" said Debra.

* * *

"Are you thinking what I'm thinking?" asked Billy Pigeon.

"Yep," said Debra Sanders.

* * *

"Dad, could you do me a big favor?" asked Billy.

"And what's that, son?" asked Walter.

"Keep your eyes open for a nice stream. I want to have an evening fly-fishing, get my mind off work, and collect my thoughts," said Billy.

# 28

## A Change of Plans

Billy received a call from Paul in Seattle.

"What are you going to do with those eighty rotten apples in the middle of your pie?" asked Paul.

"That had crossed my mind, too," said Billy. "I think we should get rid of them."

"That's our feeling exactly," said Paul.

"We either have to bury the eighty apples in the ground," said Billy, "or we could elevate them so they're sitting way up on top of the pie. That way the birds can eat them!"

"I like feeding the birds the best!" said Paul.

"Me too," said Billy.

\* \* \*

"Do you think my smoking will be a problem this time around?" asked Dustin Hoffman.

"It probably will!" said Robert Redford.

\* \* \*

Billy told Walter to pull over for another pee break near a truck stop at the side of the highway. He passed an overflowing green garbage can, with garbage littering the ground by the can. He walked fifty or so feet from the highway and found some bushes, his security detail from Spokane watching his every move. With his back to them, Billy emptied his bladder of all of Julie's delicious lemonade.

Billy saw the twenty or so little mounds of dirt piled up around his feet in the short grass. He saw a little gopher stick its head up from a hole by one of the mounds of dirt. This is what Billy thought: *I'd hate to be a gopher when we start our construction!*

Billy watched as the gopher sensed danger and disappeared from view, then stuck its head up from another hole a good twenty feet away.

"Now there's an idea!" thought Billy Pigeon.

\* \* \*

Billy really liked the idea of *go west young man*, of starting from scratch like the early settlers, of building where no one had built before, of being somewhat away from a major American city.

He showed Walter his map of the U. S. of A. He made a rectangle with an orange felt marker. He told Walter to take a drive around the new site for Billy's World. He wanted to spend the majority of his time here before the pretend debate to get a feel for the land, every inch of it. He wanted to pay special attention to the soil texture, the vegetation, and the creatures that inhabited it, that called this place their home. He wanted to study their living habits and their migration patterns. His Billy's World would be a showcase for the world, of industry and nature co-existing side by side, intermingled, man still in awe of nature, the way it should be. A gopher would be able to go in one hole in one hub, and then come out another hole in another hub. The deer and the antelope could do the same, only being able to go through game tunnels or game overpasses from one hub to another. There would be no lawns to cut at Billy's World; everything would be natural, with 25 percent of each hub made up of roads and buildings, and the other 75 percent left the way it was, the way it should be. Billy's World would easily be able to work around the Sandhills region of Nebraska and the Ogallala Aquifer, the way it should be!

Billy had a lot of work to do: major modifications to make to his initial drawings. The task was daunting; nothing that a little elbow grease and midnight oil couldn't fix! Billy and Debra had both agreed that they would be proactive with the environmental movement, that they would let them have a big say in the final design of Billy's World, and that Billy would be able to convince them of its merits, politically, economically, and morally. Billy had impressed everyone so far; one more group shouldn't be that much of a problem, especially if he listened to their concerns and worked with them, not against them.

Billy began the same day. He was on Google; he Googled all the names of the plants, the birds, and the animals of the region. He began a detailed list in a special hard cover notebook he carried everywhere he went: on every trail he walked, every body of water he looked at, and every tree and plant he touched. He titled his book, *Environmental Impact of Billy's World.* He would work on another 250 page report for Paul, which Paul would implement with the architects and engineers. The report was over 250 pages in the first week, then 275, then 350, then 400, then 455, the final notes stopping at 500 pages, with sketches, information, and possible environmental impact on the various birds, animals, plants, and water sources, with a unique way to incorporate all of them comfortably into Billy's World. The report was impressive; it had a list of 75 detailed recommendations that would be followed. Paul was absolutely blown away and said the following to Billy Pigeon: "The Keystone XL pipeline guys should have hired you as a consultant, young man!"

Billy said thanks, told Paul that he was hoping to set up a meeting soon with a large group of well-known American environmental activists, and that they would not end up at the front gates of Billy's World, disrupting construction, staging sit-ins, and making life miserable for everyone living in the construction tents and trailers. The environmental movement would be staunch supporters of Billy's World, not staunch enemies. They, too, had a say in the future of America. They also had the right to protest if they felt their concerns were not being taken seriously, their democratic rights and freedoms run all over by Big Business, by capital *C* corporations, in bed with Big Government—enough said.

\* \* \*

The Birdmobile headed west to Cheyenne, then up Highway 85, past Torrington, past Fort Laramie, past Lusk, then on Highway 20, then Highway 18 past Newcastle, all the way to Deadwood, and then back on Interstate 90. Billy did another count of all the Wall Drug signs to see if Julie's count was correct to make sure she had really won the bet. They headed east as far as Sioux Falls, then south on Highway 29 back down to Kansas City, then west again on Interstate 70 all the way across Kansas and all the way back to Denver, Colorado, and finally up Highway 85 back to Cheyenne—right back to where they started!

When that little drive was complete, Billy wanted to go east again, stay on Interstate 80, go to Omaha, drop down to Kansas City, take Highway 35 through Des Moines, see what was between Des Moines and Omaha, then go back to Des Moines, then go all the way up to the Interstate 90 again, then head west to Seattle, maybe check out Badlands National Park, do another day or two with all the tourists at Mount Rushmore, and maybe go say hi to Robert Redford in Sundance and see how he was doing with his new movie!

Billy had originally wanted to be back in Seattle by June of 2012, spend the next month or so immersed in the drawings and layout of Billy's World, put some final touches on his real debate homework preparations, book his flight to Washington and get ready to rock the world!

But that had all changed. The pretend debate would probably happen in late April, early May of 2012, months earlier than the real debate. Billy's schedule would also be bumped up. But that was later; this was now. Billy wanted to see all the small towns on the outskirts of Billy's World, to, in the immortal words of that iconic Canadian rock band, Trooper,

"Stay for a good time,

Not a long time!"

And a good time they had. The residents of all the small towns were thrilled that a future president was in their midst, not just hitting the big cities in big airplanes, but actually talking to regular folks. Billy was signing autographs to beat the band, with Julie massaging his right hand every night after dinner. All the trees in the little western towns gave them lots of cover for hanky-panky and Newfoundland kisses in Julie's Jeep Wrangler. Their campaign donations now approaching $500 million, with only $69,500,000,000,000 more needed to pay off the U. S. federal debt, with time flying by!

\* \* \*

"Dad, what do you think of pulling up stakes and moving to Billy's World to help take care of my money there, to make sure I have more revenue than expenses, and to keep Billy's World solvent?" said Billy.

"Sarah's going to be there working. I'm sure your Mom would go for one of those nice homes in your service city. She'd have lots of lady friends to talk to. I don't see a problem with it," said Walter.

"I'll give you a big office in the administration building just below Clint's; that should make for lots of fun!" said Billy.

"It depends," said Walter.

"On what?" asked Billy.

"On how fast or how much shit runs downhill!" said Walter.

"Oh, don't worry, Dad; you and Clint will be best of friends, buddy, buddy in no time!" said Billy.

"I hope so," said Walter. "I could buy him some really good cigars for Christmas!"

"I'm sure he'd appreciate that!" said Billy.

"What would my salary be?" asked Walter.

"I was thinking of starting you at $250,000, with bonuses for reaching certain profit levels," said Billy, "a mere pittance when compared to all the bankers on Wall Street!"

"I accept your generous offer," said Walter Pigeon. "Get me lots of sharp pencils to calculate all my bonus money!"

"Bravo!" said Debra.

Walter Pigeon was one happy camper; he had raised one hell of a kid. He would follow his son all the way to Washington for his big swearing-in ceremony on the steps of Congress. It would be the proudest moment of his life!

\*\*\*

"Paul is coming to see us tomorrow!" said Debra.

"What's up?" asked Billy.

"He needs to meet with you in person, to go over some important modifications to Billy's World, he told me to tell you *not* to lose any sleep over it tonight," said Debra. "He said everyone was really impressed with the way you handled the environmental issues, with no lawns to water, no grass to cut, keeping everything natural in between all the manufacturing hubs. They thought it was a brilliant idea."

"So that means we're staying in a motel tomorrow night," said Julie.

"Absolutely!" said Debra.

"I'm glad they like my handling of the environmental issues," said Billy Pigeon, with the Birdmobile by the side of the highway in an open field for the night. Walter, Julie, Debra, and Billy were sitting outside on their lawn chairs. The field was a mixture of sand and grass, with an antelope watching them—a coyote, too—with a big old hawk flying high above. The gophers were a little edgy, sensing danger for sure. The sun was going down; the prairie grass was alive with the sounds of nature. The sound was music to their ears, fascinating in its simplicity and regularity. There was a warm, gentle wind, the subtle movement of the grasses, and then darkness.

"The YA kids will be able to look out their dormitory windows and see nature," said Billy. "I think it will be awesome!"

"Billy, I have to hand it to you," said Debra. "Most developers I know would *pave paradise and put up a parking lot,* but not you. That's what makes you so unique; that's why I keep tagging along. I never know what you're going to come up with next!"

"Me, too," said Julie.

"Me, three," said Walter.

Julie walked toward the Birdmobile when the conversation fizzled; it was time to go to bed. She carried the real live, one-legged pigeon in her metal cage. This is what she said to Billy: "Look, Billy, your bird wants to go to bed with me!"

"You wish!" said Billy.

\*\*\*

One of the security Suburbans was headed to the busy airport to pick up Paul. It was a medium-sized airport in a medium-sized town. They said they would have Paul at the Birdmobile for breakfast.

\* \* \*

Paul hugged Debra. Debra hugged Paul, Julie hugged Paul, too. Paul shook Billy's hand, and then Walter's. He joined everyone inside the Birdmobile as they headed out for the day.

"I'm impressed!" said Paul. "I was expecting chaos. I see total organization: dishes done, clothes hung up, everything where it should be, and lots and lots of money. I don't know what to say!"

Paul continued to talk; everyone listened, especially Billy.

"I had to catch up with you guys, but what I have to say I really have to say to Billy. That's why we need to have a coffee and go for a walk the next time you see a quiet place away from the beaten track," said Paul.

\* \* \*

The quiet place was about ten miles down the road: a path going down to a bank and a big old log by the edge of a stream. Paul and Billy sat on the log; they sipped coffee.

"What I have to say," said Paul, "is much too complicated for code words over the cell phone. We've had to make some major logistical changes to Billy's World, mostly involving the manufacturing hubs."

"What about them?" asked Billy.

"Right now, as it stands, you've got five thousand hubs, each with a dormitory, a factory, a mall and a hotel. We're going to scrap your big recreation center. There just isn't enough time in the day for the four thousand kids in each hub to get there from all the five thousand hubs. It's impossible, especially considering the distances they would have to travel.

"We're going to have a recreation center, sports field complex with each hub, as well as its own fire and ambulance station. We're also going to split up your military complex into three components. The main military base in the southeast corner will be a separate training facility for American troops preparing for war if you ever have to send them overseas or protect our country if foreign boots land on our shores. We're going to add a small military facility to each of the five thousand hubs so the military people you want assigned to your dormitories for discipline will sleep at each hub in their own dormitory. They will also have their own kitchen facility, separate from your main kitchen and dining hall, beneath your main dormitory. The military facility will house one hundred military personnel, two military people for each of the forty rooms in your large dormitory—that's eighty soldiers—and we're throwing in twenty more for special leave, holidays, illness, troop rotation, things like that, so that way we cover all the issues without having to draw on manpower from other hubs or from the main military training center.

"The one hundred military personnel in each hub can shop in your mall, use the hotel to bring their wives or husbands or any other family members and will also have access to the recreation center without having to travel hundreds and hundreds of miles every day, wasting a lot of valuable time.

"We will also have a military outpost at each of the 210 checkpoints along the perimeter of your fence line; each outpost will have separate sleeping and eating facilities. There will be a helicopter pad at each outpost so new soldiers can be brought in from the main military training facility to practice everything the military teaches them. They'll work four days on, four days off. They'll also have Humvees to patrol the fence line and Apache helicopters for 24-hour surveillance.

"Now this is a huge change to your original diagrams. We are scrapping your tunnel system from the main food distribution center to the five thousand hubs. We're going to use trains and trucks instead, above ground. They're much more practical for transporting food and garbage and can carry more food and garbage than forklifts pulling covered containers on wheels. They can also run 24/7 and involve less manpower.

"All the hubs will be connected to one main highway, running north and south. The main highway will connect to the airports, the buses, the trains and the trucks making for better and more efficient distribution of goods and raw materials to the factories in each hub.

"We'll have 2,500 hubs on one side of the main highway and 2,500 hubs on the other side. Everything else you have is doable and will be centralized around and below the main 20-mile-long runway," said Paul.

"Wow," said Billy, "that's a lot of changes!"

"Better now than building everything and then having to rip it all up and start all over again from scratch. We're still keeping the five hundred hospitals and dental centers. The hospitals and dental centers will completely surround the five thousand manufacturing hubs. Each hospital and dental center will serve 40,000 kids. We're still going with the five thousand satellite admin offices assigned to the factories. We're going to stay with one gigantic water filtration system, one gigantic waste water treatment plant, one gigantic garbage incinerator, one gigantic fuel depot, and one gigantic laundry and clothing distribution center. We're scrapping the nuclear power station and diesel generator back-ups. We want to avoid having to dispose of nuclear waste. We're going green big time; we're contracting Nalcor Energy from Canada to design and build one gigantic wind-solar-hydrogen power station with back-up, practically zero emission, natural gas generators, wind and solar providing power for the electrical grid for Billy's World, with unused power diverted to create hydrogen through electrolysis, using water and electricity to create oxygen and hydrogen gasses. The oxygen will be released into the atmosphere and the hydrogen stored in pressurized cylinders to be converted into electricity when needed. The hydrogen will burn emission-free in internal combustion engines to make electricity. The process is in its infancy, but we're 100 percent sure we can have it ready for the grand opening of Billy's World in six years. If not, we have our back-up natural gas generators releasing zero emissions into the atmosphere. We're going to have one humungous parts distribution center for the planes, trains, trucks, and buses, which will be connected to four gigantic service centers for each of the forms of transportation. The main military base will still be run as a separate entity requiring all the same amenities. We're recommending that the service city house 2 million service workers. I know we were a little unsure of that number; we thought one, maybe two million, but we'll definitely need two," said Paul.

"What about Interstate 80 going east and west—our 80 rotten apples—and what about the rail lines crossing the construction site?" asked Billy.

"We're not sure yet," said Paul. "We could lift them; we could build tunnels underground. We could get rid of them completely and force people and goods to go all the way around Billy's World, or we could also fence them on both sides and run overpasses over them to run our own highways and rail lines, which we think is the most practical and the least expensive way to go. We could also go under them. Either way you're going to have cars, trucks, buses, and trains going right through the middle of your complex. We're going to have to really beef up security, but it can be done—no problem."

"Lots to think about," said Billy Pigeon.

"Hey, cheer up, your idea is fantastic. I thought that the first time I read your proposal and saw your diagram on my living room floor. I especially admire the way you're integrating industry and nature. I admire your goal of changing America politically, economically, and morally with one stroke of your pen in the Oval Office. We just have to make changes as we see fit, one step at a time, one problem at a time," said Paul. "There's no reason in the world to believe that you won't open Billy's World on time, on budget, the way it was meant to be."

\* \* \*

"My God, this bed squeaks!" said Paul.
"Tell me about it!" said Debra.

\* \* \*

Billy and Julie sat in the motel room next door to Paul and Debra.
"Mommy and Daddy are having hanky-panky without a condom," said Julie. "I wonder if we should tell them about Newfoundland kisses."

"No, sweetie, let's leave that to Tom Cruise in *The Kiss* movie!" said Billy.
"My God, they're noisy!" said Julie. "I think we should go for a walk."
"I agree!" said Billy.

\* \* \*

Billy, Julie, Walter, and Debra drove to the airport. They watched Paul's plane lift off and head into the clear blue sky, west to Seattle. The little Lear jet soon disappeared from site, a trail of engine exhaust still floating in the sky. Debra spoke to Julie; this is what she said: "Your dad and I enjoyed our little visit. I just wish for once your father would stop reading, turn out the lights and go to sleep, like any other normal man his age!"

# 29

## What's for Supper?

"Did you hear that on the news?" asked Debra.

"Hear what?" asked Billy.

"That 45,000 Verizon workers are talking strike," said Debra.

"That's a lot of ticked off employees," said Billy, "but not an issue at Billy's World, not now, not ever. Billy's World is not set up for unions; it's set up to give the young people of America a fighting chance in the real world, to teach them how to work hard, to live with less, to respect other people, to have their financial house in order, and to give them financial equality. If they go work for a union when they're done their five-year stint with me, then so be it. Unions have their place in the system, to look out for the rights of the worker, but they have to do it in such a way that they don't bankrupt the companies they work for—end of story!"

"But what about the six thousand construction companies you have to hire on to build your complex? What if they go on strike during the construction phase or have work slow-downs? That could be a real issue for us," said Debra. "It's something we should be thinking about now; you're going to have them on site for four long years."

"We'll have an iron-clad contract with every single company, with a no-strike clause built in," said Billy.

"Or we could use all non-union companies," said Walter.

"We could bring in non-union companies from Canada and Latin America," said Julie.

"Honest, guys, I don't think we're going to have an issue. They'll be happy with all the work. They'll be making competitive wages, and you've got 20 million young Americans who would take over their hammers and shovels and saws in a heartbeat if they thought they were going to have to wait any longer than six years to go to work! Push comes to shove, we'll let Jack and Arnold do the negotiating. Arnold can pack that big old sword he used in the *Conan the Barbarian* movie; he'll smarten them up!" said Billy.

\*\*\*

Stephen Colbert and Jon Stewart both got on Letterman's case about his misadventures in cowboy land trying to capture the real live, one-legged pigeon. Stephen Colbert actually cut Letterman some slack when he said the following: "Good thing he wasn't Wyatt Earp in Dodge City!"

Jon Stewart, on the other hand, was totally disgusting, hitting Letterman way below the belt.

"I got a bird he can grab onto! I'll even get inside a cage if he prefers that!" said Jon Stewart.

\*\*\*

"Did you know that for every dollar Washington spends, 40 cents of it is borrowed?" asked Debra.

"I knew it was high, but I didn't realize it was that high," said Billy. "No wonder we're going broke!"

\*\*\*

Billy watched CNN. He listened to Wilbur Ross, one of the most respected names in American business. Wilbur said that because of all the political brinkmanship that went on in Washington during the debt-ceiling debate that there would be an anti-incumbent vote against both the Republicans and Democrats in the 2012 election.

"That makes my job a whole lot easier!" thought Billy Pigeon.

\*\*\*

After they talked to Wilbur Ross, CNN announced a warning from Standard &Poor's that they could cut the debt rating of the U. S. of A. another notch to AA from $AA^+$ if their first warning wasn't taken seriously.

"And the good news just keeps on coming!" said Billy Pigeon to himself.

\*\*\*

So while the Birdmobile was motoring along its merry way checking out the perimeter of Billy's World, getting a real feel for the lay of the land, meeting more folks and trying to convince them to vote for Billy Pigeon in 2012, collecting more campaign donations for Walter to count, still stopping at dingy motels, still eating good healthy food on the run, pondering all the structural changes Paul had made to their original concept drawings, thinking about their big upcoming meeting with the environmentalists and then the pretend presidential debate, another group of Americans were slowly, but surely, making their way around the perimeter of Billy's World, too. Not the bird watchers—they had all gone home, hoping that the real live, one-legged pigeon would fly the coop again. No, I'm talking about Clint Eastwood, Jack Nicholson, Tommy Lee Jones, Arnold Schwarzenegger, James Garner, Chuck Norris, Donald Sutherland, Lee Marvin, and Charles Bronson, all on horseback, all heading west from Broken Bow. Their journey had taken them fifty or so miles so far, their every move followed by the press in their 4x4 pickups, and their dune buggies. Lee Marvin spoke for everyone when he spit some chewing tobacco on the ground and said the following: "I wish they'd all fuck off and leave us alone!"

\* \* \*

It was Jack and Chuck's idea that they go for the ride, to learn every inch of their proposed fence line, every gully, every rock cropping, every stream they had to cross, every place a bad guy could possibly hide from the soldiers in their big old Humvees and the pilots in their Apaches.

Our nine American originals were soon joined by more riders. The new riders kicked up a pile of dust as they caught up with Clint: Sylvester Stallone, Bruce Willis, Harrison Ford, Steven Seagal, Vin Diesel, The Rock, Stone Cold Steve Austin, Brian Boswell, John Cena, The Undertaker, Randy Couture, Tito Ortiz, Chuck Liddel, John Riggins, Larry Csonka, Dick Butkus, Howie Long, and Jack Lambert, all excited as hell about tagging along with Clint, 18 more riders all eager to explore the wild, wild west, with The Undertaker along to bury any dead riders or dead horses or dead Indians. Steven Seagal, the cook, was in the chuck wagon, which was pulled by six big old strong horses and filled to the brim with food, pots and pans, and other supplies. Steven Seagal had packed on way too much weight to ride a horse!

The press was impressed; so were all the people gawking at our 27 riders along the trail. Our riders were mean-looking, some with as much as four days growth of beards on their chinny-chin-chins, with big old cigars and little cigars and rolled cigarettes dangling from their mouths, some preferring chewing tobacco, spitting big old gobs of saliva and chewing tobacco on the ground way down below them, with the press convinced that the name of Clint's new movie would be *The Dirty Two Dozen, Plus Three, Cowboy Style*, a long title for a movie for sure, but who the hell was going to argue with these cowboys!

Jack was a little concerned about the five ex-football players that Clint had brought along for the ride, players he planned on using at Billy's World to supervise fence line security and to scare the shit out of the 20 million YA kids when need be. He was concerned that because they wore helmets all the time, and because they were all way past their prime, the YA kids might not recognize them like a Tito Ortiz or John Cena or an Arnold. The kids might just walk past a Howie Long, a Dick Butkus, a Larry Csonka, a John Riggins, and a Jack Lambert just like they were regular Joes.

Clint told Jack to relax, go smoke one of his big old cigars, have a shot of whiskey, and dream about getting a blow-job from a superior officer! He said the YA kids would have no idea what was coming their way, what those five football legends would have in store for them, especially Lambert.

"That fucking guy is crazy!" said Clint.

"Crazier than me?" asked Jack.

"He'd give you a good run for your money!" said Clint.

\*\*\*

Vin Diesel approached Jack on horseback; this is what he said: "Aren't you guys bringing any motor homes—a place where we can shit, shower, and shampoo?"

"Not on this trip, my friend," said Jack. "We're camping out, just like I did in *Easy Rider!* The only difference is I get to wear a big old cowboy hat, not that stupid fucking football helmet they made me stick on my head!"

\*\*\*

A member of the press got a call on his iPhone from Daniel Craig. Daniel Craig told the press guy to tell Clint that he enjoyed doing *Cowboys and Aliens* so much with Harrison Ford that he was wondering if he could come on this shoot, too, to do another far-out cowboy movie, that he had a lot to offer, that the thought of running into real live Indians didn't bother him one little bit!

"Tell him there's not a woman to be had in this movie!" said Clint.

"Daniel Craig said, 'Oh'!" said the press guy.

"So is he coming, or is he not coming?" asked Clint.

"He's going to take a pass; he said he's going to stick with the Bond girls!" said the press guy.

\*\*\*

Bruce Willis told his big old horse to giddy-up. Bruce Willis was now riding alongside Clint.

"Do you want me to round up some more people, maybe some women?" asked Bruce Willis. "I could call up the ex. Demi could get another eleven women for sure. We could call our new movie *The Dirty Two Dozen plus Three and the Clean One Dozen, Cowboy Style!*" said Bruce Willis.

"Like hell you will!" said Clint. "I'm not having pussy, titties, and tampons on this ride—no fucking way!"

\*\*\*

"Billy, this is Sarah Palin. Do you know who I am?" asked Sarah Palin.

"Sure, you're the lady Tina Fey makes fun of on *Saturday Night Live;* you're the one beating the big old halibut to rat shit with that club of yours up in Alaska!" said Billy Pigeon.

"That would be me!" said Sarah Palin.

"So what can I do for you?" asked Billy.

"I thought maybe you'd like someone to be your vice presidential running mate. I've got a great sniffer. I can smell the winds of change a mile away. I see all the people giving you campaign donations on TV," said Sarah Palin.

"I thought you were a Republican," said Billy Pigeon.

"I'm not quite sure what I am, Billy. I know I'm an opportunist. I know I can pull in the Tea Party votes for you; so what do you say?" asked Sarah Palin.

"I already have a VP picked out and raring to go!" said Billy Pigeon.

"Oh," said Sarah Palin.

\* \* \*

Billy Pigeon watched the business channel in his run-down motel room, one of the worst motels on the trip, with cockroaches running here, there, and everywhere; Debra was screaming to high heaven. Rick Santelli of Tea Party fame made a really neat comment about the state of politics in America.

"Iffy world—iffy leaders!" said Rick Santelli.

"I promise, Rick, I won't be an iffy leader!" said Billy Pigeon.

\* \* \*

Billy was on Google; he was brushing up on America's education system. He was intrigued by the catchy phrase, "No Child Left Behind."

"Trust me," said Billy, "there will be no child left behind in my America!"

"I like that attitude," said Walter.

"Me, too," said Debra.

"Me, three," said Julie.

\* \* \*

"Clint, I'm going to stop for a shit!" said Chuck Norris.

"Tell someone who cares!" said Clint.

\* \* \*

Billy watched the Dow Jones Industrial Average frantically trying to find a bottom.

"We need Mark Haines," said Billy Pigeon, "but he's gone to the pizza parlor in the sky!"

\* \* \*

Billy saw all the business journalists on TV second-guessing all the politicians in Washington, wondering why all of the politicians were on vacation while Rome was burning!

"Shouldn't they be in Washington now, when Americans really need them?" asked one of the savvy business journalists.

"You're goddamn right they should be in Washington!" yelled Billy Pigeon. "I'd fire them all; kick their sorry asses right out onto Pennsylvania Avenue, right now!"

"Calm down, Billy, calm down; that's no way for a future president to talk!" said Debra, making another note in her day planner.

"Bump up Anger Management Course in Seattle before he goes to pretend presidential debate; maybe take two courses from two different instructors!"

\* \* \*

"What's for supper?" asked Arnold.

"Beans!" shouted Steven Seagal, having a tough time breathing through his red, cloth handkerchief wrapped around his face. The six big old horses in front of him were kicking up dust, big-time!

\* \* \*

Billy stopped at a little tiny post office in a little tiny one-horse town. He gave the little old lady behind the little wooden counter a little envelope to mail to his mother, Sally, in Seattle.

"How much for a stamp?" asked Billy.

"Which arm do you want to give me?" asked the little old lady.

"Seriously," said Billy Pigeon, "how much for the stamp?"

"I could have asked you for an arm and a leg," said the little old lady. "That'll be 60 cents even."

After Billy paid the little old lady for the stamp, licked it and stuck it on the envelope, Billy asked the little old lady how long it would take for his little letter to get to Seattle.

"Would you like the slow horse or the slower horse?" asked the little old lady.

\* \* \*

While Debra and Billy focused on which environmentalists would get an invite to a secret meeting at a secret location in Colorado, Clint and Jack were dealing with a major issue of their own.

"So what do we do about the Mexicans?" asked Clint.

"I'm ten steps ahead of you!" said Jack. "When they find out that we're going to wean 20 million YA kids off drugs, they're going to want to get to those kids. They're also going to want some of their jobs. We're going to have to see that they don't get anywhere near Billy's World. We're going to have our hands full."

"I agree," said Clint.

"Since I'm in charge of your fence line, I'm going to build it the way I want. We're going to have two fences: an outer fence and an inner fence. They'll both be 20 feet high. We'll have rolls of really sharp wire on top. There'll be a forty-foot-deep, five-foot-wide, alarmed concrete wall under the first fence. The concrete will be reinforced with one-inch-thick rebar crisscrossed at six-inch intervals a foot apart. Then under the second fence will be an eighty-foot-deep, five-foot-wide, alarmed concrete wall with the same rebar reinforcement. Then inside the complex, across the four-lane highway for our Humvees to do their patrols will be another 20-foot-high fence, with more really sharp wire on top, and below the third fence will be a 120-foot-deep, alarmed concrete wall, ten feet wide, with the same rebar reinforcement, and in the 100-foot area between the outer and the first inner fence, which I will call no man's land, I'm burying landmines every ten or fifteen feet apart. I'm also having drug-sniffing dogs at all the 210 security checkpoints. I'm having state-of-the-art Apache helicopters with spotlights and infrared cameras with instructions to shoot to kill any fucking Mexican who tries to get across or under my fence line, and when I get my first dead Mexican, I'm going to stuff him in a body bag, drop him off on the front lawn of the first drug lord I can find in Mexico. There will be a big old sign on the body bag that is going to say, 'Remember the Alamo, you mother fuckers!'"

"That should just about do it!" said Clint.

\* \* \*

Jack was on a roll. "At every checkpoint, all 210 of them, a U. S. soldier will get out of his or her Humvee and raise two big old flags: one will have the red, white and blue stars and stripes of the United States of America; the second will have the red, white, and green of Mexico, and written in big black letters on the white section of each Mexican flag will be four words. This is what each Mexican flag will say." Jack reached into his shirt pocket and passed a folded piece of paper to Clint. Clint unfolded the piece of paper; this is what he saw:

| |
|---|
| FUCK OFF, |
| WE'RE |
| FULL! |

"Do you think we should let the business owners own their own homes inside our service city, or should we charge them rent like everyone else?" asked Billy.

"I think we should do rentals for them, too," said Walter. "Why should we let them own inside your service city when they could decide to pack it in anytime, do a midnight move, or sell their businesses to someone else, and be long gone before we find out about it? I say save the houses for the service people with young families. We rent to everybody; the rental income goes to pay off your $70 trillion debt, just like you talked about. We own everything; we're obligated to no one. We don't want the service city crawling with real estate agents trying to sell vacated homes."

"Makes sense to me," said Billy. "Two million people in a small city outside a really big, big, big city called Billy's World, with everyone in the little city having their own schools, hospitals, churches, strata councils, libraries, recreation centers, fire halls, ambulance stations and shopping malls. The only people coming inside Billy's World from the service city will be the ones catching a bus or a train to go to work, to service Billy's World. They'll be paid the same wages as anyone else in the private sector, with the same benefits, the same medical and dental, the same self-controlled pension plans. There will be a healthy federal government in Washington with its financial house in order, no longer having to worry about its next dollar, or how they're going to take care of their American families, and take care of future obligations to them.

"And even their kids will be working inside Billy's World, pledging five years of their lives to America, to produce Made in America products, to have $50,000 in their blue jeans when they've completed their first tour of duty in my War on Jobs, to be debt free when they leave and go out into the real world.

"I can't wait to see Sarah after five years," said Walter.

"She said she might do ten!" said Julie.

"Well after ten then!" said Walter.

\*\*\*

"What's for supper?" asked John Cena.

"Beans!" said Steven Seagal.

"That's what we had last night!" said John Cena.

\*\*\*

Warren Buffett, the King of Omaha, was on TV. He said, "As far as I'm concerned, the U. S. of A. is still Triple A to me."

"Now there's an idea," said Billy Pigeon. "I've got to approach him, see if Berkshire Hathaway wants to invest in Billy's World, maybe get him to provide the financing for all my rental units, and do one big mortgage over 30 years for every home, condo, town house structure, and apartment building for my two million person service city. What a business opportunity for the King of Omaha!"

\* \* \*

Jack Vogel, founder of the Vanguard Group, was also on TV. He was also commenting about the ups and downs in the market, especially the down part!

"The rule in a financial crisis is don't stand there; do something. I say don't do something; stand there!"

"Now there is one smart hombre," said Billy Pigeon to himself. "Now we know how he made all his money!"

Mr. Vogel also quoted Winston Churchill in that same interview. This is what Mr. Churchill so eloquently said: "Americans always do what is right only after they try everything else!"

"He sure had that right," said Billy Pigeon to himself, "and the American who does it right the first time will be me!"

\* \* \*

"Julie, I swear to God, if you get any more birds on top of this motor home, and a good wind comes up, we're going to lift off like a helicopter!" said Walter.

\* \* \*

Walter and Billy were kicking back in their motel room. They watched Wall Street close for another day, with Maria Bartiromo on CNBC saying the following to her TV viewers: "And it is four o'clock on Wall Street; do you know where your money is?"

"In the tank, down the toilet!" said Walter.

"In my mattress!" said Billy.

\* \* \*

It had been a long, dusty day on the trail. Our 27 riders had swallowed a lot of dust and were starving to death!

"What's for supper tonight?" asked Jack Lambert.

"Beans!" said Steven Seagal.

"The last time I saw you on TV, you were a cook on some fucking American destroyer!" said Jack Lambert.

"So?" said Steven Seagal.

"So, if I come back for supper tomorrow night and I see beans in that fucking frying pan of yours and nothing else, I'm going to personally rip your fucking head off. I don't give a shit how much fucking karate or kung fu you know!" said Jack Lambert.

\* \* \*

After their third night of beans and a farting session that would put the *Blazing Saddles*' boys to shame, Jack got into a bottle of whiskey and was soon half-pissed. Slurring his words, Jack told anyone who would listen a cowboy joke.

"Did I ever tell you guys about the cowboy who was riding across the Great Plains, just like we are, and came across a big Jesus white hat sitting on the ground in the middle of nowhere?"

"Never heard that one before," said The Rock.

"When he lifted up the hat, there was a head under it, and a set of eyes looking at him.

"'What happened to you?' asked the cowboy.

"'A bunch of Indians got me. They took all my guns. They left me buried here for the buzzards to pick out my eyeballs!' said the set of eyes. The cowboy started to walk away. The set of eyes asked him where he was going.

"'I'm going to get a shovel and some help to dig you out,' said the cowboy.

"'You'd better get more than one shovel,' said the set of eyes.

"'And why's that?' asked the cowboy.

"'Because I'm standing on my horse!' said the set of eyes."

There was laughter all around the campfire. Donald Sutherland said the following to anyone who would listen: "Fuck, that's funny!"

# 30

## Rules of Engagement

Debra told Billy a couple of interesting bits of information at his next 9:00 a.m. briefing.

"Did you hear there were 13,000 people attending a big job fair in Florida?" asked Debra.

"Tell them to hang in there," said Billy. "Tell them they'll be canceling all the job fairs soon. Tell them they can all come and work for me and help me build Billy's World. They can sleep in the construction trailer and tent cities, pee and poop in Porta-Potties, work hard all day, get paid real good money, then eat some good liver and onions, or some good mashed potatoes and Salisbury steak!"

\* \* \*

Then Debra told Billy about David Letterman being in the news again. A frequent contributor to a jihadist website was threatening David Letterman. He was urging all Muslims to cut the tongue off the late night host because of a joke the comic made on his CBS late night show about a drone strike in Pakistan that had killed al Qaeda leader Ilyas Kashmiri. Billy said the following to Debra Sanders about David Letterman: "Is there anyone he hasn't pissed off?"

\* \* \*

Billy also listened to a reporter talking about all the economic problems in Europe. He said the problem was so complex that even the great statesman Henry Kissinger would say, "What number do I call?"

"That's a good line by a smart man!" said Billy. "I think I'll record it in my Scrapbook of Life."

Billy recorded another phrase he found in a newspaper that day, a phrase which went like this: "Nothing in life is to be feared; it is only to be understood." The statement was from Marie Curie.

"That's exactly how I feel right now about Billy's World!" thought Billy as he entered that phrase under Henry Kissinger's phrase in his Scrapbook of Life.

\* \* \*

Billy also added three more comments from newer wise men, men of the modern era, much younger than Henry Kissinger—phrases written by bathroom poets in the shitter stalls of America.

"Eat shit, asshole!"

"Unless you're a hemorrhoid, get off my ass!"

"Opinions are like assholes; everyone has one!"

Billy was somewhat perplexed by the growing use of the word ass in modern American culture. Billy started to brainstorm; he wanted to see how many ass words or ass phrases he could come up with. Maybe he could do an ass poem for Julie, just like her hanky-panky poem! As words and phrases popped into his mind, Billy added them to his Scrapbook of Life.

- Kick-ass
- Ass-wipe
- Horse's ass
- Asshole
- Jackass
- Nice ass
- Piece of ass
- Your ass is grass
- Fat ass

Billy was out of ass words and phrases for the moment. He would brainstorm some more as he cruised across America. He would definitely collect enough of them for that ass poem for Julie—you never know!

\* \* \*

Billy remembered David H. E. Smith's poem in the *Moustafa and Me in World War III* book, titled "My Outdoor Shitter." He knew now why his mind was focused on the ass word and why he was doing his own list of ass words. You just know the way a fertile mind works: once you have read something or have seen something or have heard something, that something is stored in your memory forever. It might be two days, two months, two years, or twenty years, but when the moment is right and all the stars line up, and all the *T*s are crossed and the *I*s all dotted, and something triggers your memory, out it comes, from left field, and you are absolutely astonished. Weird things go on in the universe that can never be explained, like when Billy came up with the YA symbol and he went crazy and he yelled hell ya, hell ya, hell ya. Well guess what Stone Cold Steve Austin said to Clint when Clint asked him if he wanted to tag along on that horseback ride they're on as we speak. Stone Cold Steve Austin shouted to Clint "Hell ya, you can count on me!"

Who knew that the YA kids at Billy's World would be taken care of by Billy Pigeon and Stone Cold Steve Austin? Maybe Billy saw one of Stone Cold Steve Austin's performances on *Monday Night Raw*. Maybe he heard Stone Cold Steve Austin yell hell ya; maybe it was Steve's hell ya that influenced Billy. Who knows who cares? Or maybe Billy was just downright brilliant and had never seen or heard Stone Cold Steve Austin before in his life. Confusing, isn't it? To some it is, to others it's as clear as a bell—fate, serendipity, something from the *Twilight Zone*—enough said!

Let me read you one verse from "My Outdoor Shitter" to show you the influence it might—and I say might—be having on Billy Pigeon's fertile mind.

"I pray for my asshole,

Every other day,

My asshole is truly grateful,

I wasn't born gay!"

Maybe Billy got such a laugh out of that verse that he was looking in the shitter stalls all across America for a better one. As of today, he hadn't found what he was looking for!

Billy would have a similar experience with his father, Walter, way down the road, way, way down the road, one that came right out of the clear blue yonder at an unexpected moment in time. You watch for it!

\* \* \*

"Billy's World is going to be awesome!" said Billy to himself. "I don't know where my head was when I was thinking I'd have to sink my shovel in Nevada or New Mexico or Arizona. The real live, one-legged pigeon was bang-on when he sat on top of that big rock near Broken Bow. This place is perfect for what I have in mind."

"I agree!" said Walter.

\* \* \*

Debra received a call from Wolf Blitzer from CNN. Wolf Blitzer said he was setting up the rules of engagement for the pretend debate at George

Washington University. Wolf Blitzer said that the Republicans had agreed on five minutes each for an opening speech from each of their ten speakers. The other twenty Republicans sitting in the background had to listen only; they wouldn't get five minutes to speak like the other ten Republicans, but those twenty could participate in the question and answer session if they felt that they had something relevant to say. The thirty Democrats on the other side of Billy had agreed to the same conditions. All we had to do now was to agree that Billy would do a five-minute opening speech and then we could get on with the more important question and answer session.

"No, no!" said Debra Sanders. "If the Republicans get fifty minutes for their opening speeches, and the Democrats also get fifty minutes for theirs, then it's only fair that Billy Pigeon be given fifty minutes, too, time that he probably won't ever use, but nevertheless is available to him if he so chooses. Billy is the one that America really wants to hear from the most—the one who is going to blow your TV ratings through the roof! America has heard the same old, same old from your twenty other speakers for years now. Billy Pigeon should be entitled to some catch-up time!" said Debra.

"Anything else?" asked Wolf Blitzer.

"Billy goes last!" said Debra.

"I'll get back to you," said Wolf Blitzer.

"You do that!" said Debra Sanders.

# 31

## The Hungry Wolf

Billy scratched "bad ass" on a piece of paper; he would write it in his Scrapbook of Life later.

\*\*\*

The days flew by, with Billy constantly reworking the numbers, the logistics, their final choice of a location for Billy's World was of the utmost importance, with no room for error.

"Look at the map," said Billy Pigeon. "We have the Missouri River as a water source. We have the Platte River coming out of the mountains to the west. We have Lake McConaughy and look at this: the Platte River goes all the way across to Omaha. And the rail lines are exactly where we thought they'd be. We just have to hook into them, and there's tons of natural gas to the north and to the east. We can get all our supplies in Denver, Cheyenne, Omaha, Wichita, Lincoln, and Kansas City, This place is perfect!"

"I agree," said Walter. "We have everything we need!"

\*\*\*

Hold onto your horses, Billy; you are just about to get another important telephone call from Paul in Seattle. Paul just returned from a meeting with Tim Hickman. The final length and width of Billy's World was now in the computer, the numbers matching perfectly to all their needs. Tim Hickman was pumped. Tim Hickman was about to pass more bad news to Paul. Paul parked his precious BMW, walked into his beautiful home, was about to pour a scotch and water, and then call Debra.

"Billy, you have a call from Paul," said Debra.

*What now?* thought Billy.

Billy took Debra's phone; he began the conversation.

"Hi, Paul, what's up? Long time no hear from!" said Billy.

"Smart ass!" said Paul. "I hate to tell you this, Billy, but you have to bake an even bigger pie than the bigger one you're baking. The record for the one you are baking was broken yesterday in Canada!"

"No problem," said Billy. "I had a funny feeling you'd call. I know exactly what you're going to say, too. You're going to tell me I have ninety more rotten apples to deal with. I suggest we still keep our options open like we did with the other eighty rotten apples. I've got a lot more ingredients and ninety-four big, big apples to buy up in Bismarck, North Dakota," said Billy.

"We heard about those big, big apples in Bismarck, too, but we think you should go further north and buy even bigger and better ones in Minot," said Paul.

"Really, that far?" asked Billy.

"You won't believe how good the apples taste there; they're well worth the trip!" said Paul.

\* \* \*

Billy scratched "smart ass" on another piece of paper; he would add it to his Scrapbook of Life when he got a chance!

\* \* \*

When Billy and the Birdmobile reached Sioux Falls and Interstate 90, Billy kept on going north to Fargo, then all the way up Highway 29 to Grand Falls. Then he turned northwest and cruised through Devil's Lake, Rugby, Minot, and Stanley before hitting Highway 85 near the Montana border. Then turning south once more, Billy and the Birdmobile stopped for two whole days in Theodore Roosevelt National Park, with Lake Sakakawea to their left, and the Missouri River beginning its long journey south, there was more water for Billy's World than he could ever have imagined. Billy and the Birdmobile continued all the way south on Highway 85 to Spearfish in the Deadwood country, only a hop, skip, and a jump from Sundance, Robert Redford's hangout, a fitting ending for their trip through North Dakota.

\* \* \*

Billy scratched "dumb ass" on a piece of paper; he would record it in his Scrapbook of Life when he got a chance!

\* \* \*

Two hours later, Billy was on a roll, his mind going here, there, and everywhere; his mind was on fire. Where they all came from in such a short period of time was incredible—beyond belief. Billy scratched the following list on another piece of paper:

- Kiss my ass
- Sorry ass
- Bite my ass
- Tight ass
- Shit-ass luck
- Ass-kicking
- Kiss ass
- Haul ass
- Morass

Billy was definitely done with ass words now. He had plenty to write his ass poem for Julie!

\* \* \*

Billy told Debra to call the press guy following Clint to get Clint a message; tell Clint that their ride had just gotten longer, that when they hit the mountains, they were to head north, way, way, up north, way up to Montana as far as Culbertson. Then they were to head east into North Dakota, cross through Minot and Devil's Lake and go all the way to Grand Forks. They would be just below the Canadian-U. S. border, and then they were to head south, all the way through North Dakota, South Dakota, and Nebraska, all the way down to Kansas. They should arrive for the construction of Billy's World in about two years. The trip would certainly toughen them up physically and mentally. They should have just about enough time to park their horses, get changed into their Marine uniforms, head straight over to the site of the new administration building, get set up in their military tent, supervise the fence construction, and do crowd control. Billy told Debra to give Clint his best and tell him he could buy lots of beans and black coffee along the way; they had already been there and done that!

\* \* \*

Clint got word of the route change from the press guy. Clint didn't say anything; he just spit a big old gob of chewing tobacco on the ground and mumbled something to himself.

Vin Diesel was privy to the conversation between Clint and the press guy; he was a little more expressive than Clint.

"My fucking ass is killing me already, and we haven't even gone three hundred fucking miles! And now we're going two fucking years and I get to sleep under a fucking tree if I can find one and eat the shit that Seagal is pumping out of that chuck wagon. Fuck that noise! Why the hell couldn't you do a car movie with lots of explosions, lots of girls, and lots of action? Who was the bright fucking idiot who thought this up anyway, to ride around the prairies on a fucking horse?"

"That would be me and Jack, asshole," said Chuck Norris. "I haven't kicked someone's behind in a long time. You want to go, right here, right now? Come on, let's go!"

"Settle down, boys, settle down!" said Bruce Willis.

"Who the fuck asked you?" said Vin Diesel, with Dick Butkus and John Riggins standing up and walking toward Vin Diesel; Larry Csonka and Jack Lambert joined them, too.

"Should I kill him, or are you going to do it?" asked Dick Butkus.

"No, no, you go ahead. I'll watch!" said John Riggins.

"I saw a big fucking wolf this morning," said Larry Csonka. "He looked real hungry to me."

"That's a great idea," said Jack Lambert. "I'll just rip his fucking leg off first to see if the wolf likes it. If he does, then I'll rip the other fucking leg off, then each fucking one of his arms!"

"That should make the wolf happy!" said Dick Butkus.

\* \* \*

"Julie, would you like something to do?" asked Billy.

"Sure," said Julie.

"Count all the places on the map from Interstate 70 in the south all the way up to Highway 2 in North Dakota; that's half of Kansas, part of Colorado, all of Nebraska, all of South Dakota and three quarters of North Dakota. Go from Highway 29 on the east side, all the way across to Highway 25 on the west side," said Billy.

"Every one of them?" asked Julie.

"I don't care if you miss the odd one; just give me a ballpark," said Billy.

\* \* \*

"Got your number!" shouted Julie, completing her count in five minutes. Her map was full of $X$s drawn in pencil.

"Already done?" asked Billy.

"You bet I am!" said Julie. "There are about 146 towns if you don't count the towns along the main highway making up your border."

"Hmmm," said Billy, "not as many as I expected."

\* \* \*

Ring, ring, ring…

"Hi, Debra Sanders speaking."

"You got your fifty minutes!" said Wolf Blitzer. "And Billy goes last!"

"Great stuff!" said Debra.

\* \* \*

It was one of those rare moments in time shared by all, a beautiful moment on a long stretch of lonely highway, with Julie finding an oldies, but goodies radio station, and the Beatles singing one of the greatest songs ever recorded, the song starting out like this:

"Hey, Jude, don't make it bad,

Take a sad song and make it better,

Remember to let her into your heart,

Then you can start to make it better."

Walter and Debra knew all the words to "Hey Jude." Billy and Julie were blown away, quiet as two church mice, their eyes looking at each other, their mouths ajar. Walter and Debra sang "Hey Jude" at the top of their voices, singing in unison once more:

"Hey, Jude, don't be afraid,

You were made to go out and get her,

The minute you let her under your skin,

Then you begin to make it better.

And anytime you feel the pain, hey Jude, refrain

Don't carry the world upon your shoulders

For well you know that it's a fool who plays it cool

By making his world a little colder

Nah nah nah nah nah nah, nah nah nah,"

Walter and Debra knew each and every word of "Hey Jude," singing the fourth and fifth and the sixth verses and then singing:

"Nah nah nah nah nah nah, nah nah nah, hey Jude" sixteen more times, the final "Nah nah nah nah nah nah, nah nah nah, hey Jude" as important as the previous fifteen. The song came to an end, with Debra and Walter high-fiving each other, the way it should be, and Billy and Julie still in shock and awe, their heads shaking in disbelief—go figure!

* * *

Billy was on the Internet. He read, with great interest, about the European astronomers who found a new planet capable of sustaining life in the Goldilocks Zone. The new planet was about 3.6 times the mass of Earth; temperatures there range from 30 to 50 degrees Celsius with plenty of humidity. The new planet was called HD855126 and closely circles a star about 203 trillion miles away from Earth. Billy was excited. He told Walter about what he had read, and then he said the following: "Glad we don't have to drive the Birdmobile there!"

"You got that right!" said Walter.

\* \* \*

The following morning, Billy Pigeon pulled the Birdmobile into one of those 146 one-horse towns Julie had crossed on her map with the letter $X$. The one-horse town was in South Dakota. The residents of the one-horse town welcomed Billy with open arms. One of the little old ladies wore a big old white T-shirt. It had some writing on the front; this is what it said:

THE ONLY THING
GOLDEN ABOUT
MY GOLDEN YEARS
IS MY URINE!

When Billy saw the T-shirt, he said the following to himself: "Am I ever going to make her happy!"

\* \* \*

The residents of the one-horse town thought it was wonderful that a future president would take the time to grace them with his presence. They waved American flags, asked Billy for his autograph, and shook his hand. Their handshakes were firm from a life of hard work, trying to make something from nothing, from scratching out a living in their little one-horse town.

Billy was invited for a free lunch at their only restaurant in their only general store next to their only motel next to their only gas station. Billy took them up on their offer, knowing that he wasn't dealing with the mayor of Chicago, and no political favors were going to be asked for by these residents. About thirty or so of the hundred or so residents stuffed into the little restaurant; the residents were all ears when Billy Pigeon spoke.

"So what if I offered you way more money than you would ever dream possible for your home and land in your tiny town, and also promised to give you free rent for the rest of your lives, in a fully furnished, one, two, or three bedroom condo with nice friends and a swimming pool and fantastic air conditioning and wheelchair access? And if you don't want to retire, I'm going to offer you a job with a great salary and benefits and medical and dental and a self-controlled pension plan working in a brand new complex I'm going to build and living in a brand new city I'm going to build right next to my complex—what would you say to that?" asked Billy Pigeon.

"I'd say would you like some ice cream on your apple pie Mr. President," said the owner of the little restaurant. "Would you like your apple pie heated up?"

"Are you serious?"

"You're kidding me right?"
"When do we leave?"
"Can I bring my cat and my dog?"
"How soon do you want me to sign on the dotted line?"
"You have my vote, Billy Pigeon!"
"You can't get me out of this one-horse town quick enough!"
"Can I give you a big kiss?"
"Can I pour you a second cup of coffee?"

\* \* \*

"Actually, there is something I do need," said Billy Pigeon. "We're out of crunchy croutons for our real live, one-legged pigeon!"

"Come over to my house, dear. I bought a whole case of them when I was in town last week. They're all yours, you sweet little thing!" said one super-duper nice old lady, the same lady who wore the Golden Years T-shirt.

"And there's one other thing," said Billy Pigeon. "Loose lips sink ships. I need you to keep quiet about my little offer until I become president, or my offer goes down the tube!"

"Don't you worry about that with us. We're not going to screw up a chance of a lifetime. This is better than winning a big old lottery!" said another nice old lady.

"And besides," said the lady in the Golden Years T-shirt, "there's no one else here to talk to anyway besides us chickens!"

\* \* \*

Billy grabbed a newspaper as he left the little restaurant. He saw that McDonald's sales had grown 5.1 percent in the last quarter.

"We've got to work on that," said Billy Pigeon to himself.

\* \* \*

Billy discussed McDonald's with Debra at their afternoon briefing. He told Debra that maybe they should make some phone calls, tell a company like Whole Foods Market that it was in the best interest of the country that they take a run at purchasing McDonald's, and give McDonald's a new lease on life!

"Even better," said Billy Pigeon, now thinking way out of the box, "why don't we, when we form the government, enact new legislation in Congress forcing fast food companies like McDonald's, Burger King, Taco Time, Kentucky Fried Chicken, and Papa John's to place awful labels on their packaging just like they do to the tobacco industry. We could have pictures of really fat people sitting down, their behinds hanging over the seat of their chairs; we could have them pricking their fingers with their blood glucose readers!"

"I'm sure the fast food industry would love you for that, Mr. President. No, I like your first idea better. Confine the YA kids to Billy's World for the next five years: 20 million young Americans eating hot, healthy meals, with no junk food to be had, with our resident psychiatrist on staff at each of the five hundred hospitals ready to deal quickly with the ones suffering from withdrawal symptoms, affecting the quality of their work!" said Debra.

"Out of sight, out of mind!" said Billy.

"Exactly," said Debra.

\* \* \*

After Julie and Billy worked up a sweat with more Newfoundland kisses, which led naturally into some good old hanky-panky with a condom in the back seat of Julie's Jeep Wrangler, Julie asked Billy how he came up with the name Newfoundland kisses.

"When I was at Headwaters talking to David H. E. Smith, the Canadian author," said Billy, "I asked him how he came up with all those out of the box solutions to problems in the world. He said it wasn't easy, that it was hard work, that I should pick a couple of new problems of my own, try racking my brains out for a solution, that a solution will come after a lot of soul searching, gut wrenching, brain storming sessions using some elbow grease and some midnight oil!

"So I chose two: I tried to invent a new kiss with my imagination and I tried to find a new way to get rid of plastic when I heard about all the albatrosses swallowing all the plastic floating debris in the Pacific Ocean and dying horrible deaths."

"That's why you pick up all the plastic pop and liquor bottles, isn't it?" asked Julie. "So animals won't chew on them or swallow them whole!"

"You're partly right," said Billy. "I also don't like lazy littering, and the money is an added bonus!"

"You've obviously solved the new kiss problem. What about the plastic problem?" asked Julie.

"I have a chemical engineer friend named David. He's just starting at U-Dub. We're real close to a new formula that disintegrates plastic when it comes into contact with salt, just like when you put it into a burning fire, only this does it without all the black smoke and the noxious fumes. It's like melting ice, like something out of *The Terminator* movie when the bad cop just turns into mush. David and I are going to open a new company one day when we patent the formula. David and I are going to make a mint!

"So that still doesn't answer my original question: why Newfoundland kisses?" asked Julie.

"Because David H. E. Smith was born in Gander, Newfoundland, the same little town of 10,000 people that opened up its heart and its homes to nearly 6,700 airline passengers and crews who were stranded in Newfoundland after all the flights were grounded in the chaotic aftermath of 9–11, the attack on the World Trade Center in New York and the Pentagon in Washington, D. C.

"I named the kiss after him for teaching me how to think out of the box, and in appreciation of what his hometown of Gander did for the U. S. of A. in our time of need. So now you know the rest of the story!" said Billy.

"Amazing!" said Julie.

\* \* \*

Debra also informed Billy of the explosive situation in London, England. The riots there were expanding throughout the city. Prime Minister Cameron was getting really uptight and young people were going absolutely nuts, burning whole sections of the city down, looting more stores, and scaring the beJesus out of the townsfolk.

"I have got to start working on an English version of Billy's World," said Billy, "or I have to fit them in over here!"

"Young people in the world need hope that there's something positive for them down the road," said a concerned Walter.

"I think you're spot-on," said Debra.

"Thank God for Billy," said Julie.

"Ditto," said Debra.

"Another ditto," said Walter.

\* \* \*

Then Debra showed Billy a Washington Post headline, the headline read: "If Only We Had a Triple 'A' Leader!"

"I'm coming, I'm coming," said Billy Pigeon, "but I can only drive so fast!"

"Should we worry about the rest of the world, too?" asked Billy.

"Sure we should," said Debra, "but focus on America first. Let's get our own house in order; let's show the world what a great leader you are before we do anything else. Trust me, Mr. President, your model of success will be copied the world over. You won't even have to leave Washington to have your ideas for political, economic, and moral change embraced the world over. Billy's World franchises will be in hot demand!"

"You really think so?" asked Billy.

"I know so!" said Debra. "Now go get some rest; we have a long day tomorrow."

"I'm glad you're thinking about the rest of the world," said Julie.

\* \* \*

Billy also read another newspaper article on his laptop. The newspaper article said that President Obama was doing such a lousy job as president that he should give back his Nobel peace prize he received in Oslo.

"Politics is a cruel business!" said Billy Pigeon to himself. "One day you're king of the hill; the next day, they want to throw you to the wolves. Yikes!"

\* \* \*

And speaking of wolves, Vin Diesel let his big old horse drift back to the end of the line. He rode a little bit ahead of Steven Seagal in his chuck wagon. Vin Diesel was wide awake, watching every move that Jack Lambert made!

\* \* \*

Billy was reminded of a quote he had recorded from a prominent Seattle businessman. I'm sure you know him. His name is Bill Gates. This is what Bill Gates once said: "Success is a lousy teacher. It seduces smart people into thinking that they can't lose!"

"I have to remember that," thought Billy Pigeon, "maybe I should e-mail a copy to President Obama. Nah, I'm sure he's got lots of fine people giving him plenty of good advice! I also have to remember, he's my competition—big-time."

\* \* \*

"Did you see the two dogs by the gas station back there?" asked Julie.

"I did," said Billy.

"The poor big golden doodle dog was squished into the little dog house, his front feet a foot out onto the dirt; the little beagle dog was sleeping comfortably in the middle of the big dog house!" said Julie.

"It's called little dog syndrome!" said Billy Pigeon, with Debra busting a gut, with Walter busting a gut too!

\* \* \*

"Billy, it's Paul again."

"What's up, Paul?" asked Billy.

"We're going to work around and up over the 80 rotten apples and the 90 rotten apples and the 94 rotten apples, too. We think they'll make your apple pie even taste better. I have that from an apple pie expert. He feels that if we set up apple stores everywhere, tourists will flock into your apple stores like crazy to look around to see exactly how you make your apples. They'll probably even pay an admission fee of $20 that you can put into a big old glass bottle and use to pay against your student loan. Even better, you can put all those $20 bills toward that big rainy day account that you were talking about so you can go to graduate school and never have to deal with any more student loans, ever! They'll probably want to buy a sandwich and a coffee, too, and maybe stay at a local hotel overnight. That should really help out the local hotel business!" said Paul.

"That is one fantastic, unbelievable, incredible, brilliant idea!" said Billy Pigeon.

"Ditto!" said Debra.

"Ditto, ditto!" said Walter.

"Ditto, ditto, ditto!" said Julie.

\* \* \*

"That is one interesting proposition young man!" said Warren Buffett, the King of Omaha. "I'll tell you what: I'm going to go out on a limb on this one. I'm not even going to discuss it with anyone else at Berkshire Hathaway. I've been a risk-taker all my life; I'm in. I'll set up Berkshire Hathaway Financial. I'll do your one, 30-year, big mortgage for your two million people service city!"

"Thank you, sir!" said Billy Pigeon.

"If you're ever on my home turf again around Thanksgiving, drop by my house with our family for turkey dinner!" said Warren Buffett.

"I will," said Billy Pigeon. "I promise. One more thing: mum's the word till I'm elected president."

"Mum's the word," said Warren Buffett. "I didn't get where I am today by being a blabbermouth, Billy. I like to surprise people—catch them off guard!"

"Me, too!" said Billy Pigeon.

\* \* \*

Billy had heard through the grapevine about General Jessep's plans for the fence line construction. He thought the plan was brilliant, especially the two flags flying over each of the 210 security checkpoints.

As the Birdmobile drove through another quaint little one-horse town, this is what Julie said: "Look at those flags, Billy; that is just so cool. Look at the American and the Mexican flags flying together on the top of that garage. He must be American and she must be Mexican, or vice versa."

"That's nice, said Debra. "It's almost inspirational in a way, wouldn't you agree, Walter?"

"If you say so," said Walter.

"What do you think Billy?" asked Debra.

"I don't know what to think," said Billy. "I'll have to give that one some thought!"

\* \* \*

Julie read from Billy's Scrapbook of Life. This is what she read: "An audience of one thousand was in an auditorium in Ottawa, Canada. There were TV cameras, too. The moderator was on the microphone to the two finalists of the national poetry contest. One of the finalists was a Harvard English professor from Boston, but born in Toronto, the other finalist a fisherman from Arnold's Cove, Newfoundland.

"The moderator told the two finalists that the final poem to decide the winner should be four lines long, have rhyming couplets and end in the word Timbuktu. The moderator passed the microphone to the Harvard professor first. The professor was quiet; then after a minute or so, he said the following:

"Across the desert sand,

Trekked a lonely caravan,

Men on camels, two by two,

Destination Timbuktu!"

The audience stood up; they applauded the professor. He took a bow before sitting down.

The fisherman from Newfoundland was next. He took the microphone. He too was quiet. He scratched the back of his hairy neck and then his chin, with a grin appearing on his face. This is what he said to the hushed audience.

"Me and Tim a-hunting went,

Spied three whores in a pop-up tent,

They was three, and we was two,

So I bucked one and Timbuktu!"

Walter and Debra were still busting a gut when Julie asked Billy the following question: "Where on God's green Earth did you find that story?"

"From my writer friend in Penticton!" said Billy Pigeon. "He told me I could use it for a laugh some day in front of a large audience."

"So will you use it when you're president?" asked Julie.

"Yes, I think I will!" said Billy.

*\*\**

"What's Donald Sutherland doing with us?" asked Bruce Willis. "I thought he was Canadian."

"He is," said Sylvester Stallone, "but he's pretty tight with Tommy Lee and James Garner and Clint. Clint says he spends more time in the states than he does in Canada. He's more American than he is Canadian as far as he's concerned. I think I even read somewhere that he obtained his American citizenship, but don't quote me on that."

"So I guess the Canadian stays," said Bruce Willis.

"I guess so," said Sylvester Stallone.

"So, changing the subject, are you doing another Rocky or Rambo sequel?" asked Bruce Willis.

"I might; it just depends on how my investments are doing," said Sylvester Stallone. "How about you, do you have any sequels lined up to go?"

"Not me, I'm done!" said Bruce Willis. "I've had enough lights, camera, action for two lifetimes, but thanks for asking!"

"How long are you going to stay on this ride?" asked Sylvester Stallone.

"It depends on the cooking, my man; it depends on the cooking!" said Bruce Willis.

\* \* \*

Julie was into pizza again.

"The vegetarian for me," said Debra.

"Me, too!" said Billy.

"Me, three," said Julie. "I'm trying the spinach one! What about you, Walter; what do you want to order tonight?"

"I'm not sure; maybe I'll try something different. I could use a little meat in my diet," said Walter.

Billy knew his father was a lost cause, would never change his ways, and would never stick to the vegetarian pizza.

"Then try the Mexican one," said Billy. "I hear it's really good!"

\* \* \*

"Don't forget the goddamn receipt!" yelled Walter.

# 32

# The Men in Black

Steven Seagal was also thinking about food as he purchased a big old pig from a farmer in a tiny, one-horse town along the trail. The pig was soon on the spit, over a bed of hot coals, his twenty-six companions happy as can be, knowing that they were about to chow down and chomp on big, thick, juicy cuts of fresh pork to go along with their plate of beans.

As Clint chowed down on his dinner, his eyes were soon focused on the two sets of legs parked in front of him. The two strangers were dressed in black, with black boots, black pants above their ankles, black jackets, white shirts, black ties, long beards and tall top hats with flat brims.

"Sorry to bother you, sir," said one of the men in black, "but we're from New York City. We heard that there were more Jewish people in the area! Have you seen any in your travels?"

"Do I look like the American ambassador to Israel?" asked Clint.

"Don't mind him," said Tommy Lee Jones. "Would you like to stay for dinner?"

"No thank you, sir, we'll pass!" said one of the men in black. Sylvester Stallone was busting a gut, spitting all his beans out of his mouth. The mouthful of beans landed all over the back of Jack Lambert's clean shirt that he had just changed into!

\*\*\*

"Look at that," said Walter, "gas prices are going down, big time!"

"At least there's one positive thing happening in America!" said Debra.

\*\*\*

Billy watched another commentator on CNBC; this is what the commentator said: "The compass is spinning; the stock market is turning upside down. This is a time when fortunes are made!"

"That's easy for you to say!" said Billy Pigeon.

\* \* \*

"Sarah just called and asked if she could use some of our campaign donations to pay her Visa and MasterCard bills!" said Walter. "I told her to go right ahead!"

"You didn't!" said Debra.

"No, of course I didn't. I told Sally to pay ours with it!" said Walter with a smile.

\* \* \*

With the exception of Billy's white shirt, which he was saving for special occasions only, the collars on both his other used shirts were really getting frayed and were coming apart at the seams.

"Start looking for a Thrift Store," said Billy.

"What for?" asked Julie.

"I need two more shirts; mine are falling apart," said Billy.

"Let me buy you a couple of new ones," said Julie.

"We can probably write it off as a legitimate campaign expense," said Walter.

"Nope, I'm buying them used again. I'm buying them with my credit card, and then I'll pay it back to zero. I have to set that example I want my 20 million YA kids to follow. I have a promise to keep to myself. It's tempting, but no thank you!" said Billy.

\* \* \*

"Here's a question for you," said Debra.

"And what's that?" asked Billy.

"How many kids in London, England, under the age of 25, have never worked a day in their lives?" asked Debra.

"I have no idea," said Billy.

"Try 600,000!" said Debra.

"Holy shit!" said Billy.

"Holy shit is right!" said Debra.

"Did you know what one teacher there said about them?" asked Debra.

"I have no idea," said Billy.

"She said nothing is expected of them," said Debra.

"Well, if they ever make it to my world, life will be a hell of a lot different!" said Billy Pigeon.

\* \* \*

The crowds in and around Deadwood were awestruck with Billy Pigeon and his Birdmobile—the four-foot-tall, carved, one-legged pigeon, the two Billy Pigeon for President signs. One young lady from the Deadwood area said the following to Billy Pigeon: "We're stoked; me and my brother both signed up to go to your War on Jobs. We figure to stay for a good ten years and come back home with over $200,000 in our blue jeans!"

"I'm stoked, too!" said Billy Pigeon.

"We've already chucked out all the raunchy CDs we had. We're not watching any more porn on the Internet. I even bought a bra to go inside my T-shirt! My mom was so proud of me. My brother Teddy sold his two dozen marijuana joints he had hidden away. He got five bucks each for them. He took the $120 and opened a savings account at the bank; he has over $146 in his account as we speak!" said the young lady from the Deadwood area.

"Good for him!" said Billy. "Good for you, too!" said Billy, biting his tongue, trying to keep his eyes off the two beautiful breasts inside the bra of the young lady from the Deadwood area, her nipples still bulging, still pushing out through her bra for the world to see!

"So why can't you tell us what we're doing and where we're going?" asked the young lady from the Deadwood area.

"You have to wait another year or so till I'm president, and then I'll spill the beans," said Billy.

"And then we have to wait four more years after that," said the young lady from the Deadwood area.

"And you'll be all grown up by then!" said Billy Pigeon.

"I'm all grown up now!" said the young lady from the Deadwood area, her hard nipples now at six inches and counting from Billy's nose. Billy was hard-pressed to get out of Dodge!

\*\*\*

"Were you flirting with that girl?" asked Julie.

"She was flirting with me!" said Billy.

"If I ever see her doing it again, I'm going to punch her one!" said Julie.

"On national TV?" asked Billy.

"On national TV!" said a ticked-off Julie.

\*\*\*

At the next stop down the road, Billy instructed all twenty of his security detail from Spokane to keep a minimum five-foot buffer zone between him and his loyal followers. There were to be no exceptions—none!

\*\*\*

At a small restaurant, Billy took a breather from people. He caught up on the news. He saw the wives of the Navy Seals and the U. S. Marines killed by the Taliban on that night raid in Afghanistan balling their eyes out and their children balling their eyes out, too, knowing that they would never see their daddy again. Their daddy would just be another name on another cross in a cemetery called Arlington, filled with thousands and thousands and thousands of dead American soldiers. Their Daddy was there because he was probably one of those thousands and thousands and thousands of young Americans who didn't have the grades to go to college, or couldn't find a good paying job. So when the military recruiters came calling in their community, they got caught up in all the excitement and the hoopla and ended up in places like Vietnam, Iraq, and Afghanistan, and ended up in wooden boxes at Dover Air Force Base on their way to Arlington because of stupid policy decisions made by their own government leaders.

Then Billy saw Jamie Dimon on TV. Jamie Dimon, the somewhat arrogant head cheese at JP Morgan Chase, who, on the same day in America that the soldiers and sailors and airmen's wives and children were balling their eyes out, was riding in a big old fancy motor home three times the length of the Birdmobile, maybe even longer, in his blue jeans, holding a cup of Starbucks coffee, full of smiles for the press. Jamie jumped out of the motor home with joy, giving handshakes, high-fiving and giving big old hugs to waiting admirers who were employees of a brand new JP Morgan Chase bank branch opening in California. Jamie Dimon said something like this: "I don't see any problems in America. Everything is hunky-dory. Our banks have lots of capital. There is good liquidity in the system; loan losses are going down, down, down. There's lots to be thankful for in America, so don't worry, be happy!"

"There's something wrong with this picture: a tale of two cities," thought Billy Pigeon. "I am bringing our soldiers, sailors and airmen home. I mean what I say. I want all of America to be happy, especially the children. They're only going to war if it is absolutely necessary to help a friend in need, or if a foreign power steps its boots on American soil. We will use our technology to attack and defend. We will keep a strong military presence in America, ready to defend and protect with their lives, if need be—end of story!"

\* \* \*

Billy had seen a lot of people on his trip around America: a lot of people standing on the side of the road looking for handouts, wearing cardboard signs on their chests, with string around their necks, to catch the attention of motorists and pedestrians alike. Some of the signs were creative, but in Billy's humble opinion, and certainly worthy of his Scrapbook of Life, was this sign, the best sign yet:

---

**NEED MONEY**

Too hungry to travel,

Suck at stealing,

Too ugly to prostitute!

---

Howie Long pulled his big old horse up next to Clint's horse. He told Clint that his behind was getting sore and that his Chevy Silverado back home in his garage would have been his preferred choice of travel. Clint was not impressed, not even remotely!

"I thought you Raider boys were real men, not a bunch of fucking pussies! Now get your ass back in line, quit your goddamn whining, and suck it up like the rest of us!" said Clint.

"Sorry about that!" said Howie Long.

"Shut the fuck up!" said an angry Clint. "I've got enough fucking problems of my own!"

\*\*\*

"Are you okay?" asked a concerned Jack.

"I'm okay; I just hate whiners!" said Clint.

\*\*\*

"Now gas prices are going up again!" said Walter in disgust. "What the hell is going on with the world?"

"Who the hell knows?" said Debra.

\*\*\*

When Billy exited from another restaurant in another one-horse town on another day on the campaign trail, he ran into another card-carrying member of the RPA, a YA kid with a comment.

"There's a rumor going around that you're not going to allow any junk food in Billy's World when we go to work there in another five or so years."

"That's correct," said Billy Pigeon.

"Just so you know, my mom says that's a good thing!" said the YA kid.

"You tell your mom I like her already," said Billy. "Tell her I'll look forward to meeting her when she comes to visit you."

"Will do," said the YA kid.

\*\*\*

At the same restaurant stop, after Billy had emptied his bladder and washed his hands in another run-down washroom, another YA kid caught up to Billy. He was huffing and puffing; he caught his breath, adjusted his glasses, and spoke to Billy.

"Mr. President, Mr. President, do you have any investment ideas for all that money we're going to save, or are we on our own? My mom is saying muni-bonds, my dad is saying good American blue chip companies like IBM, Johnson & Johnson, and Merck, companies that pay a healthy dividend, my sister says gold, and my little brother, who's only four, says keep it in my piggy bank!" said the YA kid.

"Stick with your little brother!" said Billy Pigeon.

\* \* \*

At the same restaurant, Billy couldn't help but notice the T-shirt of a big old beer-bellied trucker. This is what his T-shirt said:

DON'T ACT STUPID,
WE HAVE ENOUGH
WORLD LEADERS FOR THAT!

*Don't worry,* thought Billy Pigeon. *I'll be in a league of my own.*

\* \* \*

"Did you know that there are roughly 300 million people living in the U. S. of A. today and only 153 million are working?" asked Debra.

"I hadn't heard that stat," said Billy, pulling out his little pocket calculator. "So if the numbers are correct and only 9 percent of American workers are in the manufacturing sector that means there are only 14. 8 million Americans producing Made in America products today. So if I add another 20 million workers at Billy's World in five more years, the percentage goes up to 23 percent, if I add another 20 million more in 9 more years, the percentage goes up to 35 percent, and if I add 20 more million in 13 years, then the percentage goes up to 48 percent. That's where I want it to be; that's where I have to be to get our $70 trillion federal government debt to zero in 24 years!"

"And how are you going to do all that?" asked Debra.

"Already baked into the cake!" said Billy Pigeon.

\* \* \*

"So, Billy, let's play Devil's Advocate," said Julie.

"Let's play," said Billy.

"What happens if one of your YA boys meets a YA girl and they go off to one of your five thousand hotels and they have hanky-panky without a condom and nine months later the YA girl has a little baby boy or little baby girl—what are you going to do with them then?" asked Julie.

"If that happens, which it won't because I'm going to be big on safe sex and because all the YA kids are going to know that if that does happen, then out they go, to a rented apartment in the service city, their dream of $50,000 each in their blue jeans after five years will be gone, gone, gone. They'll spend their Friday evenings changing poopy diapers and listening to a baby cry when they could be out on the town having a good old time!" said Billy.

"What if the girl says she can take some time off and have an abortion and then be right back to work?" asked Julie.

"I don't like that idea one little bit!" said Billy. "It's an easy way out in today's world of sexual promiscuity. I hate the thought of dead babies as much as I hate dead soldiers," said Billy.

"Right on!" said Walter.

"Good for you!" said Debra.

\* \* \*

It didn't take Howie Long forever to find out why Clint had a big burr up his ass earlier in the day, that it wasn't just the Chevy Silverado comment that was upsetting Clint. It was all about saddle bags; the majority of the saddle bags were filled with Samsung lithium batteries instead of beef jerky. His cowboys were constantly talking on their cell phones, more focused on the action on Wall Street than the lay of the land, the call of the wild. Bruce Willis, Sylvester Stallone, and The Rock were getting hourly updates on their investment portfolios, which were tanking as we speak. The pressure on a lot of our pretend cowboys was mounting: do I hold or do I sell. Almost everyone in Clint's trail ride was in the same boat, with the majority of Clint's cowboys soon to be on a Lear jet and heading back to L. A. or wherever. A final decision would be made over a hot meal of beans and three-day-old, leftover pork, with *The Dirty Two Dozen Plus Three, Cowboy Style* movie soon to be renamed *The Dirty Half Dozen Plus Five, Cowboy Style* or *The Dirty Dozen Minus One, Cowboy Style,* take your pick!

A runway was a day's ride, with the desperate riders picking up the pace, passing Clint and his real cowboys, leaving a trail of dust for as long as the eye could see, with Arnold speaking for everyone skipping town when he said the following to Clint: "We'll be back—maybe!"

\* \* \*

When Clint saw the little Learjet fly over the remaining horseback riders, he looked at Jack, Jack looked at him, and they both spit big old gobs of chewing tobacco on the ground, with Clint's gob the heaviest, kicking up the most dust!

"Do you have any whiskey left?" asked Clint.

"Enough," said Jack.

"That's the best thing I've heard all day!" said Clint.

"What will you do if they all come back?" asked Jack.

"I'll tell them to their face, I don't want them back," said Clint. "Don't worry, you won't see them again!"

\* \* \*

When Julie took the real live, one-legged pigeon out for his early morning pee and poop and his fly-around exercise session, the real live one-legged pigeon didn't return to Julie's arm. He didn't hop back into Julie's cage like he always did; for some unknown reason, he flew, flew away and was gone, gone, gone again!

\* \* \*

Breaking news on CNN...

This is Wolf Blitzer reporting to you live from New York. CNN is first to confirm, from reliable sources, that the real live, one-legged pigeon has flown the coop again!"

Bird watchers all across America were back on the road again, and David Letterman was jumping for joy again, the terrorist threat suddenly a thing of the past, a distant memory!

\* \* \*

Even Jack wasn't immune to all the rumors on the trail.

"I own a shit-load of Bank of America stock!" said Jack.

"That's not good!" said Clint.

"Arnold said they're even talking about preparing bankruptcy papers," said Jack.

"That bad?" asked Clint. "Do you want to take a day and go dump your stock?"

"I'd really appreciate it!" said Jack.

"Just be back in 24 hours," said Clint. "I'm not waiting around to fuck the dog!"

\* \* \*

Debra told Billy that the New York Bank of Melon was laying off 1,500 employees, Cisco 2,000 employees, Bank of America 3,500 employees. State governments were also announcing layoffs like crazy; some cities were declaring bankruptcy.

"Hang in there, boys and girls, your knight in shining armor will be jumping on his big old horse real soon!" said Billy.

\* \* \*

"Gas prices are going down again!" said Walter.

"Unreal!" said Debra.

\* \* \*

Debra also read Billy the comment made by another Wall Street financial advisor. This is what he said: "We're getting close to the abyss; we have no lifeline to pull us back!"

"I've got a lifeline," said Billy. "I've got a big lifeline. I'm going to throw it real soon, trust me!"

\* \* \*

"Gas prices are going up again!" said Walter.

"Why?" asked Debra.

"Who the hell knows?" asked Walter.

\* \* \*

Billy Pigeon was all eyes and ears. He traveled from town to town, from city to city. He signed autographs. He shook hands. He could feel the pulse of America. He could see the desperation in peoples' eyes, all running like Clint's cowboys. All that it would take to really set them off was a big old earthquake in Washington or New York, to have the power go off for three or four days, with no traffic lights, no hot coffee, no showers, no hair blowers, no TV. Americans were over the edge, all stressed out. Billy could sense the nervousness in America like no other time in his life. He knew most Americans were leveraged to the nuts, their house mortgages and car loans and credit lines and credit cards all tied to the stability of the financial system. Every world economy was into deficit financing, leveraged to the nuts, too, to support the good life. American investors were flocking to gold as a safe haven, as a way to make a quick buck. JP Morgan Chase said that gold could hit $2,500 an ounce by the end of 2011. Policy makers in Washington were unable to get a grip on the fast-changing economic landscape. Wall Street was up, down, up, down, up, down on a daily basis, just like oil prices, with computers and margin calls controlling Wall Street, the stock market was in chaos. Social media were feeding information to people the world over like never before. North American investors were no longer isolated; the economy of the U. S. of A. was now global, with European and Asian problems now American's problems. A lot of really smart members of academia feared the worst, *The Doomsday Report*, the worst of the worst, the world close to economic catastrophe, the world up to its eyeballs in debt, the system like a house of cards that could come tumbling down with the push of a finger!

\*\*\*

"Gas prices are going up again!" said Walter.
"I don't care any more!" said Debra.
"Well you should care!" said Walter.
"Well I don't!" said Debra.

\*\*\*

"Find me a stream; I need to go fly-fishing again. I want to see if these prairie fish will take a Royal Coachman," said Billy Pigeon.

\*\*\*

Julie was ticked; she expressed her concerns to Billy, Walter, and Debra. She did not mince her words.

"You know, I'm really upset with Jane Fonda! I liked her once. I thought she was the cat's meow. Have you heard about her new book, *Prime-Time?* Instead of getting off her butt and going to Somalia to tell the world to do something about all the starving children there, she's sitting on her butt in her bed and telling old people to play with their sex toys! I'm pissed!" said Julie.

\*\*\*

*We need savings,* thought Billy. *We need 20 million young Americans walking into my bank and adding another $57 to their $48,000 in cash, to stand in the teller line and feel the strength of real money, to be debt free, to have normal blood pressure, and to take time to smell the roses.* A really frisky little trout nailed Billy's Royal Coachman fly in the little stream. Billy waved to a twelve-year-old boy legitimately driving a big old tractor, giving Billy the thumbs up. The young boy saw the flashing lights of the State Trooper cars, the black Suburbans, the Birdmobile and he knew exactly who was unknowingly fly-fishing on private property. This particular fly-fisherman was allowed to stay and fish for as long as he wanted—end of story.

\* \* \*

Billy Pigeon caught six of those frisky little fish and Julie cooked them for dinner. Julie was always in an inquisitive mood, always wanting to make the world a better place.

"So what are you going to do about nuclear weapons when you become president?" asked Julie.

"I'm not sure," said Billy, as he continued to pick his teeth with the hard plastic toothpick from his Swiss Army knife. "I guess as long as everyone else has them, we have to have them, too."

"We could collect them all, lease them out when countries want to use them to play their game of chicken, write out when and how long and where to use them on a signed contract, get their John Hancocks, and we're good to go. We could even write the leases off if the leased warheads actually go ka-boom!" said Walter with a grin. Debra's eyes perked up, and she said the following to Billy Pigeon: "What else would you expect from a banker?"

\* \* \*

"Gas prices are going down again!" said Walter.
"I told you, I don't care!" said Debra.

\* \* \*

On a slow news day in Washington, a secret service agent working the White House detail saw all the commotion at the big old black metal fence out front, a fence to keep all the looky-loos and the demonstrators out.

"What the hell is going on?" asked the secret service agent.

"I'm not sure," said his secret service agent buddy. "There were no protests scheduled for today, nothing that I'm aware of."

One lady outside the fence, still wearing her pitch black oil outfit from the American-Canadian Keystone XL Pipeline protest, started to let out a really loud scream, like she was going to charge the White House, like she had won a $50 million lottery prize. After she finished screaming, this is what she said to anyone who would listen: "It's him, the $100,000 bird!"

# 33

# Deep Throat

"That Margot Kidder's a real hard lady to get a hold of," said Billy Pigeon. "I've been trying her house for days."

"She might still be in jail," said Debra.

"In jail, I never heard about that!" said Billy.

"You didn't; sorry, my fault, she got dragged away by police at the Keystone XL environmental protest in Washington just recently," said Debra.

"Maybe that's why she's not answering her phone," said Billy.

"Did you leave a message?" asked Debra.

"I did," said Billy. Debra had made a dozen more calls to some of the most powerful people in the American environmental movement. She was even trying to get Robert Redford to attend the big meeting in Colorado, but his secretary said he was on the road looking for some kid named Billy Pigeon. Debra got his cell phone number; his message recorder said "all full"!

"It's time to have some fun with Robert Redford and Dustin Hoffman," said Billy Pigeon, fully aware of the two real Washington Post reporters giving Paul the gears in Seattle. Billy also saw on TV that Robert Redford and Dustin Hoffman were re-enacting their roles as the ageless wonders Bob Woodward and Carl Bernstein from the Washington Post in a new *All The President's Men 2* movie. The reporters were now looking for Billy Pigeon; the president in the movie was trying to figure out what Billy Pigeon was up to, too!

With Debra and Walter listening in anticipation in their dingy motel room, Billy had Julie make the call!

"Robert Redford, please," said Julie.

"This is Robert Redford."

In a really sensual voice, Julie said the following to Robert Redford, real slowly: "I'm your new Deep Throat!" Debra was busting a gut, with Billy telling her to shush, his finger to his mouth.

"What's your first name?" asked Robert Redford.

"Why would you want to know that?" asked Julie.

"Just in case we run into each other at night and I have to make sure it's you!" said Robert Redford.

"My first name is Lindahhhh!" said Julie, in a really, really sensual voice.

Robert Redford was quiet for a long time; he was lost for words and then he recovered.

"Okay, now that we have that out of the way, what next?" asked Robert Redford.

"Follow your intuition; go bite on an apple in sunny California!" said Julie, pressing the *end* button on Billy's campaign cell phone.

Debra busted a gut some more; Julie busted a gut, too. Billy was already busy planning his next move. Walter had a big old grin!

\* \* \*

Robert Redford was on the blower to his buddy Dustin Hoffman; this is what he said: "You're not going to believe this!"

\* \* \*

"Gas prices are going up again!" said Walter.

Debra said nothing; she continued to read her newspaper.

\* \* \*

"My God," said Debra. "People are setting up tents at Zuccotti Square in New York City; they're starting a Wall Street protest. They want fairness in America. They want financial and social equality. They say they're the 99 percent against the rich 1 percent, similar protests are popping up in cities all across America and the rest of the world."

"Unreal," said Billy Pigeon. "Contact your buddy Tom Moore at *The Seattle Times*. Tell him to put out a news release to tell the 99 percent to hang in there, that pretty soon the big banks will all be little banks, Fannie and Freddie will be shut down, the economy will be on fire, house prices will all go back to normal, people will have equity in their homes again, unemployment will be at zero, 401K plans will rise in value again, all of our young people will feel financial equality, and all the graduates from Billy's World will have $50,000 in their one pair of blue jeans. The people of America will soon have a new set of moral values; quality of life, not quantity of life, will be the new normal, the RPA will guarantee this. Any crooked politicians or crooked bankers or crooked businessmen will go directly to jail; they will not stop at GO, they will not collect $200, they will not collect big severance packages. Big corporations will no longer own and control our politicians and politicians will no longer profit on the stock market from insider knowledge. Eight-year term limits will be put on all politicians in Washington except the president. The size of the federal government will be reduced big-time. The people of America will run the Congress and the Senate. They will pay down the federal debt to zero in 24 years. We will take back our country, and you can take that to the bank—end of story!"

\* \* \*

"Wow!" e-mailed Tom Moore.
"Wow is right," e-mailed Debra Sanders.

\* \* \*

The next night on the *CBS Evening News,* Wall Street protesters were all shouting the following in unison:"Bil-ly, Bil-ly, Bil-ly!"

\* \* \*

"Maybe you'll get lucky this time around; maybe those meetings in that dark, underground parking lot might get a whole lot more interesting!" said Dustin Hoffman.
"Could be!" said Robert Redford. "To be quite honest, I haven't been this excited in years."
"I wonder what she looks like?" asked Dustin Hoffman.
"She sounded young!" said Robert Redford.

\* \* \*

After Julie heard the new breaking news on CNN, Billy headed the Birdmobile east. They were going to find the real live, one-legged pigeon one more time.
"We're coming to get you, my precious!" said Julie.

\* \* \*

"So why would she tell me to go bite on an apple in sunny California?" asked Robert Redford.
"I have no idea," said Dustin Hoffman.
"We grow grapes in sunny California; the only apple ever talked about in California is the company Apple," said Robert Redford.
"Bingo!" shouted Dustin Hoffman.
"I'm on my way!" said an excited Robert Redford.
"Do you want me to come, too?" asked Dustin Hoffman.
"No, you stay on the East Coast for now, no sense in spending all our travel money in one day!" said Robert Redford.

\* \* \*

"Billy, check this out," said Debra. "The Super-Committee is playing soccer, too; they're kicking the $1.2 trillion in required spending cuts down the road!"
"What else is new?" said Billy.
"They're even talking about kicking the automatic cuts that were supposed to come in 2013 down the road, too," said Debra.

"You're kidding me," said Billy.

"I kid you not," said Debra.

"Don't worry," said Billy, "I'll be kicking all of them down the road soon with one big, big boot!"

"Thank God!" said Debra.

\* \* \*

Debra also told Billy about the Wall Street protester who was hassling a Christmas shopper. The protester had a sign hung around his neck. This is what the sign said:

> What's in your
> bag that's more
> important than
> my education?

"Tell that Wall Street protester to come to Billy's World, work with me for five years, save $50,000, and then enroll in the college or university of his choice to get his degree!" said Billy Pigeon.

\* \* \*

Debra confirmed by e-mail to the twelve environmental big wigs that the big meeting would be in another month, give or take a few days. They would be meeting in a log home in Colorado, the summer residence of a friend of a friend of a friend of Paul's. This big meeting was with Billy Pigeon, the next president of the United States; it was a meeting that they should not miss!

\* \* \*

Billy had avoided Washington like the plague the first time around. He really wanted to build up steam before he pulled his train into the station, but this time around was different. This was the real live, one-legged pigeon, the bird that took him to Broken Bow. He was Julie's pigeon and Julie was the love of Billy's life—enough said.

\* \* \*

Gas prices are going down again!" said Walter—still no response from Debra.

\* \* \*

The confirmations for the big environmental meeting started to trickle in; Maude Barlow, Robert F. Kennedy Jr., Margot Kidder, Mark Ruffalo, Bill McKibben, Jonathan Lash and Naomi Klein had all confirmed so far, with five more to go.

\*\*\*

"Mr. Woodward, welcome to Apple; what can I do for you?" asked the pretty little secretary.

"I'd like to speak to Steve Jobs," said Robert Redford.

"He's not in today; he's not feeling great. Let me get Tim Cook, his right hand man," said the pretty little secretary.

\*\*\*

"We've just hit $725 million in campaign donations; can you believe it?" said Walter.

"That is sick!" said Billy.

"Wow!" said Julie.

"Wow is right!" said Debra.

\*\*\*

"Mr. Woodward, what brings you to our humble abode?" asked Tim Cook.

"I'm doing a story for the Washington Post. I was hoping to talk to Steve, see if he ever met Billy Pigeon, the kid who's running for president," said Robert Redford.

"Not that I know of," said Tim Cook. "Just a second, now that I think of it, he did go back east; he did play golf with some kid, some business meeting. I've no idea what it was about."

"Really!" said Robert Redford. "Can you remember what city?"

"Let me think. I believe it was Lafayette—that's right—in Louisiana; it was definitely Lafayette!" said Tim Cook.

\*\*\*

"Gas prices are going up again!" said Walter. Still no response from Debra.

\*\*\*

The Birdmobile was through St. Louis. Billy wanted to stop and tour the Lincoln Boyhood National Memorial near Evansville, Indiana. The stop was brief but inspirational for Billy. The Birdmobile was now heading for Lexington, Kentucky. Walter was stoked to know that they were almost in Davy Crockett's home turf. Billy, Debra, and Julie all agreed that Walter had contributed so much to their road trip that they should hang a right at Lexington, head south on Highway 75 to Knoxville, then find the hometown of Davy Crockett, born August 17, 1786 in Greene County, Tennessee. Walter had goose bumps as he located Davy Crockett's birthplace, He purchased a Davy Crockett raccoon hat and placed it on the dash of the Birdmobile just to the right of Billy's new TV and DVD player. Walter was happier than a Tennessee pig in shit, the way it should be. The Birdmobile was on its way again on Highway 81, with a direct line to Washington, D. C., most of Highway 81 through North Carolina, home of the North Carolina Tarheels, Dean Smith Country, Michael Jordan country, and tobacco country. The residents of North Carolina were ticked with Billy Pigeon because he was weaning young people off cigarettes. Tobacco was their big money-maker. Billy Pigeon refused to cave in or to say it was okay to smoke cigarettes. Billy told North Carolina residents that he would have better jobs for them than growing tobacco, and that the health risks outweighed making money. The Birdmobile and its motorcade passed through such wonderful southern towns as Abington, Marion, Pulaski, Salem, Buchanan, Natural Bridge, and all the way up to Strasburg and Front Royal, with nobody waving to Billy in North Carolina. Billy was an outcast. Billy refused to compromise his values to big tobacco. Billy took Highway 66 straight into Washington. Washington was abuzz that Billy Pigeon was just about on their doorstep, with the citizens of Washington and bird watchers from all across North America joining in the hunt for the real live, one-legged pigeon, not in front of the White House anymore, but sighted at three different locations: on top of the Pentagon, on the very top of the Washington Monument, and on top of a building near George Washington University, but that was the last sighting. The bird was gone, gone, gone by the time Billy Pigeon and company entered town. Julie was almost in tears. Billy put his arm around Julie. The crowds waved to Billy; Billy stopped near the White House. Billy was a celebrity, signing more autographs and collecting more campaign donations. Washington took notice, with President Obama saying the following to his press secretary: "The kid has certainly got the magic touch!"

"Do I sense a little nervousness in your tone of voice?" asked his press secretary.

"Hell no!" said the President. "We'll eat him for dinner at the pretend presidential debate; the tobacco workers will be happy, happy, happy!"

\*\*\*

While Julie and Debra spent a day in Julie's Jeep Wrangler in Washington looking for the real live, one-legged pigeon, one of the security detail from Spokane, an avid hunter named Derek, said the following to Billy: "It's like hunting a white-tail deer. You can't chase him; you have to sit and let him come to you!"

"I agree with Derek," said Walter.

\*\*\*

"This is a good time to service the Birdmobile," said Walter. "We need a couple of new tires, the brake shoes are getting down, and the fuel filter needs replacing; we should get a tune-up, a new fan belt, and just give everything a good going over."

"I agree," said Billy. They found a dad and son shop with time to take a gander at their 81 Chevy motor home. The son, named Richard Perkins Jr., did the majority of the work, doing everything Walter had requested and more. He found the receipt that Walter had lost inside the dash months before, he topped up the windshield wiper washer fluid, he washed the front windshield and back window, he tightened a loose door handle, he put some air in their spare tire, he washed all the dead bugs off their headlights and their front grill, he replaced a worn windshield wiper, he went next door to a gas station and topped up the propane tank for their stove, and he said the following to Walter: "Sorry, but I don't do toilets!"

"We don't expect you to, son; you've done way more than we asked. We really appreciate it," said Walter, paying cash for all the mechanical work on their motor home. Walter also gave the young man a $50 tip. Young Richard Perkins Jr. told Walter that he didn't have to give him a tip, that he treated all his customers the same courteous way. Billy Pigeon said the following to Richard Perkins Jr.: "You keep the money; you've earned it. We might need another oil change when I get to Washington; you never know. I just might contract you out to work on all our government vehicles!"

"Thanks, man!" said Richard Perkins Jr.

"You're welcome," said Billy Pigeon.

\* \* \*

"So?" asked Billy.

"No luck," said a down-in-the-dumps Julie.

"Do you want to stay and look another couple of days?" asked Billy.

"No, let's hit the road. It's like trying to find a needle in a haystack," said Julie. "We've got a month to make Colorado. Let's take a different route; let's head north and hook into Interstate 70. It's clear sailing all the way to Denver."

"I like that idea," said Billy.

"Me, too," said Walter.

"Me, three," said Debra.

\* \* \*

Robert Redford discussed his meeting at Apple with Dustin Hoffman. He told him about Steve Jobs and his golf game with Billy Pigeon in Lafayette. He told Dustin Hoffman to head down to Lafayette, to check out every golf course in the city, to check with the staff, the caddies, the grounds people, to find out if they saw or heard anything unusual.

"I'm all over it!" said Dustin Hoffman.

"I'm taking Danny DeVito with me. He has a way with people. He'll find out what the hell they were up to!"

"Sounds good to me," said Robert Redford.

# 34

# The Used Car Dealership

From Washington, Billy and the Birdmobile headed northwest. The autumn air was cool. Walter wore his Davy Crockett coonskin hat full-time. Billy had his baseball cap on, and Julie and Debra pulled out their turtle-neck sweaters. America was in full bloom!

"Don't you just love the fall colors?" asked Julie.

"What can I say; they're spectacular!" said Billy Pigeon.

"I agree," said Walter.

"Me, too," said Debra.

\* \* \*

"Billy, did you know that last year, Americans used enough plastic bottles to stretch around the planet 190 times!" asked Julie.

"I told you that David and I were going to make a mint!" said Billy.

\* \* \*

Highway 70 soon turned onto the Pennsylvania Turnpike all the way to Pittsburg, with Billy hooking a left before Pittsburg and heading west all the way to Columbus, Ohio, then Indianapolis where Peyton Manning was taking a year off, spending that $90 million he had tucked away in his mattress!

From Indianapolis, it was clear sailing to St. Louis, time to relax again, watch the yellow line markers on the highway, look and wave at all the well-wishers. The cash and check donations were increasing on a daily basis. Billy was almost up to $900 million, with a ton of money coming in from Washington residents fed up with government, fed up with gridlock, and fed up with the childish antics of all the Washington politicians. Walter was simply astounded with all the Washington money and all the attention Billy was garnering on his trip around America. Walter counted coins like crazy, the raccoon tail of his Davy Crockett hat flapping in the breeze, going here, there, and everywhere!

\* \* \*

"So what do you have planned for your malls?" asked Debra. "Paul said you were close to having everything finalized."

"I do," said Billy. "The mall in each hub will service all four thousand kids from the dormitory, plus the one hundred military staff, plus the kitchen staff, plus all the service workers going to and from the site.

"If you figure each YA kid will spend about $200 per month, that works out to be about $800,000 per month of income from the kids plus all the other money coming in from all the other people having access to the hub including all the people staying in the hotel. So I figure I'm pretty safe in saying that I can count on each mall having a million dollars a month in sales, probably more.

"So if I have ten retail outlets in each mall, they should be able to split that fairly comfortably, and make a nice healthy profit for a small business, and remember, I also have the option of owning the malls myself if I want to go that route. So if I own all the five thousand malls and make only a profit of 10 percent on $12 million in sales in each mall per year, my yearly profit per mall would be $1.2 million times five thousand malls equals $6 billion per year profit for me—not bad for a guy with no business experience. If we run the malls as private businesses, they would make $120,000 per year profit at 10 percent; most of them run a 20–25 percent profit margin, so you do the math!" said Billy Pigeon.

"What kind of stores do you have in mind?" asked Debra.

"I'm going to have a plain-Jane mall, with the basic necessities," said Billy. "A secondhand clothing store, a 20-seat men's barber shop, a 20-seat women's hair salon, a post office, an Apple store, a pharmacy, a gift shop, a health food store, an eye doctor with lots of glasses to buy and an insurance company, plus one big bank with fifty tellers!"

"What lucky bank in America is going to get into your five thousand malls?" asked Walter.

"My bank," said Billy, "the bank you are going to form for me and run for me from your office below Clint's. Your annual wage will be bumped up to $500,000, plus bonuses, still a mere pittance compared to the money all the Wall Street bankers are making!"

"And what are we calling the bank I am going to run?" asked Walter, his Davy Crockett hat still flapping in the wind, still going here, there, and everywhere, as Walter shook his head in amazement.

"It will be called the Bank of Billy. The YA kids will probably call it Billy's Bank!" said Billy Pigeon.

"That's cute," said Walter. "And how are you going to capitalize your bank?"

"Probably start with the leftover money from our campaign donations, money which I was going to earmark as a payment on the federal debt, but instead use it to tide us over till the YA kids first payday from the five thousand corporations. With 20 million YA kids depositing approximately $400 each, that's $8 million the first two weeks plus the other $1 billion I'll have left over from our campaign donations if we keep up our current pace. At the end of the first year, you'll have $288 billion plus my $1 billion; at the end of 5 years, you'll have $1 trillion 441 billion on deposit, and you should certainly be able to run a bank with that in your hip pocket!" said Billy.

Julie saw an incredible opportunity to get one up on Billy, to put him down a notch, to remind *him* just how smart she really was, to never be taken for granted. Julie began:

"So, Billy, what if all the kids get there on the first day and all 20 million of them want to borrow $100 from the Bank of Billy to tide them over till their first payday, and they all want cash at that very moment, that would be 20 million YA kids times $100 = $2 billion and you only have $1 billion from your campaign contributions. What would you do then?" asked a confident Julie.

Debra and Walter sensed the intellectual tug-of-war going on between Billy and Julie. It was fun to listen to. They waited for Billy's response.

"I would stall!" said Billy. "I would put a big old sign on the front door. The sign would say: Temporarily closed down to get the computers up and running properly. They'd buy that for sure, and bingo, in ten short working days, the computer glitch magically disappears, the sign comes off the door, and presto, we're in business!"

"You're kidding; you've got to give me a better answer than that. I want the truth!" shouted Julie.

"You want the truth; you can't handle the truth!" shouted Billy. Debra was busting a gut, having watched *A Few Good Men* at least ten times. Walter had seen it five, for sure, and was busting a gut, too!

"Yes I can. I'm a big girl; I can handle the truth. Sock it to me!" shouted Julie.

"Truth is: Walter is setting up a holding company. The Bank of Billy will be one entity, Billy's World will be another entity and the service city will be the third entity.

"On the day the 2,000,000 renters sign their rental agreements for the 2,000,000 condos and apartments and townhouses and houses they will rent from me, they will be required to pay me the first and last month's rent and a damage deposit. So if I only charge $200 per month for rent and get a $100 damage deposit per renter on the first day that would be $1,000,000,000 (one billion dollars), and if I add that to the $1 billion I already have from my campaign donations, that total comes out to be $2 billion, and I believe you said I would need $2 billion if all the YA kids took a run on the bank and asked for $100 from the Bank of Billy all at the same time. If I did my math correctly, I have enough to cover the run on the bank, and since I'm going to charge more than $200 per month for rent in the service city, I should have way more than enough left over to take you out to dinner. So where would you like to go and what do you want me to order?" asked Billy Pigeon.

"I hate you, I hate you, I hate you!" shouted Julie, with Debra busting a gut, and Walter busting a gut, too. Debra was busting a gut so badly that she started to bang on the cupboard doors with her hands, and then she dropped to the floor, laughing hysterically as Billy pulled the motor home to the side of the road. Debra was now outside the Birdmobile, on the ground laughing and laughing and laughing. The security detail from Spokane all surrounded Debra; the State Troopers surrounded her, too. The security detail from Spokane blocked the view of the TV cameras, shielding Debra from the camera lights. The security detail from Spokane was worried sick about Debra, thinking they had a loose cannon in their midst, a crazy lady. Julie exited the Birdmobile next, saying the following to her mother, Debra: "Mom, are you okay!"

\*\*\*

"Would you like a drink?" asked Billy.

"Sure, why not," said Walter, "we could be here for awhile!"

\*\*\*

The next day, Debra was on her laptop. She read Billy a list of the final confirmations she had received from environmental activists all across America.

"We have the last five confirmations for Colorado; they're sending a lawyer from the Advocates for the West based in Boise, Idaho, but they haven't decided who yet. Native Indian activist Enei Begaye is confirmed; so are James Hanson, Wes Jackson, and Walter Perry. So that makes twelve of the most active minds in the American environmental movement."

"That's impressive," said Billy. "So why haven't you invited Ralph Nader?"

"He's too domineering; he won't give anyone else an opportunity to speak. He's a pain in the butt!" said Debra. "Our group of twelve will eat him for breakfast. They'll shut him up after we're done. They'll put him in line, you mark my words. These twelve are tough. You're going to have your hands full; trust me!" said Debra. "So what are you up to—what are you going to say to them?"

"I haven't the faintest clue. I want to feel them out for a round or two. I'm sure I'll come up with something!" said Billy.

"I'm sure you will!" said Julie.

"One day at a time, one problem at a time," said Billy Pigeon.

*　*　*

Danny DeVito called Dustin Hoffman at their motel and told him he had been digging hard. He told Dustin Hoffman that Billy Pigeon played lots of golf in the southern states, that he had played golf with Steve Ballmer from Microsoft, that he had also played golf with Tom Cruise and Drew Brees, that the newspapers in the local towns were all over it, that he was still digging, and that he should have more good info soon!

*　*　*

Dustin Hoffman called Robert Redford, they chatted some more.

"So what do we know right now, at this very moment?" asked Robert Redford.

"We know the kid is running for president. He's on a two-year tour of America. He's collected a shitload of money. He's got Clint doing a big cowboy movie. He played golf with Steve Jobs from Apple and Steve Ballmer from Microsoft. Apple and Microsoft are loaded with cash. He's got 20 million kids all signed up on some silly Pledge of Allegiance to America. He's promising them all jobs. An FBI source in Washington told me something about the kid baking a big Apple pie; that's about it so far," said Dustin Hoffman.

"So think about it for a second," said Robert Redford. "It's Apple and Microsoft—it's a big Apple pie—there's a tie-in with Apple already. Maybe the 20 million kids are all lined up to be sales people for Apple and Microsoft. Think about it: if each kid just sold ten iPhones each at say $200 per unit, that's 20 million times ten, that's 200 million units times $200 a unit, that's $40 billion a year in sales. If each kid sold 20 units a year, that's $80 billion. That's huge; that's one big Apple pie!"

"Wow!" said Dustin Hoffman. "But how does Microsoft fit in? What's their connection with Apple?"

"Maybe they've got some hot new software product that they haven't announced to the world yet. I have no idea. Maybe the kid knows something we don't know," said Robert Redford.

"Why don't you give Deep Throat another call; see what Lindahhhh will tell you!" said Dustin Hoffman.

*　*　*

Robert Redford was hot to trot. He called 1–800–911-BIRD. Debra saw the number display on the phone and handed the phone to Julie.

"Lindahhhh, this is Robert Redford. We know about the golf game with Steve Jobs from Apple. We know that 20 million young people are involved; we think they're going to be sales people for someone. We know there's a lot of money involved—a hell of a lot of money—and that your Billy Pigeon has to be elected president to make this happen. We think it's a big trade deal with someone overseas. We know the kids can communicate with anyone these days, anywhere in the world with the click of a mouse, the push of a button. We just don't understand the connection with Steve Ballmer from Microsoft. Can you help us there; are we going in the right direction?"

"You're not doing badly!" said Lindahhhh.

"So will you help us?" asked Robert Redford.

"I'll sleep on it; give me a call tomorrow!" said Lindahhhh.

*  *  *

"So a bank manager has to do more than just collect deposits!" said Walter.

"I know that," said Billy. "So here's the way our loans will work. They've only got $200 a month to spend, so let's say you let them borrow up to $2,500 on a major item over five years. What would that be a month for their payments, say at 4 percent interest on their loan?"

"Five years = 60 months into $2,500 dollars = $41.10 per month plus interest, say $50 a month for a nice round number, but probably less," said Walter.

"Just what I figured," said Billy. "And if a kid stays on at Billy's World for ten years, he could afford a five thousand dollar loan."

"That's correct," said Walter.

"We're not doing any payday loans, but we will allow the 20 million YA kids to make one major purchase during their five or ten-year stay at Billy's World," said Billy.

"And what would that purchase be?" asked Julie, reluctant to get too involved in the conversation.

"Think about it," said Billy "What's the one thing every kid in America wants, except me?"

Their own vehicle!" said Julie.

"Exactly!" said Billy.

"So the kid comes to my dad for a loan. He says I have the discipline to live on the $150 a month I have left. I can easily afford a payment of $50 a month for a $2,500 used car. I'm even willing to stay on another five years if I can get a five thousand dollar one. My dad will ask, 'How's your behavior, son?' My dad will look into Clint's file and the file will say only one strike. Dad will say 'Your loan is approved, but I'm going to be watching you like a hawk and

I will call your loan if you strike out; you'll have to return your car or truck—game over—kiss your money goodbye!'"

"So where do you come up with good used cars and trucks for 20 million kids?" asked Julie.

"Remember my two high school classmates who chased us all the way to the Montana border when we first left Seattle?" asked Billy.

"The ones who only had $10 to make it all the way home; the ones who took the car full of fat, ugly girls home. I remember them," said Julie.

"Jeff and Ryan Smith, two of the biggest con artists in America: they could sell ice cream to an Eskimo. They can wheel and deal with the best of them. They knew that fat, ugly chicks need loving, too, that fat, ugly chicks try harder!" said Billy, with Walter and Debra busting a gut!

"That's disgusting!" said Julie. "And knowing you, you've probably got them signed, sealed and delivered, all ready to go!"

"I do!" said Billy. "For those two boys to get my used cars and trucks is a walk in the park, a piece of cake. We're going to call our dealership Smith Brothers' Used Cars and Trucks. I'm building them the biggest used car lot in America, with free living accommodations above their offices and covered carports to store all their vehicles—to keep them out of the weather—to keep the paint from fading. The YA kids will be allowed to drive their vehicles one Friday night a month; it will be car and truck night at Billy's World. The ones with good behavior can book their cars and trucks in advance, their engines all primed to go. They can hook a date, maybe go in their vehicles for a little cruise and go for a little hanky-panky with a condom. If they're lucky enough, and all the stars line up, and they've saved enough money by squeezing out the last tiny bit of toothpaste and staying away from the mall and getting their kicks totally at the recreation center after their nightly one-hour exercise session, and they were one of the lucky ones to book a hotel room, they can drive right up to the hotel, park their vehicles, get their room key, have some real good hanky-panky with a condom on a nice comfortable bed instead of on the back seat of their 1981 Ford Mustang, the way it should be!

"And when they come back to the used car lot and give their cars and trucks back to the mechanic on duty to be put away in storage, the mechanic on duty responsible for the maintenance of all the cars will probably check for oil leaks on his hands and knees, vacuum the inside of their vehicle, wash their windows, spray and wash their tires, wipe their headlights, remove any chewing gum and cigarette butts in the ashtray, take a wet cloth to the dash board, and hang their keys on a big old board big enough to hang 20 million sets of keys all at one time!"

"Ya right!" said Julie, "and where are you going to find a mechanic like that—who will do all those extra things for nothing? Give me a break!"

\*\*\*

"Hi Lindahhhh, this is Robert Redford!"

"Go follow the horses!" said Lindahhhh.

\*\*\*

"Gas prices are going up again!" said Walter.

"Shut up, I'm busy!" yelled Debra.

\*\*\*

"I like your loan idea for the used cars," said Walter, "but what about lines of credit and credit cards for buying Apple products in your mall? Those things aren't cheap!"

"Only for the very best, the top 25 percent, the hardest workers in their factories, their dorm pits immaculate during inspections, zero strikes, never complaining about anything, perfect attendance at work!" said Billy Pigeon.

"And how many credit cards?" asked Walter.

"One!" said Billy. "And always a zero balance at the beginning of each new monthly statement."

"And how do I make money if I set that rule?" asked Walter.

"Find a way; that's what I pay you the big bucks for!" said Billy, with Debra busting a gut!

"And the lines of credit?" asked Walter.

"Secured by cash only," said Billy, "with instructions to pay it down to zero as quickly as they can, preferably before the next monthly statement."

"I know the answer to my next question," said Walter, "that's why I get paid the big bucks!"

\*\*\*

"Well, well, well, what have we here: The *Sundance Kid,* in the flesh!" said Jack.

"I'll be—go to hell!" said Clint.

"What's for supper?" asked the *Sundance Kid.*

"Beans," said Steven Seagal, "beans and leftovers!"

# 35

## Wrong Horses

Billy and the Birdmobile were through St Louis, through Kansas City, and were crossing into the rest of Kansas. Billy Pigeon said the following to Julie, Debra and Walter. "Enjoy the moment boys and girls; this will probably be the last time you ever see Kansas looking like this!"

"Are you sure the residents here are okay with moving into their condos in our big service city?" asked Julie.

"One hundred percent," said Billy. "I'm getting e-mails every day at admin@billybird.com. All the Kansas residents above the Interstate 70 were itching to go; residents from the bottom half of the state were curious to know why their neighbors to the north of the Interstate were all smiles. The residents of Belleville, Mankato, Oberlin, Beloit, and Wakeeney kept their promise to Billy; there was no way they were going to screw up a once-in-a-lifetime offer like this. The people below Interstate 70—the people of Sharon Springs, Rush Center, Ness City, Iola, and Wichita—would soon learn the bad news. They would have a period of mourning and agony, but would soon get over it and realize that what Billy Pigeon was doing was right, that he was the only one with a plan for America, to change our country politically, economically and morally with one stroke of his pen in the Oval Office. The residents below Interstate 70 might even sell their own homes, go rent a place in Billy's service city, and be thankful that Billy was providing them with a good paying job, with benefits and medical and dental and a self-controlled pension plan, the way it should be. Billy knew people in Kansas were rough and tough, had John Wayne characteristics, and could handle anything. They could even handle their Kansas Jayhawks losing all their games if they had to. Not really!

Billy and the Birdmobile said goodbye to Kansas. The last piece of their puzzle was waiting for them in a beautiful log home in Colorado, one more hurdle before they could take a break for the winter, find a good place to sit in front of a crackling fire, sip on some hot chocolate, and read a good local history book!

Billy Pigeon crossed into Colorado. They were soon in Denver. From Denver, they headed north toward Boulder. They found their log home; they settled in and waited for their guests to arrive.

\* \* \*

"So how was the horseback ride?" asked Dustin Hoffman.

"The shits, but thank you for asking!" said Robert Redford.

"So what happened?" asked Dustin Hoffman.

"They acted like a bunch of spaced-out cowboys!" said Robert Redford. "Jack was drunk, Clint had a bad cold, Lee Marvin was a dickhead, Charles Bronson never said fuck all to anybody, Tommy Lee Jones spent all day laughing, Chuck Norris slept in, didn't even crawl out of his sleeping bag, Steven Seagal was gone somewhere looking for another pig, and Dick Butkus, John Riggins, Larry Csonka, and Jack Lambert played catch with a big old rock all day long!"

"So did they say anything about Apple or an apple pie?" asked Dustin Hoffman.

"Nothing," said Robert Redford. "Jack mumbled something about beans and a snake pie, but that's about as close as it got to food!"

"So it was a waste of time," said Dustin Hoffman.

"It was," said Robert Redford.

"Better give her another call; see what she has to say," said Dustin Hoffman.

\* \* \*

Billy figured the meeting would last a good two to three hours. He suggested that Walter and Julie go to Boulder for dinner, maybe take in a movie; he wanted his vice president to be at his side, to get her claws all sharpened up if he needed her help!

\* \* \*

The lawyer from the Advocates for the West bailed at the last moment; he apologized, and then said the following to Billy on his cell phone: "Don't fuck with us, young man. We'll do anything to preserve the west, to take care of the lakes and the streams and the prairies and the mountains and all the birds and animals that call the west their home. I don't know what you're up to, but tread carefully; you're on sacred ground!"

*What a great start to the evening!* thought Billy Pigeon. Billy told Debra about his cell phone conversation with the lawyer from Boise. Debra invited the remaining eleven environmentalists into the spacious living room: a mount of a big old elk on top of the rock fireplace in front of their eyes as the environmentalists sat on eleven leather chairs, the floor adorned with mountain goat rugs. Billy was in more trouble, even before he began to speak!

"There's a lot of dead animals in here; I don't care much for the setting of our little get-together!" said Naomi Klein.

"I don't mean to offend you ma'am," said Billy. "I just wanted you to be comfortable. I wanted a place where we could talk and not have to worry about distractions from phones and people."

"America is a mess," said Billy.

"We know that!" said Maude Barlow. "And we had nothing to do with it!"

*Holy shit,* thought Billy, *what a tough crowd!*

Debra Sanders sensed what was happening. She stood up and gave a little lecture to the environmentalists. She did what a good vice president should do: she spoke her mind!

"Now let's stop this crap right here and now! You've got to give Billy a chance to speak. He's earned it. We don't need to sit here and exchange insults. If I wanted that, I'd go to Washington and sit down with all the fucking idiots there!

"Our country is a mess, and I want you to show a little courtesy and listen to what your future president has to say. Then if you have any questions, which I'm sure you will, we'll answer them, one at a time, one person at a time. I won't tolerate your we-they attitude. This is our country; we're trying to make it better, not worse. We have to work together for the good of America, not bicker like a bunch of school children, or try to lay blame for something Billy didn't create!

"I've listened to everybody. I know why you are protesting. I know how Washington is controlled by big business. I've heard no one with a vision for America—no one except Billy. We're here this evening to work together, to make our country a better place, to give the youth of America hope—end of story!" said Debra Sanders.

Debra took her seat. Billy Pigeon stood up; his audience was all ears!

"As I was saying, American is a mess," said Billy Pigeon.

Billy spent the next hour talking. He talked about America; he talked about his government in Washington, of the $70 trillion hole we were all in, about all the unemployed in America, about the way the rest of the world thought about Americans: that Americans were bullies, and they carried a big stick. He said it was time to bring our troops home, to start working again, to start saving and not spending like drunken sailors, that he had all the parts of the puzzle together for Billy's World, with $5 trillion all set to go, with $2.5 trillion from his newly elected RPA government and $2.5 trillion from the private sector. Billy's World would house 20 million YA kids and all the people in all the small towns in Billy's construction zone were happy campers. Billy would work around environmentally sensitive areas like the Nebraska Sandhills region and the Ogallala Aquifer. All the people were willing to step aside and let Billy construct, over a four year period, the largest military, industrial, manufacturing complex the world has ever seen, from Interstate 70 in the south to Minot, North Dakota in the north, from Highway 29 in the east to Highway 85 in the west. Billy's World would be completed gated, with five thousand manufacturing hubs, each hub with a factory, a dormitory, a mall, a hotel, a recreation center, a military compound, an administration center, and five thousand corporations in the U. S. of A. all committed to building a state-of-the-art factory in each of the hubs, many of them wanting access to more than one hub. All the corporations were signed up, with a service city of 2,000,000 people all set to go, two service workers for every ten YA kids, with 20 million young Americans all set to work for minimum wage, to sign a five-year Pledge of Allegiance to go to fight his War on Jobs. The kids would save 80 percent of their wages, and pledge to eat no fast food, watch no porn, use no drugs, bully no one, never take part in hazing, and only drink when they're twenty-one in a proper bar or tavern or lounge in Billy's World, and smoke cigarettes or cigars in designated areas. The kids were committed to daily exercise, to wear YA uniforms and coveralls, to bust their butts in the five thousand factories, to work forty-hour weeks, to have their nights and weekends off, to make Made in America products in factories with good lighting, a great big coffee room, a first aid station, and great air conditioning. The American factories would never be called sweat shops. The 20 million kids would all have $50,000 in their blue jeans when they finished their five-year commitment, with financial equality in America, and the option to stay another five years and leave with $100,000 in their bank accounts. All of the profits from Billy's World, from the leases in the malls to the room rentals in the hotels to all the rentals in the service city would go to pay down our $70 trillion federal debt. All the $20 bills collected from all the tourists touring Billy's World would go to setting up two gigantic accounts for the people of America: one a rainy day account for tough times down the road, the second to deal with global warming issues. All the construction jobs over a four-year period would set America on fire, put the unemployment rate in America at zero, and create wealth on the stock market for all Americans, who would see 401ks go up, up, up in value, not down, down, down in value. The American debt of $70 trillion would be at zero in twenty-four short years. Americans would no longer run government deficits; our governments would always be in surplus. America would be Number One in the world again. Our troops would run Billy's World. They would have their own military training center. All the boots were coming home, and they would get ready for war here. They would only go to war if they were asked to help a friend or if foreign boots invaded our soil. We would keep some strategic military bases around the world for our sailors and airmen and their stealth bombers. Each ocean would only have a couple of submarines, a couple of aircraft carriers, and a couple of warships full of American marines to rescue Americans in danger in foreign countries. Technology would defend and attack for America. Billy's World would change America politically, economically, and morally. He would kill three birds with one stone. All Americans would be proud of Billy's World, especially the environmental community; three environmentalists would be on the Board of Directors for Billy's World, with a gigantic environmental office set up in Billy's World to deal with any environmental issues. The environmental office would be staffed and run by the environmental movement. Their salaries would be covered by Billy's World. Billy's World would have the latest in green technology with a massive, twenty-second century, wind- solar- hydrogen power station providing all the electricity, with zero-emission, natural gas generators for back-up, with millions of solar panels and wind turbines completely surrounding Billy's World in a fifty-mile wide power grid, all bringing clean energy, with all the garbage at Billy's World being burned in a state-of-the-art, green garbage incinerator. The incinerator would provide more energy for the hubs and service buildings, with the preservation of nature's ecosystem the number one priority at Billy's World. Everything would be left in a natural state, with no grass and lawns to cut, with the least possible human footprint, with animals and birds wandering freely, unencumbered amongst the five thousand manufacturing hubs, each 25 square mile hub fenced, but with game tunnels connecting each hub on the north, south, east and west, a game tunnel built every half mile, the seven major components of each hub also fenced, with game tunnels going under the train tracks, the main roads and sidewalks, the animals and birds going here, there, and everywhere, living, breeding, dying—the way it should be—with game tunnels and fencing and lighting protecting the animals and birds at Billy's World, with a gigantic state-of-the-art veterinary clinic a priority. It would be a place for all the injured and sick animals and birds to go to get help, with state-of-the-art, specially designed helicopters and trucks ready to transport the animals and birds, 24/7, 365 days a year, with hundreds and hundreds of specially designed recovery pens built by the veterinary clinic to help the animals and birds get well before they were released back to the wild. All 20 million kids in the five thousand dormitories would be able to look out their windows and witness the beauty of a sunset, see an antelope, a coyote, a jack rabbit, or a prairie chicken. Billy's World would be open to the public, which would marvel at America, proud of its technology, its commitment to nature, but most of all, proud of its youth—20 million kids who have changed America politically, economically, and morally, who have made America proud. Learn from the past, deal with the present, and the future will take care of itself!

Debra stood up, walked up to Billy and gave him a big old hug, Billy liked the feel of her breasts. Naomi Klein, Maude Barlow, and Margot Kidder hugged him, their breasts feeling really good, too. Enei Begaye, Jonathan Lash, Mark Ruffalo, Robert F. Kennedy Jr., Bill McGibbon, James Hanson, Wes Jackson, and Walter Perry all shook Billy's hand, congratulating him for a job well done, and wishing him well as their new president!

The eleven environmental activists left the beautiful log home after three more hours of wine and cheese, and hundreds of questions to Billy about Billy's World. There were questions about the wind-solar-hydrogen power station, about the state-of-the-art factories, about the green garbage incinerator, about the refocused generation of American YA kids, about the future of America as a world environmental leader, about Billy's quality of life, not quantity of life vision, about the vehicles at Billy's World all operating on propane and natural gas and electricity, not Middle Eastern oil, about a society of savers not spenders, about a country not controlled by corporations or big labor, about the Reality Party of America, about the rainy day account for global warming, about the future of American technology and education, about a refocused generation of Americans able to handle tough courses in college, now able to compete with China and India, about the role of the environmental movement in a Billy Pigeon government, about term limits on politicians, about the Nebraska Sandhills region and protecting the Ogallala Aquifer, about the environmental office Billy was setting up at Billy's World, about the three spots he was leaving for environmentalists on his Board of Directors, and about preserving space inside Billy's World for farmers and ranchers to grow corn and wheat and raise cattle. The farming and ranching issue was a no-brainer as far as Billy was concerned, with 100 hubs and 400,000 YA kids all ready dedicated to process meat, corn, and wheat, Billy was already ten steps ahead of the environmentalists. His 25 percent/75 percent hub space utilization plan accounted for any and all no-brainers to pop up, with adjustments to no-brainers being made as we speak back in Seattle, no-brainers like space for existing Indian reserves, for existing state and national parks, for shale natural gas production in North Dakota, and for Wall Drug. Billy's total commitment to work with everyone affected inside the construction zone, to step on no one, to make everyone happy campers, everyone in America to benefit from Billy's World—the way it should be. Billy told his eleven guests that mum was the word, that all the 20 million YA kids were still in the dark, that all the people in the 146 towns in the construction zone were mum, that the five thousand CEOs of all the corporations were mum, that he would spill the beans at the pretend debate at George Washington University in the early spring of 2012, that he needed the environmental people mum, too. The environmental people were now committed to Billy, and promising to be mum, too. Billy and Debra finally shooed them out the front door, with snowflakes falling. The eleven members of the environmental community were still buzzing about Billy's rainy day account for global warming, a thunderbolt which struck from left field without warning and made a direct hit!

\* \* \*

"Let's have a glass of merlot," said Debra.
"Great idea," said Billy.
"A toast," said Debra.
"To the real live, one-legged pigeon, wherever he may be!" said Billy.
"To the real live, one-legged pigeon!" said Debra.

\* \* \*

Walter and Julie arrived home. They'd gone to a movie; they watched *The Social Network*.
"So how was the movie?" asked Debra.
"It was okay," said Julie.
"It was all right," said Walter.
"And how was your night?" asked Julie.
"Piece of cake!" said Debra.
"Walk in the park!" said Billy.

\* \* \*

The following morning Robert Redford dialed 1–800–911–BIRD. Julie saw the number on call display.
"Lindahhhh, this is Robert Redford."
"Hi!" said Lindahhhh.
"I found Clint Eastwood. I spent all day with him and his buddies. I learned nothing. I don't understand," said Robert Redford.
"Wrong horses!" said Lindahhhh.

\* \* \*

"Billy, come here; look at the news on TV," said Debra.
"What's up," asked Billy.
"Steve Jobs just died," said Debra.
"You're kidding!" said Billy.
"Nope, he's gone," said Debra.

\* \* \*

Two weeks later, Billy Pigeon received a telephone call from Tim Cook, the new CEO at Apple. Tim Cook told Billy that Apple would still be taking 20 hubs, that Billy's World was still a go as far as they were concerned, that they were already doing the planning to bump up their numbers in phase 2 and 3, and that hopefully, down the road, all Apple products would be Made in America and designed by American engineers!

"Thanks," said Billy Pigeon. "I appreciate it."

"You're welcome," said Tim Cook. "I look forward to meeting you soon. Good luck!"

# 36

## Jingle Bells

Christmas 2011 was spent in the mountains near Deadwood, one of the most interesting places in America as far as Billy Pigeon was concerned. The snow had shut them down. Billy found a neat old motel, with a big old fireplace in the lobby, a natural wood floor, a big old comfy couch, no TV, no nothing, only the sounds of the crackling fire in the fireplace, and the odd visitor checking in. There was one landline for the entire motel, but still cell phone coverage. Debra told Paul the following: "We'll be home soon."

"I can hardly wait!" said Paul.

\*\*\*

Danny DeVito took time to see Clint, too. Clint still had a cold; the cold was getting worse. Clint said the following to Danny DeVito: "What the fuck do you want?"

"Are these all the horses you have?" asked Danny DeVito.

"We started with a lot more, but all the pussies riding them left Dodge!" said Clint.

"And where did they go?" asked Danny DeVito.

"How the fuck should I know!" yelled a pissed off Clint. "Go find them yourself!"

"And who exactly am I looking for?" asked Danny DeVito.

"I don't know, there were so many of them, I can't remember," said Clint.

"Arnold was one of them," said Steven Seagal. "They were all losing their shirts on Wall Street!"

\*\*\*

Dustin Hoffman called Robert Redford. He told him about Danny DeVito's visit with Clint.

"Steven Seagal said that all the guys who left were losing their shirts on Wall Street, and that Arnold was one of them," said Dustin Hoffman.

"Good work," said Robert Redford, "now we know what Lindahhhh meant by wrong horses. She was talking about Arnold and his buddies who headed for the hills!"

"So if I hear you correctly," said Robert Redford, "now we have Apple involved, 20 million young kids involved, Microsoft involved, Wall Street involved, and now the ex-governor of California involved. This is getting really interesting!"

"I agree," said Dustin Hoffman. "And a lot of Hollywood stars and wrestlers and hard-core UFC fighters have lost their shirts; so how do they fit in?"

"Get DeVito out to see Arnold and see what he has to say," said Robert Redford.

"Already done," said Dustin Hoffman.

\* \* \*

Billy Pigeon had revisited the Custer Battlefield. He and Julie had frozen their butts out in the cold, the winds howling; fall was close to turning into winter. Billy told Julie on the Custer Battlefield that he hoped everything he was planning for America would work out, that he hoped he didn't have to go to Plan B: to build a new log White House, paint the logs white, bring in his 20 million YA kids, have them help him form a revolutionary government, circle the wagons, and start the second American Revolution!

\* \* \*

On their second trip to Mount Rushmore, Billy Pigeon shook more hands, signed more autographs, collected more money for Walter to count, spent hours going through the historical museum, and reading all kinds of newspaper articles of the day showing all the ups and downs of carving out the four American presidents. Billy's eagle eyes were all over the mountain, imagining another new carving going on, just like the one up the road of Crazy Horse, one of the great Sioux warriors.!

Billy's new carving was of himself—Billy Pigeon—way, way up there, a gigantic caricature with the one-legged pigeon standing in his outstretched right hand, which was a perfect place for thousands of real pigeons to sit on their annual pilgrimage to Mount Rushmore. Millions of Americans two hundred years from now would say that Billy Pigeon had more balls than a brass monkey, was the greatest American president in history, and the greatest political figure the world has ever seen—bar none!

\* \* \*

"Arnold was down in the dumps man; his muscles were aching. He said he lost a bundle on the stock market. He was receiving death threats from crazy Californians; life was all about family, and his family was a mess. There was big trouble brewing!" said Danny DeVito.

"Big trouble brewing for his family probably means the big divorce coming up," said Dustin Hoffman.

"It could also mean he's talking about *her* family, not his," said Robert Redford.

"You mean the Kennedys?" asked Dustin Hoffman.

"Maria Shriver is a Kennedy, isn't she?" asked Robert Redford.

"Sure she is, and there's also Robert F. Kennedy Jr.," said Dustin Hoffman. "He's out there big-time with the environmental movement; maybe the Mob is after him like his father and his uncle!"

"Could be," said Robert Redford, "maybe the Mob and the environmentalists are at each other's throats over something we don't know about."

"Holy shit, is that what all this is about?" asked Dustin Hoffman. "Now we've got Microsoft and Apple involved, 20 million young kids involved, Wall Street involved, an ex-California governor and his ex-wife involved, his wife a Kennedy, a Kennedy in the environmental movement, the Mob hating the Kennedys—where do we go and look next?"

"I think we should just calm down and relax, maybe think out our next move," said Robert Redford. Joined at the hip, Robert Redford and Dustin Hoffman spoke the same words at the same time:

"You and I should go visit Robert F Kennedy Jr.!"

\* \* \*

At a local truck stop, Billy and Julie stopped for a coffee. They were driving their Jeep Wrangler. They had four of the security detail from Spokane with them in their Suburbans.

"Let me tell you a good Obama joke," said one of the truckers sitting on a stool by the counter.

"You don't have to," said Billy.

"Sure I do," said the trucker. "It's the best one I've heard yet, and I've heard lots; trust me!

"Barack Obama dies and goes to heaven. St. Peter meets him at the pearly gates and says 'Welcome. And who are you?'

"Obama says 'My name is Barack Obama and I was president of the United States of America!'

"St. Peter, clearly showing amazement, says, 'That's unbelievable; a black President? When did that happen?'

"Obama looks at his watch and replies, 'Oh, about 14 minutes ago!'"

\*\*\*

"Go ahead, Frank, tell him one more; they're funnier than shit!" said another trucker.

"Question. What Bruce Springsteen song always makes Obama grin?"

"Answer. 'Born in the USA'!"

\*\*\*

"Tell him one more. The kid's not going to be offended; they say he's tough as nails, smart as a whip. Go on, tell it!" said another trucker.

"The good news is that Obama has finally created some jobs. The bad news is that they're all in India!"

\*\*\*

Billy and Julie also took time to stop in and visit Robert Redford in Sundance. Julie was going to knock on the door and say, "Hi, I'm Lindahhhh!"

But a nice lady who knew Robert Redford said Robert Redford was still away. He was still trying to catch up with some kid named Billy Pigeon.

\*\*\*

Billy had never really seen his father, Walter, three sheets to the wind, but here was Walter, half-pissed on Jack Daniel's with his Davy Crockett raccoon hat on, telling Mexican jokes to Julie, Debra, and Billy. Everyone was cutting Walter some slack. He was a trooper on their trip. He had four boxes of their expense receipts on the back seat of Julie's Jeep Wrangler. He had $947 million all tucked away with Mrs. Larson at her bank in Seattle in CDs and Treasury bills. He had driven lots of miles around America. No one disagreed with Walter when he said he deserved one night off, one night on the town, to kick back, cut loose, as he shouted the following: "Fantastic, wunderbar—I finally get to drink in peace!"

\*\*\*

"Why do Mexicans have small steering wheels? So they can drive with handcuffs on!"

"Why don't Mexicans play hide and seek? Because nobody will look for them!"

"What's a Mexican's favorite book store? Border's!"

"Why do Mexicans wear their baseball caps with the brims up? So they have a place to keep their taco!"

"Why do Mexicans put their names on their cars? So they won't steal them!"

"Why do Mexicans wear pointed boots? Because it's easier to get over a fence!"

"What is the difference between a Mexican and an elevator? One can raise a child!"

"What's the difference between a Mexican and a bucket of crap? The bucket!"

"What do you call Mexican basketball? Juan on Juan!"

"What do you call a pool with a Mexican in it? Bean dip!" said Walter.

"Good night, Dad," said Billy.

"Good night, Walter, sleep tight," said Julie.

"Good night, Davy Crockett!" said Debra.

\* \* \*

Billy was intrigued by all the local history, reading every book he could find about the wild, wild west, the old gold days, the old prospectors, and their relationship with the Indians.

The Dirty Half Dozen Plus Five were also near the mountains. They were up to their waists in snow, with Lee Marvin and Charles Bronson in the lead. Charles Bronson was an expert in the mountains in the snow. Jack said the following to Clint: "Where the fuck is he going now?"

\* \* \*

We wish you a Merry Christmas,

We wish you a Merry Christmas,

We wish you a Merry Christmas,

And a Happy New Year!

Julie raised a wine glass to toast her sweetheart, Billy Pigeon: "To 2012, to the best and most exciting year of your life!"

"Here, here!" said Walter.

"Ditto!" said Debra.

\* \* \*

Clint Eastwood, Jack Nicholson, Lee Marvin, Chuck Norris, Tommy Lee Jones, Charles Bronson, Steven Seagal, Dick Butkus, John Riggins, Larry Csonka, and Jack Lambert were still in the mountains the same night Julie made her toast to Billy. They were up to their eyeballs in snow, their horses under a big old tree, and freezing their nuts off. Steven Seagal's six big old pulling horses were under a tree, too, his chuck wagon surviving the mountains. Steven Seagal was now a lean, mean cooking machine, in the best shape of his life; his days were spent pushing and pulling his horses and his chuck wagon through the snow!

What dry branches and scraps of dry wood they could find were fueling a smoking fire. Since the tree branches were green, the fire was a bitch to keep going. Jack's precious supply of whiskey was just about toast, with Jack saying the following to his buddy Clint: "Where the fuck are we?"

"Who the fuck knows?" said Clint.

"Who the fuck cares?" said Charles Bronson.

\* \* \*

"I can't believe there hasn't been a sighting of the real live, one-legged pigeon," said Julie. "It's been months and months now; I'm getting concerned!"

\* \* \*

"Fuck, it's cold tonight!" said Jack. "We have got to find a place to sleep with some cover."

"We're not going to last three more days like this!" said Tommy Lee Jones.

\* \* \*

Danny DeVito called Dustin Hoffman; this is what he said: "There's something I forgot to mention to you that time I went out on the trail to find Clint. On my way back, I stopped in a little restaurant for a coffee and struck up a conversation with this middle-aged lady.

"She said she was from Boston and she was visiting her sister, and her sister said to her that she was really excited that she was finally retiring, that someone had bought up the whole town, was giving them a shit load of money for their places, that they were all moving to some new city with free rents and all kinds of service jobs.

"I checked around, asked a few more questions, nobody anywhere was saying a thing. It's probably nothing, but I thought you'd like to know anyway."

\* \* \*

Like anything Billy Pigeon did, there was a method to his madness. The little motel in the hills had their best January and February ever, with a steady stream of vehicles arriving, the majority of them from Seattle. The guests were all architects and engineers and computer science people all working on Billy's World. The sudden rush of guests were up all hours of the night with Billy Pigeon and Debra. Billy was tweaking this and tweaking that, adding the new used car lot, the mile-long car ports, the fifty bay garage and the really cozy apartments on top for Richard Perkins Jr. and his young mechanic friends from Washington, D. C., There was a lot of midnight oil being burned, with Billy's World just about ready to go to tender, the tenders all on the computer, the stakes all cut and ready to be hammered into the ground. Weyerhauser was happy to have the extra work cutting all the stakes in a shitty economy. The bulldozers were ready to level 146 towns, all waiting for that magic word *go* from their president, the computers with e-mails all set to be sent to construction companies and sub-trades all across America. Billy Pigeon was about to unleash the greatest and most audacious construction project the world has ever seen. The name Billy's World on all the documents was not just a figment of someone's fertile imagination anymore!

\* \* \*

I have to tell you about horseshoes up your ass; you're not going to believe what happens next in our little story! The day after they just about froze to death in the mountains, Lee Marvin spotted Charles Bronson standing by his big old horse. Charles Bronson was waving his arms like crazy to his buddy Lee, telling him to get his butt up here because Charles Bronson had spotted a small opening in the snow, an opening which led into a cave, which was really the entrance to an old mine shaft that had not seen a human's footprint in over 150 years!

"We're up here guys; there's shelter!" yelled Charles Bronson, as he and Lee Marvin began to throw away rocks to make the entrance to the cave bigger. Once inside, with a nice fire going and wood crackling, Jack decided to go explore a little bit with his trusty Bic lighter! About 200 feet inside the mine shaft, and Jack half pissed, he saw a one-inch-wide yellow streak going across the wall of rock above his head. There were two dusty Winchester rifles on the ground and the skeletons of two people in leather cowboy boots!

"Clint, Clint," yelled Jack, "come quick!"

All ten of Jack's buddies came a-running, their Bic lighters leading the way.

"What the hell's wrong now?" asked Lee Marvin.

"The ten sets of new eyes saw the two skeletons, the Winchester rifles, and the incredible vein of gold running above their heads.

"Holy Christ!" said Tommy Lee Jones.

"Holy Christ is right!" said Charles Bronson.

The boys had stumbled on one of the greatest gold deposits ever found in the U. S. of A. The deposit was worth thousands—sorry, millions—sorry billions—maybe even trillions of dollars with today's price of gold!

The mine had been dug in 1862, the mine shaft dug by hand and all the rock packed out to the entrance by wheelbarrow by the two skeletons on the ground. The two skeletons on the ground were killed by local Indians, their throats cut, their heads scalped, their bodies left in the mine to rot. The cave entrance was almost completely covered over by rocks. The Indians were all over the case of whiskey they had walked away with; the two Winchester rifles and all the gold in the mountain were meaningless. The Indians were ready to P-A-R-T-Y, big-time!

Jack and Clint and their nine other cowboys on the trail of life all shook their heads in disbelief. They sat by the fire; they smoked cigars, ate cold beans, drank the last two bottles of Jack's whiskey, laughed, and farted all night long!

Jack summed up the feelings of everyone around the campfire when he said the following: "Fuck, those other guys are going to be pissed!"

\* \* \*

Twenty million YA kids at Billy's World would be mesmerized by Clint's story of the gold mine told after dinner before their exercise session. In the massive dining hall below the dormitory tower, Clint spoke to four thousand YA kids, telling the same story at 4,999 other dormitory dining halls over a 14-year period, with Clint getting questions like:

"How come the Indians left the guns?"

"What brand of whiskey did they take?"

"What did you guys do with the cowboy boots?"

"Did General Jessep save his Bic lighter as a keepsake?"

"I bet Jack Lambert cuts a mean fart!"

"What have you done with all your money?"

"What did Arnold say?"

At the end of each story to a different group of YA kids, the YA kids looking fabulous in their sharp-looking outfits, stress-free and confident as can be with their bloated bank accounts, Clint would always tell the YA kids that success in life was all about hard work, discipline, doing without and struggling towards your goal when most people would pack it in, call it quits, and go home when the going got tough.

"And don't forget about eating your beans and the horseshoes up your ass!" shouted one young lad from Colorado.

"And that, too!" said Clint with a grin, and with all 4,000 YA kids in the dining hall busting a gut!

# 37

# Put the File Away

"Robert F. Kennedy Jr., do you mind if we come in?" asked Dustin Hoffman.

"We're putting together a story for the Washington Post about Billy Pigeon, the kid from Bellevue who's running for president. We know he's doing something big. We know Apple and Microsoft are involved. We know he's promised work to 20 million young Americans. We know someone is buying up towns on the Great Plains. We know Arnold was involved in, we think, some promotional ride with Clint Eastwood. We know a lot of people have lost a lot of money on Wall Street. You know Maria Shriver—she's a Kennedy—we thought you might be able to shed some light on the matter. We know you're big in the environmental movement. Are you possibly involved in that big apple pie Billy Pigeon is baking? Maybe you guys are against it because there's Mob money involved. I'm hoping you could help us out," said ace reporter Robert Redford.

"Sorry guys, I'd like to help, but I know nothing!" said Robert F Kennedy Jr.

\* \* \*

"Do you believe him?" asked Dustin Hoffman.

"Nope," said Robert Redford.

"Me neither," said Dustin Hoffman.

"I think we should check out the travel habits of one slippery Robert F. Kennedy Jr.," said Robert Redford.

"Already done—Danny should have an update real soon!" said Dustin Hoffman.

\* \* \*

"He booked a flight three months ago to Boulder," said Danny DeVito.

"One of my favorite towns!" said Robert Redford.

\*\*\*

In Boulder, Robert Redford tracked down an old friend who ran a restaurant in town. He showed her a picture of Robert F Kennedy Jr. She said he had been there, in her restaurant with ten other people about two or three months ago—no it was definitely three months. They were all waiting for one more guy—a lawyer from Boise—but he called and said his flight was canceled and then they all took off to some big meeting at a private residence not too far from here!

"Bingo" said Dustin Hoffman.

"So who in Boise is big into the environmental movement?" asked Robert Redford.

Dustin Hoffman was on Google; he Googled environmental activists. Guess what came up on his screen?

"Advocates for the West, a group led by prominent lawyers and scientists committed to the preservation of the west as we know it!" said Dustin Hoffman.

"Boise is one of my favorite towns, too!" said Robert Redford.

\*\*\*

"Hi, we're from the Washington Post. We're trying to track down the person from Advocates for the West who canceled on a flight to a meeting of environmentalists in Boulder about three months ago," said Dustin Hoffman.

"That would be David Horton," said a cute little secretary named Judy.

"You wouldn't happen to know where his office is?" asked Robert Redford.

"Sure, just a second. I'll get you the address," said Judy.

"You're a sweetheart!" said Dustin Hoffman.

\*\*\*

"David Horton, thanks for seeing us. We're from the Washington Post. We know you were going to a big environmental meeting in Boulder about three months ago, but you canceled at the last moment. The meeting was about a big project that Billy Pigeon has planned for somewhere in the United States, we think the mid-west. We know 20 million young Americans are going to work there. We'd like to know how the meeting went in Boulder," said Robert Redford.

"I wasn't there, so how can I tell you what happened?" said David Horton.

"You must have talked to someone who was at the meeting," said Dustin Hoffman.

"I did talk to Margot Kidder. She said the meeting went well, that Billy Pigeon seemed really happy; that's all I know," said David Horton.

"Any idea how many corporations besides Apple and Microsoft are involved?" asked Robert Redford.

"The number five thousand came up! Hey, guys, I'm really busy; you'll have to excuse me. I have a two o'clock," said David Horton.

\* \* \*

"Holy crap!" said Dustin Hoffman.

"Holy crap is right!" said Robert Redford.

At the Washington Post, Robert Redford and Dustin Hoffman sat with Tom Skerritt. Tom Skerritt played the role of Ben Bradley, the editor of Washington Post in *All The President's Men 2.*

"We have got to talk!" said Robert Redford.

"About what?" asked Ben Bradley.

"What do you think we're going to be talking about?" asked Dustin Hoffman, smoking a cigarette. Dustin Hoffman was as excited as a cat on a hot tin roof.

"This is the biggest story since Watergate!" said Robert Redford. "We're onto something really big!"

Dustin Hoffman laid out all the facts: about their crisscrossing America by plane a couple of times, about the exceptional digging by Danny DeVito, that all they had to do now was to make one of the most important decisions of their journalistic careers!

"Are you certain of your facts?" asked Ben Bradley.

"One hundred percent!" said Dustin Hoffman.

"One hundred and fifty percent!" said Robert Redford.

"So we're between the proverbial rock and a hard place!" said Ben Bradley. "We can sink the kid's plan for America, unveil all the secrecy, tell the world what we know and then the kid's on the run. He's hounded by Fox and MSNBC for details and they try and screw everything up for him. We get the Republicans and the Democrats trying to crucify him—they probably do—and then we get the same fucking assholes running the White House, pumping out the same old shit to our country that they've pumped out for years!"

"So what you're saying is that we give the kid a chance," said Robert Redford.

"Give him till the pretend debate in the spring. Let's see what he's got hidden up that sleeve of his: why he was able to get five thousand corporations on board, 20 million young Americans on board, towns in the Great Plains on board, and the environmental movement on board. I mean, this has *got* to be good. This should be the best night on TV in our lifetime!" said Ben Bradley.

"This certainly is a switch!" said Dustin Hoffman. "We usually dig up the information to make news; now you're telling us to put the file away, to make no news!"

"My call!" said Ben Bradley. "You guys did one hell of a fucking job! You're still the best of the best anywhere in the world. You can be proud of what you've accomplished in such a short time, but my decision is final. I'm giving the kid a chance; I want to see what he's got!"

\* \* \*

"Oh, by the way, what did you say her name was?" asked Ben Bradley.
"Lindahhhh!" said Robert Redford.

\* \* \*

When the snow finally started to melt, the warm winds of spring arriving right on schedule, with Billy, Julie, Debra, and Walter having hibernated for three relaxing months, with all the pieces of the puzzle in place for Billy's World, with Billy having completed all he had set out to do on his two-year whirlwind tour around America, it was time for Billy, Julie, Debra, and Walter to hit the road, to head home, their campaign donations now in excess of one billion dollars. Billy fired up the Birdmobile, the engine sputtering after being idle for three long months, with all of winter's snow swept off the four-foot-tall, carved, one-legged pigeon on top of the motor home, and Billy choosing his John Denver cassette tape to get them started that first day of April 2012, April Fool's Day. Julie's bikini top was taped on the radio antenna outside the Birdmobile. Julie said the following to Billy Pigeon: "Happy April Fool's Day, sweetie!" In his airplane in the sky, John Denver was singing,

"Country roads, take me home,

To the place I belong!"

that place being Bellevue, with Billy Pigeon enjoying the moment, and the Smith brothers, Jeff and Ryan, waiting for them at the Montana border in a kick-ass used car, a 1975 black Mustang, the first for their used inventory at Billy's World and sure to get $2,500 on opening day. Ryan Smith said the following to Billy Pigeon: "There's a lot more where that one came from!"

Ryan Smith was spinning doughnuts on the dirt road next to the highway for a little celebration, with the State Troopers giving him the evil eye. Billy had his fly rod out again, ready to hit some of the northwest streams. The anticipation of Billy's return was picking up steam big-time. The State Troopers looked sharp in their pressed uniforms. The security detail from Spokane was so close to home that they could spit on it. Billy and the Birdmobile went through the little neck of Idaho and into Washington, with people lining the highway and waving American flags and giving Billy Pigeon the thumbs up. Billy entered the mountains, with Debra adamant that she was not returning to the motel with all the spiders, and that they were camping out in their motor home. The Birdmobile was now on the final downhill slide into Seattle; a crowd of 40,000 was on hand as the Birdmobile was escorted into Safeco Field. The crowd of admirers came unglued, with Billy Pigeon receiving a ten-minute standing ovation, as if Billy had just hit the game-winning World Series home run. Billy was at a microphone behind second base and said the following to his 40,000 faithful and a national and worldwide audience on CNN: "It's nice to be home, Seattle. I've missed you. I'm only staying for awhile. I have a plan for America. I have plenty of work to do before I can rest!"

Billy, Walter, Julie, and Debra finally pulled the Birdmobile into Billy's driveway at their home in Bellevue. Sally and Sarah were there to greet them, with hugs and kisses all around; the front lawn of their home was filled with TV cameras, and security guards from Seattle. The 2012 pretend presidential debate was just around the corner. President Obama was watching the scene unfold on his own TV, his underarms starting to sweat. Billy unloaded his suitcase and the four boxes of expense receipts from Julie's Jeep Wrangler. The Jeep Wrangler was filthy, dirty as can be. Billy took out the box from the closet of the motor home with the five thousand letters of intent from corporate America signed that night in Las Vegas. President Obama said the following to the FBI Director: "Where the hell is his big apple pie?"

# 38

## The 1800 Boxes

"Are you nervous about standing on the same stage with sixty seasoned politicians and media giants and political analysts and past presidents all at the same time?" asked Wolf Blitzer in an exclusive interview with Billy Pigeon on CNN.

"Not one bit," said Billy.

"You'd better do your homework, young man," said Wolf Blitzer. "I've got questions for you on being president, on dealing with a collapsed economy in a fast moving economic world, on deficits and debt and political gridlock in Washington!"

"Bring it on!" said Billy Pigeon.

\*\*\*

"Cocky little bugger, isn't he?" said Wolf Blitzer to his CNN News producer.

"He sure is!" said the CNN News producer.

\*\*\*

"So what's he up to today?" asked President Obama.

"He's still riding his old mountain bike around Seattle. He picked up a bunch of aluminum beer cans and put them in a plastic bag. He spent some time chitchatting with a guy in a car wash, and had a cup of coffee across the street at the McDonald's store with the manager," said the FBI Director.

"That's it!" said President Obama. "What's he doing at night?"

"Going to the movies, taking a walk in the park with his girlfriend, taking photographs along the Seattle waterfront—that's about it!" said the FBI Director.

"I just don't get it; he should be pouring over his notes, surrounded by political advisors like me, preparing for the pretend debate. Something is wrong; I can smell it. This is some type of diversion to keep me preoccupied. I'm being set up by the Republicans; they're probably all laughing at me as they ramp up their political machine!" said President Obama.

"Who knows," said the FBI Director. "He's a tough kid to figure out!"

\* \* \*

"How are you feeling?" asked Debra.

"Number One!" said Billy.

"Are you nervous?" asked Debra.

"Nope!" said Billy.

"Well I am!" said Debra.

\* \* \*

Billy watched an interview his mother, Sally, had taped for him. He listened to a business dude saying that companies in America's future will choose technology over talent, that there is no future for long term employment growth in America.

This is what Billy Pigeon said to himself after he watched the interview of the business dude: "Really!"

\* \* \*

Billy packed his suitcase again. He thought of what the two nice ladies said to him in his two anger management courses. He took two deep breaths; he smiled. He placed his two extra shirts and one extra pair of pants, his shaving kit, his toothbrush and tooth paste, his comb, two pairs of white socks, and two pairs of underwear in his suitcase. He closed his suitcase, crawled into bed, closed his eyes and slept like a baby!

\* \* \*

Over at Paul and Debra's house, the entire living room floor was full of boxes. Five of the security detail from Spokane were all over the house, five were at Billy's and the other ten were sleeping, getting ready for the day shift. Paul's neighbors were curious as hell, knowing from the *CBS Evening News* that Paul, Debra, and Julie were on their way to Washington with Billy Pigeon, Walter, Sally, and Sarah for the pretend presidential debate.

\* \* \*

Paul and Debra taped the boxes: the A Boxes containing the Pledges of Allegiance made by the 20 million YA kids all across America, the B Box containing the five thousand contracts e-mailed by corporate America to Debra, the C Boxes containing the real estate deals signed by all the residents of all the one-horse towns across three-fourths of North Dakota, all of South

Dakota, all of Nebraska, a part of Colorado and one-third of Kansas. The boxes were all marked on the outside with a big old, black felt marker. Eight large courier trucks showed up at Paul and Debra's home at seven o'clock the following morning. The boxes, all 1800 of them, were loaded into the eight courier trucks and delivered to SEA-TAC Airport in Seattle, with a Boeing 747 cargo jet waiting on the tarmac. The 747 soon lifted off from SEA-TAC after Billy Pigeon received a tumultuous goodbye and good luck send-off by Seattle residents at the airport. All 1,800 boxes were safely on board in the belly of the beast. Ten members of the security detail from Spokane protected the boxes; the other ten were sleeping.

Billy, Julie, Walter, Debra, Sally, Sarah, and Paul were all upstairs behind the pilots and navigators, relaxing and chitchatting. The flight across North America was a hell of a lot quicker than driving the Birdmobile. There was chaos at Washington National Airport as Billy's plane touched down. The 1,800 boxes were loaded into eight waiting courier trucks, the twenty members of the security detail from Spokane watching every box being unloaded and then reloaded. The press from all over the world was astounded by all the boxes. The security detail from Spokane were now in ten rented Suburbans, all of them black, with five Suburbans riding in front of the eight courier trucks, two Washington State Troopers in front of the five Suburbans, Billy Pigeon and his merry band of Washingtonians from the northwest in two other rented Suburbans, five other black Suburbans following those two black Suburbans—a total of twenty-two vehicles slowly making their way to waiting dormitory rooms on the campus of George Washington University.

"My God, he's even acting like the president!" said Wolf Blitzer. "The best political team on television" was blown away by the twenty-two vehicle motorcade through Washington and the 1,800 boxes in the eight courier trucks. The boxes were the talk of the town, with "the best political team on television" stumped as to what was inside the boxes, and with the rest of the world stumped too!

\* \* \*

"What's with all the boxes?" asked President Obama.

"I have *no* idea!" said the FBI director.

"You're fired!" yelled President Obama.

"Maybe he has a piece of apple pie for all of us!" said the FBI director's assistant.

"You're fired, too!" yelled President Obama.

\* \* \*

Billy Pigeon entered the George Washington University campus to another hero's welcome, with thousands and thousands of students standing on both sides of the street, American flags being waved everywhere, all the students screaming and yelling at Billy in his rented Suburban, with iPhones and cameras and video recorders recording history in the making!

\* \* \*

Billy had another great sleep; he slept like a baby once more. The following morning, he went to join the student body in the student cafeteria for bacon, eggs, toast, and black coffee, with students of all shapes and sizes, of both genders, of all colors yelling support to Billy Pigeon, trying their best to motivate Billy for the pretend debate scheduled on campus for seven o'clock that evening. The students minced no words:

"Give 'em hell, Billy!"

"Kick their butts!"

"Don't take any prisoners!"

"We got your back!"

Billy toured campus after breakfast. He even sat down and listened to an old English professor with graying hair lecture to his class. The book of choice in today's lecture was *Slaughterhouse-Five,* an American classic by Kurt Vonnegut, one of Billy's two favorite authors, the little book about the horrors of war, about the Allied bombing of the German city of Dresden in World War II. The old professor welcomed Billy Pigeon to his class and said he was honored to have a possible future American president in his classroom. He asked Billy if he had anything to say. Billy stood up and said the following:

"I hate war too, sir. I'll tell you all about it tonight!"

The professor told Billy that he had a front row seat for the pretend debate on campus, that Kurt Vonnegut himself would have loved to have written a novel about an eighteen-year-old boy who was running for president, who drove around America in a motor home with a four-foot-tall statue of a one-legged pigeon on the roof, who was impressing the hell out of Americans everywhere, who had collected over a billion dollars in campaign donations in two years, who was willing to debate sixty of the best political minds in the country on national TV, who would be surrounded like Custer at the Battle of the Bighorn, but hopefully, with a different result!

\* \* \*

You just knew it had to happen: guess who showed up on the window ledge of Julie's dormitory room? You guessed right—the real live, one-legged pigeon! But you're only one-third right. Next to the real live, one-legged pigeon was a real live, female one-legged pigeon and a real live, baby one-legged pigeon, the mother and the baby pigeon having absolutely no idea what all the fuss was about!

Billy looked at Julie; this is what Billy said: "No wonder we couldn't find him. The little bugger was out having hanky-panky without a condom!"

Julie went bananas; she called everyone to the room. Debra spoke for everyone when she said the following: "OH, that is just *so* cute!"

Julie opened the window. She let all the pigeons inside the little dormitory room. She asked Walter to go to the dining hall to get her three or four bags of crunchy croutons!

"It's a sign, Billy. Honest to God, it's a sign from above. You're going to win the pretend debate. You're going to become the next president. We're going to move into the White House!" said Julie.

\*\*\*

It was 4:30 p.m. in Washington. President Obama was on the blower to his new FBI director.

"So what's he doing now?" asked the president.

"He took a pillow with him. He's having a nap on the grass in front of his dormitory room, surrounded by four big security guys!" said the new FBI director.

"A nap!" said the president.

"A nap," said the new FBI director.

\*\*\*

It was 6:45 p.m. in Washington. The TV lights were on; there were sixty-one chairs on the stage. There were thirty chairs to the left of the chair reserved for Billy Pigeon; there were thirty chairs to the right. Each group of thirty chairs was divided into three groups of ten; all three rows of ten chairs angled toward Billy's chair. The audience was able to have a super profile of all the people on the stage. The organizer of the sixty-one chairs had done a heck of a good job!

The Democrats entered stage left at 6:50 p.m. : the Rev Jessie Jackson, Jessie Jackson Jr. , Barney Frank, Patty Murray, Governor Jerry Brown, Robert Gibbs, Al Gore, Larry Summers, Tim Geithner and Rahm Emanuel filling the back ten seats first, with the audience applauding gently. Then they were followed by Howard Dean, James Carville, Debbie Wasserman-Schultz, Mario Cuomo, Elijah Cummings, John Kerry, Chris Matthews, Rachel Maddeaux, Lawrence O'Donnell and Ed Schultz, with the audience applauding gently. Then they were followed by President Jimmy Carter, Robert Reich, President Bill Clinton, Hillary Clinton, the Rev Al Sharpton, Nancy Pelosi, Harry Reid, Vice President Joe Biden, Michelle Obama and President Barack Obama, with the audience applauding gently. The Republicans entered stage right: Gary Johnson, Larry Kudlow, Ann Coulter, Mrs. George Bush Sr., President George H. W. Bush Sr., President George W. Bush, Jeb Bush, Karl Rove, Eric

Cantor, and Rick Santelli filled the back row, with the audience applauding gently. John Boehner, Paul Ryan, Rand Paul, Bill O'Reilly, Dick Chaney, Glenn Beck, Rush Limbaugh, Tina Fey, Herman Cain, Donald Trump, and Thaddeus McCotter filled the second row, with the audience applauding gently. Herman Cain, Sarah Palin, Rick Santorum, Newt Gingrich, Mitt Romney, Michele Bachmann, Tim Pawlenty, Ron Huntsman, Ron Paul, and Rick Perry filled the front row, with the audience applauding gently. Billy Pigeon entered the stage to a standing ovation from the audience, shaking hands with all twenty opponents in the front rows. Billy was wearing his Sunday best: his white short-sleeve shirt, his dark brown belt, his pressed blue jeans, his white socks, his dark brown leather moccasins. Billy grinned, as cool as a cucumber, and took a seat!

A hush came over the crowd as Wolf Blitzer entered the stage. Janet Jackson entered the stage too to sing the national anthem, doing a lovely rendition of God Bless America, all of the world waiting for another wardrobe malfunction, but it never happened. Janet Jackson waved to the audience as she left the stage. Wolf Blitzer was now in control, his hair and beard looking real good, his outfit dapper as can be, his shoes shined. Wolf took the microphone, standing tall, with no chair required for this New York commentator. He welcomed all of America and the world to the first ever pretend presidential debate, an historic night in American politics. Wolf Blitzer thanked President Obama for bending the rules, for giving a nineteen-year-old boy an opportunity to pretend he was running for president. President Obama acknowledged Wolf Blitzer's comments, taking a bow, milking all the political points he could milk out of the moment. Wolf Blitzer read the Rules of Engagement: each of the twenty speakers in the two front rows was given five minutes for an opening statement, Billy Pigeon was allowed fifty minutes for his opening statement, he would go last, with the other forty speakers in the pretend debate only allowed to participate in the Question and Answer portion of the debate. Wolf Blitzer told his first twenty-one speakers that he wanted the opening statements of all twenty-one speakers to focus on the American economy and that he wanted to hear what each speaker would do to jump-start America's economic engine. All the members of the audience were allowed to Tweet their comments about each of the speaker's comments. The Tweets would be posted on a large screen on the west wall of the auditorium and also posted in a lower caption on each television set in America and around the world!

Jimmy Carter spoke first. "Sorry, you were supposed to speak about the economy, not peace in the Middle East!"

Robert Reich was next. "Sorry, go back to your teaching job at Berkley!"

Bill Clinton was next. "Sorry, you had your chance; you blew it!"

Hillary Clinton was next. "Sorry, you always play second fiddle to your husband!"

The Rev. Al Sharpton was next. "Sorry, stick to preaching!"

Nancy Pelosi was next. "Sorry, bad hair day!"

Harry Reid was next. "Sorry, you could use some pep pills!"

Vice President Joe Biden was next. "Sorry, been there, done that!"

Michelle Obama was next. "Sorry, keep your focus on being a good mom!"

Wolf Blitzer introduced President Barack Obama next. He sensed his need to talk, to have one of those really great bullshit sessions of his. Wolf would cut him some slack; allow him to go past his five minutes if he rambled on!

President Obama spoke for six minutes and thirty-four seconds. "Sorry, you look presidential, you talk the talk, but you just don't walk the walk!"

The audience was restless; they had endured 51 minutes and 34 seconds of the same old rhetoric on the economy. They heard it all from the left: from protecting good union jobs, to gays in the military, to abortion, to the peace process, to another big stimulus package, to preserving the big three—Social Security, Medicare and Medicaid—that we had to spend our way into recovery, that running a deficit was not a sin, that there had to be a balanced approach, that there had to be new taxes in the mix, that any new taxes could not come on the backs of the poor, that they had to come from the filthy rich, from the 1 percent, from anyone making more than $250,000 per year, that the thought of giving back control of the Senate to the Republicans was repugnant!

"Thank you very much, Democrats. I would like to hear now from all ten Republican candidates for president. I realize there are more than ten of you, but I can only fit in ten tonight; maybe try again in the real presidential debate or again in four more years!" said Wolf Blitzer.

Herman Cain spoke first. "Sorry, Nine Nine Nine = 27, the number of women you've played around with!"

Sarah Palin was next. Tina Fey also stood up at the same time; the crowd was not sure exactly who was who. "Sorry, still crazy after all these years!"

Rick Santorum was next. "Sorry, relax, chill, you talk way too fast for me!"

Newt Gingrich was next. "Sorry, go play in the Greek Islands, admire your Tiffany jewelry, say hi to your friends at Fannie and Freddy!"

Mitt Romney was next. "Sorry, but flip-flopper, flaky, fidgety, and fortune-finder equals failure to me!"

Michele Bachmann was next. "Sorry, but you're way too right wing for me!"

Tim Pawlenty was next. "Sorry, boring, boring!"

Ron Huntsman was next. "Sorry you look and talk like a church minister!"

Ron Paul was next. "Sorry, your simplistic approach to problems is too complicated!"

Rick Perry was next. "Sorry, great hair, but you're a little too slow for me!"

The audience was even more restless. They had endured 51 minutes and 34 seconds from the left, Wolf Blitzer for another minute, and now 50 minutes from the right, telling the audience that taxes weren't the answer, that we had to cut spending by four trillion dollars, that we had to cut, cap, and balance the U. S. federal budget, that deficits had to be eliminated, that we had to drill, drill, drill, that we had to pipe, pipe, pipe, that we had to strengthen our military, that we had to buy more of the best technology that Boeing and Lockheed Martin and Northrop Grumman could pump out for the war machine, that only the private sector could create jobs, that they should have a corporate tax holiday, a payroll tax holiday, an R&D tax holiday, an income tax reduction plan, and that the Democrats had just finished running the country into the ground with all their stimulus spending. The sniping and cat-calling started slowly with the twenty Democrats and the twenty Republicans behind the twenty speakers, with Rush Limbaugh giving the finger to Lawrence O'Donnell, with Lawrence O'Donnell giving it right back, with Glenn Beck standing up and telling Bill Clinton to pull his pants down, to take a fucking bow on national TV, with Al Gore giving George Bush the choke signal, with Debbie Wasserman-Schultz sticking her tongue out at any Republican who would look, with Sarah Palin throwing her purse at Hillary Clinton, with Hillary Clinton throwing the purse back, with Sarah Palin throwing the purse again and hitting the Rev. Al Sharpton, who said the following to Sarah Palin: "Go to hell, witch!"

The war was on, with all thirty Democrats standing and shouting, with all thirty Republicans standing and shouting, too. Donald Trump told President Obama that he couldn't run a pig farm on the outskirts of Chicago, let alone a country; Hillary Clinton yelled "And what the hell do you know about China?" to Donald Trump. Glenn Beck threatened to come across the aisle and beat the living shit out of Ed Schultz. Ed Schultz took off his jacket, loosened his tie, and told the Republicans to "Come on over, come on over, you bunch of assholes; let's get it on, right here, right now!" The Rev Jessie Jackson shook his head in disgust; Jessie and his son both sat and shook their heads together in disgust. All the other 58 Republicans and Democrats were acting like little children, like spoiled brats, with the war of words heating up, with the F-word used, then the B-word, the D-word, the C-word, three more F-words, the B-word again, with insults and cat calls and racial slurs, with the slings and arrows of Washington politics front and center. Jimmy Carter stood and pleaded for peace. *Politicians Gone Wild* was sure to be the next reality show on TV, with one of the security detail from Spokane running up on the stage and giving Billy Pigeon a battle helmet and a protective jacket, the stage in absolute pandemonium, exactly as Debra Sanders planned. Debra Sanders gave Billy Pigeon the thumbs up, and Billy Pigeon gave the thumbs up back to Debra. Debra and Billy were smiling, but Wolf Blitzer was in panic mode, his days as a big event political moderator in America in jeopardy, big-time!

"Gentlemen, ladies, I realize the economy is a difficult subject. I realize you all are under a great deal of pressure to perform, but this is ridiculous!" The audience was now on its feet, the TV ratings sky-rocketing, all of the world watching the audience going boo, boo, boo, boo!

"Settle down—settle down—settle down!" yelled Wolf Blitzer. "Let's be calm; let's be calm. Billy Pigeon still has fifty minutes to speak!"

While all the political infighting was going on, Debra Sanders had all 1,800 boxes brought into the auditorium on dollies. The dollies were pushed by hired help, all students on campus looking for some extra spending money. The one-hundred students were responsible for eighteen boxes each. The 1,800 boxes soon filled the middle aisle of the auditorium, both side aisles, all the available space in front of the stage, with the B box in front, the 30 C boxes behind them, and the 1,769 A boxes spread all over hell's half acre!

When everyone on stage had finally settled down and realized they had made an ass of themselves in front of the entire world, the sixty participants in the pretend debate were in shock and awe when they saw the 1,800 boxes in the auditorium. Billy Pigeon was about to speak—about to get his turn at the microphone. Billy had his pointer and his Garth Brooks microphone; he was going to give a power point presentation. Billy Pigeon was about to become our next president!

Billy Pigeon had fifty minutes; he was in no rush. He began to speak.

> Good evening, ladies and gentlemen, my name is Billy Pigeon. I will be twenty years old on my next birthday. I'm from Bellevue, Washington, and I want to be the next president of the United States! I want to return America to its glory days, to where it once was, the greatest country on the planet Earth!

The audience applauded enthusiastically. Billy continued.

> I am a high school graduate from Bellevue High in Bellevue. I have three shirts and two pairs of pants to my name. I ride a bicycle everywhere I go. I have $49,000 cash in the bank, money I have worked for and saved since I was four years old.

> I have no debt. I have a line of credit and one credit card; they both have a zero balance. I feel real strength when I walk into my bank and place another $57 into my savings account. I am stress-free. I don't have a worry in the world!

I look at my country—your country. I see an America in a political, economic, and moral crisis. We have a government that is in gridlock. We have a $15 trillion federal debt. We have unfunded liabilities of $56 trillion. We owe a grand total of $71 trillion to someone!

We have a total of 15 percent of our work force unemployed if you crunch the real numbers, if you take into account all the people in America who have stood in too many lineups looking for work, who have attended too many job fairs, or who have given up looking for a job. We have a younger generation of Americans who are obese, lazy, addicted to alcohol and spaced out on drugs, who show no respect whatsoever for other people or other peoples' property, who have no idea of what they can achieve with hard work and discipline, and who have no goals in life.

America, we have a problem—a really big problem! I have listened tonight to twenty of, supposedly, the most brilliant minds in American politics. I have heard nothing new, just the same old, same old bag of promises. Even the same old bag of promises can't be counted on because of all the political posturing, the political brinkmanship, and the grip that special interest groups have on our politicians: the gridlock in our system.

I am different from those politicians. I do have a plan, a real plan. I will lead the RPA, the Reality Party of America: real people with real solutions to real problems. We will not be puppets on a string. We will not be worried about being elected in the next election. We will be risk takers. We will take the bull by the horns. We will build Billy's World!

The day I become president, with one stroke of my pen in the Oval Office, I am going to give every unemployed American a job. I am going to teach discipline and hard work and how to save and not spend money to 20 million young Americans. They will all have $50,000 cash in their blue jeans after a five-year commitment to me. America's youth will have financial equality. They are going to fight a war here in America—my War on Jobs—not die in some foreign land like Iraq or Afghanistan.

As your president, I am going to unleash the entrepreneurial skills and incredible technology of America. I am going to oversee the largest construction project the world has ever seen: a massive military, industrial, manufacturing complex built in the heartland of America. The heartland of America will pump blood into the life of every American, with $2.5 trillion coming from my government, $2.5 trillion coming from the private sector: $5 trillion already set to go, $5 trillion all set to build my vision for America!

I will use one-third of Kansas, part of Colorado, all of Nebraska, all of South Dakota, and three-fourths of North Dakota. I will have 6,000 American construction companies using every unemployed American they can find over a four-year period. I will have 10,000 sub trade companies. Every factory and manufacturing facility in America will produce all the products needed to build Billy's World: all the steel, the aluminum, the concrete, the plastic and copper pipe, the electrical components, and the machinery. Every unemployed American will be working either building Billy's World or making all the products needed for our military, industrial manufacturing complex: all the products made in America by Americans!

Bring up a B Box please," said Billy Pigeon. Billy sipped on a glass of water as he waited for one of his security detail from Spokane to deliver the box to the stage, open it with a pocketknife, and give Billy the first piece of paper he saw at the top of the box. Billy continued.

I have thirty boxes of signed real estate deals from all the people presently living in the 146 towns in the construction zone, each piece of paper containing the signature of one or two happy campers who will get twice as much money for his or her property than it's worth, and then will live in a new two million person city I am building to service Billy's World. They will be put up in hotel and motel rooms at no charge during the construction phase. Their condo or apartment or townhouse or home of their choice will be rent free in my service city, for as long as they live. They will have first dibs on any service job in Billy's World. They will receive a competitive wage, with benefits and free medical and dental and self-controlled pension plan. They will work for me; they will work for you!

Bring up Box A, please." Billy removed the top piece of paper in Box A and showed the piece of paper to the world.

In Box A, I have five thousand signed contracts from five thousand of America's biggest and best corporations. These corporations will unleash $2.5 trillion into Billy's World to construct five thousand manufacturing hubs. Each hub will have its own factory, training facility and raw material warehouse; each factory will be state-of-the-art.

Outstanding American companies like Apple, Microsoft, General Motors, Caterpillar, John Deere, Nike, DuPont and 3M will all manufacture Made in America products at Billy's World. These corporations have been forced to take their jobs elsewhere and build new plants overseas because of wage costs, benefit costs, medical and dental costs, and pension costs, all the workers' money going to pay for the American Dream of a house here, and a house there, three cars, seven TVs, four bathrooms, and clothes coming out of our ying-yang. We don't need all that stuff to be happy. We need a roof over our head, a bed to sleep on, some food to eat, and some clothes to wear. Happiness is not about the pursuit of material things. Happiness is being stress-free, debt-free, having money to pay your taxes to a government that is debt-free, not so far in debt that they, too, are driving companies from America with their regulations and their insatiable appetite for tax dollars, a federal government forcing American corporations to look elsewhere for lower wage costs and tax savings.

These five thousand corporations are committed to Billy's World. They are willing to give me a lot, and in return, I am going to give them a lot; it's a win-win situation. I'm going to give them 20 million young Americans—YA kids—to all learn a trade, to work in their factories, to produce Made in America products, with comfortable chairs to sit on, coffee breaks and safe working conditions and super air conditioning. There will be no factory sweat shops at Billy's World. American companies will never, ever, have to look to the rest of the world for its employees, ship their jobs overseas, or build factories in foreign lands.

I want to introduce three outstanding Americans to you tonight," said Billy. Clint Eastwood and Jack Nicholson walked onto the stage, looking fabulous in their Marine outfits, their four and three star general badges, their crew cuts, their polished shoes, their serge caps at their sides. Clint and Jack were joined on the stage by Tommy Tucker in his YA uniform, his brown boots, his dark green pants, his beige shirt, with Sarah's YA decals on his sleeves, and his dark green baseball cap fitting snugly on his head.

Tommy Tucker also wore a microphone. Tommy Tucker read his modified Pledge of Allegiance to America:

I, Tommy Tucker, from Buffalo, New York, age ten, agree to make a five-year commitment to my country America, to work in Billy's World, to be a soldier in President Pigeon's War on Jobs, with President Pigeon providing me with food, clothing, shelter, and free transportation for those five years, with me making a commitment to learn a trade, to work for a company of my choosing, to go where I am told by General Highway if all the 4,000 jobs in my manufacturing hub of choice are filled, to not even think about questioning his decision, to say, 'yes sir, put me to work, sir!'

I will receive minimum wage, with no other benefits. I will put 80 percent of my wages into the Bank of Billy every payday, with the other $200 a month given to me as spending money—$50 a week—that I have to budget, to spend on what I want, where I want in Billy's World.

I will do no drugs, watch no MTV, bully nobody and not take part in any teen hazing. I will watch no porn, drink no alcohol in public till I'm twenty-one, and if I choose to smoke cigarettes or cigars or chew tobacco, it will be in designated areas only. I will eat no junk food for the five years I am at Billy's World. I will eat hot, healthy meals only. I will exercise for one hour every evening under the command of my military dorm supervisor. I will work forty hours a week, from 8:00 a.m. till 4:00 p.m. I will have my evenings and my weekends off. I understand The Golden Rule: four strikes and you're out. I will be confined to my dorm for two weeks without pay if I get three strikes; if

I mess up again after three strikes, I'll get a free flight home from Billy's World, never to return!

I make this pledge tonight to America. I am looking forward to working hard for five years, for the corporation that gives me a job, to never complain, to produce Made in America products for people all over the world to buy, to leave Billy's World with $50,000, and counting, cash in my blue jeans, with an option to sign on for another five years if I want to, to come back home with $100,000 in my savings book, my five thousand dollar 1980 Chevy Camaro all paid for, ready to move onto the next phase of my life, to have a head start, thanks to Billy Pigeon. I am ready to go to war for America, to rebuild America's manufacturing sector, to kick some Asian and Oriental butt!

Tommy Tucker shook Billy Pigeon's outstretched hand. He saluted General Highway and General Jessep; both generals saluted Tommy back.

"Good job, kid!" said Jack.

Billy then ordered two more of the security detail from Spokane to set up for the power point presentation. A gigantic 30 foot by 30 foot screen was lowered from the ceiling. The 61 chairs on the stage were now out of sight, out of mind. This was the first bird's eye view of Billy's World ever seen by the public. The lights were turned down, way down; the only thing you could see in the whole auditorium was Billy's lit up screen and his red power point. Billy resumed his conversation with the world.

I have 19,999,999 other Tommy Tuckers all signed up, their Pledges of Allegiance to America in all the boxes around this room, all 20,000,000 young Americans ready to serve in my War on Jobs, to serve under General Highway, General Jessep, General Jones, General Norris, General Bronson, General Marvin, General Seagal, General Butkus, General Riggins, General Csonka, and General Lambert—the YA kids—all ready to go serve their country, to do what they're told, to the best of their ability, to listen to and respect their elders.

So before Tommy Tucker catches his flight in Buffalo and lands on our 20-mile runway at one of our four gigantic airports, let's talk about Billy's World. Let's start with the fence around the perimeter.

General Jessep will have a fence line to protect, stretching 350 miles at the south end, 350 miles at the north end, 700 miles of fence line to the east, another 700 miles to the west, for a total of 2,100 miles, with guard checkpoints for tourist and service worker entry and military personnel at 210 locations—one every 10 miles—with U. S. Army personnel at all checkpoints to check for ID, to keep out illegal immigrants, and to watch for any type of terrorist activity.

Billy's World will be double fenced, with General Jessep having total control of fence line construction into our complex, with U. S. military helicopters also patrolling our fence line 24/7, 365 days a year, with U. S. Army and Marine personnel also driving Humvees and flying Apache helicopters between each checkpoint. Our military personnel will stay in their own military compound, over here in the southeast corner of Billy's World. They'll also have housing accommodations at each of the 210 military checkpoints along the fence line so they can drive or fly in and work four days on, four days off. I'll be bringing 95 percent of our troops home. We'll keep a couple of submarines and a couple of aircraft carriers with U. S. Navy fighter aircraft and U. S. Navy Seals and a couple of destroyers with U. S. Marines (for rescue operations of Americans in hostile territories) in EACH of the major oceans of the world and we will keep strategic military bases for our stealth bombers. We will bring all our boots home except for our special ops and CIA operatives. We will use our technology to attack and to defend. We will lead the world in technological advances for the military.

The military training facility at Billy's World will be the largest military training facility in the world for soldiers and airmen. It will be self-contained—a fence line within a fence line. It will be totally out of bounds for our 20 million YA kids, but it will have a profound influence in their daily lives. Our YA kids will look like soldiers and will act like soldiers. They will be a lean, mean, working machine! The U. S. military will train here and will then report, if necessary, to bases in the United States to be ready for war, to protect our country if foreign boots step on our soil, or to go somewhere to help a friend in need.

The U. S. military, with its proud tradition, will be the backbone of Billy's World. It will protect our 20 million young American workers from harm's way. Our workers will salute every U. S. military personnel they come into contact with. Our military personnel will be under the command of General Highway. General Highway will have an office on the top floor of the administration building. It will be here, close to the southern fence line. The admin building will be forty stories high, will be the administrative center for our entire complex, and will house secretaries, accountants, computer operators, corporate liaisons, and military personnel. There will be five thousand smaller admin sites attached to each of the five thousand manufacturing hubs, but we'll get to that later!

Oh, and next to the admin building will be a private residence for the president and his family; we will call it White House 2. It will be plain-Jane: a couple of floors, nothing special! So let's get back to Tommy Tucker. He lands on the 20-mile runway. He is picked up at one of the four airports by military personnel and he is transported to his manufacturing hub. So we go this way, all the way up here where we hook into the main transportation highway going north to the end of our complex. The highway is wide, 40 lanes in total: 20 going north, 20 going south. The highway will be 500 miles long!

On the right hand side of the main transportation highway will be 2,500 manufacturing hubs, each five miles by five miles, a total of 25 square miles. There will be 100 hubs going north, 25 hubs going east, and on the other side of the highway, to the west, we will also have 100 hubs going north, and 25 hubs going west, another 2,500 manufacturing hubs on this side of the highway, for a total of five thousand manufacturing hubs.

Each of the five thousand hubs will contain a ten-story dormitory to house 4,000 young American workers: 400 per floor, 100 per room, separate rooms for male and female workers. Each room will have separate washrooms, separate showers, separate laundry facilities for a quick cleaning of their three shirts and two pairs of pants and their two pairs of work coveralls. The 100 kids in each room will have separate pits, with a single bed, a footlocker and a desk with three drawers.

There will be ten elevators going down to a massive underground dining hall, which will seat 4,000 workers at one time. The workers will be up at 6:30 a.m., eat their hot, healthy breakfast, work in their factory from 8:00 a.m. to 4:00 p.m. They will take a bag lunch to work with them. Dinner will be at 5:30 p.m. A daily exercise session will follow. Lights will be out at 10:00 p.m. during the week, 11:00 p.m. on weekends. The kids will work forty-hour weeks and have their weekends off.

One hundred military personnel will also be housed at each hub. They will have their own separate sleeping and eating facilities next to the main dormitory. Two military personnel will be in charge of each dormitory room.

Each hub will also have a state-of-the-art factory, with an elaborate, hands-on, training center for all new workers, and a warehouse to store raw materials. Each hub will have its own mall. Each mall will have a Bank of Billy, a 20-seat male barber shop, a 20-seat female hair salon, a post office, a gift shop, an Apple store, a used clothing store, an insurance company for YA kids to buy insurance for their used vehicles, a pharmacy, a health food store and an eye doctor store with a variety of eyeglasses to try on and buy.

For visiting parents, tourists, corporate executives, factory staff, prospective clients, suppliers, sales people, and for workers to have the odd bit of hanky-panky with a condom, each hub will also have a one thousand-room hotel, with restaurants, lounges, a swimming pool, gift shops, and a car rental office. Billy's World will give General Motors a $1.8 billion order for 45,000 Chevy Sparks, with nine electric cars ready to rent at each of the five thousand hubs, General Motors gets an order, not a bail-out—the way it should be!

For the workers to relax and enjoy at night and on the weekends, each hub will have its own recreation center, with facilities for every type of sports activity you can imagine, plus an extensive library with a book and video component, and tables and tables of free computer terminals for worker use.

Bottom line: when Tommy Tucker checks into his hub, he's good to go for five years. He has everything he needs within a twenty-five-square-mile area. He does not have to go anywhere, but he can visit any of the other 4,999 hubs on weekends by personal vehicle or by bus or mass transit. Bicycles will be provided for him to roam around as he wishes in the hub he is visiting, and if General Highway finds out that he hasn't returned the bicycle to the spot he borrowed the bicycle from, then it certainly would be one strike against him—that I'm certain of. General Highway nodded his head in agreement, with General Jessep and Tommy Tucker nodding their heads as well.

All of the food and supplies will be brought to each of the five thousand hubs by train and trucks. All of the garbage will be returned the same way, with a circular roadway shooting here and there, east and west from the main transportation highway. That roadway will be six lanes wide, with the trains, buses, and trucks running side by side. The highway and train tracks will completely circle the 2,500 hubs on each side of the main highway, with shorter spur roads and rail lines connecting to each of the five thousand hubs. The trains and the trucks and the buses will run 24/7, 365 days a year!

All of this takes up about three-quarters of our complex, so let's talk now about the other one-third. Oh, I forgot the hospitals and dental centers: there will be 500 of them, three miles apart, all the way around the 1,500 mile highway and train track system surrounding the five thousand hubs. The furthest any sick worker or a worker needing a dentist would have to travel to get medical or dental care will be 250 miles north or south, and 125 miles east or west. For real emergency procedures, each factory—all five thousand of them—will have a helicopter landing pad on the roof, as well as one on the top of each one of the ten story dormitories!

If you look here in the northeast corner of our diagram, you will see a water filtration plant, the biggest in the world, and then going further south, here, a waste water treatment plant, also the biggest in the world, and next to those, the most elaborate garbage incinerator ever built by man, and I'll get to that in a bit. Our cell phone towers are located here and now we're into our 200 mile by 250 mile service area for all the five thousand manufacturing hubs, and you'll see, north of the main military training center, a veterinary shelter for sick and wounded birds and animals—we'll get to that in a bit, too. Here is the computer center, the communications center, a train service center, a truck service center, a bus service center, and as you get further west toward the twenty-mile runway, a series of gigantic hangars to store and service all makes and shapes and sizes of aircraft. On the other side of the twenty-mile runway, right here, we have the fire and ambulance service center, the clothing distribution center, the air traffic control center, the highway maintenance center, and the weather center. Over here, in the southwest corner, we have our energy center, with a massive twenty-second century solar-wind-hydrogen power plant, with back-up natural gas generators, thousands of them, and then the elaborate grid system of solar panels and wind turbines surrounding the entire complex all the way out to the perimeter fence line, a fifty-mile-wide zone stretching the entire 2,100 miles around Billy's World. Then go back over here, right here, you'll see the massive fuel depot with diesel, regular gasoline, propane, and natural gas. With 95 percent of the vehicles in Billy's World running on natural gas or propane or electricity, that should certainly make Boone Pickens happy. Two gigantic underground pipelines will go north and east to the two largest underground supplies of natural gas in the United States, avoiding environmentally sensitive areas, with two more above ground pipelines piping fresh water from the Missouri and Platte Rivers and the Ogallala Aquifer to the massive water filtration plant. Then north of the fuel depot, right here, is the biggest building in the entire complex, probably the biggest building in the world: the food distribution center, operating 24/7, 365 days a year, with so many workers you won't believe it, most of them privates in the military, with food loaded on trucks and trains on its way to the five thousand manufacturing hubs. All the food will be good healthy food—no crap food full of sugar. And last, but not least, the largest used car storage facility on the planet Earth, with the largest used car dealership in the world, named Smith Brothers Used Cars And Trucks, with the world's finest mechanic on duty, seven days a week!

Billy Pigeon looked at the clock on the wall. He sipped on his glass of water and then continued.

In my pocket, I have a letter.

Billy took out an envelope, opening it up, and taking out a piece of paper.

This is a letter of support signed by eleven of the most prominent environmental activists in the United States. I met with them recently, told them about Billy's World, about the twenty-second-century solar-wind-hydrogen power plant and back-up natural gas generators, the garbage incinerator which burns all the garbage, the smoke and the heat from the fire turned into energy to run our service buildings and to heat our water in all the hot water tanks in our complex. Then I explained to my eleven environmental friends, in great detail, that Billy's World and nature will exist in harmony, that more attention will be given to the environment at Billy's World than anything else, that 25 percent of each manufacturing hub will be buildings and roads, the other 75 percent will be left in its natural state, that man's footprint will be kept to a minimum, with animals and birds being reintroduced to Billy's World after the construction phase, with animal underpasses and animal bridges beneath and over all the roads and the train tracks, with animals and birds roaming all the spaces between the five thousand hubs, with the hubs all fenced, with all the components of each hub fenced, too, the animals and birds free to go as they like to live, to reproduce, to die at Billy's World. Injured or sick animals will be airlifted by helicopter or by animal ambulance to the magnificent veterinary hospital, with its hundreds and hundreds of wire-mesh-covered outdoor cages for the injured or sick animals to recover. The environmentalists are working with the architects and engineers and computer experts as we speak, tweaking this and tweaking that, making sure that when all 20 million young Americans look out their dormitory windows at sunset, they will see the animals, hear the owls, watch the birds in flight, watch the ranchers herd their cattle, see the farmers grow their wheat and corn, watch the natural gas men working their rigs, see the tourists going into Wall Drug, and watch the sun go down on the Great Plains—the way it should be!

Billy was almost at the end of his presentation; he had a few more loose ends to tidy up.

Twenty-five successful Americans have been approached and have agreed to serve with me as my board of directors—successful Americans in their own right from all aspects of society. I would like to announce their names to the world tonight:

Mrs. Steve Jobs
Steve Ballmer
Tim Cook
Henry Aaron
Jack Nicklaus
Arnold Palmer
Robin Williams
Whoopi Goldberg
Tom Hanks
Richard Thomas
Mika Brzezinski
Larry King
Warren Buffett
Margot Kidder
Maude Barlow
Naomi Klein
Bill Gates
James Taylor
Paul Simon
Tom Cruise
Robert Redford
Dustin Hoffman
John Elway
Stephen Colbert
Jon Stewart

I would like to thank these outstanding Americans for serving on my board. I'm certainly looking forward to my first meeting. I may even bring along General Highway to keep them in line and have him bring his .357 Magnum!

\* \* \*

Then Billy Pigeon asked the governors of Colorado, Kansas, Nebraska, South Dakota, and North Dakota to stand up in the audience and take a bow. The governors were all sitting together, all looking spiffy in their new cowboy hats and new cowboy boots, all smiling, already to kick back, put their feet up on their big old oak desks, to count all the tax revenues about to pour into their respective states from Billy's World. The five governors all gave Billy Pigeon the thumbs-up sign, all at the same time, the scene impressive as hell!

Now I want you to look here, in the southwest corner of my diagram, outside the fence line. I want you to imagine a beautiful new city of two million people, the first all-green city for the twenty-first century, with all of the service city workers catching buses and mass transit trains to go to work each day to provide the services necessary at Billy's World, to earn a living, to get a competitive salary, with benefits and free medical and dental and self-controlled pensions, not having to worry where their next paycheck is going to come from, to go home to their families and live in more than reasonable rented homes and apartments and condos and townhouses, the mothers and children doing what all mothers and children should do, the city with everything a city should have, the way I want it to be!

In conclusion, I will make a profit of $1.5 trillion my first year of operation at Billy's World. In twenty-four short years, I will have completed Phase 2 and Phase 3. In twenty-four years, the American federal debt of $71 trillion will be at zero. All of the $20 entry fees paid by tourists from all over the world to visit Billy's World will go into two gigantic rainy day accounts: one for the people of America in case we have a financial emergency, the second a fund to study global warming, to stop it in its tracks!

In five short years from now, 20 million young Americans will have 200 billion dollars in their savings accounts after their first year of working at Billy's World, our federal deficit will be eliminated, our federal debt will be going down, down, down, our soldiers, sailors, and airmen will receive an unbelievably big, fat, much deserved pay increase, our Congress and Senate of RPA politicians will operate like it never operated before, bills will actually get passed, we will not be controlled by big business or big labor, we will pay off our $1.2 trillion debt to China, we will put term limitations of eight years on our politicians, something will actually get done, every worker in America will have a job, and unemployment will be at zero. I will kill three birds with one stone. I will change America politically, economically, and morally with one stroke of my pen in the Oval Office. We will learn from the past, deal with the present, and the future will take care of itself. My name is Billy Pigeon. I want to be your next president. God bless you all, and God bless the United States of America!"

\* \* \*

When the lights came back on, and the giant 30-foot by 30-foot screen was rolled all the way up to the ceiling, there were only two people left on the stage. One was Wolf Blitzer, the other was Billy Pigeon. The sixty chairs to the left and right of Billy Pigeon's chair were empty. For some strange reason, the pretend presidential debate had come to a sudden, screeching halt!

\* \* \*

The last official act of President Obama's short term in office as president of the United States, and the last official act of the elected officials of the Congress and the Senate before everybody ran out of Washington with their tails between their legs, was to sign a constitutional amendment allowing a 19-year-old teenager to become president of the United States. The bill was passed into law the day after the pretend presidential debate at George Washington University. No one voted against the bill!

Ben Bradley, the editor of the Washington Post, had a conference call with both Dustin Hoffman and Robert Redford.

"Now we know why they pay you the big bucks!" said Robert Redford.

"Ditto!" said Dustin Hoffman.

\* \* \*

General Nathan Jessep called General Highway. This is what he said: "I can't wait till those Mexicans see all my 'FUCK OFF, WE'RE FULL' flags!"

\* \* \*

Robin Williams jumped for joy on his big old bed. He shouted the following: "I'm going to Billy's World; I'm going to Billy's World!"

\* \* \*

Billy Pigeon, Julie, Walter, Sally, Sarah, Paul, and Debra spent the night at George Washington University. Billy took a walk around the spacious dormitory. He came back to his little room. He called Julie inside. This is what he said: "Want to have hanky-panky with a condom? Everybody else is doing it!"

\* \* \*

Seven days later, on the steps of Congress, in front of thousands and thousands of people, and with a worldwide audience watching on CNN, Billy Pigeon was sworn in as the youngest president of the United States. Debra Sanders was sworn in as the first female vice president. It was one of those magical moments in time. Billy had the real live, one-legged pigeon sitting on his outstretched right hand!

Seven days later, Billy and Julie were married in a small ceremony in the White House. Walter, Sally, Sarah, Paul, and Debra were there. The manager of the Seattle car wash and his wife were there. The manager of the Seattle McDonald's and his wife were there. The manager told Billy that McDonald's was preparing a brand new green menu as they spoke. The 20 members of the security detail from Spokane were there permanently. The Smith brothers, Richard Perkins Jr., the old geezer from Washington, and the owners of the motel from Deadwood were there. Clint Eastwood, Jack Nicholson, Tommy Lee Jones, Lee Marvin, Charles Bronson, Chuck Norris, Larry Czonka, John Riggins, Dick Butkus, Jack Lambert, and Steven Seagal were there, all decked out with their new gold rings. Stephen Colbert and Jon Stewart were there. Tim Hickman was there. Dustin Hoffman, Danny DeVito, and Robert Redford were there. Wolf Blitzer was there reporting for CNN. The real live, one-legged pigeon and the mother and baby pigeon were there, too, all three pigeons sitting on a small table full of croutons!

It was a wonderful wedding, with Billy and Julie exchanging vows, the minister wishing Billy and Julie a long and happy and prosperous life together, and Julie's bouquet thrown and then caught by Sarah. Sarah was thrilled, telling her father Walter that she wouldn't dare think about getting married till she finished her first five years at Billy's World. Walter said the following to his daughter: "Good!"

*\*\*\**

At the reception outside on the White House lawn, with a 12-foot head table at the front, with Billy and Julie and the minister and the family of pigeons sitting in their place, with Billy looking dapper in his white, short-sleeved shirt and his new used tie, bought specially for the occasion at a local thrift store, with everyone else drinking wine and hard liquor on their comfortable, white plastic lawn chairs, Julie did a toast to the groom. It was a wonderful toast. Walter and Sally were in tears, especially Sally!

Billy stood up, reached into his shirt pocket, and pulled out a folded piece of paper. He would toast the bride; he had written a poem for Julie.

"How sweet!" said Sally.

"That's my boy!" said Walter.

This is Billy's poem he wrote for Julie. I'll let you guess the title. Billy read the poem out loud to the people gathered on the lawn. The people were quiet as a church mouse.

*If you marry me,*

*I will worship thee,*

*If we think as one,*

*They'll be plenty of laughter and fun!*

*If you start a fight,*
*I won't fight with thee,*
*But if you throw things at me,*
*I will put you on my knee!*

*If you mouth off to me,*
*I will hide your vehicle key,*
*If you complain to me,*
*I will get pissed at thee!*

*If your tears fall on me,*
*I will comfort thee,*
*If you cry constantly,*
*I will tie you to a tree!*

*If you talk on the phone,*
*I will leave you alone,*
*I will sit in my room,*
*I might even take out a broom!*

*If you want some food,*
*You can eat all you can see,*
*But if you get fat on me,*
*I will bug you constantly!*

*If you let off gas,*
*I will forgive thee,*
*But if it's over and over again,*
*I will tell a gossipy friend!*

*If you smoke in front of me,*
*I'll walk away, you'll see,*
*But I'll have a drink with you,*
*You can have a drink with me!*

*If you sleep with me,*
*I will sleep with thee,*
*If you get up to pee,*
*I will walk with thee!*

*If we go on expensive trips,*
*You can put coloring on your lips,*
*You can wear your bright bikinis,*
*But you must cover up your tits!*

*If we have a babee,*
*And his diaper is all poop and pee,*
*I will watch and see,*
*How you help our nice babee!*

*Why should you do all this*
*For a boy named Billee?*
*Because if you think of me,*
*I will give myself to thee!*

*When you marry me,*
*I will love and honor thee,*
*But if you cheat and lie,*
*You can kiss my ass goodbye!*

Debra busted a gut so badly that her plastic chair fell over. Paul tried to grab her; one of the security detail from Spokane said the following: "Here we go again!"

\* \* \*

Alone in their bedroom at the White House on their wedding night, Billy in his boxer shorts, with no one watching from above, with his pecker hard as a rock, Billy said the following to Julie: "We can have hanky-panky without a condom; everyone's gone home!"

"Go work on your construction plans!" said Julie.

"Ah come on sweetie, it's our wedding night. I was only teasing; everybody else thought my ass poem was funny. You saw how much your mother laughed!" said Billy.

"You're not married to my mother!" said Julie.

"Sweetie, you've got to lighten up and have some fun. I can't work all the time; you've got to try and not be so sensitive," said Billy.

"Well I am sensitive; you hurt my feelings today!" said Julie.

"If I said I was sorry, would you forgive me?" asked Billy.

"I'll think about it," said Julie.

"I'm sorry, sweetie. I won't embarrass you in public like that anymore; I promise, cross my heart!" said Billy. "Do you feel better now?"

"A little," said Julie.

"What if I got into bed and gave you a big hug and rubbed your shoulders—would that make you feel better?" asked Billy.

"It might," said Julie.

"Why don't we give it a try!" said Billy.

"Okay," said Julie.

\* \* \*

Julie had her worm box built on the back lawn of the White House and a big old pigeon coop built next to the worm box. The real live, one-legged pigeon and the mother pigeon and the baby pigeon were all happy campers, with daily flights around Washington for exercise. Washington was now the bird watcher capital of the U. S. of A. The three pigeons had lots of cold water in their dishes, and lots of crunchy croutons, too!

Billy had a gigantic twenty-foot statue of a one-legged pigeon carved and painted by the same carver in Seattle who carved the four-foot-tall, one-legged pigeon for the top of the Birdmobile. Billy had the new carving shipped out to Washington and placed on top of the White House. The carving was the talk of the town, with Washington pigeons coming from here, there, and everywhere to sit on top of the big old pigeon, to get a bird's eye view of all the happy Americans outside the White House gate!

Billy placed the $100 bill the old geezer from Washington gave him on his secondhand oak desk in the Oval Office. He also placed John Elway's football there, too, sitting on a wooden base. He also had his piggy bank that his father, Walter, gave him when Billy was four years old. He had his Scrapbook of Life on his desk, too, and also the five self-published books by David H. E. Smith, Billy's writer friend from Penticton, British Columbia, Canada. He also had every novel ever published by Kurt Vonnegut. He tacked Walter's Davy Crockett hat on the Oval Office wall, along with his prized graphite fly rod!

The Birdmobile, complete with the four-foot-tall ,carved statue of the one-legged pigeon went to the Smithsonian so people the world over could come to Washington, take pictures of the old 81 Chevy motor home. The old 81 Chevy motor home was all polished up and it looked spic and span. It was all cleaned up by you-know-who. It now had its final resting place. Its legend would go down in American history along with Charles Lindbergh's airplane, the space shuttle Columbia, and Henry Ford's first automobile!

\* \* \*

The RPA did not have to run any candidates in the elections for Congress and the Senate: there were no candidates from the Democratic Party or the Republican Party to run against them. Billy just appointed members from the RPA from all over America—half boys, half girls, from all ethnic origins—to fill all the vacancies in the Congress and Senate. Billy Pigeon had total control of everything and everybody in Washington—everybody except Julie!

A site was located at Mount Rushmore for President Pigeon and the one-legged pigeon sitting on his outstretched right hand. Construction and carving on the mountain began even before Julie had her worm box and her pigeon coop built. The tourist business in and around Mount Rushmore was booming like never before!

\*\*\*

Robert Redford was having a Jeremiah Johnson moment. He was all by himself in the mountains. His cell phone had three bars. He dialed 1–800–911-BIRD; Julie answered the cell phone one final time before having it disconnected.

"Hi, this is Robert Redford."
"Hi, this is Lindahhhh!"

\*\*\*

"She said it one more time, just for me!" said Robert Redford.
"Wow!" said Dustin Hoffman.

# 39

## Let the Work Begin

President Pigeon flew on Air Force One to Wichita, Kansas, then took a Suburban ride on Highway 135 to Interstate 70, then hung a left and went as far as Grainfield in northern Kansas.

He pushed a shovel into the ground and scooped up a pile of dirt. He began four years of construction on Billy's World, with all the displaced landowners now staying in free rooms all over Las Vegas, with oodles and oodles of cash to burn. They had four years to P-A-R-T-Y before President Pigeon let them into their free rentals in his new service city to retire for good or go to work in Billy's World.

President Pigeon scooped a second pile of dirt for the press. The shovel for the ceremony was brought to Billy by the old geezer from Washington, who told Billy at his wedding that he wanted the president to use it to dig worms or to shovel up pigeon poop, but most importantly, he wanted the shovel to shovel no bullshit. President Pigeon told the old geezer that there would be no bullshit to shovel in Washington as long as he was president. The old geezer's shovel was all cleaned up by you-know-who after the shovel ceremony in Grainfield and then mounted permanently on the Oval Office wall next to Billy's graphite fly rod!

As I was saying, before I slid off course, the minute after President Pigeon pulled the shovel out of the ground, and construction began on Billy's World, the Dow Jones Industrial Average soared five thousand points; the computers were unable to keep up to all the stock buyers. Caterpillar stock went through the roof; any stock having to do with construction went through the roof, too. The American economy was on fire, big-time.

The perimeter fence line was under construction first. Millions and millions of stakes cut by Weyerhaeuser were driven into the soft clay. The 146 one-horse towns in the construction zone were leveled to the ground. Thirty construction tent and trailer towns spread out all around the perimeter fence of Billy's World, with tents and trailers moving onto the site from here, there, and everywhere, six thousand construction companies and ten thousand sub trade companies showing up with 6 million American workers happy to finally have a job. The Porta-Potty business was on fire; 100,000 American military personnel from Germany and Korea arrived to do site security, tickled pink to be back home in America. The military personnel set up a tent city of their own.

The gigantic hangar was built by the proposed 20-mile runway, specifically to lay out the miles and miles of architectural drawings. Another tent and trailer city was setting up to build the service city outside the main fence line with more building blueprints arriving by courier every hour, with thousands and thousands of computers set up. Power to all the computers in the massive hangar was provided by portable diesel generators; the generator business was on fire. The scene all over Billy's World was surreal. The digging was underway for the underground pipes and the underground electrical cables, the material delivery site set up for all the building materials arriving, with separate material collection sites set up at each of the five thousand hub sites and all the service building sites. The main delivery site was being filled with rebar rods, concrete bricks, the plywood for all the cement forms, the steel guiders being laid out; the steel industry in America was on fire. The list of stuff coming onto the site going on and on and on and on and on and on and on and on and on and on and on and on and on and on and on. The footings were now being poured for all the buildings inside the five thousand hubs, the roads laid out, the train tracks laid out, and the underground game tunnels for all animals were underway. All the prep work alone for all the construction took up the whole first year.

The Dow Jones Industrial Average was now at 30,000 and climbing, with the 401ks of all Americans exploding through the roof. All of America was alive and well, the down days of the past done and over with; America had a new lease on life. The second year of construction saw all the construction cranes brought in, the construction crane business on fire, with new building cranes being ordered in on a daily basis. There were 20 million young Americans chomping at the bit to get to work and kick some Asian and Oriental butt. Young Americans were watching the factory buildings go up, up, up and up, the airports coming along just fine, the 20-mile runway now paved and up and running, the underground pipes to the natural gas fields and the overland pipes to the source of the Missouri River and the Platte River all good to go, the solar-wind-hydrogen power plant coming along Jim dandy, and the back-up natural gas generators in place.

The third year of construction was underway, with the walls and the windows going up and in, the roofs getting tarred, and all the roads and sidewalks completed. The fourth year of construction saw the painters and the tile and carpet layers and the millwork guys on site, all the beds coming in, the kitchens being completed, the plumbing and electrical tested, the millions and millions of computers going in, and the factories starting to get organized. All the construction materials, the construction tents and trailers, and the Porta-Potties were picked up and heading home. The service city was all ready for renters. Billy's World was a done deal, the Dow Jones Industrial Average at 100,000 and counting. Clint was at his desk in the administration office smoking a big old cigar. All that was needed now was for President Pigeon to arrive, to officially open up Billy's World!

\* \* \*

It was the year of Our Lord 2016. It was the big day, with 20 million YA kids standing on the west side of the 20-mile long runway, all looking spiffy, their brown boots all polished up. General Highway was in his green Chevy 4 by 4, with General Jessep right behind him in a little green military Jeep. The five thousand heads of all the American corporations at Billy's World were all lined up, too, with the twenty-five Board of Directors standing next to them, all ready to congratulate President Billy Pigeon for a job well done, for setting the economic engine of America on fire, for having zero unemployment in America, for giving America a bright future, and for restoring its Number One ranking in the eyes of the world. Air Force One landed right on schedule, touching down on the 20-mile long runway and beginning the long taxi to Airport #1, with General Norris decked out in his Delta Force uniform, his black coveralls and his black boots, on his dirt bike chasing Air Force One, and doing wheelies. A rope was lowered out the back door of the big old 747, the 20 million YA kids roaring their approval as General Norris climbed the rope, was lifted inside, and the big old 747 came to a stop. President Pigeon exited Air Force One and slowly walked down the boarding ramp to the runway tarmac, carrying the cage with the three pigeons. Julie walked down the boarding ramp, too, with an adopted Somalian girl on one hand, and an adopted Somalian boy on the other hand. The president of the United States was saluted by and then shook the hands of General Highway and General Jessep. The president and his pigeons got into General Jessep's little military Jeep; Julie and her two adopted children from Somalia hopped into the Chevy 4 by 4 with General Highway. The inspection of the 20 million YA kids began. The YA kids saw General Highway and General Jessep for the first time. The generals were mean-looking, not cracking a smile, and the YA kids started talking amongst themselves:

"Oh my God!"

"Holy shit!"

"We're toast!"

"No way, Mr. President,

"Not those two! We thought you were kidding at the pretend presidential debate!"

General Highway had a big old cigar in his mouth. The two vehicles were five miles into the inspection when General Jessep received an emergency call on his cell phone. General Jessep told General Highway to stop, let the president into the front seat with his wife and kids, and throw the cage with the three pigeons in the back of his pickup truck!

"What's going on?" asked Clint.

"The first Mexican has arrived," said Jack. "I want to deal with him personally!"

"I understand," said Clint. "I'll see you when you get back!"

An Apache helicopter landed on the runway, with General Jessep inside and heading to the military checkpoint. General Highway and Julie and President Pigeon and their two Somalian children and the three real live pigeons continued to inspect the 20 million YA kids. Then when all that was done, they drove toward the five thousand heads of all the corporations at Billy's World. President Pigeon was pooped when all the handshaking was done—he shook the hands of the twenty-five board members, too—and returned to White House 2 for dinner and some bedtime stories for his two Somalian children and some well-deserved hanky-panky without a condom in his private bedroom!

\*\*\*

General Jessep made the 175 mile helicopter ride to the southwest corner checkpoint, the young Mexican lad held at bay by four U. S. soldiers, their guns locked and loaded!

General Jessep exited the Apache helicopter and walked quickly up to the young Mexican, who was 20 years old, maybe older.

"What's your name, son?" asked General Jessep.

"Pedro!" said the terrified Mexican.

"What are you doing here?" asked General Jessep.

"Came to get a job, man!" said the young Mexican.

"Ever worked in a military, industrial, manufacturing complex before, son?" asked General Jessep.

"No, sir!" said the young Mexican.

"Ever worked at a real job before, son?" asked General Jessep.

"No, sir!" said the young Mexican.

"Ever seen a real American really work, son?" asked General Jessep.

"No, sir!" said the young Mexican.

"Can you read English, son?" asked General Jessep.

"Yes, sir!" said the young Mexican.

"Look up at the Mexican flag flying next to the American flag, son, and read the words on the white part, right in the middle!" said General Jessep.

The young Mexican looked at the Mexican flag.

"Oh!" said the young Mexican.

\* \* \*

At 2:00 a.m. the next morning, a land mine went off between Checkpoint 13 and Checkpoint 14. An Apache helicopter was sent out to take a look!

\* \* \*

Forty-one days after the opening of Billy's World, the first tunnel, twenty feet under the ground, hit the first five-foot-thick, alarmed reinforced concrete wall.

"Fuck!" shouted Carlos.

\* \* \*

Ninety-nine days after the opening of Billy's World, the second tunnel, sixty feet under the ground, went under the first fence, reached the second fence line, and hit the second five-foot-thick, alarmed reinforced concrete wall.

"Fuck, fuck!" screamed Antonio.

\* \* \*

One hundred and ninety-eight days after the opening of Billy's World, the third tunnel, one hundred feet under the ground, went under the first fence, then crossed under the second fence, then under the four-lane perimeter highway, and then hit the third alarmed, reinforced ten-foot concrete wall.

"Fuck, fuck, fuck this noise. I'm going home!" yelled Juan.

\* \* \*

A week after the third tunnel reached the third alarmed, reinforced concrete wall, two F-16s were scrambled to intercept an unidentified aircraft approaching Billy's World from the southwest. The Cessna had filed no flight plan. The pilot would not communicate with either of the F-16s. The Cessna, with five Mexicans on board, was blown out of the sky by the U. S. Air Force as it approached, and subsequently crossed, the outer fence of Billy's World. Seven land mines exploded, too, as parts of the Mexicans and the Cessna hit the ground between the first and second fences!

\*\*\*

A week after that, seven Mexicans, all wearing disguises, all dressed in coveralls and looking like real plumbers, were stopped at the mass transit train station leaving the service city by armed U. S. soldiers just as the Mexicans were about to enter the train on a busy Monday morning. The seven Mexican plumbers did not know that *Billy Boob* was the code word to get into Billy's World! They did not know that the service workers also had another code to get back on the train after work and go back home. The code for that afternoon train ride was Billy Bottom.

On Tuesday: Billy Ball, Billy Boy

On Wednesday: Billy Bob, Billy Betty

On Thursday: Billy Beer, Billy Box

On Friday: Billy Bait, Billy Baby

On Saturday: Billy Belt, Billy Biscuit

On Sunday: Billy Bird, Billy Goat!

\*\*\*

A week after the seven Mexicans were caught at the train station and sent home, Navy Seals were scrambled to investigate an alarm that had gone off at Checkpoint Charlie, one mile from the water filtration plant, coming from inside the six-foot-diameter pipe above ground bringing water into Billy's World.

Upon further investigation, the team of Navy Seals could clearly hear some banging and clanging going on inside the water pipe. One Navy Seal climbed the six-foot ladder to the top of the water pipe. He opened a four-foot latch after he had unlocked the three gigantic padlocks holding the latch in place.

He could see lights going here, there, and everywhere; he zeroed in on one light. His Navy Seal partner was on the top of the pipe now, shining a big old light of his own inside. With their light, they could see a diver's head with a pair of goggles wrapped around it, a set of eyes inside the goggles, and a body behind the head, dressed in scuba gear, his or her head and goggles banging and clanging against a six-foot-wide metal grill inside the pipe. The grill was made of one-inch-thick steel. The current in the pipe was too great to allow any of the thirty-three Mexican scuba divers stuffed up against the metal grill like sardines in a can to turn around, swim back where they came from, take off their heavy waterproof packsacks full of drugs they were carrying, or take a well-deserved breather, start all over again, and maybe bring a cutting torch this time!

\*\*\*

When General Highway was told about the thirty-three Mexican scuba divers, this is what he said to General Jessep: "I told you so!"

"One more thing," said General Highway.

"And what's that?" asked General Jessep.

"Did you cover the tour buses?" asked General Highway.

"Oh shit," and General Jessep, "I didn't even think about them!"

"Better get your ass in gear!" said General Highway.

# 40
## A Letter for the President

Ex-President Obama had lunch in Chicago with his buddy Rahm Emanuel, now the mayor of Chicago.

"So?" said Rahm Emanuel.

"So now you know what $71 trillion can build!" said ex-President Obama.

*　*　*

Billy Pigeon was back in the White House, with his dark brown leather moccasins kicked up on his desk; he had some quiet time. There were stacks of letters to read, congratulating the president and telling him what a kick-ass job he had done with Billy's World. Billy Pigeon read all the letters; this one really caught his eye.

> God bless you, President Pigeon! Please find room for my boy, David, at Billy's World. Take my daughter, Betty, too. Take them away to war! Put a uniform on them, keep them both for five years, teach them to save their money, and teach them to show respect for other people and other peoples' property. Give them what for if they need it. I really enjoyed that Gunnery Sergeant Highway movie on TV. I think you made an excellent choice for your top general.
>
> I am flat out tired of dealing with mouthy teens who spit in your face, do drugs, carry cans of open beer wherever they go, urinate on my rose bushes, sleep in all hours of the day, stuff themselves with pizza, vandalize property, write graffiti on any wall they can find, and carry knives and guns. I'm getting scared. I'm afraid to go out at night, or even to open my door.

David and Betty used to be good kids, but they won't listen to me anymore. Their dad got killed in a car accident two years ago and things have gone from bad to worse. They both feel somewhat guilty that I'm so upset, so there's hope. They said they would give Billy's World a go if you can get them in. I know you're all filled up for the next five years. They just need a job and a good swift kick in the behind!

Yours Truly,

Betsy Milan
Los Angeles, California

Billy Pigeon replied to the letter, hand written on presidential letterhead. This is what the letter said:

*Dear Mrs. Milan,*

*Send your kids, ASAP! I talked to General Highway. He told me he would squeeze them in somewhere, somehow. He told me he would pay special attention to them, give them hell when they deserved it, teach them a trade, shape them up, work their butts off, and make you proud of both of them. He said he might even take them for a weekend horseback ride!*

*Yours Truly,*

*Billy Pigeon,*
*President of the United States*

\* \* \*

Three short years later, General Highway called President Pigeon at the White House.

"We have a problem—a big problem!" said General Highway.

"And what's that?" asked Billy Pigeon.

"We can't handle all the orders coming in from all the small and medium sized businesses in America who want our kids to make their Made in America products, too! We're even having requests coming in from other companies in other countries! I have to turn down business; there's no way we can do it," said General Highway.

"Let me let you in on a little secret," said Billy Pigeon. "When we did the initial engineering plans for Billy's World, we called for footings in every building to hold three times the weight they're carrying now. Phase 2 kicks in, in 2020, Phase 3 kicks in, in 2030. By then, the dormitories will be thirty stories high and the factories three stories high. We will be working three shifts, five days a week. All the other buildings in each hub will go up, too, way up.

All the service buildings, the water filtration plant, the waste water plant, the garbage incinerator, the underground and above ground piping, and the electrical were all set up for 60 million workers. The airport has space to be 60 miles long, to hold 12 airports!"

"I should have known!" said General Highway.

\* \* \*

President Pigeon also attended the first graduation ceremony at Billy's World. It was just like the Grand Opening, with the hotels overflowing, 20 million graduates all lined up on the runway, General Norris ripping up the runway on his dirt bike again, climbing up into a moving Air Force One, just like he did at the Grand Opening. The 20 million YA kids went nuts again, with President Pigeon personally presenting 20 million graduating certificates to 20 million graduates: four thousand certificates given to each of the military leaders of each of the five thousand hubs. The four thousand certificates were in a big old box, and handed out later that evening in the five thousand dining halls. The four thousand graduates at each hub had successfully completed their first five-year Tour of Duty at Billy's World. The graduates all threw their baseball caps into the air at the same time. The scene in each of the five thousand dining halls was surreal, with General Highway and General Jessep smoking big old cigars in one of the dining halls, both generals cracking a smile—the way it should be!

\* \* \*

Five million graduates decided to stay on for a second Tour of Duty at Billy's World, to go for the $100,000 in their savings account at the end of ten years, to pay off their $5,000 used vehicles, to continue to sharpen their life and work skills, and to be part of one really big, lean, mean, working machine—one big, happy, American family!

The other 15 million graduates headed out into the real world, their savings accounts all at $50,000 and counting, all with a trade, a work ethic bar none, self-discipline, proper manners, drug free, in great physical shape, porn free, with respect for their elders and fellow workers. All left with one used suitcase, three used shirts and two pairs of used pants. The one used suitcase was placed in the trunk of their used car. Their $2,500 used vehicle was all paid for and in tip-top mechanical condition, thanks to Richard Perkins Jr. Their cars and trucks looked fantastic, all waxed up, all clean and shiny for their ride home to say hi to mom and dad—the way it should be!

\* \* \*

Tommy Tucker worked at the Cummins factory at Billy's World making diesel engines. He did such a fantastic job that he was the first graduate of

Billy's World to be hired on by Cummins at their biggest plant in Seymour, Indiana—the way it should be!

\*\*\*

Irene George and David Bellows worked at the GM factory at Billy's World. They were married when they returned home to Detroit in David's used Camaro—his Camaro all paid for. They bought a foreclosed home in a Detroit suburb for a steal. The bank was pleased as punch that they both had a total of $100,000 in their joint savings account and that they had plenty to put a down payment on their new home.

Irene and David also landed jobs at a GM plant in Detroit. They were absolutely thrilled when they found out that they were both going to be making $16 an hour, twice the amount they made at Billy's World.

They fixed up their rundown starter home: they cut the lawn, repaired the fence and the cracked windows, removed the graffiti, and painted all the rooms. They both agreed that their little starter home was all the home they would ever need.

They filled their modest home with secondhand furniture; they paid cash for everything. They saved coupons to help with their grocery bills. At the end of their first year in Detroit, Mr. and Mrs. David Bellows had another $12,000 squirreled away in savings. Their only credit card had a zero balance, too. They had no debt except for their mortgage. They had a few bills to pay every month: for their house, insurance and gas for David's car, food, and that was about it—the way it should be!

\*\*\*

Michael Zimmerman was one of the 80,000 young American workers who worked at an Apple factory at Billy's World. He was trained by Apple to make iPhones. Michael was so intrigued by Apple products that he decided to go to college after Billy's World and use his $50,000 to pay for tuition. He worked hard at college and burned the midnight oil. He did not take geography and social studies; he took engineering. When he graduated, he drove to California in his used Ford Taurus and landed a job with Apple. He was assigned to a design team working on a new Apple iPad—the way it should be!

To Billy Pigeon's surprise, and certainly unexpected, 29,999 other young American workers who worked in the Apple factories at Billy's World did exactly what Michael Zimmerman did. Apple had 30,000 new engineering graduates to hire. Tim Cook was ecstatic. He told the 30,000 Chinese engineers that their services were no longer required; Apple had all the American engineers it needed. Apple was increasing the number of its hubs at Billy's World from 20 to 115 when Phase 2 was completed in 2024. All Apple products from then on would be Made in America by Americans—the way it should be!

\* \* \*

Peter Hellier worked at a Boeing factory at Billy's World, making wings for gigantic Boeing planes. On the weekends, Peter would go to the airports at Billy's World and watch all the planes taking off and landing; he was intrigued with flight.

He used the $50,000 he had saved at Billy's World to take his pilot's license; the rest is history. Peter Hellier is presently flying a small turboprop commuter plane for United Airlines, hoping to get into the big birds real soon, possibly a new Dreamliner—the way it should be!

\* \* \*

Sydney Frost worked at a 3M factory at Billy's World. He made tons of earplugs. He delivered boxes of earplugs to the military base at his hub. Sydney was intrigued by military life, by their swagger, so much so that he joined the Army after his five year tour of duty with 3M. He trained at Billy's World and was ready to defend America. He was assigned to fence line security under the command of General Jessep. He was on the military payroll. He had a bed to sleep on, a roof over his head, clothes to wear, and food to eat. He had his $50,000 invested in the bank, earning compound interest. He would never touch that $50,000, He would be a millionaire when he left the Army—the way it should be!

\* \* \*

Sarah Pigeon returned to Bellevue. She used her $50,000 to set up The Bird's Nest, a small sewing shop in downtown Seattle, with a four-foot-tall, carved, one-legged pigeon gracing her small front window. The crowds lined up around the block to have their sewing done by their president's sister—the way it should be!

\* \* \*

Betsy Porter worked in the Sara Lee factory at Billy's World. She won President Pigeon's one million dollar contest for the most money saved by a factory worker at Billy's World. Betsy was an inspiration for the 19,999,999 other YA kids. Her picture went on President Pigeon's Wall of Fame in White House 2. She was hired by President Pigeon to serve in his cabinet in Washington, to teach Americans of all ages how to save money. She ran a weekly TV show and was the hottest woman on television—the way it should be!

\* \* \*

Billy-Jean McGregor worked at the John Deere factory at Billy's World. In the evening after exercise class and on the weekends, Billy-Jean was on the

Internet. She completed all the university equivalent courses necessary for her accounting degree. She left Billy's World with her accounting degree and $50,000 cash in her blue jeans. Billy-Jean headed to St. Paul, Minnesota in her used Honda Civic, which was all paid for. A job at her uncle's local accounting firm was all ready and waiting for her—the way it should be.

* * *

I could tell you a million other stories, but you get the picture. Enough said. Nope, hang on for a second. I have one more story to tell you. It's one you all need to hear about. Keith Bussey, Jerome White, LeRoy Peddle, and Carl Waterman, four best friends, graduated from Billy's World with a new attitude, their energies now focused on quality of life, not quantity of life. They took President Pigeon's advice. They drove home to Chicago, pooled their $50,000 together, and paid $200,000 cash for a foreclosed four-bedroom home in suburban Chicago. The home was legally registered to all four owners, each with a 25 percent share in the home.

They all found $12/hour jobs at a local manufacturing plant making kitchen cabinets. On their bi-weekly payday, they pooled all their money into one bank account: over $3,000. On their third Saturday together, after sleeping on foam mats, they paid cash for four single beds, four used dressers, and four used desks for their four bedrooms, which cost them $400. For their kitchen, they bought a large, used table with four used chairs; for their living room, two large used couches, one used TV, and four used metal TV tables. That cost them a grand total of $740. Their house was furnished.

They devised a budget for utilities, telephone, groceries, entertainment, car insurance and gas for their four used vehicles. Their vehicles were from Billy's World, all paid for. That came to just over $2,000 per month. The other $4,000 was invested in a bank CD earning them 1.5 percent, with a proper investment councilor being lined up as we speak.

They worked hard at their jobs. They went to movies at night, and went to the Black Hawks games, the Cubs games, the Bears games, and the Bulls games; they had fun! They ate at a different restaurant in Chicago each week, having sampled the food at 52 different restaurants over a full year.

They took a two-week vacation in Florida, had a blast, went fishing, tried scuba diving, and were super rested when they got back to Chicago, ready to get back to their jobs. They wrote President Pigeon after their first full year away from Billy's World and told him they were all working full-time making $12 an hour, that their house was all paid for, that they had no debt, that they had another $48,000 cash, and counting, at the end of their first year together, that they were having the time of their lives, and that he was right, that quality of life was more important than quantity of life.

President Pigeon made a special trip on Air Force One to Chicago. His presidential motorcade stopped in front of Keith, Jerome, LeRoy, and Carl's mortgage-free home. The story of the four young Americans went viral on social media, with millions of Billy's World graduates quickly joining forces, pooling their cash and snapping up homes all over the country. Architects all over America designed four-plex homes in the $200,000 range: the two-bedroom four-plex plain Jane. The graduates of Billy's World and their new American four-plex homes were all set for the addition of a mom or a dad and a kid or two, mortgage-free. Quality of life was the new normal in America, the new American Dream. The big banks were in deep doo-doo; Fannie and Freddie were in deep doo-doo, too, soon to be closed down by the new RPA government. Big banks were no longer in the mortgage business; house mortgages had gone the way of the dinosaur. A new generation of Americans was forcing all the big banks to break up into little banks; debt was an ugly word to this generation. Little banks were now the life-blood of the American economy, with Billy's Bank the biggest of the little banks. There was no more too big to fail in the financial sector—the way it should be!

As promised, Billy's World went through the two big expansions, the first completed in 2024, the second in 2034, and in 2039 there were 60 million factory workers at Billy's World, with 6 million workers in the expanded service city. Billy knew Julie was tickled pink when he hired workers from America and every other country around the world, especially China. Chinese factory workers lost the War on Jobs and wanted to come to America to get six times the wages they were getting in China. With Chinese factory workers flooding into America to work at Billy's World, to go back to China in five years with $50,000 in their Made in America blue jeans, the Chinese economy was struggling even more without all of its workers. Billy's World became a virtual United Nations of young factory workers. There were no more riots in London, England, Israel, Egypt, Syria, Greece, Spain, Portugal, or Libya, and no more starvation in Africa. Young people the world over obtained proper documentation and work visas and passports to enter the U. S. of A. legally, including the Mexicans, their paperwork double and triple checked by General Jessep. Young people the world over were leaving Billy's World after five short years with $50,000 and a new moral code of conduct. The American dollar was now truly King Dollar, the way Larry Kudlow always wanted it to be!

The American federal debt was actually at zero in twenty-three years, not the twenty-four years that Billy Pigeon had boldly predicted in 2012. The American government under the RPA was actually in surplus, taking in way more money than it was spending; it had more money than it knew what to do with. President Billy Pigeon called the chairman of the Joint Chiefs of Staff into the Oval Office and gave all the military men and women working at Billy's World and serving America overseas in their stealth bombers, submarines, aircraft carriers, destroyers, CIA posts, and Special Ops posts another big fat raise. Billy topped up the pensions of all the retired American military big-time—bigger than big-time. The military men and women in America were making almost as much as doctors and lawyers and accountants, but still not as much as Wall Street bankers. Wall Street was still on fire thanks to Billy Pigeon, with capitalism still the best path to prosperity. Billy Pigeon was still up watching *Morning Joe* and *Squawk Box;* old Joe Scarborough was still giving Mika a hard time—the way it should be—Billy Pigeon still liking Mika's pretty blond hair, her long legs, her sweet lips, her sensitive side, and her brilliant mind!

# 41

## Another Bare Ass

Billy Pigeon retired from politics in 2040; he had spent seven terms as president of the United States, five more than most presidents, not an issue for Billy and his RPA-dominated Congress and Senate. Debra Sanders was still his vice president. Billy and Julie had lots of serious hanky-panky moments without a condom and had three boys of their own: Tom, Dick and Harry, all attending college. Harry was about to get married and have children of his own. Their two Somalian children were all grown up, too, were doctors now, and were back home in Somalia caring for the sick and elderly—the way it should be!

When asked what he was going to do in his retirement at the tender age of 47, Billy Pigeon said he wanted to fly fish, maybe buy another used motor home, take another trip around America with his sweetheart Julie, see what effect his presidency had on America, and he would certainly stop at Mount Rushmore and have a look-see!

\* \* \*

At Mount Rushmore, Billy asked one of the workers there what took them so long to do the carving on the face of the mountain.

"We had a bitch of a time getting that pigeon of yours to stand on one leg!" said the worker.

\* \* \*

On Walter's seventieth birthday, Billy decided to spend the day on the Seattle waterfront with his father, take a couple of lawn chairs, maybe get some fresh fish for dinner, and take a few photographs with his old, old Kodak instamatic camera if something really interesting popped up.

Suddenly, right out of the blue, all these years later, while staring at the behind of a cute young lady passing by, Billy Pigeon said the following to his father, Walter: "You snuck into my room, didn't you?"

"I don't know what you're talking about," said Walter.

"Sure you do," said Billy. "That's where you got the Bill Clinton joke, the one about his underwear down to his ankles! You read my books!"

Walter was quiet; he listened to his son, Billy, as he spoke again.

"You read *Party On, Dudes!*" said Billy.

The cat was finally out of the bag after all these years!

"Yes, Son, I did. I hope you don't mind. I read all five of his books. He's such an unpredictable writer; I couldn't get enough of him!" said Walter.

"You read them all!" said Billy. "I didn't think you were that much of a reader."

"I wasn't," said Walter, "but once I got started, I couldn't stop! I know now why you put that four-foot-tall, carved, one-legged pigeon on top of your Birdmobile. The five thousand kids at that August Long Weekend party in Tulameen were disgusting, but you fixed all that. I couldn't get over how big that dick got in *A Perfect Person on Planet Earth;* that 50 or 60-page sentence blew me away, and surprise, surprise, just when you think you've seen everything, he writes *Land of the Bear,* a little love story, with hardly any swear words, no dicks, no WFDS, no explosions, no chasing al Qaeda in the hills behind Osoyoos—just a simple story of a big old bear and a man and a woman madly in love with each other."

"What did you think of the cabin scene at the end of the book?" asked Billy.

"Unreal!" said Walter. "Honest to God, I thought the guy was toast!"

"What did you think of David H. E. Smith's bare ass on top of that pile of grizzly bear shit in *Moustafa?*" asked Billy.

"That's why you mooned the Chinese and told them to kiss your ass!" said Walter.

"I'll never tell," said Billy.

"You don't have to," said Walter.

\* \* \*

"Come on, Dad, let's go home; it's been a long day," said Billy.

"Want to hear another Mexican joke?" asked Walter.

"Sure, why not?" said Billy.

"What do you call four Mexicans in quick sand?" asked Walter.

"I have no idea," said Billy.

"Cuatro cinco!" said Walter.